Currents of Destiny

A novel

by

Frank Piñeiro

2nd Edition

Currents of Destiny

ISBN #: 978-0-578-00239-2

This is a work of fiction.
Any similarities to people,
living or dead, is purely coincidental.

This book is dedicated to my immigrant parents and to all those through the ages who have had the courage to leave everything behind in order to create a better life for their descendants.

-FJP

Chapter 1

December 8, 1941

When the first news accounts of the Japanese attack on Pearl Harbor crackled urgently over the Phillips crystal set in the parlor, Carlos slumped into the old leather chair in front of the flickering fireplace but felt as if he was falling into a well. He listened with alarm but without surprise. He had been expecting this for some time; since mid-October, almost two months before it actually happened. At that time he had witnessed in a nightmare the gigantic ships, bigger than the municipal palace building, exploding and sinking into the sea, engulfed in flames and thick, billowing clouds of acrid smoke. He saw, all around him, the grimacing, contorted faces of the dying sailors, and he heard the panic in their cries, emanating from a burning sea and echoing from the bowels of the mighty crafts that for so many of those sailors would become their tombs. Then, he awakened in a panic, gasping for air as if he too was drowning. His wife, Catalina, startled from a deep slumber, had to shake him and call out his name several times before he snapped back to reality.

"It's okay." she said, handing him a cloth to dry his perspiration. "I'll make you some tea."

She went into the kitchen to make a pot of chamomile tea, already dreading what the news would be. Her husband's nightmares were never just nightmares. Inevitably, they were skewed visions of some calamity that would befall their lives.

Sitting on the edge of the bed, Carlos drank his tea, sipping it slowly and Catalina waited patiently until he finished. Then she asked him about the content of his nightmare.

"I' don't know," he lied. "I can't remember."

"It's all right," she insisted. "You can tell me. Was it about the baby?"

He looked at her swollen belly. "No, no. Nothing like that. Just some stupid things that didn't make any sense. I probably just ate too much."

She knew that he was hiding the truth, which only made her worry more, but there was no sense arguing about it, so she dropped the matter for the moment. Carlos pretended to fall back to sleep but in fact slept little the remainder of that night or during the ensuing days. He recognized his nightmare as much more than just the result of his accumulated worries. This had been one more of those dark premonitions that tore into the fabric of his life at the most inopportune moments: Convoluted visions, sometimes of the past, more often of the future; annoying revelations he could never fully understand and over which he had no control. He too had learned to dread these moments because by the time they made some sense it was too late to alter their course.

Clearly, he had witnessed the beginning of a terrible war, probably between the United States and Germany, since that had been the speculation of the foreign relations experts in Mexico City for some time. And he assumed the revelation had come to him because of his plans to go to the United States. Was it a warning to stay away because of the dangers of war? Did it mean that the United States was going to lose the war?

The only thing he knew for certain was that if he related any of it to Catalina she would instantly decide he must not go. She had been against his plans right from the start.

Now, he thought, his nightmare was finally to come clear. He sat transfixed near the radio, listening to the mounting reports of the previous day's surprise attack on Pearl Harbor.

He was surprised to hear that it involved the Japanese and not the Germans. Yet, when the broadcast ended, he had no greater insight into the meaning of his nightmare.

Naturally, when Catalina heard the news, which soon included confirmation that the President of the United States had declared war on Japan, she became adamant that Carlos should at the very least postpone his plans.

"It makes no sense to travel right into the middle of a war," she'd say.

Carlos' cause was not helped by the news reports and expert assessments that followed for weeks. It would be a long protracted war, they said. Very costly not only in terms of material but also in human lives. And they all agreed that the greatest danger for Mexico was that as a neighbor to one of the combatants, it might somehow be drawn into the fray.

It was only when a professor from the Autonomous University of Mexico City was interviewed on the capital's XEQ radio station one afternoon, that Carlos received some help for his contentions.

The professor said that this war would be fought far away, in the European theater and in even more distant parts of Asia. He insisted that Mexico would remain, if not totally neutral, certainly outside the realm of active war. Of more relevance to Carlos, he speculated that Mexico's greatest involvement would come as a supplier of laborers to the United States, to fill the void already being created by that nation's inscription of young men into their army.

"You see?" Carlos pointed out to Catalina. "This is what I've been trying to tell you. I'm only going to work there. I can make much more money there than here, and I'll send you all of it. We'll finally be able to make some progress."

Catalina looked away with a sigh and cautiously touched a sore subject: "Your father says that all the men who go to work in the United States are treated like servants or slaves."

"Oh, what the hell does he know? He's never been beyond Mexico City."

"Well, what about the men from around here that have gone?

They all come back with stories about how they were mistreated by the Gringos."

"First of all. . . who are those men? They're barefoot peasants with no education. Most can't even read or write. Besides, things are different now. The Gringos will pay us better and treat us with respect because now they need us. We'll be working with a contract.

Catalina fell silent. She knew it was no use to argue with him now that he had made up his mind in spite of whatever it was that his nightmare had revealed.

Carlos Cansino had been plagued by those strange and unexpected visions that sometimes arrived in the middle of a peaceful sleep, like common dreams, and at other times attacked him in plain daylight, through a fog that temporarily numbed his senses, leaving him with the dread and foreboding of a coming storm. It started early in his childhood. In fact, now that he found himself at a crossroad in his life, between jobs, twenty seven years old, married, with two children and another on the way, he could no longer recall a time when he had been free from the influence of these episodes. He did remember that in those first years, back even before the persecutions, he looked forward to those dazzling, semi-conscious, imaginary journeys because they were not only a source of solace in his unhappy life but indeed an exciting diversion from it. And they became also his great secret; not because he had intended them to be, but because he was unable to explain them clearly to anyone else. Those strange daydreams were usually about complete strangers doing so many mysterious things that, as a child, he could seldom understand, let alone describe.

Then, at the age of twelve, one day in school, his dreams suddenly burst fully into the current of his life. He could recall the exact moment when it happened: It was a Tuesday morning in the early spring of 1926, before recess. The teacher, Mr. Cupertino Meneses, distributed new textbooks to the excited class while announcing with great ceremony that the day's civic lesson would be to learn about the wonderful old city that was their home.

"Why?" he asked rhetorically, pacing the creaky floor boards of the one-room school house and gazing past the weathered walls, the broken window and the empty, dusty playground, to the distant mountain tops beyond. Once certain that all eyes in that room were attentively upon him, he turned and continued:

"Because the world is changing! Great things are happening. Right this moment train tracks are being set down all over our beloved country. Thousands of kilometers of track! Already they have reached the edges of our region and one day they will pierce those mountains and enter this old town."

Some of the older students glanced skeptically at each other.

"And then," he continued, lowering his voice for effect and peering gravely at his students in an effort to inflame that sense of wonder that had captured his own imagination so many years before.

"You'll be able to leave your home, walk to the plaza and board one of those ambulatory parlors--which can carry fifty people at a time--and travel comfortably for days, across mountains and valleys, until you reach some great and distant metropolis: Mexico City, Monterrey, New York City, Chicago, Wichita. . ." He snapped his fingers. "just like that!"

Now the students knew they were in for a long morning lecture, because the future and all that was modern were Don Cupertino's favorite subjects. Soon he would rhapsodize about sky scrapers that he'd personally seen, homes which had their own private telephones or man-made rivers that would make it possible to build towns anywhere at all, and a host of other things that his students had to strain to imagine.

Carlos, however, lived for these moments. He longed for those fantastic places that he had never seen and shuddered at the thought that he might never see them. The attraction was tremendous; almost frightening. The old teacher's descriptions of these mystical places tugged at the very core of his existence. He felt it with his heart racing, just as it did the time he was caught in the rapids of the Usumacinta River, gasping for air and fighting for life.

9

"Some of you," Don Cupertino said gravely, "are destined to travel to far away lands, and then people will want to know about the place that formed you."

Carlos was certain those words were directed specifically at him, even if the melodramatic old teacher might not realize it. Overtaken by curiosity, he dove into his new book without waiting for permission, hoping to find in it some drawings or perhaps even the reproduction of a daguerreotype. He knew that this irresponsible act could cost him dearly, because whenever he took home anything short of perfect marks on his report card, his father, the venerable Don Carlos Cansino, would tie him to a tree in the patio and flog him with a wet leather strap. In spite of that, he raced ahead, looking for the future, and there, on page 24, he found the first illustration and stumbled deep into a past that sent a chill reverberating up his spine.

It was a full-page artist's rendering of a man with shoulder length hair, a thin mustache and a pointed goatee; and Carlos recognized him immediately although the drawing did not do justice to the angular features of his face. Yet, even if in the drawing the man had not been wearing the strange outfit that moments later would elicit laughter through the classroom, Carlos would have recognized him still. He had seen him in his dreams just as clearly as he could now see his teacher, standing a few feet away.

With his heart still racing, Carlos read ahead to discover all he could about this figure that had haunted him so long. The man wore a metal shell over his torso and very odd-looking short pants that ballooned like pumpkins at the hip over long stockings that made his legs look like those of a sparrow. He cradled an odd metal helmet under one arm, held an ornate shield and a huge sword in the other, in order to pose in an aloof yet menacing stance. His name was Diego de Mazariegos, and he was a Spaniard that the book insisted on calling a *Conquistador*. According to the story, in the spring of 1528, year of Our Lord, during explorations on behalf of his Spanish king, he and his men had entered the valley of Hueyzacatlán and camped upon it's floor. So pleasant was their stay in that idyllic valley, festooned with yellow butterflies, that on March 31, before moving on, Mazariegos stuck his lance into the fertile ground and founded thus the town which he christened Villa Real.

The book did not specify, and Mr. Meneses did not know, exactly when the city's name had changed to *San Cristobal de Las Casas*. The schoolmaster speculated that it must have been upon the death of the town's most illustrious inhabitant: "Our first bishop, Friar Bartolomé de las Casas, at whose urging the town adopted San Cristobal as its patron saint. So you see, children, the new and current name of San Cristobal de las Casas honors them both."

Carlos had always known his home town simply as San Cristobal. Except for the worst years of the persecution, when the government only allowed it to be called *Ciudad de las Casas*, (City of the Houses). Now, for the first time and partly due to one of his strange dreams, some pieces were falling into place for Carlos and a few things started to make sense. It was all so exciting to him that he jumped at the chance to volunteer additional information during the day's lesson. He blurted out that the boots pictured on the drawing--black with an upturned toe--were incorrect.

"How do you know?" he was asked.

"Because I saw them." he answered without hesitation, only to suddenly realize that he had said too much. Everyone was staring at him. Now he was speechless.

"Surely, what you mean," intervened the professor, peering over his spectacles, "is that you've seen other depictions of the Conquistadors."

Carlos nodded timidly, and his classmates' fickle attention turned elsewhere. "Well," Mr. Meneses concluded with a chuckle and much to the amusement of those in the class who were still listening, "I'm sure that our Spanish ancestors had more than one pair of boots."

Embarrassed, Carlos clung to his new book for the rest of the day but did not dare reopen it until he was alone, on his way home from school. He stopped at the Friar Bartolomé Park, sat on a wooden bench near the legendary old bishop's

11

statue and watched the sun disappearing by flickers through the eucalyptus grove on the far side. There, in the park where he had spent many afternoons playing with his friends and classmates, he turned again to page 24 and again found that old, familiar figure with the baleful eyes and aquiline nose staring back at him. It absorbed him so completely that his next sensation (for it was more a feeling than anything else) was that of walking into a dark room inhabited by dusty figures, like mannequins or statues stored in some long-forgotten museum.

He walked among them, each of whom, he somehow realized, represented someone from his dreams, until he came upon the gaunt figure of Diego de Mazariegos.

Carlos was surprised at how much more tattered the Spaniard looked in comparison to his portrait. At least now he had color. His velvety clothing was mostly black and maroon, setting off the dull gray of his scratched and dented breastplate. His stockings, torn at several places, were also a dull gray and his boots, brown not black, were in fact not pointed or upturned at the toe. A large, frilly collar that once must have been white, sustained the head of this man worn well beyond his years. His brown hair, now dry and matted by the elements, framed an olive complexion deeply furrowed, more by disillusion than by time.

Carlos found him now, once again surrounded by seventeen of his men; the broken remnants of a battalion that had numbered two hundred when they landed on the eastern coast of the Yucatán peninsula fourteen months before. He saw them descend from the surrounding mountains, through the morning fog, not as a proud group of conquerors wrapped in glory, as the history book suggested, but as the sad remains of an army decimated by malaria, intestinal fever and other tropical deceases still unknown back in the old world. Several Spaniards had drowned in the swollen rivers of the rain forest and some were swallowed by the quicksand of the jungle swamps. Dozens were killed in skirmishes with the local Maya tribes they had mistreated, exploited and tried to subjugate, while others starved to death in the unforgiving, burning deserts of the Yucatan. Two had simply lost their minds and wandered away.

That had been the price of their greed and their arrogance; the price they paid in exchange for the gold they plundered from the temples and the graves of the ancient Maya people they so callously desecrated. Now, camped in the valley of Hueyzacatlán, on the edge of a long-existing Maya village whose occupants they used even now as mere servants, many of the soldiers spoke openly of longing to return to Spain, to the women and the families and the safety they had left behind. However, Mazariegos insisted on spending three more months searching the southern mountains for the fabled city of Xibalbá, rumored to exist there and to contain the most fabulous treasure of them all. So, in a ceremony marked by heavy consumption of *Chicha*--an Indian beverage made from fermented corn--he claimed the village for king and country, naming it Villa Real in honor of his majesty's summer home. But he actually did it less as homage to their monarch and more to establish a point of reference to the spot on the edge of a lagoon where, on a moonlit night, he and three of his most trusted men buried the cumbersome crates of gold, jade and precious stones that were once again stirring their insatiable greed and fueling their deep mistrust of one another.

On that park bench in 1926, Carlos realized three things of great significance that day: First of all, his nightmarish dreams, which had never made much sense to him before, were in fact based upon reality, like some magic window into other times and places. Secondly, he apparently had the ability not only to recall but also to experience once again those revelations. And finally, by an incredible coincidence that even Professor Meneses had overlooked, the date was March 31, which made that very day the 398th anniversary of the founding of their town.

He closed his book, turned up the collar of his coat to ward off the drizzle that had started falling moments earlier and which awakened him from the vivid recollection of his dream, and he headed home. Walking past the statue of Friar Bartolomé, he felt a sudden warmth wash over him and, out of fear, he dismissed it quickly as something caused by his elation from the day's events and his discovery of those strange powers. Nevertheless, when he dared himself to look up at the statue, he could not find the courage.

He hurried home, looking forward to sharing his discoveries, convinced that even his father would find them terribly engaging.

However, he was surprised to find his home already filled with more than its usual chaos and commotion. His father was in the library, meeting with some visitors, while several of his sisters stood outside the doorway straining to hear their every word. The discussion inside centered on the news that the government had ordered the deportation of several Spanish Roman Catholic priests. At the same time, in Mexico City and across several central states, a number of Catholic schools had been shut down for "failure to provide the prescribed lay instruction".

Furthermore, it was rumored that in the state of Tabasco, several temples and their surrounding lands had been confiscated from the Church by the government and a limit had been set upon the number of priests that would be allowed to practice there.

Don Carlos Cansino paced in front of the raging fireplace and puffed on his Cuban cigar. "There can be no doubt," he told his visitors, "Those sons of a whore are preparing to launch another round of persecutions."

Carlos' sisters looked at one another with dismay. Some of them attended Catholic school, most of them attended Catechism classes and all of them attended church on Sundays. Now their life too was about to change.

In view of that, none of them was interested in hearing about Carlos' dreams, so he walked out to the patio and up the stairs to the deck where his dad's hammock swayed silently in the night breeze.

He stood there for a long while, his chin on the railing, gazing beyond the white walls and red tiled roofs, at the old church of San Cristobal, atop a distant hilltop, disappearing amid the fog and the drizzle and the darkness, just like the last vestiges of his childhood were disappearing from his unhappy life.

Fifteen years later, as the radio repeated accounts of the brazen Japanese attack upon the United States navy and various experts again speculated on the repercussions this might eventually have upon Mexico, Carlos, knowing that his own life was about to change dramatically once again, lingered at that other early and pivotal moment in his life; that night of his discoveries in 1926, in the San Bartolome´ Park, amid the drizzle and the San Cristobal fog.

Chapter 2

March 31, 1928

On a fateful Sunday morning, exactly two years after young Carlos discovered the truth about the founding of his town, all of San Cristobal's church bells rang out with a particular urgency, not only calling the faithful to mass but to officially invite the entire citizenry out to celebrate the four-hundredth anniversary of that founding. They began ringing at five in the morning, starting with the high-pitched peal of the bells from the church of San Cristobal, followed by the unmistakably deep, sonorous tolling of the bells from Santo Domingo, which seemed to reverberate deep inside one's chest with mournful sadness. They were joined by the joyous, pristine clanging from the twin towers of El Carmen as still others, not as distinctive, followed suit, echoing off the surrounding mountain tops in the distance and repeating their call every fifteen minutes from every corner of the sleepy town.

Alberto Sanchez awoke with the first chorus and was unable to return to sleep. He could hear his stepfather, Don Romulo Gallardo, snoring in the master bedroom down the hall. The notorious Municipal Prosecutor wouldn't be going to work that day, and that thought alone filled Alberto with dread. He knew the snoring would soon turn to bouts of shouting and barking of orders generally accompanied by personal insults, leading to the inevitable arguments and ugly confrontations that would keep the entire family in a high state of tension for the remainder of the day.

Angered by the anxiety already rising inside him, Alberto rolled out of bed, lit a kerosene lamp and ambled to the marble-top dresser in the corner of his dreary room. He poured cold water from a white enameled pitcher into a matching basin and proceeded to wash away his lingering thoughts of sleep. He dressed quietly, glancing only once at his reflection on the broken mirror. He was thin, his ribs still evident, and somewhat small for his thirteen years of age. In contrast, he seemed older than he was, due partly to the constant frown already etched into his brow and as familiar to his few friends as the rigorous absence of his smile.

Once dressed, he carefully opened a window and climbed down the vines of ivy to the garden. The same window and the same vines that his older half-brother, Fernando, often used when sneaking back into the house to visit their mother, Doña Rosa, ever since being banished from the house by the rancorous old prosecutor.

Fernando was the result of Doña Rosa's first marriage, to Candido Suarez; a union that lasted less than a year. For that sin, he bore the brunt of Don Romulo's infamous temper over many years, until, at the age of sixteen, he stood up to the old man and confronted him as an equal. That was more than the embittered old lawyer could endure, so he ordered the youth out of his house, threatening to throw out the rest of the family if he ever returned. Fernando left, but only after issuing a warning of his own to the tyrant, that if he ever struck his mother again, as he had done on several occasions in the past, he would return to kill him.

All of that occurred the previous year. Since then, Fernando Suarez had earned a steady job with a local metalworker and was living in a rented room in the mostly indigenous Barrio of Cuxtitali, on the outskirts of town. But every week or so, he would sneak back into the house to visit his family while the prosecutor was at work. When possible, he would leave Doña Rosa some money to make up for the meager stipend that she received from her miserly husband. Those surreptitious visits were as much a treat for the five-year-old twins, Amerigo and Amelia, as they were for Alberto and their mother. However, with Fernando gone, the old man's temper tantrums had turned increasingly against Alberto, himself the product of a scandalous affair Doña Rosa had with a married man--the notorious Don Carlos Cansino--two years before her marriage to Don Romulo.

When the bells tolled six o'clock, Alberto was making his way along the still empty streets of *El Cerrillo*, a working-class neighborhood renowned for its tanneries, leather works and saddle makers. But those shops, which had made silver-trimmed saddles for some of the most famous people in Mexico, were quiet now. The empty streets only echoed the activity within the houses as he passed, and he tried to imagine the families inside, eagerly preparing for church and the subsequent celebrations, without shouting, without anger, without fear. The contentment that emanated from those humble adobe homes as naturally as the smoke from their chimneys or the aroma of baking bread wafting from their earthen ovens was something that Alberto had either never known or already forgotten, and that thought filled him with envy, self-pity and anger.

He skirted the more affluent central barrio of Guadalupe, which always made him feel uncomfortable with its pristine whitewashed walls, Spanish wrought-iron balconies, neatly tiled roofs and meticulously maintained cobblestone streets. Alberto found this area pleasing to the eye but cold and forbidding to the soul, and he sensed that from behind every window curtain, eyes were watching him pass and questioning his presence.

Instead, he crossed the old stone bridge, commonly known as lover's bridge, since the days when disillusioned lovers started throwing themselves from its walls into the cold alpine currents more than a century before, and he followed the aqueduct back up to the marketplace. By then the road was filling up with ox-drawn carts loaded with coal for the town's ovens and resinous *ocote* wood for the torches to be used that night in the procession up the San Cristobal hill.

The town's few automobiles--considered as much a nuisance as an expensive fad that would soon pass--had to navigate around mule trains bringing the town its life blood: cacao beans across the mountains from Ocosingo and sugar cane from Yucatan, whilecoconuts, corn, melons and yams from Guatemala arrived through Comitan, and fresh fish, wrapped in moist banana leaves, from the coast past Tapachula. Poultry, beef, fruits, vegetables, coffee, dry goods and even hand-carved furniture, all arrived from the surrounding mountain villages like *Tenejapa, Chamula, Zinacantan*, and *Teopisca*, usually on the backs of the very Natives who produced them. They carried it all in huge netted bundles several times their own size, perched precariously on their hunched backs and held in place with a *mecapal*, the leather sash that wrapped around their forehead. Like army ants, they trudged in single file down the treacherous mountain trails that eventually converged in San Cristobal's very heart: the *mercado*.

By eight a.m. that marketplace was teeming with merchants already hawking half a dozen types of avocado and many varieties each of tomatoes, potatoes, corn and citrus fruits. The pungent smell of fresh green onions intermingled with the tart aroma of tamarind, the essence of cinnamon and the scent of clove, creating new and unique fragrances that would remain in Alberto's memory tied forever to those moments and that place. He took a seat at one of the sidewalk food stands, ordered a cup of *atole*, and allowed himself to be swept away from his misery by the colors, the sounds and the aromas of the only place on earth where he would ever feel completely at peace with himself.

He was a familiar figure to many of the mercado's vendors, for they had watched him grow from a sad and lonely child into amorose, dejected youth. And he would have been surprised to know that many of those Indian peasants felt sorry for him, for they sensed that something deep inside him was terribly amiss.

"He drags a heavy shadow," one of them would say, "even when there is no sun."

Carlos Cansino would later recall that on that fateful morning he found his younger half-brother sitting on a stairway of the marketplace, looking as serious and inscrutable as ever. He knew that Alberto felt a greater affinity to the native Indians than to *Ladinos*, as the mestizos were commonly called. But whatever amount of native blood ran in his veins, his features betrayed him as clearly Spanish in extraction: curly hair, olive skin and longish nose. That kept him separate from the strong, gentle, copper-colored people he loved most and it gave him one more reason to hate the father that had disowned him from the start.

Carlos also knew that Alberto hated to be touched, so when he put his hand upon his shoulder he did it to underscore the authority over him that his age conferred; authority that Alberto accepted only grudgingly.

"Is it true you've been expelled from school again?" Carlos asked.

"Yeah."

"For fighting again?"

"Yep."

He sat down beside him. "Alberto, when are you going to stop this shit?"

"When they stop fucking with me."

"You talk like a fool."

Alberto ignored him, staring straight ahead, motionless except for his right index finger rubbing insistently back and forth against his knee.

"What did the old man say?

Alberto shrugged his shoulders.

"Well, when can you go back to school?"

"I'm not. I'll find a job and move out; away from that snoring pig!"

"A job doing what? You have no skills. You'll be an apprentice. How will you support yourself?"

"I can move in with Fernando for a while."

"No! You can't. It's not that simple. Fernando has enough problems."

The index finger rubbed faster and deeper into his knee.

21

"Look, Alberto, I know it's tough with that old man, but just hang on a little longer and I'll see what I can do. I'll ask father to help."

Alberto glanced at his brother with an incredulous smirk.

"Father? Are you joking? You know damn well he'd never do crap for me. He won't even admit I'm his son."

It was true, and Carlos knew it. So, their conversation drifted off to things less important but more pleasant, and in the end the most important things of all were the things they left unsaid; Those things that dealt with social standing and each person's place within that very clearly defined structure.

Carlos and Alberto were both sons of Don Carlos Cansino, the heir and head of one of the town's most distinguished families. The Cansinos could trace back their roots many generations, to the *madre patria* in the old world; to Galicia, Spain. But unfortunately, neither Carlos nor Alberto were among Don Carlos' ten legitimate children.

They belonged instead to a less exclusive club, since Don Carlos was reputed to have sired, not to say fathered, more than twenty illegitimate children, scattered throughout the region.

They were bastards, both, and nothing could change that. It automatically placed them in a lowly social category. And yet, even within that group, further class distinctions would be made. Carlos' mother was also a member of an old, respected family, whereas Alberto's mother, Doña Rosa Sanchez, came from humble, lower middle-class stock. Furthermore, Carlos was--for some still unknown reason--the only one of all Don Carlos' illegitimate children to have been publicly acknowledged by Don Carlos as his own, and brought into the family home, at the age of five, to be raised along with the legitimate Cansino offspring. Now, nearly ten years later, many townspeople were unaware of that fact and naturally assumed that young Carlos, as the oldest son, was the legitimate heir, if not to the family fortune, which had been largely squandered, then certainly to the family honor, which was far more precious in that town.

Alberto, on the other hand, officially had an unknown father and therefore no paternal name, but although he resented

Carlos' good fortune he kept that to himself. He endured the stigma of his birth with a stoic indifference that some considered a sign of maturity while others recognized it as a time bomb of emotions.

The fact remained that in San Cristobal nothing of importance ever happened without the social standing of all involved being brought into the balance, and it was given far more weight than ability, potential or any other factor. Those, like Alberto, who had no recourse but to use their mother's maiden name, could hope for little from the very society that produced them with such profligate abandon and discarded them with such disdain. "We all have to know our place." they said. It was the catch-phrase of the day, and had been so since the days of Spanish conquest and glory.

Even Doctor Ruben Novojoa, who had received his medical degree from Leipzig University with honors, was shunned by San Cristobal's upper crust, except during extreme emergencies or delicate matters of secrecy, like venereal diseases or surreptitious abortions. Otherwise they would patronize Dr. Ezequiel Asturias, an incompetent dandy who could nevertheless still slur his esses like a proper Spaniard.

Sharing a bag of walnuts, the two brothers strolled a few blocks to the central plaza, stopping under one of the twenty palm trees that the new mayor had ordered planted there in spite of the horticultural society's assurances that they would die in the cool San Cristobal climate.

"Sometimes I feel a little like these poor palms." Alberto said. "Out of place in this town."

"Yeah; and in this century." sighed Carlos, catching himself by surprise. He too had always felt out of step and out of time in his life, and his adolescent years had only magnified the symptoms, leaving him with a nauseating helplessness and sometimes rapid palpitations of his heart.

They remained quiet for a moment; both of them wondering about their future and each knowing that the other was contemplating the very same things.

"Look, Alberto," Carlos finally said, "just give me a little time. I promise to work things out. I'll talk to my great aunt.

She still has a lot of influence, especially with her sons. Maybe I can get you a job at their new pharmacy. Give me a few days."

Alberto nodded a tentative agreement which Carlos sealed quickly with a handshake and an awkward hug. "In the meantime, just avoid the old man! Keep your tail away from his rocker." The younger brother allowed himself the hint of a smile and with that they headed off in different directions.

The concern Carlos had for Alberto was not new by any means, but it had grown much stronger during the previous week and he didn't really know why. Later he would recognize it as a premonition, but as he crossed the central park it just felt like an annoying weight lodged in the back of his head.

He hurried back home, not only because he had to prepare the six horses and supplies for a trip that Don Carlos was to take to Tuxtla, nor because he had to keep an eye on all his sisters--a chore that had been added to his duties some years before--but because one of his sisters' friends had started to cause him sleepless nights and now he thought that he would die if a day passed without seeing her; even if only a brief glimpse from a distance. He needed something, anything that would at least carry him to the next day.

Meanwhile, Alberto headed for the church of Guadalupe, on the east end of town, simply because that parish--being the home of the nation's patron saint, The Virgin of Guadalupe, the mother of all Mexico--usually put together the best celebrations. The church bells were already announcing the ten o'clock mass and the streets were already bustling with the pilgrims from outlying communities as well as the local faithful, and those simply out to enjoy the celebrations. It all left very few people at home and it occurred to Alberto in passing that there would be many burglaries that day.

As he passed the Barrasa family home, a single story mansion which took up an entire block, he couldn't keep from glancing through each balcony window into the rooms. All had shimmering, dark hardwood floors inlaid with a variety of intricate patterns and covered partially by plush, thick rugs imported directly from the kingdom of Persia. Every room had a specific designation and use, such as the sewing room, where he once saw Isabel Barrasa crying quietly into her embroidery. Alberto tried to decipher the use of the rooms as he passed them. Some were easy, like the prayer room which resembled a chapel, full of icons, old portraits of saints hanging on the walls in gold leaf frames and statuettes inside glass cases lined with votive candles. Others were less obvious. The interconnected rooms all opened out to a marble corridor that surrounded the central garden/patio, separated by massive Greek columns supporting the high, overhanging roof. The patio with its central fountain that spouted water from the mouths of three sea serpents ferociously guarding a beautiful mermaid who was strumming a harp with glistening strings made of falling water.

An oak and several old elms provided a high canopy of shade for the rich variety of flowers that blossomed with lush abandon in the garden. In the branches above lived a royal cockatoo and several Guatemalan parrots that had been taught to speak with a Spanish accent.

This was the house where the President of Mexico always stayed when he visited San Cristobal or passed though the region. It was also rumored that the Archbishop Cardinal of Madrid, personal envoy to the Pope, had often been a guest; however, in those days of conflict between church and state, such a rumor was never repeated openly in public.

Just as Alberto approached the main entrance to the house, the massive wooden portals adjacent to it swung open, old lumber creaking, and a matching pair of stallions pranced proudly into the street, towing one of the Barrasa family carriages. Elena, Isabel and Laura Barrasa sat at the back of the open buggy, impeccably attired in the latest Paris Fashions: long, frilly, pastel-colored, short sleeved gowns with matching parasols and elbow-length white gloves.

Don Miguel, wearing a severe gray suit and top hat, sat across, facing his daughters and next to his sister, Doña Elvira, who in rigorous black was still mourning for her sister-in-law, Doña Placencia, who had died under mysterious circumstances three years before.

The carriage passed an arm's length from Alberto, and as it did, his eyes met with Laura's for a second that stopped his heart and passed through his mind like an eternity. The youngest of the Barrasa sisters, at thirteen, Laura was already a match to her two older sisters' legendary beauty. Her hair, set in long curls that dangled past her shoulders, was light brown with golden highlights that glinted in the morning sun. Her smooth skin, Alberto would later recall, was like amber; a perfect setting for her limpid eyes, blue as a summer sky, and a pink, pouty mouth. When she looked into Alberto's sad eyes, she smiled with an easy honesty that paralyzed him and found no possible response from his suddenly mixed-up emotions.

Long after the carriage disappeared among other vehicles on Villa Real street, Alberto would reproach himself for having been too cowardly to answer her disarming smile, and he hoped--in vain as it turned out--that he would get another chance.

From the narrow side streets connecting the outlying barrios to the central part of town, the peasants--mostly highland Indians-- streamed forth, wearing their finest clothes in order to impress the Ladino's gods, who, they had come to realize, apparently responded better to appearance than sincerity. With slight variations dictated by their particular tribe, their dress was similar. The men wore plain, ankle-length, white cotton pants and matching shirt under their woolen ponchos. The *Chamulas*, as the Ladinos called all the native people from the town of Chamula, were distinctive by the fact that their ponchos, or tunics, regardless of design, were always black and white. The Chamula men were short, powerfully built, wearing *caites*; a type of sandal made from hardened leather, which produced a strange clopping sound as they trudged upon the town's cobblestones. On the other hand, the *Zinacantecos*, (from the town of Zinacantán) tended to be tall and slim, though just as muscular, and their skin was of a darker shade of copper. They wore the most colorful attire, with a fringe and tassels on each corner of their finely woven, red and white cotton tunics. Their hats were actually thick, flat discs of woven straw with just a slight dome in the middle from which multicolored ribbons fluttered in the wind as they trotted by, which they did in preference to walking. That image was a good reflection of their happy and lighthearted ways; They always seemed to be laughing or smiling. But it also reflected their pride, as they were the only group still re fusing to wear the pajama-like trousers that the other tribes had adopted in deference to the Ladinos. They clung to their traditional garb, even though it looked more like a huge diaper. The men all carried long staffs made of the hardest wood and mounted with a long metal tip. They used it to aid their climb along the mountains but, whenever necessary, also as an effective weapon to bring down a mountain lion or any other enemy.

The women, generally barefooted, wore long black skirts with a colorful fringe that matched their broad, woven waist sashes. Their blouses, spotlessly white, were embroidered around the collar and sleeves in traditional designs that traced their lineage back to the days when only their people inhabited these lands. Most of them wore shawls which doubled as baby carriers on their backs. Their raven-black hair, shimmering steel-blue in the sunshine, impeccably clean and perfectly combed, was usually parted in the middle, braided with ribbons at each side and wound in a circle at the top of their head. And always, behind those gentle faces and bashful smiles was a look of great resilience and resignation that had brought them through centuries of change and suffering and seemed to promise that they would still be here long after the European invaders perished.

In a cleared field, adjacent to and just below the towering church of Guadalupe, vendors had set up rows of stands, and a carnival atmosphere was already in the air. Pastry and candies made with fruits and spices abounded, as did the hot or cold beverages to enjoy with a variety of foods already exuding tantalizing aromas.

Handmade masks, wooden toys and games for children and adults were arranged in tiers to attract customers, while the night's fireworks displays, set up at the field's perimeters, were being inspected one last time. In the center, near a moss-covered fountain that bubbled forth in fits and starts, a pinewood bandstand with a conical oak roof, had been decorated with bright streamers and banners, as was the whole backdrop of trees along the stream that disappeared behind the old temple. In a clearing to one side, several native children ran back and forth, screaming with joy, chasing a large yellow kite with rainbow colored tail that they had been given by one of the vendors. In front, all the streets leading into the basin were decorated with intricate, multicolored rice-paper cutouts that hung on wires strung from one rooftop to another and which fluttered with a nervous buzz in the morning breeze.

Already a virtual parade of horseless and horse-drawn carriages was pulling up to the base of the church's long staircase ceremoniously delivering the cream of San Cristobal's society, while the bulk of the faithful--poor and middle-class Ladinos and "Los Indios"--climbed either side of the grand staircase and entered the temple through one of the smaller arches flanking the central portico. The central staircase remained tacitly reserved for the people of influence and importance: politicians, wealthy landowners and venerable aristocrats; people who had controlled the town in one way or another since the time of Diego de Mazariegos, exactly four centuries before.

The crowd strained to get a rare glimpse of Don Erminio Contreras, an obese, white-haired old man whose land holdings were said to stretch clear to the Guatemalan border and who often explained his ever expanding girth by bragging that he had promised to retire just as soon as he outweighed the stock of solid gold that he had accumulated in his safes. He was carefully helped up the stairs by his two heirs and their families. They were followed by the black 1922 Reo of Don Abelardo Schwartz, the Austrian merchant who owned several rubber and coffee plantations in the southern mountains. The Rojas family, who controlled the cacao industry exports for the entire region, arrived in a landau coach pulled by four white horses wearing harnesses that virtually dripped with the purest silver from the Taxco mines.

However, the males in the crowd were most appreciative when the Barrasa family arrived, because it wasn't often that one could get so close to such exquisite charm and feminine beauty as that of the Barrasa girls. Don Miguel, a wily political tactician and behind the scenes manipulator, was aware of his daughters' growing fame and justly proud of it, but did not yet understand its full implications since other aristocratic families were already avoiding them due to their own daughters' reluctance to endure direct comparison to Elena, Isabel and Laura.

When the last bells chimed for ten o'clock mass, most of the important people had taken their places in front pews reserved for them and in some cases with their family names inscribed upon them in bronze plaques for all to see. The lesser families, like the Silmars, who owned the dry-goods store, the Santiagos, who owned the town's distillery, and other merchants or people of means but not of pedigree, filled the back rows of that middle sections.

Outside, at that moment, another of the important figures of San Cristobal's power structure appeared from a side street. Astride a handsome gelding and wearing his dress uniform, General Celestino Aramenta cut a most imposing figure. He was a man of about forty, well tanned and very fit. He had appeared in town two years earlier as the head of a military contingent sent by the federal government to implement the policies of the provisionally appointed Governor of Chiapas, following the death of the sitting governor during a peasant uprising along outlying parts of the state. The General arrived amid a flurry of rumors about him which only grew and solidified with time.

It was said that he had cut his military teeth fighting in the north alongside the legendary rebel, General Francisco 'Pancho' Villa, until the famed general retired peacefully to his ranch under a specially arranged government pardon.

Aramenta, then a colonel, suddenly switched his allegiance and joined his former enemies in the government. It was whispered that he had earned his rank of general by arranging Villa's assassination in July of 1923. It was also rumored that he had several mistresses because no single one of them could satisfy him, that he slept with a gun under his pillow and one eye open, just as General Villa himself had done, and that he could put a bullet between a man's eyes from fifty paces, every time. No proof of any of this was ever offered and the General himself never confirmed or denied a word of it.

All that was known with certainty was that he lived in a house near the barracks on the other side of the aqueduct and that he was a harsh taskmaster with his enlisted men. He loved to parade through town on his favorite horse, wearing his dress uniform, as he did now, which included German riding boots, a pearl-handled American revolver and a chest full of medals. During these rides he had taken to dropping in unannounced upon the town's most prominent families. Lately, he could be seen visiting Don Miguel Barrasa nearly every day.

Now he rode up to the church stairway and the crowd parted before him, but he had no intention of entering a place he held with undisguised contempt. To him, all such temples were a crude reminder of the inherent weakness of the masses and their inability to face the normal travails of life. God, in all his forms and disguises, was just a creation to appease their fears. Religion, he often said, was the greatest controlling devise ever invented by man.

Just then, several elegant young ladies passed in front of him and his sneer immediately became a smile. He greeted them with a tip of his military cap and some pedestrian remark about their beauty. The ladies hurried by, giggling and whispering among themselves.

General Aramenta turned his horse triumphantly and headed down a narrow trail towards the stream, well aware that he was now the center of attention. Not fifty meters ahead, in a small ravine, he came upon a group of youngsters playing marbles in the middle of the path. When they saw the horse approaching, all but one of the youths scampered up one embankment or the other. Alberto Sanchez, the one whose turn it was to shoot, remained on his knees, absorbed completely by the game. His playmates yelled at him, warning of the approaching horse, but he ignored them.

"Out of the way, you snot!" the General growled. Alberto ignored him too, and continued to line up his next shot. The officer, used to having his orders instantly fulfilled and aware that the crowd was still watching, was enraged by the impudence of what appeared to be nothing more than a lowly servant. He urged his mount forward with the whip but the animal refused to trample the boy and even under the painful jabs from its rider's spurs would only approach him sideways, neighing and rearing up in protest and alarm.

"Can't you hear, you bastard?" Aramenta yelled, and his insult hit a mark which he could not have known existed. Alberto jumped immediately to his feet and glared up at the horseman.

"Why the hell don't you just wait?" he screamed.

The audacity of such disrespect brought audible gasps from some onlookers. From the General it brought a swift kick to the side of the boy's face, which sent him sprawling to the ground.

"Maybe that'll teach you to respect your superiors!" the officer exclaimed, more for the public's consumption than for the insolent youth he was already leaving behind. What he didn't realize or anticipate was that Alberto, with blood running from his mouth, had already scrambled to his feet and scampered up the embankment. He ran around a large oak tree after the horseman and flung himself from a branch down upon the unsuspecting rider. He landed on Aramenta's back, clawing viciously at his face. The horse, startled as much as it's rider, reared up, dropping both man and boy to the ground, and sprinted away in a fright.

The General, dazed by the fall, sat up and was in the process of getting to one knee when his attacker pounced on him again, like a wild animal, flailing away with punches to the side of his face and the back of his head. It sent the officer face down into the ground, but reaching back with one hand, he managed to grab his attacker by the shirt, and although the boy continued to hit him he countered with a single blow that sent Alberto reeling back several feet. This time Aramenta regained his feet, and seeing his adversary falling on his knees to the ground he reached for him only to receive two handfuls of dirt flung violently and with accuracy at his face.

Blinded now and furious, he screamed at the youth: "You son of a bitch!" and was immediately struck on the side of the head with a large rock, which sent him for the third time to the ground. Alberto was on top of him in an instant, hitting him as hard as he could and spitting his own blood at him like venom.

Desperately now, the General grabbed blindly for his gun only to find an empty holster. Then he reached into his right boot and his hand emerged with a dagger, but Alberto saw it in time and lunged at his hand. They wrestled for the weapon momentarily but the General was obviously far stronger, so Alberto sank his teeth into the soldier's wrist, biting him with all his might. With an angry cry, Aramenta released the weapon, but in his semi-blinded state still managed to grab the boy by the hair and he began to shake him violently. He didn't realize that the boy had already picked up the knife until he suddenly felt the pain of his own weapon tearing into the flesh of his thigh. Automatically, he reached for the site of his pain, only to then feel the disorienting havoc of sharp steel tearing through the muscles and vessels of his throat.

Years later, Alberto would comment that it sounded and felt like slamming a knife into a watermelon.

General Celestino Aramenta fell back onto the reddish earth one last time as strange noises sputtered and gurgled through the blood that was already streaming from his throat, mouth and nostrils.

The disbelieving crowd fell silent for a moment; shocked and mesmerized by the surreal scene. Slowly, they approached and surrounded the dying man and the young boy who was still standing over his victim, glaring at him with clenched fists, as if expecting the battle to continue.

"You'd better get out of here, kid!" someone in the crowd advised. "The authorities will be coming and they will all be on his side."

Several others muttered their agreement. Alberto looked at them in bewilderment until he found a familiar face.

"Pedro, you explain it to my mother." he said, "and to my brother Carlos too."

"Hurry, boy!" someone yelled. "Go quickly or they'll kill you." In a flash, Alberto disappeared through the crowd. No one in San Cristobal would see him again for nearly four years.

That was the first time Alberto Sanchez took the life of another man.

The General was dead. Someone knelt down to cover his contorted face just as the church bells tolled again. At the bandstand, nearby, where the musicians had been setting up their places and preparing their instruments, the lead trumpet proceeded to play taps until the bandleader turned to glare at him, whereupon he returned calmly to polishing his horn.

Carlos did not receive the news until several hours later, just before the police arrived to interrogate his father. Don Carlos invited them into the parlor for a drink and calmly denied any relation to or even any knowledge of Alberto Sanchez, but he offered his permission for them to search his house, which they declined after a second drink, assuring him that it would not be necessary.

Only then did Carlos realize that the reason Alberto had been so much on his mind the past several days was due to another of his dreams. It was of a celebration taking place inside some dark, cavernous hall. Many of the guests wore strange costumes: some had dirt and leaves painted on their clothes and even on their faces, others hid their identity behind knitted masks, like large stockings fitted over their heads with two holes for their eyes. Still others danced around a bonfire, feeding the flames with books, scrolls and ancient manuscripts handed up to them by priests from open graves where Indians slept. Brightly colored piñatas hung from the rafters and Ladinos wearing suits fought for the chance to break them, only to then be showered with thick tar that oozed out, caught fire and spread the flames in all directions. There was a stampede for the exits and many people were trampled. Carlos, caught up in the panic, ran out with the first group but noticed that one of the trampled victims was his brother Alberto. He looked back but did not stop to help him. And it was that guilt which had kept him troubled but unable, or unwilling, to remember.

In reality, he searched for Alberto several days--discreetly, in case he was being watched or followed--but his brother had disappeared without a trace. The speculation grew through town that the authorities must have found him and executed him on the spot to avoid drawn-out legal complications. It happened all the time.

The quadri-centennial celebration turned out to be the most memorable ever seen in San Cristobal in spite of--and some would say because of--the unfortunate incident that sent General Aramenta so unexpectedly early to his grave.

By the evening of that historic Sunday, nearly all of the town's people were engaged in the celebration in one form or another and large groups of people from Comitán, Ocosingo, Tuxtla, Tapachula and even some dignitaries from Mexico City, had arrived to join them. Photographers representing various local, regional and even a few national journals, scurried to set up their large wooden cameras along various parts of the city in order to record for posterity the sight that would identify San Cristobal for decades to come: The procession by more than fifteen thousand people circling its way up San Cristobal hill, carrying torches in the crisp night air. It began at six in the evening with groups leaving from each of the town's fourteen churches. The groups grew steadily along the way, drawing people from their homes like magnets as they passed.

Eventually all the groups came together at the central plaza and headed for the church of the town's patron saint, atop San Cristobal hill on the south end of town. The tail end was still streaming onto the plateau three hours later, long after the church itself had filled to overflowing.

In his sermon, Bishop Osvaldo Uribarren--the latest clergyman to inherit the celebrated mantle of Friar Bartolomé, along with the traditional title of 'Defender of the Indians'-- never mentioned his old enemy, Celestino Aramenta, who had jailed him years before for secretly preaching the gospel in a mountain village, and then had him tortured for refusing to publicly recant his beliefs and his faith in any power other than the power of the government. Nor did he mention the young boy who, hours earlier, had sent that nonbeliever prematurely to account to the ultimate judge for his deeds upon the earth. The bishop knew that it had been just one more incident adding to the polarization of the inhabitants of this tortured land--the exploiters versus the exploited--which had started four hundred years before in a frenzy of greed and would not stop until it exploded and spread like wildfire through the entire world within another century.

Carlos, sitting with the entire Cansino family at the back of the small church, sent up a prayer for his brother, Alberto, and another for Anna Maria Valdemiro, who was sitting nearby, among his sisters, apparently still oblivious to the simple fact that he loved her madly.

In fact, she knew it very well, but did not care. Like many of the other young girls in the church at that moment, Anna Maria was only concerned with attracting the attention of a very shy but extremely handsome young man named Fernando Suarez, who was standing alone, near a side entrance. She had no idea that he was the maternal half-brother of the suddenly famous Alberto Sanchez, who in turn was the paternal half-brother of Carlos Cansino, her greatest admirer.

The mass, which to appease the government was called a commemoration of the founding of the town, but which everyone knew to be a celebration of the Catholic faith, lasted nearly two hours. By then, the crowd inside the church and the thousands of candles they carried in, had used up so much of the oxygen that several people fainted, including Catalina Guirau Olea, a pretty, ten-year-old girl sitting directly behind Carlos. He didn't even notice her, because he was too busy fighting back the tears of unrequited love.

Three months later, a young girl that Carlos barely knew, greeted him in the park of the Immaculate Conception with an unexpected embrace, and slipped a note into his pocket.

"I am alive," it read, "and no longer troubled by the old pig's snoring." There was no signature and none was necessary.

Chapter 3

Catalina Olea was born in 1918 in Chilón; a tiny village hidden in the central mountains of Chiapas, in the south of Mexico. She was the first and only child of Magdalena Guirau Olea, a pretty young woman with large green eyes, who was as frail as she was attractive. The few people in Chilón who got to know Magdalena during the short time she was among them, remembered her as a melancholy girl who displayed flashes of the vivacity and exuberance that had obviously been central to her nature sometime in her past.

The story that they pieced together after her death was that, as a sixteen-year-old, living in Valparaiso on the Chilean coast, she had come down with pneumonia, not for the first time, after an impulsive romp in the frigid ocean waters. She had then come under the care of a handsome young doctor who, while curing her malady, had infected her heart with the far more serious illness of love.

However, Magdalena's father, Don Jose Iturbide Guirau, an old-fashioned and very stern Catalán, would not even consider such a union. His opposition was fierce not only because his daughter was so young, but also because, as his only child, she was the promise of the fulfillment of his dreams, for which he and his wife, Doña Natalia, had sacrificed so much.

As a young couple expecting their first child and struggling merely to survive the economic decline that had swept Europe and would eventually culminate in World War I, they decided to confront destiny on their own terms. So, on a rain-swept winter night, they boarded a ship in Barcelona and sailed for the new world with only the clothes on their backs, the hope in their hearts and the price of passage. Magdalena was born on the ship, delivered by the Swedish Captain on the afternoon of the first day of the new century.

They landed in Cartagena, Colombia, and settled there, just blocks away from the old Palace of the Inquisition and the slave market that centuries before had served the Spaniards as the major transfer point between Spain and the new world, bringing slaves from Africa and returning home with plundered gold and precious stones.

"And now," Don Jose had told his wife with a wry smile, "it is we Europeans that arrive on these shores to become slaves; paying for the sins of our fathers."

Don Jose, a mason by trade, slaved away in Cartagena for the next seven years, struggling from one scarce job to another. Then, in 1907, upon learning that a series of earthquakes had destroyed most of the city of Valparaiso, on the coast of Chile, he envisioned a great demand for skilled masons emanating from the ruins of that misfortune. So, severing their roots once again, the Guiraus traveled by boat, raft and canoe along treacherous rivers deep in the great Cauca valley and then on horseback through uncharted, snowcapped mountains and finally down into dense jungles inhabited only by wild animals and elusive tribes of headhunters, until they reached the port of Buenaventura on the Pacific three weeks later and boarded The Lazarus, a broken-down old Portuguese merchant ship that took them to Valparaiso.

This, their second major transplantation, turned out to be a long-shot gamble that paid off handsomely. Within ten years, Don Jose Guirau had become owner of his own construction company and had earned the right to call himself an architect. He moved his family to the exclusive hillside neighborhood of *Los Cerros del Alhambra*, into a large, colonial house overlooking the sea, which reminded Doña Natalia of the French seacoast of her childhood.

From their bedroom balcony they could gaze down upon the marketplace surrounding the statue of Juan De Saavedra, the Conquistador who, it was claimed, stood on that very spot in 1536 and changed the name of the little Indian fishing village of *Quintil* to *Valle del Paraiso*, and then, to commemorate the occasion, ordered a dozen natives chained together to take back to Spain.

The Guirau's daughter and only child, Magdalena, attended the exclusive Valparaiso French Academy where she was taught French, music and the fine art of being a lady. Under such care and guidance she blossomed into a delicate beauty worthy not only of her parent's sacrifices but even of their tremendous pride.

By then, Don Jose and Doña Natalia were often being included in the invitation lists to Valparaiso's most exclusive social functions and upper-class affairs, and if they avoided discussing their expectations for their own future even with one another, it did not prevent them from reading them in each other's eyes when they gazed upon the cream of Chilean society in all its elegance and glamour.

It was for all those reasons that when Magdalena so unexpectedly professed her love for this very nice but very common young doctor, her father momentarily lost his self-control and flew into a rage; and it was only his wife's remarkable composure that prevented what could have been a sad and ugly family tragedy.

The thought to Don Jose that his daughter would even think of marrying a man so clearly beneath their hard-earned social status was an outrage, and even when he had calmed down several days later, his decision was clear: He forbid Magdalena to ever see the young doctor again.

Magdalena, always as stubborn as her father, proved to be equally resourceful, and she found ways of circumventing his orders just as fast as he formulated new ones. Soon, it became a war of wills, more entrenched and bitter with each thrust and parry.

Caught helplessly in the middle, Doña Natalia was left to wonder where it would all end.

Her answer came one day when Don Jose announced that he had sold everything and now the three of them would be taking a trip.

He would not say to where or for how long.

Their meandering journey took them first by ship back to Cartagena, passing through the newly completed Panama Canal which Don Jose considered one of the modern wonders of the world and said so to all who would listen and some who would not.

Throughout the cruise, Magdalena remained locked in her cabin, crying tears of rage and throwing up the food that her parents and the ship's doctor kept forcing her to eat.

After two weeks spent in Cartagena visiting old friends and two more weeks in Caracas, attempting to interest his daughter in the latest wonders of the industrial revolution, it became clear to Don Jose that his daughter's only interest was in reestablishing communication with the doctor at any opportunity and at all costs.

That was when he decided to search for the most hidden away, least accessible place he could possibly find and to remain there for as long as it took to bring his daughter to her senses.

"Twenty years, if necessary!" were his last words on the subject.

So it was that on a sweltering afternoon in June of 1917, Don Jose Iturbide Guirau emerged from the dry riverbed outside the village of Chilón, in the southernmost Mexican state of Chiapas, at the head of a small and tattered caravan. Wearing boots and trousers caked with dry mud up to his hips and a white, long-sleeved shirt turned brown by the reddish dust hanging in the air, he pulled along a scrawny horse carrying his wife. She wore a long satin gown that only hinted at past glory through the rips and stains accumulated in the dense thickets of the Central American mountains.

She also wore the solemn look of defeat, having finally accepted the total futility of trying to reason with her husband and the thought that it was all her punishment for having married a man she had never truly loved. They were followed by two Guatemalan *Kiché* Indians carrying Magdalena, semi-conscious with fever, on a makeshift stretcher of branches and twigs. Several other Indians, including two women and a child, brought up the rear, herding three mules loaded down with all of the Guiraus' remaining possessions. Four other loaded mules had been taken by the Mexican rebel forces they encountered several days earlier in the mountains, along with all the money and jewelry that was found in their possession.

Their caravan trudged down the village's only real street, looking like an apparition from some nether world, eliciting wary glances from the few people still outside braving the stifling afternoon sun. They stopped at the dusty central square where Don Jose, knowing he had reached the limits of his wife's tolerance as well as those of his own pride, proclaimed: "This is the place!

"We'll build our life here!"

No one listened. No one cared. Least of all his daughter, who was dying of dysentery, peeling from the blistering sun and shivering from the freezing cold that emanated from the marrow of her bones.

Crossing the square, Don Jose entered the town's only store to inquire about food and lodging. He was greeted by Florinda, a wide-eyed Ladina with an easy smile and a round, rosy face. She informed him that the nearest such accommodations would be in the town of Yajalón, another six hours up the road.

"Young lady," echoed Doña Natalia's ghostly voice, "my daughter is dying. We need help."

The young woman immediately turned to a back door, even as she removed her apron. "This way, please." she said, leading them past a courtyard full of ducks and chickens and through a rusty gate in a rear, ivy covered wall, then up a terraced hill to a large, imposing house with tall, white, sentinel pillars flanking its entrance where crimson and orange bougainvillea flamed over the veranda to the polished cedar porch.

With quiet efficiency, Florinda set in motion all the necessary procedures as she passed. Servants emerged to carry Magdalena to a spacious bedroom while others led the horses to the stables and ushered the Indians into the servant's quarters to be fed. Florinda explained that the nearest doctor was days away in San Cristobal and, in any event, it was doubtful he could be persuaded to make the trip. However, there was a very trusted *curandero* in Yajalón, and when Doña Natalia asked if he could be sent for, Florinda said it had already been done.

She introduced the couple to her mother, Doña Juanita, a plump, graying woman who had been out in the orchard supervising the pruning of the citrus trees, and who turned out to be as affable and gracious as her daughter, if somewhat more reserved. Then, in recognition of their obvious fatigue, they were taken to a guest cottage behind the main house, where they were amazed to find two large wooden tubs, set side by side and already filled with cool well water, pine fronds and almond oil for their baths. Dinner, they were told, would be ready by sundown, giving them about two hours to relax and enjoy their first real bath since leaving Guatemala City, nearly a month before.

So thorough was the sudden reversal of their situation that Don Jose wondered if it might all be delirium caused by the grueling sun, but the refreshing bath waters, redolent of mountain springs, reassured him enough to fall asleep in the tub, holding his wife's hand. When he awoke she was gone, and she returned as he was dressing for dinner, to report that Magdalena's fever was still high but an herbal tea had stopped her shivers and she was resting quietly for now.

"Don't worry," he told her, "she's much stronger than she looks."

"Perhaps in mind, but not in body." Doña Natalia answered with a rueful anger, having already felt the first premonition of her daughter's death.

In the dining room, one end of a large, elegant table that could seat twenty people was set for the four of them, separated from the unused portion by a Turkish candelabra made of silver. Doña Juanita presided at the head of the table with the Guiraus at her right, across from Florinda. They were served a five course dinner that included a stew of local beef, cured ham from San Cristobal over rice, smothered with forest mushrooms seasoned with bay leaf and accompanied by a hearty red wine from Argentina. The meal concluded with a rich chocolate dessert made from cacao beans grown on the premises and a genuine sherry from *Jeréz*.

When Don Jose remarked upon the impressive layout of the house, with its spacious hallways and views of the town below from almost any window, Florinda explained that it was all built to the specifications and requirements of her father, Don Trinidad Olea.

She said that she would be happy to give them a tour of the house but that it would probably be more interesting if her father did so himself the following day, when he should be returning from a hunting trip with her three brothers.

After dinner, Florinda mentioned that they could adjourn to the parlor for a game of chess if they desired, but if they preferred to turn in early and rest after such an arduous trip, it would be quite understandable and very prudent. They opted for the latter and, after checking on Magdalena one more time, being assured that someone would stay with her through the night and inform them of any adverse change in her condition, they were led by a servant with an oil lamp back to the guest cottage.

However, they did not go to sleep for several hours. Instead, they made love for the first time in months, and while caressing each other in silence under the golden glow of a flickering oil lamp, they rediscovered feelings that had somehow been misplaced more than a dozen years before.

At about three or four in the morning, Don Jose got out of bed very slowly, careful not to awaken his wife. He put on some clothes and slipped out of the house in his bare feet. Stealthily, he made his way in the darkness, aided only by the moonlight, past the garden and the orchard to the stables. Only there, inside, did he light a lamp to continue his mission. He searched each stall until he found the old, decrepit horse that had carried his wife across the Guatemalan Sierra.

After making certain that he hadn't been followed, he pulled a long iron chisel from his pocket and proceeded to pry off the horse's right front horseshoe. Once he succeeded, he used a knife to pry off the center of the hoof, like a lid, to reveal a cavity that had been hollowed out and which was filled with his wife and daughter's best jewelry and a handful of diamonds and rubies he had bought in Cartagena with the money from the sale of their home and their possessions.

The curandero arrived early the next morning. He was a Kiché Indian, dressed in old and worn Ladino clothes, and he carried a burlap sack filled with an assortment of things that he laid out on the floor near Magdalena's bed. There were plants, some fresh and others dried, and small bones like those of a bird; rocks painted with various designs and several small bottles filled with liquids, varying in color and consistency.

Magdalena was awake but still quite feverish and didn't seem to know what was happening or to have any interest in any of it. Her parents, upon seeing the medicine man's kit, exchanged skeptical glances. Don Jose asked the man what he was going to do but was ignored completely. At the foot of the bed, the native woman who had remained up all night with the patient, pulled a rosary from within her blouse and proceeded to pray in a droning whisper.

The curandero took a small, wooden ceremonial bowl that his ancestors had carved centuries before and placed it on the bed near Magdalena's elbow. He filled it with the liquid from two of the bottles and the mixture immediately produced a strong pungent smell that filled the room. Then he chose a particular twig, lit it on fire with the flame of an oil lamp and dropped it in the liquid. It produced a sudden flash of light that blinded everyone for a moment but also left behind a sweet and rather pleasant almond aroma that would remain in the air for several days. Moving with some urgency now, the young man sprinkled the dust of some dried leaves into the flame that still flickered in the bowl, causing sparks and plumes of smoke of different colors to rise up and saturate the darkness that had returned to the room; first an eerie yellow, then purple and finally an iridescent green.

Don Jose, who had been gazing at the effects of the colors upon the shadowy figures of the room, looked back at the young man and was startled by the shaman's transformation.

His face had become contorted and grotesque, as if all its features had swelled to exaggeration. His brow protruded forward and his cheekbones to the sides, and the muscles of his jaw could be seen writhing under his taut, glistening skin. His eyes looked bigger while deeper-set at the same time, and they reflected clearly the flame's flickering light. He seemed to be possessed, or in some kind of trance, and he was chanting something in his native tongue which sounded like an unearthly moan echoing from deep inside his chest. This he continued for several minutes, accompanying himself with a gourd rattle, until all the liquid in the bowl evaporated and the flame died. Suddenly everything returned to normal, as if none of it had ever happened, and it was only later in the day, when Doña Natalia remarked about the terror she had felt during the process, that Don Jose could be sure he had not imagined it. The curandero ended by taking a black residual paste that had remained in the bowl, and gently rubbing it on Magdalena's forehead, her belly and the soles of her feet. Then he packed all his things back into the sack.

"Well?" asked Don Jose, "Is she going to be all right?"

The young man replied in his native dialect, much to Don Jose's consternation, since he couldn't understand a single word.

"He says," came a voice from behind them, "that she will be fine, but it will take some time because the spirit has left her very weak."

It was the deep, confident voice of Arturo Olea; at twenty four, the oldest of the Olea sons. He introduced himself and went on to explain that the medicine man would leave some herbal remedies for their daughter and visit her every few days, but that she should not be moved until she regained her strength completely, which would take several weeks. Don Jose was immediately impressed with the handsome young man with wavy brown hair and deep blue eyes that seemed to smile from behind wire-rimmed glasses. Doña Natalia, on the other hand, realized right away that his inadequate glasses forced him constantly to squint.

They were joined at breakfast by Arturo and Florinda's younger brothers, Jacinto and Nicandro. Both of them were taller and darker than Arturo, and Nicandro was every bit as talkative. Jacinto, in turn, was extremely shy, but in time Don Jose would find him to be the most intelligent, able to speak with confidence on almost any subject while choosing his words with care. But neither of them possessed the charm or the self-confidence and poise that came so easily to Arturo.

Doña Juanita proudly explained to her guests that all of her children were hard workers, helping to run the store, the house and the ranch as well as their coffee plantation. Arturo was also the town's postmaster, a job that required him to open the post office for at least an hour every weekday. Nicandro was in charge of keeping the store stocked up for Florinda; a job that Jacinto would soon have to assume because Nicandro was about to get married and move to another town.

Doña Natalia said little, as usual letting her husband hold up most of the conversation, but she observed the Oleas carefully and was impressed by what she saw. It was nice, she thought, to find a family getting along so well together, where each member clearly had such affection for the others. The respect that all of the children demonstrated for Doña Juanita was also captivating because it was so natural and unforced. However, it was Florinda's love for her three brothers that moved her the most. Watching the young woman flitting around the table, anticipating the young men's every need like a doting hen caring for her brood, made the French woman wish she'd had more children of her own. Perhaps then Magdalena would not be so miserable, she thought.

Arturo proclaimed their hunting trip a great success. They had brought down three full-grown stags and a mountain lion. However, the prize they wanted most--a jaguar--had eluded them once again. Nicandro felt that it was that disappointment, rather than the rigors of the trip, which had kept Don Trinidad from joining them for breakfast.

Two hours later, Don Jose was standing at a balcony overlooking the main garden where their hostess was showing his wife the great variety of plants and flowers she had collected over the years, when Don Trinidad Olea joined him, preceded by the aroma wafting from his pipe. He apologized for his absence at breakfast.

"On the contrary," countered Don Jose, "it is I who must apologize for coming out of nowhere and disrupting your lives as we have done. Your family's hospitality to complete strangers is as rare as it is kind, and we shall never forget it."

"Nonsense! My daughter did what any Christian in this town would do. Now you are our guests and welcome in my home until your daughter is fully recovered."

"In that case, Don Trinidad, I must insist on paying for our stay."

His host puffed gravely on his pipe. "Well, if you insist," he said, betraying himself with a twinkle in his eye, "I think two games of chess each evening should just about cover it."

Don Jose laughed. "You'll forgive me for saying it, but that is so kind it's almost foolish."

"Oh, not at all." Don Trinidad assured him, "You see, I'll be doing all I can to destroy you." He blew smoke from his nostrils like a bull preparing to attack. "Especially since I can no longer defeat any of my sons." he concluded meekly.

The two men shared a laugh that seemed to seal the success of their first meeting and the beginning of a great friendship.

That was indeed the case. Within days they were addressing each other as Trinidad and Jose, and that soon evolved into just Trini and Ché.

Chapter 4

Don Trinidad introduced his new friend, Don Jose, to all the people who mattered in the little highland village of Chilón. Most of them were related to him in one way or another, usually as *compadres*, because he was the godfather to one of their children or they to one of his.

Ultiminio Aguilera, the one-armed *Alcalde* of Chilón, explained to Don Jose one afternoon over coffee, how for the past sixteen years either he or his Compadre Trinidad had held the mayor's office, switching every couple of years.

"At first the people voted, with all the ceremony of a midnight mass. He won that first time, and I defeated him two years later."

"Then I won again," Don Trinidad said, "and it went back and forth like that."

"So, pretty soon the people decided to dispense with all that bullshit and they told us to just decide between ourselves."

"Forgive my impertinence," said Don Jose, "but what does a Mayor do in a place like Chilón?"

"Not much." the two compadres answered in laughing unison.

"Oh, we get disputes sometimes," admitted Don Ultiminio, "about land boundaries or water rights, and we make a decision."

"We do try to be vigilant when it comes to the undercutting of the price of coffee or cacao to the exporting companies, because something like that could ruin the economy of this whole region. The exporters are always trying to play one grower against another."

"And where does the Mexican government fit into all this?"

Don Ultiminio took a slow sip of mescal. "The government in Mexico City changes more often than a whore changes customers," he said, "so, my compadre here decided long ago that we would have as little to do with them as possible."

"Whores or governments?"

"Well, one seldom minds getting screwed by a whore, but by the government . . . that's different".

"For example:" Don Trinidad explained, "whenever the government mounts another of its crusades against the church-- their favorite scapegoat--we effect a system that warns us if someone suspicious approaches town, and then we hang a chain and padlock on the church door."

"Yeah," the Mayor added, "and we put up some anti-catholic signs that the priest himself paints for the benefit of those buffoons who claim to run this country. Meanwhile, we use the side door to attend mass until it all blows over. It always does."

"What about the revolutionaries?"

"We stay out of politics." began Don Trinidad, "They stay out of Chilón." the Mayor concluded.

It seemed an idyllic life that appealed to Don Jose more as each day passed. Some of those days he spent on horseback, along dangerously narrow mountain trails that led to coffee plantations in fog-shrouded mountainsides. Afterwards, it was down through gorges, past waterfalls, into canyons that finally opened out upon the vast cacao tree forests that produced the large seed pods used here as currency by the ancient Maya Indians a thousand years before.

In the buzzing heat of the day and through sudden afternoon thunderstorms, Jose Guirau slowly regained a passion for life that had been dwindling from his heart since the day he left Valparaiso forever. In the evenings he could be found in the Olea parlor or front porch, contentedly marshaling his chess troops and quietly planning his next counterattack, enveloped in an aromatic cloud of smoke from his friend Trini's pipe.

In the meantime, their wives were also spending long hours together, mostly in the kitchen. To Doña Juanita Olea's delight, her new guest turned out to have an uncommon interest in the local cuisine. She was somewhat of an accidental cooking expert, having lived in so many different countries, and could usually find similarities between a new dish and something in her past gastronomic experience, be it French, Catalán, Chilean, Venezuelan or Colombian. Nevertheless, her interests in the food of Chiapas, which had more in common with the cuisine of Guatemala and the tropics than with that extending to the rest of Mexico in the north, was genuine. Once Doña Juanita was convinced of that, she reclaimed command of her kitchen from her daughter and her cooks in a way reminiscent of her days as a young bride.

Before long, and to everyone's delight, savory dishes that had been relegated to the menus for special occasions were emerging from the Olea kitchen on a daily basis. A newfound energy swept through the household. Amid clouds of smoke and flour, host and guest became teacher and pupil. This allowed Florinda to spend her spare moments away from the store at Magdalena's bedside, providing care, comfort and companionship.

Surprisingly, they found great similarities in one another. Both had grown up accustomed to keeping their feelings to themselves, bottled up until it seemed that they would burst. Although Florinda was not, like Magdalena, an only child, there was a limit to the things she could confide comfortably to her brothers. In each other they found the sister neither ever had.

And so, within a month of the Guiraus' inauspicious arrival, the Olea household had undergone a total and unexpected revitalization. There was an effervescent joy in the mansion on the hill, and for the first time in a long time, all of its occupants--with the possible exception of its harried servants--awoke each morning looking forward to the day ahead. This became especially true once Magdalena was fit enough to leave her bed and make forays to other parts of the house. Her delicate good looks, which had never completely abandoned her, even in the depths of her illness, returned now to their most captivating glory. Even the frailty of her convalescence appeared instead as an understated elegance never before witnessed in Chilón.

"She can make a room glow," Don Trinidad once pompously remarked, "simply by entering it." And it was lost on no one that the three Olea brothers, always in a rush to leave the house, were suddenly finding many reasons to remain.

All of this provided the perfect atmosphere for Nicandro's wedding, which as previously decided, the Olea's would host. The first invitations had gone out months before to those who lived the farthest away, not by mail--which was terribly slow and very unreliable in the mountains--but by letters entrusted to travelers, merchants and mule drivers. These were the people who brought back news from the outside world to remote places like Chilón.

Lately the news had centered around rumors of great turmoil in the distant kingdom of Russia and suspicions that the European conflict was boiling over to what the most pessimistic were already calling a world war. But all that was set aside, if not completely forgotten, as Nicandro's wedding day approached.

It was soon evident that the entire town would be directly involved in the celebration, not only because they were all invited but also because between sixty and a hundred guests were expected from outside and they would need accommodations. Don Trinidad made it known that he would reimburse all costs to those who provided any of his guests with a place to stay, but no one would hear of accepting recompense from a man they so admired and respected. Instead, the whole town mobilized to make their little village the jewel it had long been in their imagination. Walls were whitewashed, tile roofs repaired, drainage ducts cleaned and the four wooden benches in the central square were repaired and painted a pallid green to blend in with the newly planted shrubbery.

The main street--all three blocks of it--and the alleyways around the square, were washed and scrubbed until their cobblestones reflected the light from the new oil street lamps. Simon Salinas, a young deaf-mute who until then had led an aimless life, was put in charge of lighting the lamps every day at sundown; a job that filled him with so much pride that he never missed a day until his tragic death twenty-two years later when electricity was installed, making him redundant, and he attempted to get even by sabotaging it, but managed only to electrocute himself.

It was as if the whole town had been waiting for an excuse to renovate itself. All the homes, including the most humble on the village fringe, were given a thorough cleaning, if only to keep up with the neighbors. Their earthen floors were carpeted with fresh pine needles--soft, green and fragrant--to enhance the look, feel and smell of every room while providing them with a natural insecticide. Colorful flower groupings and arrangements made their way to the window sills and doorways, giving the village a joyful charm that became legendary and which it would never again match.

All this activity was reflected manifold at the Olea's home on the hill. During the last few days, both outside ovens were kept working day and night. Besides three dozen chickens to be served in the region's famous *mole colorado* sauce, two pigs and several young goats were slaughtered on the final day, to be cooked on open spits or wrapped in banana leaves and steamed in underground ovens that sealed-in the natural juices and left the meat so succulent and tender that it would fall from the bone with a mere stare.

Large kettles of *Tachilguil*--the thick Mayan stew that, like the mole, required countless herbs and several days to prepare-- were completed only moments before the ceremony. The servants worked right up to that last moment, setting up the tables and chairs under palm canopies in the main courtyard, adjacent to the orchard, even as the wedding ceremony got under way in the central garden beneath clear blue skies.

A string quartet, under the direction of the Swiss chemist and plantation owner, Don Ubaldo Hessig, played for the ceremony, while two marimba bands, imported from San Cristobal, set up in the yard under the lush and fragrant mango trees to welcome the newlyweds and provide music throughout the subsequent feast.

In the end, over one hundred and forty guests arrived from out of town, due to a larger than expected contingent from Salto de Agua, the bride's hometown in the steamy eastern lowlands and the place where the couple would make their home after the honeymoon.

The ceremony, presided over by Father Ezequiel Juarez del Alba, a retired but still influential octogenarian priest who had baptized all the Olea children, lasted over two hours but was completed without mishap, except for the two young ladies who fainted from either too much sun, not enough breakfast or--if you believed the local wags--a broken heart.

Don Trinidad Olea, wearing a suit tailored in Buenos Aires and given to him by Don Jose Guirau, had never looked so handsome as when he stood near the makeshift altar and gave the newlyweds his blessing. Doña Juanita, who had stood with him at another altar more than a quarter century before, was seen, for the first time in the town's collective memory, to shed a tear. Almost everyone there wrongfully assumed it was a tear of joy.

Magdalena, who had been prevailed upon to become one of the bridesmaids, witnessed the entire ceremony impassively, and remembering with every heartbeat the man who had been taken from her. She never noticed at what point she bit through her lip, only that when the blood slowly filled her mouth she became convinced that it was the metallic taste of hatred.

The celebration opened with the uncorking of two dozen bottles of genuine French champagne brought from San Cristobal's best hotel and used to start the toasts to the young couple. Don Leoneldo Moncada, the father of the bride and Salto de Agua's biggest chicken farmer, was by tradition given first honors and, upon seeing that the large gathering before him was not merely attentive but hanging on his every word, decided to forgo his succinct prepared statement in favor of an extemporaneous outpouring from his heart.

Nearly ten minutes later, by which time he was reaching back to memories of his own childhood, the increasingly uneasy crowd was rescued by a nod from Arturo Olea to one of the men in charge of the fireworks. With a loud hiss that caught everyone by surprise, a rocket rose into the sky, leaving behind a trail of white smoke that dissipated slowly in the wind. Seconds later the trail ended with an explosion that rolled like thunder through the hills and elicited appreciative applause from all the guests. Pretending to assume that the applause was for the speaker, Don Leoneldo was ushered off, giving way to the groom's father.

To the delight of his guests, Don Trinidad Olea was truly concise. Raising his glass to the newlyweds he said: "In these troubled modern times, a truly happy marriage is becoming rare. May God grant you both the kind of love it takes not only to create but to maintain such a partnership."

His words, applauded earnestly by all who knew him, were to Doña Juanita, like daggers plunged into her heart. Afterwards, instead of returning to her side, Don Trinidad joined Don Jose and the two of them talked, laughed and drank along with each new toast and long after the last one, finding greater freedom with each bottle that they emptied.

The number of people in line to propose toasts had been endless, but long before it ended the music struck up and the dancing started. Almost immediately, Magdalena became the partner most sought after, and she would later say that of all the remedies she had been given in Chilón, the attention she received that day had been the greatest tonic.

Meanwhile, at the far end of the courtyard, under Florinda's supervision, a succession of piñatas was provided for the enjoyment of the children. They were laden with candies that had been carefully wrapped so they wouldn't get soiled when burst from their colorful containers and showered to the ground.

The meal--sumptuous even for such an event and such a family--was served in the afternoon and continued long into the evening, accompanied by the sounds of the marimba bands playing old favorites as well as some new melodies already popular in the nation's capital.

It was then that Don Trinidad noticed Don Jose's fascination with the fireworks; especially the rockets that were periodically sent roaring into the sky.

"Would you like to try it?" he asked, and his friend jumped eagerly to his unsteady feet.

While a group of curious guests gathered in anticipation, Don Jose was handed one of the rockets. He inspected it carefully, having never seen one up close before. It was made from a section of bamboo, about ten inches long and an inch and a half in diameter, which had been hollowed out except for the very top. The man in charge of the fireworks explained that the explosive charge was inserted first and the remainder was filled with loose gun powder that served as the propellent. It was sealed at the bottom with paraffin wax, through which a small wick protruded. To this cylinder was tied a thin, flat piece of wood, about a meter long, which served as a stabilizer giving the rocket its relatively straight trajectory.

The man showed Don Jose his technique: Holding the rocket by its barrel in one hand and keeping it pointing up, he lit the wick with a cigarette. Immediately, a plume of smoke and sparks shot out of the bottom of the cylinder and toward the ground with a loud and growing hiss of such intensity that it made everyone back away instinctively. The man held on to it for a couple of seconds more, even as it squirmed, trying to break away. When he finally released it, it shot off into the air, straight up, leaving a spiral trail of smoke that the whole crowd followed with its collective eyes until it seemed to disappear into the blue. There was a momentary silence after the hiss died away, and then, finally, came the thunderous explosion that echoed and reverberated through the hills, and again made the audience applaud with delight.

"Now you." the old man said, with a mischievous smile, handing Don Jose the next rocket. He took it with obvious trepidation and then glanced sheepishly at Don Trinidad as if asking for help. The crowd was amused. His friend Trini just smiled with a shrug that indicated it was out of his hands.

Instead, it was the old man who offered a way out. He suggested that the rocket be stuck into the ground by its tail so that he would only have to light it, and Don Jose did just that. He pressed the tail firmly into the ground about six inches and even stamped down on the surrounding dirt with his shoe. Then he took a lit cigarette and brought it carefully to the wick, moving it quickly away as soon as the plume of fire appeared. He stood back a few steps and watched with everyone else as the plume of fire roared to life. However, after a few seconds of increasing roar, the rocket had not moved and the wide-eyed spectators realized in unison that it was planted too firmly and would explode right where it stood. Covering their ears, they tried to run away, crashing into each other in the effort. Just then, the rocket finally shot into the air, traveling only twenty meters before exploding with a deafening concussion that rattled every window of the house.

The subsequent laughter that rolled through the crowd was subdued with relief. Don Jose, embarrassed by his obvious mistake, put up one hand, asking for patience and then requested another opportunity. This time he looked for softer ground just as the crowd reclaimed its place to witness his redemption. Don Jose pressed the projectile gingerly into the dirt. Before lighting it, he shook it to make sure it was not stuck. Finally he lit it and moved away.

The hissing shower of sparks emerged but at the same time, and to everyone's horror, the rocket began to lean forward. It continued to do so until it was aimed straight at one portion of the crowd. Screams rang out. Some people were trampled and others were seen diving under tables and jumping over chairs. The crowd barely parted in time as the rocket roared past them and followed a horizontal trajectory through the dance area where it sent several couples sprawling to the ground. It continued past petrified marimba players and disappeared over the courtyard's far wall into the neighboring property of Don Gonzalo Moya. The crowd held its breath.

The rocket crossed the Moya courtyard, scattering the chickens with its roar, and entered the kitchen through a window just as the maid, Luisa, was preparing Don Gonzalo's dinner. There, it exploded with a thunderous blast that sent pots, pans and dishes flying and crashing to the ground. Not a single window pane was left intact, and when Luisa appeared through the smoke, dazed and confused, she tripped over the kitchen door which was laying on the ground.

It would take the maid over a year to recover her hearing, although she was back to work within a week. On the other hand, the orange tabby cat that had been sleeping, curled up under the chopping table, disappeared like a shot into the forest and was never seen again.

Don Trinidad Olea immediately dispatched a servant to offer his apologies to Don Gonzalo, the town's cantankerous historian and amateur philosopher, along with a promise to pay for all damages.

The celebration then resumed just as before, except that the fireworks were put safely back into the hands of the experts.

It was long past midnight before things started to wind down and people slowly headed off to sleep. When Nicandro and his bride rode away on horseback to their honeymoon in the isle of Cozumel the next morning, only their immediate relatives, nursing monstrous hangovers, were up to see them off. The celebration resumed that afternoon and continued unabated for nearly a week.

After that, several more days passed before the last group of wedding guests left Chilón and a few more before the little town was truly back to normal. By then, Don Trinidad, his two remaining sons and Don Jose had gone off to hunt wild boar. They stayed in a hunting cabin that Don Trinidad had built just for that purpose in the hills not far from his coffee plantation.

Their first day was fruitless and consisted mainly of preparations and tracking to ascertain the general whereabouts of the herds of boar. Since they never actually saw any of their prey or confirmed the few tracks they found, Don Trinidad felt certain that due to the dry spell they would have to go further down into the valley to find them. Arturo disagreed.

"Boars just don't like to be out in the open because they become easy targets for the Jaguars." he said.

"Yes, but all their water holes have dried." explained his father, "They have no choice but to make for the riverbanks and the lagoons."

So, they got an early start the following morning and extended their range into the valleys. They returned to the cabin long after sundown, tired and dirty but filled with the joy of success, carrying two male boars and a sow. They could have had a bigger kill, but decided to take no more than one adult from each herd.

Chilufo and Paula, the caretakers at the Olea's plantation, had dinner waiting for them and the men devoured it with glee. Afterwards, the four hunters sat on the front porch, in the darkness, drinking Mescal, easing it down with bites of salted lime. They were still laughing about some of the day's events and arguing about the accuracy of each retelling.

Apparently, when they found the first herd of boar, Don Jose, as the guest of honor, was given the first shot. He was standing next to a small tree so he placed his elbow on a limb in order to steady his rifle. His three companions stood back, glancing at each other, wondering how long it would take him to realize that the tree limb he had chosen was actually a large snake resting away from the hot ground. Now, looking back, Don Jose was willing to acknowledge that when the snake moved and he realized his mistake, he was startled and jumped back. However, Jacinto insisted that he had jumped at least ten feet and that they all had to duck to keep from being shot by his rifle flailing wildly in the air.

"Well," he countered, after the laughter died down, "At least I didn't shoot at some poor tapir."

"No, no, no! I swear it was a boar!" Arturo defensively insisted, trying to keep the tide of derision from turning his way. It was too late.

"Sure it was." Don Trinidad agreed with a wry grin. "A huge boar, with a long nose and stripes."

"It's a good thing there are no giraffes in Chiapas," Don Jose added, "or they would be in real danger during Arturo's Jaguar hunts."

Even Don Trinidad did not escape some remarks amid the laughter regarding his erratic marksmanship, but eventually the merriment died down, as the liquor slowly wore away their deeper barriers and the conversation went from jokes to reminiscence and from memories to more intimate confessions.

Arturo recalled the first few times his father took him hunting:

"The days were great, but I dreaded the nights. You see, Don Jose, I was scared of the dark. Afraid of the animals that might be lurking there. I was frightened by every noise, every sound. When we laid down at night somewhere in the mountains or the forest, no matter how tired I was, I couldn't sleep. Then I would hear my father snoring and I'd really fall apart. Sometimes I would cry. . . as silently as I could. The trouble was. . . that no matter how frightened I felt, I was much more afraid of letting my father know that I was scared."

Don Trinidad listened quietly but never said a word.

"I'm not afraid of the dark," Jacinto confessed, "just the evil spirits."

"You believe in evil spirits?" asked Don Jose with surprise.

"Sure. Don't you?"

"Well, I don't know. I mean, I've never seen one."

"Papa has."

"Really? Well," laughed Don Jose, "I'd sure like to hear about that."

Then, from the darkest corner of the porch the tobacco glowed red in the pipe bowl, followed by a slow, deliberate exhale that cleared a path deep into the past.

"I was about nineteen." Don Trinidad's deep, soothing voice began, "coming back to my father's ranch near Verapáz with my cousin Nacho after a weekend of . . . let's just say discovery and enjoyment, at the harvest fair in Simojovel."

His rapt audience chuckled collectively in the dark.

"Anyway, we stayed longer than we should have, so we had to ride all night on the way back. It was long past midnight when we crossed the Suchiate river near the ranch. Nacho was ahead of me and when I passed under some trees on the riverbank I saw her from the corner of my eye."

"Saw who?"

"A woman, wearing a shawl and crying. I stopped and asked her what was wrong and she looked up at me. I saw her clearly in the moonlight. She was Indian, about my age, and she was the most beautiful woman I had ever seen; with huge dark eyes, which made me think she was probably a *Juchiteca*. I dismounted, but when I approached, she turned and ran sobbing into a corn field. Nacho was already gone, so I tied my horse to a tree and went after her.

The corn was tall and thick but somehow she moved through it with ease, barely making a sound, and no matter how fast I ran she stayed ahead of me. Finally I stopped. I was exhausted, ready to give up; but she stopped too, and then she turned and smiled--just a gorgeous smile--and I realized that she was flirting with me. I don't know if I'd ever been more exited. So, I ran after her again and finally caught her by the arm. I could feel her trembling like a nervous fawn, and I was trembling with anticipation."

"What happened then?"

"Well, she grasped my hand but kept hiding her face from me.

Look at me, I told her. I was trying to reassure her. Don't be shy. Don't be afraid."

He paused to draw a breath through his pipe. "She finally turned around. . . and all there was under her shawl and inside her clothes were bones, a skeleton without an ounce of flesh; a skull with holes where her eyes had been. It had big teeth and its mouth opened and let out a loud, hideous laugh that echoed through the field and into the forest."

"What did you do?"

"I was petrified. I tried to scream but nothing came out. Her grip on my left hand was like a vise. I had to struggle to get loose and then I ran, as fast as I could. She was right behind me, screeching; a piercing screech that stabbed into my ears. I've never run so fast but I could feel her right behind me, surrounded by an awful stench, like rotting meat. When I reached the place where I left my horse, it was gone; it ran away, My legs felt like sacks full of lead, getting heavier all the time, but somehow I continued to run. I thought sure that I was going to die, I was so tired. The only thing that kept me going was my terror, and I kept running all the way to the ranch. The people who saw me arrive that night said I was trembling, unable to speak and white as a newly painted wall.

The next day my left hand was purple, almost black, and swollen to twice its normal size and we eventually discovered it had several broken bones."

"*La Llorona*." Don Jose remarked.

"Yeah." Don Trinidad agreed. "Of course, I grew up hearing such stories. Who hasn't? I never paid much attention to them because I don't think I ever really believed them. I've often told myself that maybe it was just my imagination playing tricks on me because I was so tired, or that it was the result of all the liquor we drank at the fair. But I know what I saw and under that full moon it was as clear as daylight."

"Why do you think she picked you?"

"I don't know. I've often wondered about that. Was it to teach me a lesson? To show me that my life was taking the wrong path? Who knows?"

"I've heard people say that she's sent by the devil," Arturo said, "to collect souls to keep hell's fires burning."

"Yeah," Nicandro chimed in, "just like that mermaid that entices sailors to their death."

The porch remained silent in the darkness for a moment. The crickets around the cabin were chirping non-stop.

"How did you ever get over that?" asked Don Jose.

"Time. Lots of time. Then, one day you just laugh about it. What else can you do?"

"Would you walk into a cornfield on a moonlit night now, Dad?"

There was a long pause. "Not even with this gun in my hand."

Arturo and Jacinto went off to sleep soon after that, but the two older men stayed up a while longer to enjoy the sounds and aromas of the forest air. This was a place that Don Jose Guirau found incredibly sublime.

The following night, sitting on the front deck among twinkling fireflies, he asked his great new friend, Trinidad, to sell him that parcel of land so that he could build a home there for his family. He felt compelled to confess that after all his travels and experiences he had come to realize that this quiet, uncomplicated life was the ideal place and manner to raise a family, and that he hoped one day to have the kind of family life that the Olea family so naturally enjoyed.

Don Trinidad listened quietly, puffing slowly on his pipe. After an uneasy pause, he explained that while he had never considered selling the place, he could not now think of a better use for it than that which his friend proposed, and therefore he would gladly turn it over to him. However, he went on, it was time for some honesty among friends. Don Jose was puzzled by the remark, and moments later was left stunned beyond belief.

Don Trinidad told him that his life was not what it seemed. He said that he and Doña Juanita had not lived as man and wife for many years; That for unknown reasons his wife had lost all interest in physical contact all those many years before and no amount of medicine, reasoning, counseling or witchcraft had succeeded in reviving the normal passions that as a young woman she had joyfully expressed. All that was left, he added, was the dissolution of their marriage, which although very difficult and complicated within the church, was well underway thanks to his wife's completecooperation and the influence of the Archbishop of Chiapas, who was an old friend of the Olea family.

Don Jose was stunned speechless. After a long night of reflection he could only console himself with the thought that this would certainly be the biggest shock he would suffer for a very long time. He could not have been more wrong.

Chapter 5

To Don Jose Guirau's surprise, both Doña Natalia and Magdalena knew about the irreconcilable state of the Olea's marriage. It seemed that only he had failed to notice all the signs, such as the fact that Don Trinidad and Doña Juanita were hardly ever in the same room at the same time, and on the rare occasion when they were, there was never the slightest sign of warmth or tenderness exchanged between them. Perhaps he had been thrown off by the fact that he had also never noticed any sign of rancor, resentment or disdain.

"They are beyond that stage." his wife told him. "They passed it years ago." In fact, all that was left was a semblance of gratitude that they had both finally accepted the inevitable in a peaceful way.

Still, it took Don Jose a long time to get over the sadness that this unexpected revelation made him feel. He was glad for the excuse that the construction work at the cabin provided for him to be away from the mansion on the hill and he threw himself into that labor with a fury.

There was land to be cleared, not only for the expansion of the cabin into a house complete with a central patio and a garden but also for a barn, a corral and eventually an orchard and a small field to plant corn and other vegetables. This required felling trees and chopping through some of the thickest vegetation he had ever seen at such an altitude. It was a daunting amount of work, but he welcomed it as if it was penance to atone for his sins. More than ever in his life, he felt that he was doing something of value for his family rather than just chasing another personal dream. It also crossed his mind that perhaps what he was really doing was running scared, hoping to avoid a fate similar to Trinidad Olea's.

To his surprise, he and the three workmen that Don Trinidad provided were soon joined by Doña Natalia; or Nati as he now started calling her. Although she had always been diligent in her duties as a wife and mother, men's work had never interested her at all. This time, however, she put on some of his old clothes, rolled up the sleeves and jumped into the fray, and he realized that she too was avoiding the big house the way people avoid a place where serious, long term illness has taken hold.

Magdalena, on the other hand, was happy to remain at the Olea's home even though she had recovered fully from her illness. She and Florinda now became inseparable. They spent most of the day working at the store, preparing and putting away stock, replenishing the shelves and attending to customers. They sold anything and everything that a small town could need, beginning with the most common foodstuffs like flour, brown sugar, salt, rice, lentils and many kinds of beans including fava and garbanzo. They had sacks of fresh-roasted coffee beans and cacao next to bins full of spices like cinnamon, clove and red *achiote*, and herbs like dry oregano, fresh rosemary, mint and laurel leaves. They didn't keep too many fresh vegetables because most people grew their own, but there was plenty of call for fresh fruit, especially that imported from the lowlands such as mango, *zapote*, quince, *nantze, jocote, anona,* guava, *guanabana* and plantain. Many of these they sold preserved dry, marinated in wine or pickled in the hard liquor called *agua ardiente*. Dry salted fish and strips of beef jerky hung from the rafters along with a variety of sausages that included *chorizo, longaniza* and *butifarra*. They had fresh pork and lamb, and if a customer wanted a chicken all they had to do was open a back door and chase one down. One section of the store had jams, jellies and preserves, along with a variety of candies made for them by an old widow who lived in Yajalón and was said to possess the secrets of the French confectioners. Another section of the store had fabrics for clothes, bedding, curtains and the like, along with the sewing needles and supplies of thread. To one side were piles of picks, shovels and assorted implements for farm or garden. A cluttered back room held stocks of coal, firewood, paraffin and rock salt. Special orders were taken for furniture, tiles, paints, leather goods and many other things which arrived weekly from San Cristobal by mule train when the weather conditions allowed.

During those days Magdalena learned to do things she would never have imagined doing years before, like manufacturing cigars and cigarettes by hand, layout and cut a dress pattern, mix feed for the horses and the cattle, milk the cows at dawn, roast coffee, churn butter, cut and wrap the chunks of chicle for chewing gum, stuff sausages and ferment grapes into wine. She did it now and enjoyed every moment. It was a rediscovery of life. Most of all, she enjoyed learning to speak in *Tzeltal, Tzotzil, Tojolobal* and *Kiché*, which were the prevalent Maya dialects in the region, so that she could talk to the natives and travelers as an equal and a friend.

In the evenings, after work, it became their custom to take long walks along the river, through the weeping willows and pine groves. Magdalena came to love the way the setting sun played in the heavens, splashing the clouds with gold and the blue sky with streaks of orange that slowly darkened, ending finally in a lovely reddish auburn that tinged the landscape and somehow coaxed the flowers and the fruit trees to release their wonderful aromas one last time.

The projected shadows of riders coming back to town or animals grazing near the riverbanks became very long, sometimes gigantic, moving silently past hillsides just before dark, and for brief moments the world again became the paradise so often mentioned in the bible that Doña Juanita read each night.

Often, they were joined in their walks by some of Florinda's friends from town, and sometimes Jacinto and

Arturo, back from their work at the plantations, would take them for a horseback ride.

On Sundays, after mass, they would prepare a picnic basket and take a buggy drawn by Florinda's fifteen-year-old swayback horse, which she named Pegasus but was better known as Old Snail throughout the region. They would go to the meadows of Lahcantzá. There, sometimes alone and other times accompanied by various friends, they passed the time among the wildflowers, feasting on whatever delicacies they had included in their baskets, chasing royal blue dragonflies or simply counting the clouds and daydreaming of a future certain to be bright.

On particularly hot days they would venture into the home of Chaac, the rain god: A dark cave with a slippery trail that wound through damp stalagmites, down into the earth about a hundred meters to a river that blew cool mists through its nostril caverns, like gigantic breaths preceded by the echoing roar of crashing waters, which could be heard for miles along the meadow. There, Arturo took special care of Magdalena, holding on to her, keeping her near, because over the years many people who fell into those waters had been carried off by the dark, swirling currents, never to be found again.

On occasion, Doña Juanita came along, and sometimes Don Trinidad would join them, but never both at the same time. Don Trinidad was living in the guest cottage behind the big house by then, and he spent most days at his office in town. His comings and goings were ghostly and though everyone pretended not to notice, to Magdalena it all seemed an insulting charade.

Things turned very quiet in the big house during those days. Magdalena sometimes felt compelled to walk on tip-toe to preserve the silence; the kind of reverent silence people observed in times of mourning.

In fact, during the evenings, the only corner of the house that came alive was the parlor where Magdalena tried heroically to teach Florinda to play the piano. It was no use.

"The cat will learn to play before she does." Arturo predicted. And then, one day, after another fruitless lesson, the cat ran across the keyboard and everyone burst into laughter. That was the last time Florinda was put through her ordeal. After that, everyone was content to sit back and listen to Magdalena play and sing.

"She sings like an angel." Jacinto observed one night.

"No." Arturo corrected him, "Even better. She sings like she looks."

Then, one day Doña Juanita suddenly announced that she would be taking a trip to Guatemala City, to visit her sister, and would stop to visit Nicandro in Salto de Agua on the way back. She expected to be gone about a month and would only be accompanied by Sarah, who had been her maid for thirty years.

When she left, her household duties were taken over seamlessly by Magdalena. There was no agreement or arrangement, or even a discussion about it; Magdalena just did it as if it was the most natural thing for her to do.

Within days she instituted a new and more daring menu and a tighter schedule for the care and maintenance of the garden, the orchard and the stables, all of which had lately fallen into disrepair. Jacinto, Arturo and Don Trinidad would find their clean, ironed clothes for the day folded neatly next to their polished boots outside their bedroom doors each morning. Their baths would be drawn and breakfast ready. Dinner would also be ready and warm no matter what time they returned home.

One night, when Don Trinidad sent word that he would not be in for dinner because he had too much work to finish in town, Magdalena packed his dinner in a basket and walked down to his office to deliver it herself. She found him sitting on the edge of an old cot in a dark room behind his office, and she set a small table for him near a window, lit by two candles she had brought. She did it all with the calm and self assurance of someone much older than her eighteen years, and she pretended not to notice that he had been crying.

He thanked her, expecting her to go.

"I didn't go to all this trouble to leave you here alone." she told him. "You'll have my company whether you like it or not.

And if you insist on eating here occasionally," she warned, "I'll have this place transformed into a proper dining room."

By then, Magdalena's parents had made great progress transforming the old hunting cabin into a proper home. The hardest part was over: The nights spent sleeping on the hard floor of a room with a wall and parts of the roof missing, at the mercy of the elements and the mosquitoes. Then waking up at dawn under covers damp with morning dew, only to find that their every muscle ached from the previous day's work to such an extent that they were nearly paralyzed, and wanting to go back to sleep and never wake again, but always being unable to do so.

Those were the days they would never forget; the days when they fell in love with each other for a second and final time. But this time it came over them calmly and quite deliberately, like the slow revelation of an ancient secret rather than the breathless excitement of a whirlwind. And it grew, not in a sudden frenzy amid the tumult of Catalonian summer nights, but in quiet moments and silent exchanges of a simple touch, a knowing smile or a wistful sigh exhaled into a virgin forest. Jose told himself that it was something in the land, in those mountains, which was somehow transforming their spirits and sharpening their appreciation of a life that all too soon was ebbing. Natalia, however, suspected that it was just the passing of time, giving them a last chance to see and appreciate life for what it was, rather than what they wished it was or pretended it to be. The result was the same: Both had known happier times, but neither had ever been so contented.

They were busy making adobe bricks early one morning, to take full advantage of the day's sun, when one of the workmen spotted a group of horsemen approaching along the hillside trail. To the Guirau's delight, it turned out to be Magdalena accompanied by Don Trinidad and his two sons.

A breakfast was quickly improvised for the first guests to the place that Don Jose had named 'Rancho del Destino'.

They ate outside, on the spot Doña Natalia had chosen for the southern veranda, and everyone agreed that it was situated perfectly, with a view of the valley stretching below them into a frothy white sea of morning mist.

They lingered long after breakfast, catching up on town gossip as well as on the latest news of the world to arrive from Mexico City, via San Cristobal. Russia's royal family had been placed under house arrest by revolutionaries. The United States had entered the European conflict by declaring war on Germany upon finding some evidence that the German government had tried to make a pact with Mexico seeking its help and promising to return Texas, New Mexico, Arizona and California in exchange.

Of greater concern was the news that an epidemic of influenza was sweeping the world and killing millions of people in its path. Nevertheless, all of that seemed so distant that its consequences might not reach Chilón for years, if ever. In the end, what was most important to the Guiraus was seeing how thoroughly their daughter had recovered. In fact, as they sat with Don Trinidad, watching Magdalena playing ball, teamed with the Olea boys against the three workmen, Doña Natalia remarked that she hadn't seen her so happy since their outings to the beaches of Valparaiso.

No one went back to work the rest of that day. In the afternoon they roasted a pair of *tepesquintles* that one of the workers trapped in the forest. Afterwards, the workmen took Arturo, Jacinto and Magdalena to explore what appeared to be an ancient Maya burial chamber they had discovered only weeks before on a hilltop an hour's ride away. The parents chose to remain in their hammocks to watch the evening's changing light. The temperature was so ideal it went unnoticed like the soothing breeze, and the fireflies too must have been happy for they were especially bright. The aroma from Trini's pipe lent the final touch of enchantment to the evening, and Nati remarked that she wished all her remaining evenings could be a copy of that one.

"You'll have to settle for about one month." Trini warned her.

"Then the rains will come, strong enough to wash away the past."

71

Nati was amused by the remark but astute enough to let it go.

"They'll be like nothing either of you has ever seen before. My word on that."

Eventually the conversation turned to more intimate matters and Trini announced that he had moved to a house in town and was in the process of refurbishing it. He said that his marriage had been dissolved; an annulment had been authorized by the church. The Guiraus were stunned, but they offered Trini their congratulations since it was obvious that he himself was delighted with the outcome.

The guests left the next morning after an early breakfast, and when they said good-bye, Magdalena unexpectedly gave her father a kiss on the cheek. It was something she had not done in over two years, since the day he ordered her to break off her relationship with the doctor in Valparaiso.

As they rode away, Don Jose stood in the doorway, watching them disappear into the forest and Doña Natalia noticed tearswelling in his eyes.

"I'm glad that's all finally behind us." she said, but he pretended not to know what she meant. Later, as they prepared for bed, he commented on Trini's astonishing transformation. "He looks ten years younger!"

"Yeah. I guess being single again can do that to a man." sheruefully agreed.

"No, Nati." he told her, "You mark my words; he won't stay single for long. Once a man has been married, the last thing he wants is to be alone again."

"Well, there are many single women in town. Any one of them would be lucky to get him."

"Yes. Trinidad is a good man."

The rains came the following month just as predicted, but by then the roof and all the main outer walls had been completed. Don Jose paid the workers and sent them home until the end of the rainy season. His plan was to spend that time working on the interior, but although there was plenty to do, he and Nati usually gravitated to the hammocks in the veranda, drawn by the surreal sight of the torrential rains that attacked every morning and often continued unabated into the night. The two of them spent hours on end watching the flurries of water that at times became so dense they would completely obscure all the surroundings.

Doña Natalia was especially affected by the sound of rain falling upon the dense forest foliage . Sometimes it was a roar that drowned out all other sounds, including their voices. More often, it was a whisper that lasted hour after hour and combined with the sullen gray haze of low-lying skies to spread a melancholy air into every corner of their home. Invariably, the afternoons brought with them the flashes of lightning that somehow penetrated that stubborn haze to reach inside announcing the thunder that sometimes shook the walls and always echoed long into the valleys. It took a while to get used to that, but it was, they thought, a small price to pay for the right to spend the remainder of their lives in those enchanted hills. That was a decision they had both already made, independently, without discussion.

For Nati, it was a decision that at first evoked great sadness, because it meant finally relinquishing the dream that sustained her through two decades of hardships: a dream that she would one day return to the sunny French hills of her youth. Now, bitten by the realities of her life, she accepted the fact that the idyllic places of her youth existed only in the nostalgia of her memory; that people and places change irrevocably with time, and that for some illogical reason no place on earth had ever burrowed so deep into her soul as the verdant hills of Chiapas, isolated from society as much by time as distance.

Meanwhile, her husband had arrived at the same decision, not with melancholy sadness but surprise. He, who had always seen his future in terms of success that could be measured in tangible assets for all the world to see, was in the end settling for a spiritual peace he had never known, or ever known he needed, in a place few people knew existed. It had taken him nearly half a century to realize the simple fact that happiness comes from within.

The rains diminished in intensity ten weeks after they started and subsided altogether by late June. Then the hills and valleys exploded in rainbows of color as the wildflowers rushed to bloom.

Under those conditions it was no surprise to see Magdalena gallop into the ranch one afternoon, accompanied by the returning workmen and Don Trinidad. They brought with them a basket full of river perch that were suddenly so plentiful the villagers could catch them with bare hands.

They decided to cook them on an open fire and Magdalena showed her mother how to prepare a marinade with limes, mango, tamarind and garlic. "Florinda taught me." she explained as she mixed the ingredients with the confident air of an old chef. Doña Natalia then found herself gazing at her child with admiration and pride.

"You've become a woman." she exclaimed. Magdalena blushed.

"Well, it's about time," she said, "Isn't it?"

After dinner, which by all measures was a complete success, Magdalena helped her mother with the dishes and the workmen went off to prepare their new accommodations in a back section of the barn destined to become the granary. Don Jose invited his old friend to the front porch to inaugurate the chess set that he had patiently carved during the long, rainy afternoons. After he lit his pipe, Trini made the first move and they both settled back to enjoy the wars that had brought them together in the first place. Halfway through the game they heard the crashing of dishes in the kitchen and the two men just smiled and shook their heads. Moments later, when Don Jose went to move his rook, his friend stopped him.

"Ché," he said, "we have to talk. It's about Magdalena."

Don Jose was caught momentarily by surprise.

"What about her?"

"Well, I know that for you she will always be your little girl, but the fact is that she is a woman in the fullness of life and ready to start her own family as the lord intended."

Don Jose sat back in his chair, no longer surprised. In fact, he had been expecting this moment ever since he watched his daughter and Arturo playing together at the Olea's home some months before. At that time he had surprised himself by thinking that Arturo would make her a suitable husband. Now, almost as if he had willed it, Arturo had sent his father to do his bidding. Jose Guirau assumed an appropriately serious air. "Go on." he said.

Trinidad Olea took a deep breath. "All right, I'll get right to the point. I'm here today to ask for your daughter's hand in marriage."

Don Jose cleared his throat. "First of all, Trini," he said, "I assume you're speaking on behalf of Arturo and not Jacinto. Am I right?"

"Not at all, Ché. I'm speaking on my own behalf."

Don Jose blanched. "What?" He sat up in his chair. "Is this some kind of joke?"

"I assure you, Ché, that I've never been more serious."

"But it's ridiculous. You're my age. She's just a child."

"She's older now than Natalia was when you married her."

"Yes, but that was different. . ."

"Don't let the age difference trouble you, Ché. Magdalena is very mature and I assure you I have a lot of life left in me yet."

Don Jose was forced to rise from his chair by the anger welling up inside him just as Magdalena appeared at the doorway.

"No! Absolutely not!" he yelled, "I will not permit it!"

"We didn't come to ask for your permission." Magdalena explained in a calm voice. "We were simply hoping for your blessings."

"Well," her father spat out his response, "you'll get neither!"

Doña Natalia entered the room, stood next to Magdalena and glared at her husband.

"I only want what's best for her." he explained.

"Oh, really?" Magdalena countered. "I seem to have heard that before, and it did nothing good for me then. Fortunately, I now have the right to make my own decisions."

There was an awkward silence that Don Jose finally broke.

"Fine," he said, "You can all do whatever in hell you want, but I'll have no part in it!" He stormed out of the room and into his bedroom, slamming the door behind him.

Four days later, Don Trinidad Olea and Magdalena Guirau, not half his age, were married by Don Ultiminio Aguilera, the mayor of Chilón, in a simple ceremony at his office. To mark the occasion, Celso Bracamonte, the town photographer, was hired to take a portrait photo of the couple and the guests in attendance. That photograph, which was promptly misplaced and eventually lost, turned up again almost two decades later at another wedding. It showed the couple, simply dressed, at the center of the small group. The groom, looking elegantly serious, had his arm around the diminutive bride whose big eyes and wide smile seemed to light the entire scene. At her side was Florinda, her great friend, maid of honor and new step-daughter. Don Ultiminio flanked the groom, while his Godson, Jacinto Olea, stood next to him. The bride's mother was the only other family member in the group. The rest were townspeople whose names had been forgotten with the passing of time.

The old photograph, yellowed and cracked by the years, had no date and no inscription, but it was heavy beyond its frayed cardboard mounting, laden with rumors and gossip and unanswered questions that time could not diminish.

It was said that Don Jose Guirau had not only refused to attend but had promised never to speak to the couple again. Rumor had it that Arturo's absence was the result of his own great distress, aching heart and bitterness caused by the loss of the only woman he would ever love in this world. Nicandro's absence was understandable, due to the distance and the fact that the rains had left the roads from Salto de Agua impassable. However, many loose tongues would later say that the tragic end to this marriage was the predictable result of one man's attempt to circumvent the laws of God, if not also of nature.

Chapter 6

Jose Iturbide Guirau spent the day of his daughter's wedding alone at the Rancho del Destino, drowning his sorrows in a bottle of mescal he had been saving for the day when he would present Magdalena with her own bedroom, to which he had been lovingly adding the final touches just the previous week.

It angered him to think he had been foolish enough to believe that she had finally realized everything he had ever done for her was for her own good. Instead, he thought, the minute he let down his guard, she took her vengeance.

He took another drink. Yes! Vengeance is what it was, he thought. It had to be. There was no other explanation. Why else would a beautiful young girl marry a previously married old man with children older than she, when she could have had her choice of any young man in the entire region?

He smashed his glass against the wall and started drinking directly from the bottle. Not only vengeance, but betrayal, is what it was. No question about it. In one fell swoop she not only destroyed any hopes he ever had for her, but also took away from him the best friend he'd ever had in adulthood. She had actually thrown away her future just to magnify his pain. With his next gulp of mescal he resolved, then and there, that he would never let down his guard again.

When Doña Natalia arrived the following day, she found him lying crosswise on the bed, fully dressed and passed out, completely drunk. When he woke up in the afternoon, she nursed him with a cup of herbal tea and several cups of coffee. He spent the rest of the day brooding in his hammock on the front porch.

In the evening, just as the fireflies emerged from the forest, his wife emerged from the kitchen and stood behind him on the doorway.

"You know," she said, "it was actually a nice little ceremony."

"I don't want to hear about it." he growled.

She remained at the doorway for a long time, listening to the sounds of the night. There was a hushed fluttering of wings as thousands of bats flew by on their way from their mountain caves to the river banks and ponds where they would feast upon a vast supply of insects. Moments later she heard a family of iguanas scampering along the roof to the safety of a burrow they had already made beside the chimney.

"Sooner or later," she admonished, "you're going to have to come to terms with the reality of things. The fact is. . ."

"Natalia," he again growled, this time in an unearthly tone she had never heard him use. "Listen to me very carefully." he ordered, without turning to face her. "I love you very much. And I still believe this is the place where we are meant to spend what's left of our lives. I will care for you and provide all the comforts available to us. All I ask in return is that you never again mention either of their names in this house or in my presence. Other than that, what you do is your business."

She thought of arguing with him, to sort things out before they had a chance to fester, but she knew that in his present state of mind there was no telling what he might be capable of doing. She remembered an old saying from Catalonia: Only a great bullfighter will fight a wounded bull, but only a great fool will fight a man with a wounded pride. She turned and went inside. Later, when he joined her in bed, she pretended to be asleep.

There were times in Natalia's life when she found it hard to believe that men could be so stupid. She knew what her husband was thinking. He actually believed that Magdalena had married Trinidad just to hurt him. How arrogant, she thought. How self-important! How easy it was for men to think that the world revolves around them and the sun rises for their benefit. She had to suppress a sudden urge to turn around in bed and slap him, and she giggled quietly to herself at the mere thought. Finally, lighthearted, she fell asleep.

However, this time she was wrong and her husband was correct. Their daughter had finally fulfilled a promise she made to herself while convalescing at the Olea's home, when it became clear that she would not be allowed to die, as she longed to do.

She had nearly managed it just days before that, traveling through the suffocating forest on a bed of twigs and branches, dehydrated by dysentery, burning with fever yet shivering from the glacial cold of malaria that twisted painfully in her bones. Maladies all which she could easily endure, but not when combined to the suffering in her heart: the debilitating agony of a lost love.

There, among the passing tree-tops, in the midst of her delirium, she felt herself approaching the relief that only death could bring. She felt the soothing light of peace; the final release, not only from the pain that ravaged her body but, more importantly, from the emptiness that tormented her soul. She surrendered herself to the feeling, but to her dismay, awoke instead in the bedroom of a home that, although strange, was still of this world.

Prayers, potions, chants, incantations and the tenderness of strangers all conspired to keep her alive, where she would have to continue enduring the pain of her great loss. So, in her anger she promised herself to make her father pay for his selfish injustice. However, the eventual result was not the outcome of some evil formulation on her part. It was more an accident of destiny that played into her hands.

The constant memory of the young Doctor she had left behind prevented her from taking seriously any of the flirtations or advances she received from Arturo Olea or the other young men she came to know in Chilón. At best, they would become her friends. Still, even that was more than the family patriarch, Don Trinidad Olea, had any reason to expect. To Magdalena he was merely an inhabitant of the alien world of adults; a world she hadn't yet realized would soon become her own.

At first she only noticed in passing that he was a striking figure for a man of his age. He was tall, lean and muscular. His light European skin had been permanently tanned by countless years of work in the fields of his plantation, and his black hair, still thick, was peppered silver at the sideburns, matching his neatly-trimmed mustache. His deep-set eyes, black as midnight, made his slightest glance seem like a penetrating stare and gave him an air of mystery and power, underlined by an erect posture and slow, carefully calculated movements. His was a figure that commanded respect, yet he had an easy manner, a surprising smile and a deep, warm voice.

Magdalena would later remember having wished her own father was more like him but giving it no more thought than that. Even after Florinda confided to her the sad state of her parent's marriage, she felt nothing more personal than sadness for them both. It was only later, when Doña Juanita went off to Guatemala and she took over the running of the household, thereby getting a more intimate glimpse into Don Trini's personal life, that her feelings for him began to change.

Although he tried valiantly to hide it, it slowly became clear to her that the ultimate failure of his marriage had left him devastated. He was wounded, perhaps beyond repair, and to Magdalena there could be no better proof of the purity of his love. She began to nurse him and, without telling him of her own pain, they grew closer with each passing day.

However, when it became clear that his feelings for her went beyond those of a grateful friend to those of courtship, she nearly laughed in his face. The only thing that stopped her was the thought of what such a relationship would do to her father. That idea intrigued her increasingly for weeks until she could barely sleep at all. Then, one day when Trinidad Olea found her conveniently alone in his garden and asked to know her thoughts, she said, "I think it's time we stopped these childish games. If you are as serious about starting a new life as you claim, we should be talking about marriage."

For their honeymoon they went to Tuxtla on horseback and then by train to Veracruz, where they spent two weeks in a grand, colonial hotel overlooking the Caribbean ocean. They were given the luxury suite on the top floor, which had a large balcony, tiled in blue and white like a reflection of the tropical sky. They enjoyed having breakfast out on that balcony and watching the procession of ships slowly approach the harbor hours before reaching the docks. They could also look down upon the harbor plaza where, four years before, Mexican forces battled North American marines sent by President Woodrow Wilson in a well-meaning but misguided attempt to aid the Mexican revolution against the illegal government of Victoriano Huerta.

The honeymooners spent most days exploring that lovely, historic old town in an open buggy drawn by a short, stout horse with reddish mane that the driver claimed was a pure-bred Mongolian mustang. Clemencio was the driver's name. He was an old man of indeterminate age, with craggy face and shaggy hair, and judging by the distinctive aroma that surrounded him, he kept himself in a perpetual state of inebriation. He was extremely talkative and had an encyclopedic knowledge of Veracruz, including the most detailed stories behind the erection of each monument, or the downfall of some important family, not to mention the intrigue behind every historical occurrence. And he told all those tales with such arm-waving gusto and such deep-voice bravado that listening to him made the couple feel as if they were present at each of those historic moments or witnesses to those salacious crimes.

Clemencio made those sightseeing outings so enjoyable and interesting that Trinidad and Magdalena went to great lengths to procure his services each morning, eventually paying him up to three times more than the normal fee; and when, after several days they realized he was making up all the stories and could not tell the same one twice to save his drunken soul, they realized also that they would not have it any other way. By then he had created for them a fascinating world, full of interesting people and defining moments; a world all their own, to carry in their memory and treasure in their hearts forever. As Magdalena summed it up: "What does it matter if it isn't true, or if it never happened? It became true in us."

It became in fact an episode of great importance in their lives. It was a memory, a piece of life that they could share with each other and with no one else; not even Clemencio, who wouldn't be able to recall it and had probably forgotten them just moments after they paid him and thanked him one last time.

When they returned to Chilón, a month later, they were followed by a team of mules loaded down with the things Magdalena had purchased in the shops of Veracruz as carefully as if they had been the shops of Venice. This included little gifts for every family member and each of their friends, including a tapestry that she bought secretly for Doña Juanita. She purchased many household utensils and bright decorations for every room of their own house.

She then set about transforming that house into something worthy of a town's sentimental patriarch and its most respected citizen. That process included buying out the neighbors on either side in order to enlarge the house enough to add several rooms and give it a proper central patio and garden. She had no illusions about matching the house up on the hill, but felt the need to prove herself an able partner and a worthy wife.

By then she was already aware that her impulsive decision to marry Trinidad was the best thing she had ever done. He was more caring and tender than she could have imagined, yet he was also careful not to suffocate her with his love.

Thinking about that one morning while she ironed his shirts, which she liked to do even though they had a maid, she realized that she was the fortunate recipient of all the things he had learned from his first marriage.

"Sure." Doña Natalia later told her, "There are two kinds of men in the world: Those who learn from experience and those who don't. And, believe me, there are far more of the latter than the former."

"Which kind is father?" Magdalena asked.

Her mother rolled her eyes skyward and the two women burst into laughter.

Less than two months later, when Trinidad returned from several days of harvesting the plantation's coffee, his young bride welcomed him with the news that she was pregnant. She assumed he would be happy but was quite unprepared for the degree of his joy.

After taking her in his arms and dancing with her through the house while he covered her with kisses, he placed her gently on a rocking chair and ran out to tell his old friend, Ultiminio Aguilera, the wonderful news.

People in town couldn't recall the last time they had seen him so happy, and it was plain that Magdalena and the prospect of a new fatherhood had rejuvenated him to an astonishing degree. His only regret was his inability to share that joy with his old chess partner, Ché.

During the ensuing months, Don Trinidad delegated more and more of his duties and responsibilities to Arturo and Jacinto in order to spend as much time as possible with Magdalena. He would take her for long buggy rides to the meadows and the valley and they would often picnic under the willows on the riverbank. There, they would spend hours remembering their time in Veracruz and laughing about the outlandish stories that Clemencio had told them and the fact that it took them so long to realize the truth.

Those were the happiest times in Magdalena's eighteen years of life, and the day she realized that fact she also realized that she loved Trinidad Olea more than she had ever loved her young doctor or even her own father, or would ever love any other man on earth. Suddenly, the thought of her original insincerity towards Trini shamed her to tears. Tears which he assumed were tears of happiness, just like the ones he felt welling up inside him, for one of the few times in his long and mostly happy life.

The following day, against her husband's wishes, since she was almost eight months pregnant, she rode her favorite horse out to Rancho del Destino, to make her peace with Don Jose.

However, her father locked himself in his room and refused to see her. Doña Natalia begged her to be patient. "Just let me work on him a bit more." she said. "I know he'll come around.

"It's been almost a year, mother." Magdalena pointed out. "If he hasn't come around by now, he never will."

They sat in the dining room to some chocolate, warm bread with quince jelly and fresh cheese, and talked about ordinary things. Then, before leaving, Magdalena stood at her father's locked door and spoke to him in a loud, clear voice.

"Father! You can punish me with your silence if it makes you feel better." she said, "But this child that I'm bringing to the world is your grandchild, whether you like it or not, and it hasn't done anything to you. I have a feeling that I won't be around to see it grow," she said, choking slightly on the words, "so I just came to ask you not to punish it for something that I did."

There was no answer, so she turned and walked out of the house. She was stopped at the front door by her mother, who was visibly shaken.

"Maggy, what are you saying? Is something wrong?"

"No, I'm fine." she reassured her. "It's just a feeling that I have. Just one of those silly feelings we women get."

Doña Natalia watched her ride away but had to hold on to the veranda to keep from falling to the ground. She was trembling; shaken by her daughter's confirmation of her own premonition that Magdalena would not live out another year.

Only three days later, Magdalena suffered her first fainting spell. The maid found her lying on the living room floor. Don Trinidad immediately sent his foreman to San Cristobal for a doctor, and another of his workers all the way to Tuxtla for the same purpose, just in case the first one failed or took too long. In the meantime, he also sent for the *curandero* in Yajalón. Magdalena protested, assuring him that it was all unnecessary, but he would not be dissuaded. Instead, he spent the night keeping a vigil at her bedside.

In the morning, she insisted on getting up for breakfast, just to show him that she was fine, but ended up fainting once again. This time he went into a panic, not knowing what to do, and that very afternoon Florinda turned over her duties to two Indian women who helped her at the store and she moved into her father's house to take charge of Magdalena's care, at least until the baby was born.

The curandero arrived that day. He prepared a concoction of oils which he rubbed on her right arm and under her left breast and over her swollen belly, and which made her skin feel warm and very sensitive. He then wrapped her arm in fresh banana leaves that were brought from the store at his request, and he spent a long time chanting over her.

Finally, he removed the wrapping from her arm to expose the skin which had become somewhat transparent, revealing the bluish blood vessels near the surface. He studied her arm very carefully.

"Well?" Magdalena asked him in his own Kiché dialect, "What do you think?"

"Your baby girl will be born a little early," he said, "but she will be healthy like a goat."

Magdalena was elated. "Did you hear that, Florinda? It's going to be a girl!"

Don Trinidad, meanwhile, was more concerned with his wife's health and its outlook but he was unable to get the young man to commit himself either way on that point, and he was angered by what he perceived was the curandero's refusal to tell him all that he needed to know.

Doctor Novojoa arrived the following day from San Cristobal. He was a curious looking man, probably in his fifties, with dark brown skin and other unmistakably Indigenous features, like high cheek bones an little evidence of facial hair. Yet, his dress and demeanor were European, as was his manner and his speech: very formal, dry and serious. He carried a black leather bag which gaped open to reveal many compartments and from which he extracted a glass thermometer from Austria, with its own gold case, and a silver stethoscope from France. Don Trinidad was impressed enough to feel a sense of relief for the first time in days.

The doctor gave Magdalena a thorough physical examination in complete privacy and emerged from her room an hour later to proclaim that she was fine. The fainting spells were not unusual, he said, for someone in her condition and in view of the fact that she was of a fragile nature. He prescribed a mixture of mineral salts, which he provided, to be taken by her at every meal. He said they would aid her digestion and metabolism. He also made a list of foods to be avoided and ordered complete rest for Magdalena until forty days after the birth of the child, whose gender, he assured them, no one had any way of knowing.

Don Trinidad, whom the doctor at first assumed was the patient's father, thanked the doctor profusely and invited him to join him and Florinda for dinner after he took his bath, which was all ready for him, as was his room for the night.

During dinner, Don Trinidad asked the doctor if he would stay until after the birth of the child. Doctor Novojoa stopped his spoon in mid-air and looked at his host in disbelief. "I'm prepared," Don Trinidad added, "to pay you five times what you would normally earn during that period."

The doctor put down his spoon and dabbed the corners of his mouth with his napkin.

"Do you realize what you are saying, Mr. Olea?"

"Okay, ten times, then."

"In effect, you are asking me to sell out my other patients, as if they were cattle or sheep. While it's true that most of them are not as wealthy or refined as you and your family, I'm afraid I'm from the old school that still believes that every human being is as valuable as another and every life as precious as the rest. Furthermore, I did not become a physician to get rich, but to help as many people as I can."

Don Trinidad was overcome with embarrassment.

"Doctor," he said, "you misunderstood me. I didn't mean to insult you."

The doctor reached across the table and put his hand on top of his host's arm.

"Not at all, Don Trinidad. I realize that your offer was not made out of callousness, but rather out of the great love that you have for your wife. I admire that. I'm merely pointing out that the poor people I tend to in San Cristobal are also capable of such great devotion."

Doctor Novojoa left Chilón the following morning with his ethics intact. Three weeks later, on a star-lit night and under the constant care of Doctor Mauro Fortunato, from Tuxtla--who had no problem accepting Don Trinidad Olea's generous payment for his extended services--Magdalena gave birth to a beautiful and healthy baby girl with dark hair and brown eyes, which she and Trinidad decided to name Catalina in honor of Catalonia, the land of Magdalena's father. It was a wasted gesture that failed to move its unforgiving and still embittered target.

At the very moment that Catalina Olea was born, a four-year-old boy sleeping in a large, dark and isolated room at his grandmother's house in San Cristobal, had a dream of a beautiful angel who entered his room and took him by the hand, stripping away all his fears with her gentle touch. It was a dream that would follow him into adulthood, reoccurring periodically until the day when it would become a revelation.

Unfortunately, there were a series of complications with the baby's birth, which only exacerbated Magdalena's precarious condition, and left her teetering on the brink of death for several days.

Don Trinidad stayed by his wife's side day and night, leaving the baby's care entirely up to Florinda. For the first month, that care included having the baby nursed by a young girl in town who had herself given birth two weeks before. By the second month, Magdalena was judged to be fit enough to take over the nursing, even though just holding the child for a short while sapped her of what little strength she had regained. Her health improved very slowly for the next several months and she suffered periodic setbacks along the way.

When the weather was nice, which was most often, Trinidad would carry her out to the patio, to a comfortable old rocking chair under an enormous elm. There he would sit by her side and tell her about all the plans he had for her and Catalina. They would travel to Mexico City, he told her, and then to Europe on one of those new ocean liners. Spain of course, he said, but also Italy and then the coast of France where some old friends owned a chateau near an ancient village called St. Paul Vence, and from whom he had a standing invitation. They would end up in Paris, where she could buy an entire wardrobe and they would stroll along the Seine like all the lovers of the world. He never mentioned the fact that the old continent was in the middle of a disastrous war and that soon none of that may be left standing, and she didn't find the need to bring it up.

She preferred to listen again to his story of being tied to the ground like Gulliver in Lilliput, and being shot by thousands of tiny arrows, only to awaken in that Veracruz hotel, being pelted by a summer rain blowing through the open balcony doors while his young bride sat nearby laughing into her pillow.

Eventually, Magdalena would fall asleep and then Trini would work on the garden around her, planting and caring for the flowers that she had come to love.

The months passed and the seasons changed but her health deteriorated despite all his efforts. She tried to get well, more for his sake than her own, because she could see that he wanted it so badly. But it was no use. She passed away quietly one morning as he enumerated once again his hopes and dreams and promises, just weeks before they were to celebrate Catalina's first birthday.

Magdalena's funeral was appropriately sad and somber, but it was in truth much more than that. It was a painful and disorienting loss to the entire town of Chilón, felt deeply even by those who had barely known her. It was a loss by proxy, because the man they regarded as the heart and soul of their little community emerged from his home that morning a broken man, this time damaged truly beyond repair.

Many, many years before, while still an awkward young man, Trinidad Olea became their leader, guiding them through one natural disaster after another--floods, droughts and crop failures--simply by his example as a tireless worker of the land, digging wells, building dams, canals and irrigation ditches with his bare hands if necessary. When even the wells ran dry, he organized caravans of horses, mules, oxen and people to fetch water from the valley in order to keep alive a portion of their scorched plantations to afterwards germinate the lands anew.

He was a shy, quiet, introspective man, but everyone soon learned to listen carefully to his few words because they were so carefully chosen, honest and direct. In time he became the moral conscience of their growing community, innately teaching them to maneuver through the minefields of constantly changing government administrations and their even faster changing philosophies: pro-church, anti-religion; pro-agrarian reform, anti-land dispersal; pro-centralized government, anti-oligarchy.

"Just tell them what they want to hear." he used to say, "Let them believe we understand and support their concerns." And sometimes, when pressed, he would explain: "One day, when they prove that their concerns are truly for the common good, and not just something they advocate out of convenience, we will indeed support them. But until then, we'll go on living according to the simple laws of nature and the directions of our conscience and the will of God."

As a result, while other towns and villages throughout the countryside were trampled by each succeeding political tide let loose by the 1911 dam-burst of the Mexican Revolution, Chilón managed to navigate virtually unscathed through the tumultuous years that ensued.

Eventually and almost imperceptibly, Don Trinidad Olea, the man, became the very spirit of Chilón. When he smiled, the town felt happy; all was well. His contentment was their joy.

Conversely, when his divorce from Doña Juanita was announced, a virtual period of mourning descended upon the town after the initial shock of such unexpected news. There was an undeniable sense of loss that ran down the streets into the alleys and increased along the gloomy darkness of the forest. Likewise, when he married Magdalena, his transformation was immediately reflected by the community which also seemed to have been rejuvenated overnight. His new happiness had been so complete and his joy so overwhelming that its sudden and tragic disappearance was almost more than they could bear. They watched him walking behind the ox-drawn cart that carried Magdalena's coffin up to the hillside cemetery and they were horrified by the sight. Overnight, his hair had become much whiter, dry and brittle despite Florinda's best efforts with lotions and pomade. His skin was pale and yellowish and the stubble of his unshaved face was, for the first time, white as mountain snow. Worst of all, the familiar gleam in his eyes was now a blank, empty stare that seemed to reach into the desolation of his soul. His pain was felt by all, especially his ex-wife, Doña Juanita, who cried alone in her room, in her mansion on the hill, more than anyone would ever know.

For all intents and purposes he died along with Magdalena, because he lost all interest in life from that day on. He existed for three more years, just a shell of a man, and he provided for his little daughter, everything except love. He didn't withhold it out of malice; he just didn't have any left to give.

Florinda had been raising Catalina, her half-sister, as if she were her own child. Don Jose died in a freak accident at his home while cleaning his rifle that winter and his wife, Doña Natalia, spent the remainder of her life at Rancho del Destino, although she was seen less and less with every passing year during which she fought a losing battle to prevent nature's reclamation of her land, so that eventually it was difficult to even find among the thick, lush vegetation the place where the path into the ranch had been.

Then, three months to the day after the death of Trinidad Olea, Florinda accepted the marriage proposal that she had been sidestepping for two years, since 1921, and moved with Catalina to her husband's home in San Cristobal.

Chapter 7

When Carlos received Alberto's clandestine note that afternoon of 1928, in the park, his first impulse was to deliver the good news to Doña Rosa, that her son was alive and safe, even if his exact whereabouts were still unknown. However, a glance at the public clock atop the municipal palace building indicated that Don Romulo would likely be home by then, so he decided to wait until the following day.

In the morning, from the small room he shared with his little brother, Antonio, and which was attached to the servant's quarters across the courtyard from the main building of the Cansino household, he headed out to the stables at the edge of town, near the Mazariegos lagoon. Running most of the way, he stopped only to steal a peach from the widow Perkins' orchard. The town's flamboyant money lender glared at him from a kitchen window.

Several of the town's servants were already at the stables, caring for their master's horses, when he arrived. They greeted Carlos with appropriate deference, removing their straw hats and bowing, but he knew that they secretly mocked him and were convinced that he was there only because his father was too cheap to hire a proper stable hand. The real reason, according to Don Carlos, was "to make a man out of him." It was the standard line he gave when anyone questioned his callous treatment of his oldest son. However, it did not prevent Carlos from feeling humiliated and he rushed through the process of feeding and cleaning the horses and mules that his family boarded there.

The morning sun was out by the time he headed home, and it dissipated his bad mood with its light. Just as he hoped, and even though he knew for a fact that Anna Maria was hopelessly in love with Fernando, he arrived home in time to see her walking down the street with three of his sisters, on their way to school. Although he could not muster the courage to speak to her, he managed to smile at her and she smiled in return.

At that instant, no one could tell him that it was only natural for her to smile at her friends' brother. In her smile he saw hope if not promise and he indulged his mind by ignoring what his heart already knew.

By the time he sat down to breakfast in the kitchen, he was in such good spirits that he amused the cooks and maids with imitations of some of the local officials that often visited his father, exaggerating their pompous gestures and their most obvious faults. Afterwards, he authorized the cook's purchases of groceries from the marketplace and ordered the supplies of coal, firewood and lamp oil for the week. Then he headed off to pay Doña Rosa that visit.

As he crossed the plaza, an uneasy feeling crept in amid the joy of his infatuation. It was the same feeling he always got when he met with Doña Rosa, because their relationship was so unclear. She was the mother of his half-brother, having been one of his father's mistresses, just as his own mother had been. But unlike his mother, Doña Rosa was from a plain, ordinary background. On the other hand, she was now the wife of one of San Cristobal's most respected legal minds; a man not only with money and old-world pedigree, but also with political power, which increasingly was the new currency of the land. How much respect was he supposed to show her?

As usual he found Don Romulo's home with all the windows shuttered and the front door barred and bolted, just as if it had been quarantined due to a new outbreak of cholera or typhus. It merely confirmed that the old man was gone. Only when he was home would Don Romulo allow the window shutters to be open. Otherwise, he suspected that his wife was seeing, or at least looking for another man, and he would fly into a jealous rage, making the most vile accusations.

Carlos knocked several times before Doña Rosa's tremulous voice asked for his identity.

"It's just me, Doña Rosa," he reassured her. "Carlos."

Even then, she first cracked open the door to verify it. She invited him in, closing the door quickly after glancing suspiciously at the street. Her nervous fear, sometimes verging on panic, was insidiously contagious. Besides, she treated Carlos with almost ceremonial deference, as if he was someone of importance, and it made him feel terribly awkward. This was why he seldom visited Alberto at his home, preferring to meet him somewhere else instead.

The cavernous house was depressingly dark, with only a flickering candle in each room. Carlos noticed that Alberto's little siblings, the twins, Amerigo and Amelia, were playing very quietly in a back room, beyond the kitchen, and their silence, so uncharacteristic for children of their age, triggered bad memories for him as well as a sympathetic sadness. He also noticed that the photo of Fernando Suarez, which previously hung prominently in the parlor, was no longer in sight and it gave him a perverse delight, followed immediately by guilt.

Doña Rosa invited Carlos to sit down and offered him hot chocolate, but the tremor in her voice indicated that she hoped he would decline; which he did.

"I just came to tell you that I've heard from Alberto, and that he's fine."

"What!" Her face came to life. "God of mercy! Are you sure?

How do you know?"

"He wrote me a letter." Carlos reached for the note in his pocket but remembered in time that she was illiterate, so he pulled out his handkerchief instead and wiped his brow.

Where is he?" she pleaded, "Tell me where I can see him?"

He didn't say." Carlos explained. "But I'm sure he'll write again, and when he does I'll let you know immediately. She thanked him through her tears and called down blessings upon him as he left, which he did almost immediately and with great relief.

Carlos had planned to go from there straight to the foundry, to give Fernando the news about their mutual half-brother. The fact was that he liked and admired Fernando, who was mature beyond his seventeen years, yet very unassuming despite his remarkable good looks. It would also be a good opportunity to ask him directly about his feelings for Anna Maria. However, the visit to Doña Rosa left Carlos depressed and his emotions were getting as convoluted and murky as his relationships, so he decided to visit Fernando some other time and headed home.

That night, hours after all the lights in his sisters' rooms across the courtyard had been doused, Carlos was still awake, bathed in moonlight on his cot, thinking of Anna Maria, whose gypsy blood was readily apparent in her smoldering eyes and flirtatious smile. When he finally fell asleep, he was visited by a new dream. It was of a beautiful young stag being chased through snowy woods by a large, hungry wolf. The chase was epic because the snow took away the deer's usual advantages of speed and footing. The stag was eventually cornered between the sheer wall of a canyon and a raging river. There was a moment in that dream, which would haunt Carlos for years, and which he would always recall with a chill. It was the instant when the frightened prey, gasping for air, sensing its predator's imminent attack, hearing the proximity of its menacing growl, suddenly stopped its desperate search for escape and turned to face its enemy. Transformed somehow, perhaps reconciled to the inevitable, the stag turned and stared straight into its attacker's eyes with an almost icy calm, suddenly devoid of all fear.

It was an instant when the world stood still and the balance of power shifted, almost imperceptibly, and the noise of the raging river disappeared; and Carlos knew somehow that the wolf had also felt that same chill traverse his body.

After that, the actions unfolded predictably. The attacks and counterattacks were swift and vicious. Sharp fangs and slashing antlers tore the flesh, drawing blood, exposing bone.

But the pivotal moment had passed and all that remained was the outcome, which Carlos never got to see.

Nevertheless, that simple dream left Carlos with a nagging unease. He sensed that this particular dream, more than the others, was specifically meant to reveal something to him, and he was convinced that it had to do with becoming a man. And becoming a man was suddenly the most important thing in his life. A man would know exactly what to say to Anna Maria whenever they met, and exactly how to say it. A man would never turn into an embarrassed fool with nothing to offer but a witless smile and an uncontrollable trembling in his gut. So, he resolved then and there to make his feelings known to Anna Maria, come what may, the very next time that they met.

He didn't have to wait long. The following Saturday evening he practically bumped into her at the entrance to the Sebadúa theater. She was in the arms of Ernesto Vindiola, the eldest son of a wealthy Turkish merchant, and she was the picture of contentment. She smiled her usual smile at Carlos as he passed, and he passed her once again unable to utter a word.

He was amazed at her ability to discard her feelings for Fernando as soon as it became clear that he didn't share them, and turn her attentions elsewhere with such ease. He tried without success to emulate her indifference. It took him a long time to get over her and his great disappointment. However, he eventually concluded that becoming a man involved, among other things, maintaining one's dignity through a complete control of one's emotions.

With Don Carlos' approval, he left school that year to concentrate on learning all there was to know about running a ranch and tending to the family properties. He convinced himself that he wasn't running from the obscure and mysterious challenges of romance, but rather taking a decisive step to the greater challenge of his future and of his place on earth, or at least within the local social picture.

When he rode out for *Los Molinos*, the family ranch near Verapaz, alongside his father and accompanied by two Indian workers from Tenejapa and a servant from Cuxtitali, Carlos felt himself breathing the clear air of manhood for the first time in his life. Don Carlos spoke to him in general terms about the responsibilities of running a ranch, farm or similar enterprise, but more importantly, he spoke to him as he would speak to other adults, calmly and without any edge of threat in his voice; almost as an equal. Carlos put on a serious and respectful facade, not only listening carefully to the advice but even exaggerating his degree of attentiveness to make it obvious that he was intent upon absorbing every bit of it. Deep inside he was ecstatic, almost giddy, with the joy and anticipation of finally achieving his clear and rightful place within the family.

At nightfall they camped on the edge of a wide stream, so shallow that its surface still clearly emulated the position of the rocks upon its riverbed, once jagged, now smoothed by the flow of a thousand years, but still able to produce the constant, soothing gurgling that lulled them all to sleep. Carlos, still excited by the new prospects of his life, was the last to surrender. For a long time, he stared at the dark, starry sky that centuries before had awed and inspired the artists, scribes and rulers of the vast Maya Empire upon which they now trod and on which vestiges of that fabled time now lay buried and unappreciated all around them. However, such thoughts also made Carlos increasingly uncomfortable, because they seemed to point out the insignificance of man upon the universe at the very moment when he was desperately trying to establish the significance of his own existence.

That night he was visited once again by the taciturn figure of Diego de Mazariegos, who had camped upon that very spot more than four hundred years before, and had stared at that very sky and searched the heavens for a sign about his own life, only to realize with a frightening finality that he would never find the happiness he sought, no matter how much gold he plundered.

Fortunately, Carlos had no time to brood about that in the morning. They were up with the dawn to a quick breakfast of river trout, cheese, apples, wild berries and black coffee. Then they followed a trail alongside the crystalline stream towards its origin deep in the mountains. Within hours the relentless sun was bearing down on them with such an oppressive strength that Carlos thought he was about to faint on several occasions. Even the Indian laborers, far more accustomed to the rigors of the land, were soaked with perspiration and breathing the thin air with increasing effort. The stillness of the atmosphere buzzed with a monotonous drone as heat rose in clear, wavy ribbons from the hot rocks and the parched earth, distorting the landscape.

Yet, as bad as the sweltering conditions made them suffer, what galled Carlos most was that it was all so ridiculously unnecessary. It would have been simple for them to stop at any moment to drink and refresh themselves in the clear, cool waters of the stream which was never more than a kilometer from their trail. All that was needed was permission from the master; a nod, an indication, a move from him in that direction. But it was not forthcoming and Carlos knew by then that it would never come. This was a test; Another in a continuous succession of tests to see if indeed he had what it took to be a man. A complaint or even a suggestion that they stop to rest would have been a disastrous failure on his part.

Once he was clear on that, Carlos resolved to prove himself no matter what the price. His greatest fear now was the possibility of fainting and falling off his horse. That too would be seen as proof of his weakness; an embarrassment to Don Carlos, and a black mark upon his character that might take years to overcome. Yet, there seemed to be nothing he could do about it. During the next hours, or what seemed like hours, he saw the world spinning around him on several occasions and had to grip desperately onto the saddle horn to keep from falling off his mount. In his disoriented state, he even considered tying himself to the saddle.

Then, without warning, the trail turned and fed down straight into the stream. The horses, not having to prove a thing, stopped immediately to drink. And just as suddenly, the whole atmosphere and climate changed as they were all enveloped in a breath of cool air that turned the sweat upon their shirts to frosty fingers on their backs. Carlos turned to find the cooling breeze emanating like a gigantic winter breath from a huge, gaping cavern that led straight into the mountainside and from which the river flowed. To his surprise, they proceeded into the cave, dwarfed even on horseback by the majestic size and splendor of the place. Its ceiling was in places higher than the dome of San Cristobal's cathedral and its walls, sinuous and moist, glittered and played with the light, reflecting it into dazzling displays. Every sound was magnified with an incredible clarity that echoed softly in the distance from every direction and hung in the air, above the soothing gurgle of the water. When the workmen, riding together about a hundred meters ahead, spoke to each other, Carlos could hear their every word as clearly as if they were talking into his ear. The temperature, so cool and refreshing, erased in a short moment all memory of the previous hours of misery. All these things at once were overwhelming. To Carlos, this awesome place felt sacred, holy, as no church or other place on earth had ever felt, and he had to struggle to hold back an onrush of tears he couldn't explain. It was a spiritual revelation and Carlos once again assumed it had to do with the transformation into manhood upon which he had finally embarked.

The great cavern became darker as it turned and twisted with the river into the heart of the mountain and the entrance and the sunlight disappeared. The workmen had brought torches, which they lit, and they rode in silence for a while, each man seemingly absorbing as much as possible the enchantment of the moment. It was then that Carlos asked his father if he was familiar with this place.

"Yes." answered Don Carlos, turning to gaze at his son's face, and for an instant looked as though he wanted to elaborate; to pass along some quaint story or perhaps relate some personal adventure, but thinking better of it, in the end just turned and rode away.

Eventually the cavern became smaller, forcing them to squeeze through in single file on several occasions and twice the water opened out into dark pools so deep that they dismounted, enabling their horses to swim through, unencumbered, yet towing them along, grasped to their mane. Later, when the water had all but disappeared and they seemed to have reached a dead end, a tiny shaft of light beckoned from a distant corner and led them out once again into the blinding sun.

It was late afternoon, most of the heat had dissipated and a welcome breeze accompanied them down into a valley. They entered Los Molinos ranch a short time later, having saved many hours by crossing through the mountain. Carlos had been at Los Molinos only twice before, many years earlier, but he had vivid memories of the place because those visits had occurred during festive occasions. His memories were of raucous music and large numbers of people dancing, eating and enjoying themselves in the open, decorated patio behind the large colonial house with walls so white that at night they reflected the moonlight, and roof tiles as red as the bougainvillea that spread over them at various places.

Now Carlos could hardly believe this was the same place. Not only did it look far smaller, but its charm had vanished and there was no trace of the vibrant joy that tinged his every memory of it. The white lime paste that covered the main building's walls like a thick skin had cracked and fallen off in many places, creating ugly, blotchy patterns and exposing its brown adobe flesh to the elements which had already started to erode it. The walking paths and horse trails leading to the compound, once neatly trimmed through the lush vegetation, were now dusty patches of parched earth, strewn with rusted tins, broken roof tiles and other nondescript and long ago discarded matter. Even the rows of large flower pots that Carlos remembered encircling the patio and the well, like a giant garland, had vanished, leaving behind nothing more than scattered shards, like those found along the desolate ruins of the Maya.

The five riders were welcomed only by three scrawny mongrels since their unexpected arrival caught everyone by surprise. Marcelo Zeta, the foreman, came out of the main house at the last minute, still holding up his pants and tying his belt. It was obvious from his hair, standing on one side and matted on the other, that he had been asleep, but he claimed none-the-less that he and the other ranch hands had just returned from the hills where they had been rounding up wild horses. He also claimed, when they entered the house, that he had just opened it and ordered the women to clean and prepare it for them. Yet, it was obvious that the house had been under constant and severe use by two and perhaps three entire families who clearly preferred its comfort to the wooden sheds beyond the orchard that were the servant's quarters.

The Patrón said nothing, and it was difficult for Carlos to read his father's silence. Even during dinner, Don Carlos made no comment, whereas Marcelo never stopped talking about the current severe drought, the previous winter's floods and the subsequent epidemics which had killed so much of the livestock and raised the prices of the fuel and grain and other foodstuffs. Carlos knew that there was truth to all of that, but he also suspected that Zeta was exaggerating all of it to cover up his incompetence, the crew's general laziness and the very common practice of diverting funds.

Carlos made a mental list of all the changes he would institute in order to return the place to its former glory.

The next morning, after a breakfast of black beans and fresh-laid eggs, tortillas hot off the *comál* and milk still warm from the cow, Don Carlos asked Marcelo how many new horses they had gathered.

"Oh, about a dozen, Patrón. There weren't too many; the drought has been hard on them too."

"Well, let's have a look at them. Bring them to the corral."

Actually, there were only eight but they looked surprisingly healthy. Don Carlos inspected them from a distance and then ordered that they prepare one of the stallions for breaking.

It took a while for the ranch hands to separate the wily animal and even longer to force it into the pen at the far end of the corral. Once they did, they quickly pressed the side fence in until the animal could barely move. Even then, the nervous horse bucked, kicked and nearly jumped out of the trap.

"This one's a lively one, Patrón." laughed Erminio, the oldest of the hands, while they waited to see which one of them would be chosen for the maiden ride. The general expectation was that it would be Marcelo, who had broken hundreds of horses over several decades as a ranch hand, but Carlos had a feeling that his father would do it himself, just to show everyone that he could.

Instead, Don Carlos turned to his son with a grin. "He's all yours." he said, catching him by surprise. Carlos immediately realized he should have expected it. It was another test; perhaps the final test before turning the ranch over to him, so he jumped into the corral, afraid that any hesitation on his part would be taken as a sign of fear. The animal looked even bigger from above and the feel of another creature on its back panicked it into such desperation that Carlos had great difficulty getting his boots into the stirrup loops of the thick rope that had been tied around the stallion's chest. Carlos tied the end of the rope tightly around his right hand and then squeezed the fingers of his left hand between the animal's back and the rope. He was so nervous that he hadn't even noticed the pain in his legs as the thrashing animal crushed them against the fence posts.

Carlos nodded to the men and the gate was flung open. Like a coiled spring the animal shot up into the air and sideways into the center of the corral, bucking ever more violently and changing direction in mid air with every jump, desperately trying to dislodge what it perceived was an attacker like the mountain lions and jaguars that preyed naturally upon them in the wild.

Meanwhile, Carlos was being thrown around like a rag doll, bouncing off the horse's back into the air only to be yanked violently back in mid-flight. His arms felt like they were being ripped from their sockets at the shoulder and there was no sign that the pounding he was taking was going to let up. Then his left hand slipped out and he decided to allow his feet to slip from the loops.

Before he finished the thought he was flying through the air, looking at the blue sky flashing by. He had time to rejoice in his freedom for only an instant before slamming to the hard ground on his back. The horse jumped over him, missing his head with its hooves purely by luck. Carlos lay writhing on the ground, unable to breathe, his lungs momentarily collapsed. The ranch hands quickly jumped into the corral to help him but were stopped by the Patron's order: "Leave him!" They turned, incredulous.

" He hasn't finished his job."

With small but increasing gasps, Carlos regained his ability to breathe and was eventually able to sit up. By then, and much to his dismay, the horse was already penned and ready once again. As he got to his unsteady feet and dusted himself, he glanced at his father and found him still sitting solemnly on the fence, looking past him, fascinated by the wild horse and apparently unconcerned about his son's condition. Carlos felt a twinge of hatred for him stirring inside but quickly reminded himself that this was just another test; perhaps the last.

When he remounted the animal, he noticed that the muscles in his forearms trembled uncontrollably, not so much from fear this time as from fatigue, and he consoled himself with the thought that the young animal must also be feeling the effects of the exertion.

The ranch hands were all smiles as they helped him settle into place. One of them even patted him on the back to encourage him; proof that he had won their respect. Another worker slipped a stirrup loop around the toe of his boot, but with a twist of his ankle, Carlos threaded his foot fully through it. The man immediately tried to slip the loop back off.

"Leave it!" Carlos told him, sounding eerily like his father, and he bent down to loop his other ankle.

"No, Patroncito!" the man protested. "Not like that. It's too dangerous."

But Carlos had made up his mind, and ignoring the repeated warnings he tightened the loops around his ankles. He knew very well that he was throwing away his only safeguard and that even experienced horsemen had been killed when a foot got tangled accidentally and they were thrown and dragged beside the horse, head bouncing on the ground and among hoofs. The alarmed ranch hands again turned to Don Carlos, expecting him to override such recklessness, but the Patrón merely raised an eyebrow of curiosity.

A nod from Carlos and the horse exploded into the corral. At first, the young rider managed to hold tightly to his mount, and by anticipating each of the horse's violent jumps and jerks he could emulate the movements and flow with them instead of using up his energy fighting to hold on. The horse rounded the entire corral bucking, twisting, jumping, kicking up its hind legs and bending its neck between its front quarters as it crashed back to the ground, yet its rider remained in place. By then the stallion was clearly tiring and the ranch hands were cheering. Carlos started to feel confident. At one turn he tried to focus on his father but immediately fell out of rhythm with his mount. Suddenly, the ride became far more strenuous for him. The movements became violent again as he was jerked down by the ropes around his ankles just as he was on his way up, and then slammed against the horse's back which was already rising again. He felt as if he was being hit on the rear end with a tree trunk. His eyes were rattling in their sockets and his arm and legs felt as if being torn from his torso.

After more than a minute of this punishment he decided to give up. He was about to release his grip on the rope when he remembered the loops around his ankles. This is it, he thought. I'm going to be ripped apart now. His body came crashing down on the horse's shoulders once more and his face smashed against the horse's neck.

He released the rope. His hands were free and he used them to push his body back up. His face was numb and his nose was bleeding. It took him another moment to realize that the torment had stopped. The horse, its chest heaving between his legs, had finally given up.

Carlos reached out and patted the horse's neck with gratitude. It was then that he noticed they had stopped directly in front of the Patrón. He refocused his blurry vision, cleared his throat and looked his father in the eye.

"Do you want me to do all of them?" he asked, in a deeper, more direct tone than he had ever used with him and with a clear edge of sarcasm.

"Later." Don Carlos answered. "You'll have plenty of time."

Carlos washed off his blood at the well, then removed his bloodied shirt and carried it into the house like a trophy, a badge of honor. He was just then beginning to feel the soreness that he knew would become almost unbearable by nightfall, but he was beaming with pride. One of the maids approached him and asked if he would like her to prepare his bath.

"Not right now." he said. "Later."

"Yes, Patrón." she said, bowing as he passed.

As he continued to his room he tried to remember if any servant had ever bowed to him with such honesty before. While he changed clothes, he kept looking at himself in the mirror, expecting to see something different. There was no doubt in his mind that he had just taken a huge step towards manhood.

When he returned to the parlor, moments later, he found the servants scurrying about with his father's luggage. Don Carlos appeared, dressed to ride.

"You're leaving now?" Carlos asked him.

"Yes. I'm going to check on the milk farm. You'll be going there next, when you are finished here."

"Fine."

Don Carlos called out to one of the ranch hands: "Tell Marcelo that I want to talk to him."

The two men stood in the Parlor, a few feet apart from each other, silently staring out into the distance, awkwardly pretending not to feel awkward.

Marcelo entered. "Yes, Patrón?"

"Marcelo, I'm leaving now. And I'm leaving my son in your charge. I want you to teach him everything there is to know about running a ranch."

"Yes, Patrón. Don't you worry. We'll take good care of him."

"No. I don't want you to take care of him. I don't want any special favors for him. Treat him just as any other ranch hand. That's the only way he'll learn. Understand?"

"Yes, Patrón. Just as you say."

Carlos was dumbfounded. Instead of being left in charge, as he expected, he was being left under the command of a servant. He felt his blood drain down to his feet with a sickening chill. His anger began to rise and he struggled to find the proper response without success.

Marcelo helped Don Carlos mount his horse and then watched the Patrón ride away. Carlos, still glued to the spot in the parlor, also watched him, not with relief as that of the foreman, but with a hatred bordering on madness. His mind was reeling with ideas for retaliation. He considered going after his father and confronting him. He thought of just running away. He even contemplated waiting for him in ambush in the hills and blowing his brains out. Or perhaps, he thought, blowing his own brains out would be the only escape from a life that seemed to promise so much only to deny it all in the end.

When he returned to his room he avoided his image in the mirror and that night he cried into his pillow, enraged as much by his father's degrading treatment as by the pain in his muscles and his joints and the idea that it had all been in vain.

His apprenticeship began the following day, and one of the first things he learned was that Marcelo, though completely uneducated, was a wily manipulator, able to tactfully get his way, one way or another.

"Look, Patroncito, "he told him at breakfast, "there's no sense moving you out of your room to the bunkhouse with the rest of the men. You wouldn't learn much from that bunch. Better you stay here, where the women can take care of you and the house at the same time."

Carlos readily agreed, even though he knew that Marcelo's real motive was to keep himself and his family also in the house.

During the ensuing months, Carlos learned to rope and brand and drive the cattle. He even learned to care for them when they fell sick or when they calved. He learned to harvest hay and alfalfa for feed and mend fences and dig irrigation ditches. He generally worked from sunup to sundown alongside the other hands and from their comments he surmised that they were working much harder than they had done previously. He also noticed that some of the livestock disappeared periodically and always when he was conveniently working at the opposite end of the ranch.

Whenever he started asking questions about such disappearances or about the strange men that sometimes rode into the ranch, the workload suddenly became much lighter, even to the point of providing him several days off to rest or go into Ocosingo for recreation.

Nevertheless, Carlos slowly imposed his will and increasingly exercised his power by engaging Marcelo on his terms and with his own tactics.

"I think we should spend some time repairing the house, Marcelo, Before the rains come."

"Oh, no. There are many other things to do. This week we need to make new fences by the river. I think that's where we're losing the cattle."

"Well, in that case, we'd better close the house down, so it won't get any more damaged than it already is."

"Well," Marcelo mulled, "Actually, we could have three men work on the fence and the rest of us could work on the house, Patroncito."

The walls were repaired and whitewashed. The roof was retiled and the garden cleared and replanted. Large vases were brought from Ocosingo, exchanged for several pigs, and set along the courtyard's perimeter, filled with a variety of flowers. Yet, before Carlos could bring the ranch back to the glory he remembered, a messenger arrived one afternoon with his new orders.

"Patroncito, Don Carlos says it is time for you to go to the milk farm now, to learn how to run that."

Dismayed but no longer surprised, Carlos said he would leave the following day.

"Get something to eat," he told the messenger, "and don't leave until I give you a letter for my father."

He repaired to his room and wrote a businesslike letter to his father, addressing him as Sir, and nothing warmer or more personal. He made a detailed report of the work that had been done and all that had been accomplished during his stay. He ended it by saying that he had found several discrepancies and suspected that many of the 'accidents' were in fact almost certainly fraudulent reports to cover up illegal transactions. He finished it by saying: "I will be able to provide details of these matters upon our next meeting."

And he simply signed it Carlos.

A week after he started working at the farm, he received a reply and he dropped it twice as he ran to the barn to read it, filled with nervous anticipation.

"You were sent to work, not to gossip like some marketplace washer-woman!" was all it said.

That single sentence, unsigned but clearly written by his father's own hand, would become a turning point in Carlos' life, but more than that, it would remain forever seared into his heart.

Chapter 8

In the autumn of 1928, a brazen roar disturbed the tranquility of San Cristobal, where before only the odd rumble and backfire of an automobile had shocked the ear or scared the animals. This, however, was no horseless carriage or tin Lizzie, but a Packard Twin-Six, touring sedan, more than twice the size and weight of any mechanical vehicle ever seen in that remote and virtually inaccessible region. It had a twelve cylinder engine in the Vee configuration with L heads and 6,950cc worth of combustion area.

Built in the United States in 1921, this model had already become one of the most popular luxury automobiles in its country of origin among people of wealth and refined taste. President Harding himself had been driven to his inauguration in one of them.

This particular car was a two tone, blue and gun metal gray luxury sedan, and it boasted a partial metal top, sealed to the elements, and partial convertible fabric enclosure to allow the enjoyment of a sunny day.

It could seat eight adults and one child comfortably in its plush leather seats and was reputed to be capable of speeds in excess of 100 miles per hour, though no one familiar with the Chiapas roads could even begin to imagine such a feat.

When it appeared over the horizon of the old cemetery road, it caught people's attention with the gleam of its chrome long before its distinctive roar could be appreciated. By the time it pierced the town's center, half a dozen children were running alongside, and when it finally came to a stop at the door of Florinda Fabre's house, a crowd formed almost instantly around it. Two strange men were sitting in the front and one of them stepped out first and walked around the impressive vehicle to open one of the rear doors, which barely cleared the high stone sidewalk typical of the times and designed both for the much higher carriages and the heavy winter storms that could turn those streets into rivers within minutes.

While the chauffeur turned off all the knobs and switches, the mechanic bowed to the gentleman barely visible in the cavernous rear section. Out stepped Gilberto Fabre, dressed in his best suit, holding leather gloves and bowler hat in one hand and a silver-handled cane in the other. Some people in the crowd actually applauded. He smiled, acknowledging their greeting and walked into the house, followed by the other two men. From a nearby window, Florinda was seen standing with the 10 year-old Catalina, gazing out with a blank stare and open mouth.

Gilberto Fabre hadn't been seen in San Cristobal for nearly four months and tongues had been wagging mercilessly with speculations as to the cause of such an unusually long absence. Had it occurred before his marriage, six years earlier, no one would have raised an eyebrow. Young Gilberto was known as an adventurer who would get involved in new, crazy and sometimes dangerous endeavors on a whim or a bet. After traveling throughout the state of Chiapas and subsequently extending his expeditions to the far reaches of the Yucatan peninsula, the Papaloapan valley and the Guatemalan Sierras, he had decided that he must see the entire world.

So, at the ripe old age of nineteen, while his own country was exploding into a prolonged and bloody cycle of revolutions, he became a merchant seaman on a ship that sailed from Veracruz to the western shores of Africa. There, after a disagreement with the Captain over wages, he jumped ship, spent a drunken week in the city of Accra, on the British Gold Coast, and somehow ended up scrubbing decks aboard a

British vessel taking palm oil and lumber to London, England, in her majesty's service.

The change was so easy and his interest being not so much to earn money but to see the world, that during the ensuing years he worked aboard a variety of ships under Dutch, Portuguese and Spanish flags, and a few others of decidedly dubious origin. Interspersed with visits back to San Cristobal, he traveled throughout the Mediterranean and around the horn of Africa to India and parts of South East Asia. Much of what he saw was blurred by liquor, which was virtually a requirement for a sailor reaching land after weeks of continuous, monotonous hard work, and Gilberto soon developed a love/hate relationship with alcohol that would stay with him to his grave.

Then, one day, in the middle of some distant ocean, his thirst for travel and adventure suddenly dried up, due to no specific reason, and gave way to a melancholy longing for the sleepy hometown he had left behind, a place to call his own and the love and companionship of a good woman for more than a few weeks at a time.

He returned that final time with enough money to buy a modest home in the growing barrio of San Felipe and still have some left over to finance for himself some kind of business. After dabbling in a variety of things, he decided to become a coffee and cacao merchant with a view to building that into an import/export business. He had seen, to his great surprise, how expensive both of those commodities were in Europe and that the demand kept growing in spite of that.

One day, on his way through the Chiapas highlands, leading a team of 36 mules loaded with sacks of coffee beans, he and his hired hands stopped in the village of Chilón to stock up on supplies. He met Florinda Olea there.

There was no immediate attraction for either of them, yet she remained in his mind and he felt enough interest to make sure his caravan stopped at that same store on his next trip to the region, even though that time Chilón was an extra day of travel out of his way. His visits to that little village, hidden away in the mountains, increased nevertheless in length and frequency, and although Florinda became very shy once his intentions became obvious, he was as patient as he was persistent.

Two years after he first proposed to her, she suddenly accepted. By that time, Gilberto had moved out of the coffee and cacao business, having found that the market was very unpredictable, unstable, and terribly susceptible to matters totally beyond his control, such as the weather and the machinations of unscrupulous buyers and exporters. He invested some money in the rubber trade that emanated from plantations in the dense jungles near the Guatemalan border because he knew some of the German capitalists who owned them, but the profits, although regular, were small.

Then he became a partner in a poultry farm and made good money the first year but an avian virus swept through the region the following year, killing ninety percent of all the fowl. In the meantime, he had met several like-minded entrepreneurs and together they formed an investment society. For several years they invested in a variety of commodities, goods, precious metal exploration and mining. They were always on the look-out for new opportunities in a land and at a time when new opportunities were becoming increasingly common. Gilberto had seen many things in the world which were still unknown in San Cristobal, and he knew they were coming. The strategy was to anticipate their arrival as well as their potential popularity.

At the time of his marriage, his scattered financial interests were returning an overall profit that allowed him, Florinda and Catalina a modest but comfortable life. That was fine for the moment, but Gilberto had expectations of something far more grand, and he gave himself a few years in which to achieve it. He felt certain of success because while the world was changing through wars, social upheavals, industrial advances and scientific discoveries, San Cristobal was still stuck in time, isolated and forgotten. Its people were still concerned only with petty personal things like their image and their honor and the opinions of their neighbors, as if nothing existed beyond the distant mountain tops.

His marriage to Florinda was everything he hoped it would be. She was strong and steady, with a sense of duty and none of the silliness that young women increasingly exhibited in those days. In a short time, she turned their house into the pride of the barrio of San Felipe, so neat and clean that the painting and decorating always looked as if it had just been done. She was a wonderful cook, accomplished seamstress and loving partner. And she had a heart of gold. Their only regret was that the child they both hoped for kept eluding them, but even that was alleviated by the fact that they had Catalina, the precocious child that more and more became their pride and joy.

When he arrived with the Packard, Catalina and Florinda met Gilberto and his companions in the corridor, just outside the parlor. He was in a loud, excited mood.

"Well, I finally made it back." he said, then, noticing his wife's puzzled expression, he introduced the two men: "This is Pedro Romero, our chauffeur, and that's Danilo Borja, our mechanic."

Far more fearful and no less puzzled, Florinda nevertheless invited the strangers into the parlor and offered them hot chocolate.

"Actually," explained Gilberto, "we haven't eaten anything since early this morning, so if Maria has anything in the kitchen to go with that chocolate, it would be a banquet for us."

They had chicken and rice in the dining room and between bites Gilberto told Florinda and Catalina about the problems they had encountered and the adventures that developed during the two and a half months that it took them to get the Packard from Mexico City to San Cristobal. That included chopping down trees and building a bridge across a gorge and a raft to cross a river. "It's never been done." Gilberto said, "And no one thought we could do it." Pedro and Danilo laughed and nodded their agreement but continued eating. Florinda said very little.

Afterwards, Gilberto said that he had to arrange for a place where the two men could stay as well as storage for the Packard. The three men drove off, carefully avoiding the deep ruts and potholes in the street that the rains had begun and the horses and ox-carts had finished.

Florinda had gotten a bad feeling when she saw the automobile through the parlor window and nothing she had heard so far made her feel any better. Maria Hernandez quietly handed her a peach brandy.

Since the end of the previous year, Gilberto had been growing impatient with his fellow investors. He complained that they were too conservative, too timid.

"You need to be audacious to get anywhere in this world!"

But his ideas and his schemes were always being voted down because they were considered too risky. By spring, when many of his bills became due and the roof needed mending and Catalina had outgrown yet another tutor, Gilberto became totally exasperated, so he broke with the investing society and sold all his shares.

Florinda was afraid that he would go on one of his drinking binges, as he had done several times before, but instead Gilberto left for Mexico City with all his money, in search of a new investment opportunity.

He didn't know specifically what he was looking for, only that it was something that could not be easily affected by politics, because the country's political strife was still explosive, with no end in sight. Only a few weeks earlier, General Albaro Obregón had been assassinated in a Mexico City restaurant, sixteen days after becoming Mexico's President Elect. Revolutionary forces were still fighting in several sectors of the countryside and the rift between the Church and the government was still deep if not as wide. But life goes on and other more positive changes were also taking place. Parts of Mexico City were already bustling with automobiles and almost anywhere you turned, streets were being paved or widened and electrical lamps were being installed. This burst of modernization was precipitated by an inexorable tide coming from the north, from the United States. Henry Ford had opened several agencies in the heart of the Mexican capital city and his competitors from Detroit and Cleveland would not be far behind. Signs and posters advertising the latest models from these northern factories were proliferating atop buildings and photographs of New York Avenues crowded with cars as far as the eye could see were very popular on the windows of businesses that were modern and progressive, or wanted to appear so. Cars were entering the country by ship and railroad and they were selling as fast as they came in.

Gilberto spent more than a week researching the matter; first of all, learning all he could about such mechanical contraptions. He also ascertained that there were already several laws pending which would require that each state take the necessary steps to build and connect new roads and repair existing ones. The writing was on the wall in capital letters and Gilberto couldn't have missed it if he tried.

He decided to invest his money and his future in this emerging industry. The questions left were where and how.

He concluded that to invest in the road-building infrastructure would require more capital than he had and almost certainly also some kind of political clout. The other option was to purchase a vehicle with which to take part in the coming boom in transportation. For that, there would be little use in buying one of the smaller, most popular and most affordable models that the Americanos were churning out. There were already a few of those in San Cristobal, and they were only good for a small family and short outings. The most popular models could barely carry four people, including the driver, and that was most often accomplished with two people seated in the trunk.

That was when he spotted the Packard. It was parked roadside, right on Insurgentes Avenue, under an orange tree, gleaming in the filtered sunshine and as beguiling as any woman he had ever seen. It seemed longer than most living rooms and it managed somehow to look both indestructible and delicate at the same time. Its lines were long and sleek and its curves sensuous.

Its owner, Don Rodrigo Reyes Ramos, was sitting on a nearby lawn, enjoying a picnic in the park with his family. When he saw Gilberto admiring his car, he introduced himself and proceeded to give him a tour of his machine with all the pride of a new father presenting his first born.

Don Rodrigo was a short, pudgy man in his forties, dressed in the latest fashion with spats, suspenders and sleeve gatherers. He sported a waxed mustache and slicked-back hair, and he was as friendly as a kitchen cat.

"I bought it from a local politician only months ago." he said.

He opened a rear door of the vehicle to show Gilberto the fine workmanship of the leather seats. The floor was covered with a carpet that seemed molded to an exact fit and the windows could be adjusted open, closed or in between by the simple turn of a crank. It had trays made of polished wood that folded out to become a personal table for eating or to write upon. There were small metal compartments to dispose of cigar ashes and a large polished metal receptacle that could hold a bottle of champagne on ice between the rear-facing seats. Foot rest bars and padded arm rests were built-in and reading lights used during night travel were also part of the design. The equally plush front compartment had a myriad of dials and needle indicators as well as buttons, handles, levers and pedals.

Don Rodrigo explained the workings of each of them and Don Gilberto nodded without understanding any of it. Suddenly he was becoming disconcerted.

"Now," Don Rodrigo said with a squint and an air of mystery, "let me show you the best part."

He opened one side of the engine compartment, folding it up like the wings of an insect, and revealed a magnificent sight. "This is the heart of the beast." he announced.

Gilberto understood little of what he saw, except that it was huge and beautiful, with shiny metal disks and levers, hoses and pipes and a propeller, pulleys and bands. But it was far bigger than the motor of any other car he'd ever seen and it was spotlessly painted in bright red and deep maroon. It looked like a work of art.

"Now, watch." Don Rodrigo said, as he leaned into the driver's panel to turn a key and press a button. With a roar that made Gilberto flinch, the animal came to life. Then it just continued with a hum, barely moving except for the propeller that spun itself into invisibility. It was an awe-inspiring sight, even more so when Don Rodrigo reached in to pull a little lever which made the beast roar and the entire motor twist in place like a ferocious bull trying to free itself from its pen.

Don Rodrigo silenced the animal with the flick of a lever and invited his guest to a glass of wine on the park lawn, which Gilberto was flattered to accept.

Rodrigo Reyes Ramos was a real businessman. He had an eagle's eye for opportunity and the conscience of a hungry wolf. He had smelled profit upon seeing Gilberto and within minutes and two glasses of wine his suspicions were confirmed. His inexperienced quarry had cash in hand.

"You're absolutely right, Gilberto." he told him, "That beauty, sitting right there, is the wave of the future. And not only that. . . here's to your health, my friend. . . but you are in an even better position to take advantage of it than I am."

"How's that?"

"Well, here in the capital, that car is not all that unusual. There's a lot of competition and anyone who can afford a nice trip in that vehicle can just as well afford to go out and buy one of their own. But out in the province it's completely different. People will be lining up to experience the thrill of a ride in that machine. I told you it can go one hundred miles per hour, didn't I? That's miles, not kilometers."

"I can't even imagine what that must be like."

"Oh, believe me, it's incredible. The trees and houses all become a blur. And you are in complete comfort and safety. What it takes your horse an hour to cross, you can do it in a few minutes, and drink your coffee on the way."

But his pigeon was unconvinced and still had many questions to answer and problems to resolve, starting with the fact that he knew absolutely nothing about automobiles, especially one as complicated as the one in question.

"It doesn't matter." he was assured. Very few people do. I didn't know a thing about it when I bought my first car. Isn't that right, honey? Yeah. Here, Gilberto, let's finish this bottle. All you have to do is hire a chauffeur. That's what they're for.

I mean, you don't do the cooking at your home, do you? You hire a cook. It's the same thing."

The next question raised was the matter of fuel.

"Over here there are places where you can go to buy gasoline, but in Chiapas I have yet to see one."

"That's a very good point, Gil. It shows how intelligent a man you are. But don't fret because I have just the answer for you."

That answer was found in the Ramos family home on the outskirts of an exclusive new district being built upon fertile, ancient lava hills. In a large shed adjacent to the garage, Rodrigo pulled back a canvas curtain to reveal nearly fifty barrels of fuel. He explained that he filled his tank with a hose and hand pump prior to any outing and he had a contract with a gasoline distributor to keep him supplied.

"Isn't this dangerous?"

"Oh, no. Just don't smoke while you're doing it. But in your case the real beauty of this is that you can make money by selling gasoline to other car owners. You can make money both ways!"

Gilberto ran out of questions and excuses, especially after Rodrigo agreed to find him a chauffeur the following day.

Over dinner they agreed on a price for the Packard, which included a large array of spare parts, since this was obviously not one of the more common models, such as the model A Ford, for example.

Pedro Romero agreed to a six month contract during which time he would be paid a weekly salary and provided room and board. The salary was higher than Gilberto expected but the driver explained that operating such an automobile required far more knowledge than normal because it was a finer, more intricate machine. To that end, he strongly suggested that Gilberto also hire a mechanic familiar with Packards because he himself could only effect minor repairs and service. So, Danilo was hired, and then special tools necessary to repair that particular model also had to be purchased, over and above the basic kit that came with the car. Only then was the journey to San Cristobal begun. A journey that they optimistically predicted would require two or three weeks. It took ten, mainly because, for the most part, there was no road other than intermittent carriage and cart paths. In stretches they actually had to cut down trees to get through and often they filled ditches and gullies by hand to get the Packard across. They carried four spare tires and used up every one of them. At one point they had to find six tall, straight trees, which they felled, trimmed and tied together in two bunches. That was used to span a river gorge and drive across in a slow and precarious balancing act. However, most disconcerting for Gilberto, was the fact that the long, heavy vehicle had a great propensity to get stuck, often in ruts or mud patches that the lighter automobiles bounced across with ease. On several occasions, they had to resort to rented mule teams to extricate the car.

On the morning when they finally surmounted the last mountain peak and descended into the valley of Hueyzacatlán, they stopped to rest at the edge of a river. Afterwards, while his driver and mechanic cleaned and washed the car, Gilberto bathed in the river and then changed into his best clothes for their triumphant entry into San Cristobal.

In fact, what they had achieved was truly historic. Up to that time, the few autos to reach San Christobal had been shipped into Puerto Arista on the southern coast and driven across only two hundred miles of treacherous terrain. Yet, only a few people in town were appreciative of the significance of Gilberto's achievement.

Ironically, most of them were dismayed by it. To them, this was the crack of the door that would eventually open wide to the chaotic world outside and which would inundate their sleepy little town, transforming it into just another loud, congested megalopolis.

Florinda saw things somewhat differently: "This ridiculous idea will be the end of us!" she predicted with a chilling certainty.

Chapter 9

Catalina could not possibly remember her mother, Magdalena, who had died before she was even a year old. But in her heart she carried a vivid image of her, as if they had known each other very well, and there were times she felt she could not have loved her more had they grown together normally. That was because Florinda never tired of telling her about that beautiful young woman who appeared in the mountains of Chiapas one sweltering day, "sent to us by divine providence," and in a short time became her best friend, her confidant and her stepmother.

"We were really like sisters, more than anything else. And in the end, just like father, I would have given half my life in order to have had her with us one more year."

It seemed strange for Catalina to think of Florinda as a sister to her mother, then in the next moment to think of her as her own sister, which is really what she was. But Florinda had a wonderful quality of adaptation and just as she was every bit a mother to Catalina through her childhood, with the passing years she would slip seamlessly into her role of big sister to the young woman that emerged.

"Do you really think that father just let himself die so he could be with her?"

"I don't have the slightest doubt of it."

"Tell me about him."

"No. No more tonight. You must get your sleep. Remember that tomorrow will be your first day at a proper school. No more tutors. Then you can tell me what it's like and we'll see if this so-called French Academy is as good as the one in Valparaiso, which turned your mother into such a treasure."

Prior to her enrollment in the Spring of 1930, at the age of twelve, into San Cristobal's French Academy, Catalina studied at home, taught first by Florinda and later by a series of private tutors hired by Florinda's husband Gilberto. This effectively insulated her from San Cristobal's endemic preoccupation with social position and birth, and the degree to which such considerations dictated everyone's life. Instead, she arrived to her first and only educational institution with her basic concepts of life and society already formed and strong enough to withstand the great pressure to change that she would soon encounter.

Catalina had little physical resemblance to her mother. She had neither the large green eyes that captivated so many people in several countries nor the delicate elegance that opened doors for Magdalena all her life without her knowing that those doors were even there, much less that they were closed to others. Catalina did not inherit her mother's strong determination, let alone her singleminded independence or her wild streak. Instead, she had a natural beauty and a wholesome radiance that made her self-assured enough to be approachable and kind. Above all, she was sincere. When she smiled at someone, it was with such unguarded openness that they felt she was able to see that special thing about them that made them unique, and they loved her for it. For the same reason, they also considered her sweetly naive.

Florinda used to say that Catalina possessed the same magnetic charm that had drawn people to Magdalena, but that she came by it in a very different way.

"It's just that your mother couldn't always control her feelings," Florinda would explain, "and they sometimes became passions, which are feelings that control us instead. You, my little angel, will live much longer and enjoy more happiness because, unlike your mother, you are in your element on earth."

Catalina was also gifted with a photographic memory and could remember certain moments in her life as if she was living them again, like the moving pictures that she would soon discover in her adolescence at the Sebadúa Theater, a block from the central plaza.

Her earliest such memory, and one of the most vivid in her life, was of her arrival to San Cristobal on a dreary afternoon, aboard a black carriage with gold fringe and tassels framing all the windows. It was drawn by two black horses that kept slipping awkwardly as soon as they entered the newly cobblestoned main street of town.

She was four years old, sitting on Florinda's lap, and later, whenever she recalled that moment she could again feel the silky smoothness of her sister's dress upon her fingertips and smell the scent of new leather from the upholstered seats mixing with the still strange sweet aroma that emanated from Gilberto, and which she would come to know as *Agua Florída*; his favorite cologne.

The carriage stopped at the main entrance to the Hotel Primavera, which at that time, 1922, was the most luxurious hotel in all of Chiapas and boasted its own stables and grooms, a bath in every wing of the Moorish building and a fully staffed kitchen for the dining pleasure of its guests at any hour. They remained there for two weeks, while Gilberto's house was painted inside and out and transformed from the disheveled and occasional bachelor's quarters it had been for years, into a comfortable home suitable for a family.

During those weeks they took daily walks through town so that Florinda could acquaint herself with the place where they would build their new life together. At least, that was Gilberto's excuse, when in fact, and as she suspected, he just wanted to show off his new bride to a world that had not always been kind. To avoid complicated explanations, they introduced Catalina as their niece; a device that Catalina herself adopted and kept well into her teens. Florinda liked San Cristobal right away and was impressed by the sheer magnitude of things. The cathedral in the center of town was larger than any church she had ever seen, and the church of Santo Domingo, which was so famous that Gilberto had been asked about it in both Europe and India, boasted an entire wall filled with ornate, frescoes, antique carvings and original statuettes, including some that good Friar Bartolomé himself had brought from Spain aboard Columbus' ship during that famous captain's second voyage to the new world. However, what made the church most famous now was the fact that all of the artwork crowded on that wall from floor to ceiling had subsequently been covered with a thin layer of pure gold. It was a bold stroke that put the little town on the map during earlier days of prosperity.

She was also impressed by the marketplace, so extensive that it overflowed into the side streets and had such a vibrancy that it seemed more a carnival or fair than just a place to shop for goods.

Yet, it was the people that interested Florinda the most. There were so many and so diverse, in comparison to Chilón, and they were all terribly industrious, always rushing about to accomplish one thing or an other.

By the time the Fabres moved into their house, a stack of invitations awaited them which, much to Florinda's dismay, Gilberto quickly decided to ignore. They were invitations to afternoon teas, in the style of the English, or music recitals, as accustomed by the French; informal get-togethers as well as formal dinners given by a variety of their wealthier neighbors. Florinda thought it was their duty to attend, out of politeness, but Gilberto, so gregarious on the street, inexplicably became reclusive once inside his home.

Ever since she was a little girl, one of Florinda's secret joys had been to see how other people lived. Whenever Don Trinidad Olea went off to visit someone in Chilón, or even better in some neighboring town, she did her best to tag along. Afterwards, she could spend hours by herself, reconstructing in her mind the things she had discovered: every room's decor and each piece of furniture's design, or what someone ate and how. It was just a simple and innocuous pleasure that took her out of the routine of her own life. Now she had her greatest opportunity to exercise that joy, but her husband stood firmly in her way. She challenged him for once and they ended up embroiled in their first serious argument. Neither would give in and they ate dinner wrapped in an icy silence. Then, after putting Catalina to bed, Florinda turned in early, saying only that she didn't feel too well.

The next morning, during breakfast, Gilberto partially relented.

"You can go, if you wish." he told her, "Just tell them I'm the one not feeling well."

"I don't like making up lies," she said, "but apparently you are leaving me no choice."

"Don't be too eager." he warned. "You're just heading into a nest of vipers."

So, upon her return from each social visit and event, Florinda made it a point to tell Gilberto how wrong he had been. The Arellano sisters could not have been nicer, and the conviviality at the Granado's dinner party was delightful. The Villa Grande family was the sweetest group of people imaginable, and so on. She exaggerated of course, just to teach him a lesson, but he just listened and smiled one of those smiles that only curl one side of the mouth, as if he knew something she did not.

Actually, at each gathering people did seem to go out of their way to make Florinda feel comfortable and welcome. They showed great interest, wanting to know everything about her: background, ideas, opinions, likes and dislikes. Whenever she took Catalina along, they quickly took an interest in her also. So, any trepidation that Florinda may have had about moving to such a large community was soon forgotten. Her husband's customary absence turned out to be of little consequence, since most of the people present at these events, other than the formal dinners, were the women of the town's upper crust. That in itself made for a more relaxed and open atmosphere than would otherwise be possible. In fact, the only thing that Florinda disliked about her newfound social world was that sometimes the free conversation and uninhibited ambiance gave way to common gossip, idle speculation and the cruel repetition of unsubstantiated rumors about those out of favor or not present to offer explanation or defense. Such lapses sometimes involved even the most private details of a person's life. Fortunately, as a newcomer unfamiliar with the people in question, Florinda could not be expected to participate, but she worried about what would happen later on.

Then, one day, at a tea social, she accidentally overheard talk in an adjoining room about some woman who apparently had a child by a man other than her husband and was now trying to pass the child off as her niece.

"Can you imagine?" one woman scowled, "As if one couldn't see the clear resemblance."

"Not only that," another voice added, "but I understand she used that child to force poor Gil to marry her."

Florinda felt the blood drain from her head.

"But I thought she came from a rich family?" said another woman.

"Oh, my dear, in the back woods any one with more than two fruit trees and a mule is considered wealthy." The comment caused titters and guffaws among the group.

"Besides, I heard that her father threw her out before he died and left everything to her brothers."

Florinda's desperate hope that they might be talking about someone else crashed and burned at her feet.

"Well, I just hope she can get her hands on some of Gilberto's money before he drinks it all up. You know what a terrible drunkard he is."

"Well, you'd drink too, if you suddenly had a little bastard to care for."

Florinda was well aware of her husband's previous drinking problems. Nevertheless, she felt betrayed, foolish and, with the blood returning to her head, terribly embarrassed.

"Well, I just hope she doesn't try to send her child to my daughter's school." was the final, haughty blow.

She walked out without a word and headed down the lonely street, convinced that the new laughter emanating from that house was again at her expense.

Gilberto listened to her story patiently that night, and embraced her when she broke into tears.

"I tried to warn you," he whispered, "I'm just sorry that I didn't do it well enough."

"How can they be like that, Gilberto?" She stared at a window facing the dark, deserted street and felt her anger rising once again.

"I should go right back and set them straight."

Gilberto was amused. "It wouldn't do any good." he told her. "You have to understand that these are women who have lots of money and time, but not enough intelligence to know what to do with either. Their husbands tend to the business, their servants do all the housework and their maids care for the children. They are bored to death and the only way they can feel important is by tearing down the competition, even if just in their own minds."

"What competition?"

"You. Yes. You should be proud of yourself. You obviously pose a real threat to them somehow."

"Is this how all big cities are?"

"No, because the really big cities have museums, and theaters and zoological gardens, and many other interesting things. San Cristobal is so isolated that it has hardly grown in a hundred years, and stagnant pools tend to become breeding grounds for all sorts of maladies."

Florinda felt as embarrassed by her ignorance as she was suddenly proud of her husband's wisdom and experience. That night she decided not to allow this malady to infect her home. By morning her prodigious energy had taken a new direction. There was still much to be done with the house before it would be ready to welcome a now very select number of friends. Then there was the matter of Catalina's education. Rather than expose her to the evil winds outside their walls, she decided to educate her at home for the first few years and then hire tutors to take over, Gilberto readily agreed, just as he also agreed to buy Florinda an American Singer sewing machine to make Catalina's clothes. So, before long, Florinda was getting orders from friends and neighbors for similar outfits for their children.

Then, her cooking ability also became known and she found herself spending much of her time making fruit preserves and other country delicacies for an expanding number of those carefully chosen friends.

Gilberto was often away on business, but when he was home he regularly had associates over for meetings that at times stretched over several hours and one or two meals. Florinda whirled through the house, caring for them without complaint, but it was Gilberto's idea, and later his insistence, that they hire a maid to help her with the chores and Catalina's care.

At first, Florinda was offended, and it took a while for him to convince her that he never doubted her ability to do the work, but that there was no reason why she should do it all herself.

"We're not rich." she would counter.

"No, but we're well off, and if my investments work as I intend, we will be. Besides, what will the neighbors say?"

"Very funny."

So, the word was put out that they were looking for a maid, and within days they had several applicants. Florinda hired and fired the first three within a week. One was simply incompetent. The second tended to be lazy, and the third because she actually struck Catalina across the face when she thought they were alone and unobserved.

When Florinda dismissed the first two, she gave them a little extra money to help them out while they found a new position, but she asked them not to use her as a reference because she would not lie on their behalf. The third one she dismissed without the extra money but with some advice and an admonition:

"I think that you should look for a different type of work," she told her, "and I will pass the word to all my friends about you, so that they won't put their children in danger."

Two days later, Florinda answered a knock at the door and found herself facing a short, stout, young Indian woman with glistening copper skin, arms like a mule driver and gold caps in her two front teeth. She was dressed in a plain and faded but spotlessly clean brown print dress, rather than the traditional Maya Indian clothes, and she wore an old pair of black slippers that were several sizes too small for her flat, swollen feet.

"I am Maria Hernandez," she announced, "and I came to help you."

Before Florinda could answer, Maria walked past her through the patio garden and was peering into the rooms. She carried a small and tattered brown cardboard suitcase, originally made to look like leather. It was held together by some sisal string.

"Where do you live?" Florinda asked her.

The young Indian woman was puzzled by the question.

"Here." she said, pointing to a corner of the patio that had once sheltered some chickens. "Anywhere."

"Oh, I see. You're a live-in maid."

By then Maria was already walking through the house, looking around in each room as if assessing its needs. Florinda, feeling as if her own housekeeping skills were under scrutiny, trailed behind her uncomfortably.

"Well, how much do you want?" she asked, attempting to retake the initiative.

"You decide." was the terse answer. "Later. . . after I work a week or two."

"Are you good with children?"

"I don't know." answered Maria Hernandez, in a voice that trailed off into her heart. "I never had any."

Florinda drew back, embarrassed, feeling she had violated the woman's privacy.

When the two women reached a small room beyond the kitchen, which Gilberto had been using as a storage room for paints, supplies and miscellany, and Maria spotted an old army cot that Gilberto bought because he was told it once belonged to General Simon Bolivar, she placed her suitcase upon it, untied the string and pulled out a well-starched apron. She put it on and walked back into the kitchen without a word, whereupon she began to wash the morning's dishes. Florinda was still standing by the archway to the little storage room.

"Yes," she said, mostly to herself, "I guess this will be your room."

Sixty-two years later, in a foreign country, thousands of miles away, this was the moment that Florinda would remember on her death bed. It was the first moment of a partnership and friendship that imperceptibly would grow so strong and steadfast that it would endure the worst that life could throw at it, last the remainder of their long lives and in some ways come to mean more to them than any other relationship they ever cultivated on this earth.

Chapter 10

By the time Carlos returned to San Cristobal, he was seventeen and he was certain that his life was coming to an end. Everything seemed to have been building up to that for years. His childhood was effectively over at twelve, as his father had already burdened him with so many responsibilities that he had little time for friends or other normal distractions. Even during the exciting and much anticipated family outings in the summer, when the entire Cansino family, joined by relatives, friends and neighbors, headed off into the country to swim in the magical lakes of Montebello, cavort beneath the falls of *Agua Azul* or explore the primeval forest of *La Almolonga*, Don Carlos expected his oldest son to help oversee all the necessary arrangements beforehand, supervise the children during, and orchestrate the cleanup afterwards. That included preparation of the horses, harnesses and carriages; packing the food, utensils, chairs and parasols, just for a start. The result was that while everyone else was enjoying the holiday, Carlos was reduced to watching them do so from a distance.

At school his father expected him to receive and maintain perfect marks. "To uphold the honor of the Cansinos," he would say, "and set an example for Antonio and the girls."

Meanwhile, at home he had to keep on top of all his chores. The penalty for any failure ranged from a temporary banishment from the main house to a bare-back whipping administered under the avocado tree in the center of the courtyard with a wet rawhide strap.

In spite of that, Carlos was mainly tormented by the fact that when other young men were deciding the direction of their lives, he was still wondering who he really was: a son being prepared for manhood or just another indentured servant.

The moment that, at the age of five, should have provided his salvation, instead turned out to be just the prelude to his greatest disillusion. His memories of that moment were vague and loaded with a sense of utter confusion. From the time he was a baby, he had lived at his grandmother's house; a decaying old mansion in the foothills of the barrio *La Merced*. He remembered it as a place of fear and interminable loneliness. The rooms, of which there were so many that he was constantly getting lost, were lifeless and dark even in the fullness of daylight, for their thick, musty curtains were kept forever closed.

The walls, yellowish brown from age and fireplace smoke, were mostly hidden by the massive wooden furniture made of dark woods; most of it with grotesque figures carved into their surface, legs or pedestals. To Carlos, each cupboard, bureau, bookcase, chest or dresser was so tall that it seemed to disappear into the shadows of the ceiling's eaves and loom over him like menacing creatures; creatures that tormented him day and night, such as the clocks with the sound of their cold, metallic, pendulum hearts echoing through the house and etching in him a fear so deep that many years later, as an adult, he would cringe at the sight of a grandfather clock.

Actually, the house was populated by several old women who dressed so severely that only their milk-white, wrinkled hands and faces could be seen among the shadows from which they appeared and disappeared like ghosts, without warning or sound. In those rooms, Carlos always had the feeling that he was being watched and he made it his habit to remain and play in the central areas, near the slivers of sunlight that sometimes managed to squeeze in and away from the dark, unimaginable voids of the alcoves.

Outside, past the courtyard, beyond the huge walls, was a world equally unimaginable and known to Carlos only by its sounds.

Once in a while, the massive wooden portals would creak open to allow a horse drawn carriage into the flagstones of the patio. It was usually one of his uncles, Horacio or Florentino, arriving to visit his grandmother and offering him no more than a passing nod of acknowledgement.

Luis Angel was the only playmate Carlos ever had in that house. He was in his twenties, adult in size and with the strength of an ox, but the mind of a two-year-old child. He communicated with grunts, moans and whimpers, and though he was generally a gentle giant, his frustrations sometimes gave way to fits of such destructive anger that several servants were required to subdue him.

Luis Angel was kept locked up at the back of the house, beyond the kitchen and between the granary and the carriage barn, in a room fitted with an iron door and barred windows. He was seldom allowed out of that room for fear that someone from beyond the outer walls might see him and confirm his existence, which until then was only one of San Cristobal's many rumors.

Whenever Carlos saw the opportunity, he would flee the stale, dreary rooms to the freedom of the patio's sunlight and fresh air, and play among the planters filled with dead or dying flowers, using bugs and insects as his toys. Somehow, Luis Angel always knew when Carlos was outside and he would pound his head and fists upon the metal door and whine like an animal, for hours if necessary, until someone, out of pity or annoyance, would let him out to join his little friend and childhood companion.

Carlos was at once attracted to and afraid of Luis Angel. He feared the steely power of his grip, but enjoyed his innocent ability to delight in the simplest gesture or most common act. Luis Angel could laugh with uncontrolled happiness at the mere wiggle of an eyebrow or the bounce of a pebble on a flagstone. Unfortunately, he would then demand its repetition over and over again, ad infinitum, and become angry should the cycle be broken. So, their moments together in the patio invariably ended with the servants having to pry Carlos from the desperate grip of the man/child who could not understand the cruelty of their separation. Beyond the pain to his body, Carlos always felt a greater pain from the sight of that ultimately defeated innocent, being dragged away, sobbing from the double grief of losing his freedom and his friend.

Sometimes, the moaning that emanated afterwards from his distant cell went on late into the night and became more like the baying of a hound, and Carlos, alone again in some dark room, felt little consolation from the knowledge that he was not the most miserable person in that unhappy home.

He would seek solace in sleep, hoping to meet once again with the beautiful angel that first appeared to him the previous year, dressed in the purest white, floating on air, with gossamer veils billowing behind her like wings. She took him by the hand and spoke to him in the most gentle, soothing voice he could imagine and promised to take him away from all his misery and fears.

Then, one day, Carlos was aroused from his midday nap by Dominga, the old servant, and taken quickly to a waiting bath and new clothes. When Carlos, still cranky from the sudden interruption of his customary rest, protested and threatened to complain to his grandmother, Doña Carmelina, he was told that it was her orders they were carrying out.

He was bathed in a hurry by two maids, and dressed in the new but ill-fitting clothes which by their smell of camphor he suspected had come directly from his uncle Florentino's store. Then he was rushed across the patio and the east wing of the old mansion, to the parlor, accompanied by Dominga carrying a carpet bag with his old clothes. The last thing he noticed before entering was that Luis Angel was pounding on his door and crying out with an especially anguished desperation.

In the parlor, Carlos found his grandmother and his uncle Horacio accompanied by a man and a woman he had never seen before. The man was sitting at a desk across from his uncle, who was known throughout the town as an attorney and a legal prodigy who seldom bothered to take on any work. The two men exchanged some papers which they signed and initialed in turn. Doña Carmelina was sitting in her favorite rocking chair and the woman sat on the edge of a love seat at her side. They were drinking coffee and the woman smiled at Carlos as soon as he entered.

"Hello, Carlos." she said to him. "Come and sit here with me." Carlos stood his ground until his grandmother nodded to him in agreement. He sat beside the woman without looking at her even when she started to caress him by running her cold hand through his blond, shoulder length hair.

"I heard that his hair was golden," she said to Doña Carmelina, "but I didn't realize he also had your blue eyes."

"They are a strange grayish-blue," his grandmother explained, "the color of lead, just like his mother's."

Having completed their transactions, the two men stood up and vigorously shook hands. Then the stranger approached Carlos, peering down at him. He was a tall man with wavy brown hair, bushy sideburns and a trimmed mustache.

"Carlos," said his grandmother, "that is Don Carlos Cansino. He is your father; and this is Doña Helena, his wife. You are going to live with them."

Carlos had no idea what his grandmother was talking about, and he remained seated and expressionless until the strange man took him by the hand.

"Come on, son." he said, "Let's go."

"Oh, that poor dog." Doña Helena commiserated as they walked for the last time across the patio. She was referring to the mournful wailing emanating from Luis Angel's room. No one corrected her.

The three of them boarded a Hansom cab that was waiting at the doorway and from which they disembarked minutes later in front of one of the few two-story houses that in 1919 existed in the town. It was the house where Carlos would spend the next ten years of his life.

Once inside, he was introduced to his six sisters, who ranged in age from seven to four months, and to the handful of servants who helped Doña Helena run the house. It would be some time before he could remember all their names, but

Carlos was immediately intrigued by the girls and their strange behavior. Not only were they constantly fidgeting, but they smiled an awful lot and kept whispering things among themselves. They in turn were fascinated by his golden hair and one of them said that he had eyes like a cat, which then set them all off into fits of giggling and bouts of curious chatter.

Doña Helena showed Carlos to his own personal room at the end of a long corridor, which Petra, the maid, had prepared. Like the rest of the house, and in contrast to his grandmother's place, it was airy and bright, with windows that not only had their curtains apart but also their panes, allowing fresh air to enter with the sun. Petra showed him a path through some shrubbery in the lower patio, leading around the servant's quarters to the outhouse in an opening beside the stables.

Then he was left alone in his room, to rest. He sat on the edge of his small bed and remained there, motionless for nearly an hour, until two of his new sisters appeared at his door to invite him to play in the yard. He told them that he didn't know how to play and they laughed. Then they took him by the hand, out to his new life.

The beginning of his life as an acknowledged member of the Cansino family was a series of happy revelations for Carlos. Where there had been loneliness there was now an almost constant and raucous companionship. After years of being the forgotten member of a strange, mysterious family, he became, overnight, the center of attention within a family with conventional relationships and defined positions.

Don Carlos was unquestionably the supreme authority of the Cansino household. His word was law and never challenged; not even by Doña Helena. He was meticulous in his dress and all things relating to his appearance, and although born and raised in San Cristobal, he exuded the charm and style of his ancestral, old world aristocracy. It was said that he had always been gregarious and friendly, especially with the opposite sex, but it was obvious that not far below the surface of his easy-going manner ran the undercurrent of a temper that required little to make itself known and little more to make itself felt.

Don Carlos was the best known member of a family whose predecessors emigrated long before from Galicia to various parts of South America, eventually ending up in Guatemala, in order to directly monitor their growing import/export enterprise. Local rumors claimed that much of that business had been illicit and the talk made mention of arms supplied to various factions and sundry revolutionary groups in Central America and beyond. The story was that eventually, Don Carlos' grandfather found himself backing the wrong side in Guatemala and was forced to flee with his family under cover of darkness, taking with them only what they could carry, which fortunately included substantial amounts of cash and gold bullion. Their enemies were supposedly waiting for them at all the roads leading to ports, expecting them to try for a ship back to Spain. Instead, the patriarch chose the arduous journey north on horseback through the mountains; an unpopular decision with his family, and one which probably saved their lives.

They planned to go to Mexico City, after a rest at San Cristobal, which was extended many times before they realized that the peaceful old colonial town had already become their home. Their children grew up there, and married and had children of their own. Don Carlos was the oldest son of a youngest son, and while most of his siblings and cousins subsequently left for the excitement of Mexico City, the romance of Buenos Aires or the superior education of some European university, Carlos Abelardo Cansino knew from an early age that he would live and die in his beloved San Cristobal.

His formal education went as far as the seventh year at a catholic school for the preparation of seminary students. He claimed that he had left school at that point when his father drowned in the Grijalba river during a hunting expedition, and he was forced to take over the administration of the lands and businesses they owned. However, there were those in town who swore that he had been asked to leave school prior to that tragic accident, when he was discovered in a compromising position with one of the novices from the convent of The Sisters of Charity next door.

Nevertheless, the limited but condensed academic education he received served him well in terms of his image, to say nothing of his self-esteem. He could quote from Shakespeare as well as the bible and his knowledge of world geography was exceeded only by his indifference towards any kind of travel. He was well versed in the philosophy and astronomy of the day and could talk at length about the current sociopolitical upheavals. He was well liked in his town, and still young when the 'Don' of respect was added forever to his name. The fact that he had a well known propensity for romantic entanglements with young women, even those beneath his social class, did nothing to diminish that respect. If anything, it only enhanced his stature and made him more admired. He was a macho in that word's most positive connotations of the day.

However, his education did nothing to provide him with a business sense or an appreciation of the value of investment.

The lands that he inherited, which included distant citrus groves, vast cattle ranches and a dairy farm, became untenable due to neglect or mismanagement and were sold one by one over the course of his lifetime, so that when he realized that he was living on borrowed time, he was also living on borrowed money.

It was long before that, however, when he openly acknowledged his paternity of Carlos--the shy child with the long, blond hair--and brought him to live under his privileged roof. No one knew why he did it, or why he chose that particular child from the many everyone knew or suspected he had fathered.

The joke around town was that he had finally grown tired of being surrounded just by females. "Even his dog is a bitch!" They laughed. As for choice, the less merciful speculated that he was trying to remind the world of his European ancestry since all his daughter's were brunettes and most of his little bastards were decidedly on the darker, more indigenous side.

The other mystery related to Doña Helena's feelings about the whole adoption matter. Some said she had been in favor of it and others were sure she had been against it. This was something Carlos himself would wonder about in later years, but it was a secret Doña Helena would take closely guarded to her grave.

She was, in almost every way, the opposite of Don Carlos. As unassuming as he was boisterous, she blended easily into the background, the place she obviously preferred, and few people had ever seen her even raise her voice. Yet, she was direct, determined and quietly efficient.

Because of her husband's indiscretions, few people in town were the butt of more jokes, but she managed to ignore it, and if she was hurt by it, as she surely must have been, she also kept that pain well hidden in her heart.

To Carlos, her only adopted child, she was always kind, but her warmth could never be confused with love and it reached only up to a specific and predetermined point. She was kind enough to make certain that he was always comfortable and well fed. During the cold nights of winter she made sure he had an extra blanket, and whenever he fell ill she didn't hesitate to send for the family doctor.

Yet, her concern seemed mechanical, like the need to fulfill a duty, not sentimental, like a worry born of tenderness.

When Carlos was first brought into the house and introduced to everyone, Don Carlos made it clear that his son was to be treated just the same as all his other children: no better and no worse.

Somehow, even at the age of five, Carlos understood the significance of that order and was grateful for it. During the first years, after the privileges of his novelty had worn away and he indeed became just one of the ever growing number of Cansino children, given to fights and arguments as much as any of the others, his dubious ancestry was sometimes evoked against him in the heat of battle. In those instances there was usually someone present and neutral enough to remind the aggressor of their father's very specific order. In time, such transgressions happened less and less.

Ironically however, with the passing years, the implications of that order, and the fact that it was required in the first place, only grew heavier and more troubling for Carlos. The question of his provenance was always there, nearby, unseen but felt, like an evil spirit waiting to pounce. He felt its presence every time he was excluded from a game or conversation, however innocent the omission might have been. Even worse, it was often there when he was included, for he would then suspect that the order of equality was the only reason for his inclusion, just as he suspected it to be the reason for everything Doña Helena ever did for him.

Then, when Carlos was about thirteen and the oldest of his sisters reached the age when their greatest concerns all revolved around the opposite sex and the crazy illusions of love as well as the endless possibilities of romance, he as the oldest male sibling was saddled with the added responsibility of "keeping an eye on the girls" and making sure they walked the straight and narrow paths that their pseudo-Victorian society prescribed. This included the task of keeping at bay the potential suitors--already circling in ever growing numbers--with threats when warranted and actions when necessary.

Carlos, who was as healthy, athletic and strong as his father had been at that age, did not mind the several street brawls that resulted from his 'shepherding' duties as much as the subsequent altercations he underwent at home with the infuriated lamb in question. By then, the oldest of his sisters were becoming warriors in society, aware of their strengths as well as the enemy's weaknesses and ever more proficient in the use of the newly discovered weapons suddenly at their disposal. Amazed by the power of feminine charm, beauty and sex appeal, they were eager to test themselves, but time after time they were stymied by their brother's vigilance.

They tried reasoning, pleading and even bribing him, to no avail. So, angered by his constant meddling, they would strike back at him where he was most vulnerable, with a well placed remark about the fact that he was not even their real brother. Sometimes they would twist the knife with a final comment that included some pointed reference to "my mother."

These attacks left him cold. Carlos had no defense against them. The ghost was there, as close and as large and as odious as ever. Taken together with the fact that their father, in spite of his own rule, demanded more from him and treated him with more severity than he used with the others--including Antonio, who at the age of nine was treated far better than Carlos had been treated at five--the conclusions that Carlos could reach regarding his place in the world were as painful as they were obvious.

Later, when Carlos met and became infatuated with Anna Maria, the events provided a welcome distraction in his life. Instead of adversaries, his sisters quickly became his allies, happy that he would finally understand the things that had been driving them. And after the disappointing discovery that Anna Maria had no interest in their brother, they were equally happy to hear of his decision to leave San Cristobal in order to tend to the ranch and the other properties.

When he returned, more than a year later, many things had changed. His oldest sister, Alicia, was engaged to marry the son of a hotel owner in Comitán. Not what Don Carlos and his wife had hoped for, but a better prospect than some of her previous suitors.

The exact place and time for the marriage had yet to be set because the war between the Catholic Church and the Mexican Government had once again intensified. Two of the local priests had been arrested and charged with insurrection, which could mean anything from using the pulpit to advise people on matters like voting, forming labor unions or protesting against certain laws, to more serious transgressions such as stockpiling weapons, materially aiding revolutionary forces or providing sanctuary to enemies of the government.

The church of El Carmen and the convent of The Sacred Heart had both mysteriously caught fire on a recent night and many devout Catholics had received anonymous threats. Needless to say, church attendance went severely down and several of the churches were soon only providing one mass each week. Already, in secret meetings, plans were being made to again celebrate masses inside private homes, surreptitiously, in preparation of the church closures that were sure to come.

Carlos was surprised by the extent of change even among his sisters. It was as if he had been away many years. Lucinda and Mariella, 18 and 17 respectively, and the two who had given him most trouble due to their wild, flirtatious nature and their passion for all things romantic, had become prim and proper ladies, attending tea parties and formal soirees with an air of confidence and a demeanor far too mature for the same young men they themselves had chased after just the previous year.

Unfortunately, Isabel, Adrianna and Mercedes, now 15, 14, and 13, had taken their place and all of them were growing faster than Carlos ever expected.

Yet, Carlos was unconcerned by all of that, because it was he who had changed most of all. He left San Cristobal with the singular purpose of establishing his place in the world once and for all, and instead returned defeated and demoralized. His quest to find, or earn or prove his manhood and his value had been thwarted at every turn by the one person whose acceptance or approval was indispensable to its success. It angered him to think about it. He had gained nothing! Over a year, completely wasted, since he had not been paid a penny for his efforts. Furthermore, even what he had learned would be of little use to him in San Cristobal.

His prospects were bleak. Going back to school was out of the question, and since he wanted nothing more to do with his father, he would have to get a job and strike out on his own. Yet, without his father's help and influence, all the positions of significance would be out of reach. So, while his friends and peers were moving into offices of their own as aides to lawyers, businessmen, government officials and the like, he would be left behind to toil in some menial position.

Worst of all, it would be right there in San Cristobal for all the world to see and talk about, and constantly remind him of his failure.

He didn't even want to think about it anymore. The final confrontation with his father would come soon enough.

Meanwhile, he just sank back into a corner of his old room--which had been completely taken over by young Antonio during his absence--and allowed his misery and despondence to overwhelm his spirit and his soul.

Several days into his stupor--for he had lost all track of time, sense of reality and interest in any of the normal rituals of daily life--Carlos' attention was captured by a sound he did not recognize. It was a girl's voice, but clearly not the voice of any of his nine sisters. And it wasn't just a voice, but one like none he'd ever heard, or actually, one he'd only heard once before but could not now remember where. It was, like the prettiest of feminine voices, mellifluous, with a lilt at the end of certain phrases, and it also had presence and warmth, and most of all, something he could only describe to himself as the clarity of truth. He heard it that time amid the cacophony of several of his sisters' voices, but it transcended them without having to be louder, and it not only captivated his ear but practically lifted him bodily from the dark corner of his misery. Before he knew it, he was kneeling at the doorway of his room, peering out through a crack, trying to put a face to that heavenly sound.

There, under the large old avocado tree, silhouetted by the evening sun, stood Adrianna, Isabel and Mercedes, surrounding the stranger and talking over each other, as frantically as usual.

Mercedes had a bottle of soap in one hand and a celluloid ring in the other, which she was using to produce long, iridescent bubbles that floated slowly in the twilight, up to the lower branches of the tree. The three other girls jumped up to burst the bubbles with their hands and laughed with glee at each success and every failure as if engaged in the most thrilling of games. Carlos strained to get a better view of the young stranger. She was as tall as Isabel but moved and carried herself with such maturity that he figured her to be at least 16. She was as playful as the others and completely uninhibited in her joy. On a couple of occasions, when she turned just right into the slanting sun he was able to see, to his great delight, that she was as pretty as her voice.

Suddenly, Carlos was gripped with panic. What if they decided to come into his room for some reason? His room was a mess, with clothes and bedding scattered all about. Trays of food, left for him by the servants over several days, were strewn in all directions. Worst of all, he himself hadn't changed clothes or washed in all that time.

He rushed about the dimly lit room, picking things up, tripping over dishes, covering the beds and hiding what he could up on the shelves and what he could not under the beds. He tore off his wrinkled clothes and slipped quickly into others, equally wrinkled but clean. Finally he ran a brush through his hair and decided that he must preemptively open the door to let the room air itself out. His heart was pounding. Flinging the door open, he stood at the doorway and gazed out at the avocado tree, the disappearing sunlight and the empty courtyard. They had gone.

Later that night, during a quiet moment in the parlor, he asked Adrianna about the stranger as casually as he could.

"Oh, that's Catalina Olea Fabre. She's our new best friend from school."

"Really? I'd never seen her before."

"Well, of course not. You haven't been around. Do you want to meet her?"

"Oh, no." he laughed. "I was just curious, because I saw her here and didn't recognize her."

It took all his will power to pretend he wasn't really interested and he regretted it even as he said it.

"Well, she recognized you." Anna Maria mentioned, as she walked out of the room.

"What?" He ran after her. "What do you mean, she recognized me?"

"Yeah. We had told her about you and she saw you when you rode into town. She knew it was you because of your blond hair; even though its not as blond as it used to be."

"Ha! Imagine."

Marianna searched his eyes, which he quickly averted.

"She comes over almost every day, after school."

He shrugged his shoulders, turning quickly away to hide a smile. He took a long, hot bath that night, after ordering one of the maids to thoroughly clean and sweep his room. "I don't

144

know how Antonio can stand to live like this!" he scowled. Afterwards, he sat next to the kitchen fireplace to eat a steak and some black beans, which turned out to be not only the biggest meal he'd had in weeks, but also the best tasting.

Long after everyone, including the servants, had turned in, he stood under the avocado tree staring at the moon and admiring the stars twinkling in the mysterious heavens, and he remembered Anna Maria and his great disappointment and the fact that he had no future, and he went to bed in order to avoid the anger and self pity that was welling up inside him once again. Forcing his eyes shut, he tried also to force himself to dream of Catalina Olea Fabre in his sleep as he already did while awake. Instead, he once again had the dream of the the hungry wolf and the stag, fighting to the death, and in the morning he was more convinced than ever that it was a metaphor for his ongoing battle to attain manhood; The manhood that to him somehow signified the answer to all his problems.

Chapter 11

Two painfully long days passed before Carlos saw Catalina again, and then it was only for a fleeting moment as she passed to join his sisters for their morning walk to the French Academy. It was, however, long enough for him to verify that she was as beautiful as he had imagined, that Anna Maria was coarse by comparison, and that just as he feared, he was already irretrievably in love with her. When, to his shock, he found out that she was only thirteen years old, it was too late to matter.

He could see, even from a distance, that she had a wonderfully sunny disposition and a ready smile, but there were many other things about her that simply fascinated him: her walk, somehow more feminine than any other; the way she would look down at the ground when someone talked with her, as if to show her full absorption in the matter; even the way she tossed her head to move aside the locks that kept sliding toward her eyes.

But as time passed and Carlos overcame his initial shyness, he could also see that the nervous excitement that took over his whole being whenever she was near, had no counterpart in her emotions. She was as happy to see and greet him as she was to greet any of her many other friends, and it was equally easy for her to say goodbye and walk away, unaware that he was grasping for ways to keep her near. It was devastating for Carlos to realize that on top of all his miseries, he might be once again snaring himself in the trap of unrequited love, and he fought to keep from tumbling back into depression.

What little he came to know about Catalina, he gleaned from conversations that he overheard among his sisters: That she lived near the Church of El Carmen with her aunt and uncle because her parents had died. That she was one of the best students at the French Academy for Girls, but somehow managed to also be one of the most popular, at a time and place when those two things seldom coexisted. In fact, the only complaint that his sisters had of Catalina was regarding her obstinate refusal to participate in the adolescent games of love and hate, where friendships and alliances were made or broken almost daily on the basis of some rumor or the outpouring of gossip.

Everything he heard about her reinforced the tender feelings that Carlos was helpless to resist, and his transformation was soon noticed by his sisters. Mariella, the third oldest, confronted him about it one afternoon, and although he halfheartedly denied it, the blush on his cheeks gave him away, much to her delight.

Within days, she and her sisters prevailed upon their mother, Doña Helena, to intercede with Don Carlos and invite Catalina formally to their house. Surprisingly, Don Carlos agreed without even asking for a reason or an explanation.

The following evening, a servant delivered a note, signed with a flourish by Don Carlos Cansino, to the home of Don Gilberto and Doña Florinda Fabre, requesting the pleasure of their niece's company at their family dinner on the following Sunday afternoon.

In the Cansino household, Sunday dinners were practically a sacred ritual . It was the one time in the week when every member of the family was expected to be present, from the patriarch, Don Carlos--who presided ceremoniously over the entire affair--to Antonio, the youngest of his children. All had to dress up, be spotlessly groomed and on their best behavior.

They took this meal in the formal dining room upstairs, and that alone made it special, since, even in 1931, theirs was still one of the few two-story homes in San Cristobal. It was a long, narrow and somewhat dreary room, due to the dark paneled walls and the fact that daylight could only enter through the two narrow doors from the deck or the single small window facing the street. Additional light, when necessary--and it was always necessary after twilight--was provided by oil lamps on the wall and candles on the table.

Don Carlos sat at the head of the long, massive table which had growling lions carved on each of its six legs. Alicia, at nineteen the oldest of his children, sat at his right and Carlos, sixteen and the oldest son, at his left. This was a privilege that Carlos would have happily relinquished to either Lucinda or Marisela, both slightly his seniors, because he had been backhanded clear off his chair on more than one occasion as a result of some minor indiscretion on his part. A crooked tie, a stained collar or even a sibling-provoked snicker at an inopportune moment was enough to trigger one of his father's mighty swats, and although the girls were not exempt from such instant punishment, Carlos had most often been used as the example.

Whether this would change now that Carlos had spent more than a year working at the family properties, no one yet knew. Doña Helena sat at the other end of the table, near the door, and the moment the grandfather clock in the parlor struck five, she would nod to the servants and they would begin serving the meal. After that, what little conversation took place depended totally upon the patriarch's mood. Sometimes the entire hour would pass in ghostly silence, save for the clicking of silverware upon china. At other times, the master of the house would reveal a lighter mood by asking questions of his children: What did they learn in school that week? What did they think of the latest news from abroad? Or something else to that effect.

Those occasions made the Cansino children very nervous, because they knew that a wrong answer could plunge the evening into a barrage of angry threats and lectures from which even Doña Helena was not exempt.

Catalina arrived promptly at four thirty, as instructed. She presented Doña Helena with a scented candle that her aunt

149

Florinda made and a small box of Havana cigars for Don Carlos from her uncle, Don Gilberto Fabre. All the girls sat and chatted in the parlor for nearly an hour, and even Alicia was impressed by Catalina's poise and maturity. She could quickly and effortlessly establish good rapport with anyone, regardless of age.

Eventually, Don Carlos appeared, followed by Carlos and Antonio, and they all repaired to the dining room. The Cansino girls were amused by the lengths to which Carlos had gone to make an impression. Wearing his most formal gray suit, an over-starched shirt that forced him to walk like a knight in armor and so much pomade on his hair that it was already starting to run down shimmering along his temples, he tried in vain to act as if this night was just like any other.

Catalina, seated between her friends Adrianna and Isabel, had been warned about the atmosphere that generally prevailed at this table, but she seemed perfectly at ease, with a warm smile for everyone, including Carlos, who sat nearly across from her and was already feeling as if he might either faint from self-consciousness or explode with joy and gratitude.

While the first course was served, Don Carlos, who had been studying his young, attractive guest, leaned toward her with a mischievous glint in his eye. "My daughters tell me that you are one of the most intelligent students at the academy." he said, and several people at the table held their breath.

"No. Not at all," Catalina answered, "I'm just good at keeping quiet in order to conceal my ignorance."

Don Carlos burst into roaring laughter. That was all it took. She had won him over just like that, and the room itself seemed to breathe a sigh of relief.

The rest of the meal was as convivial as any that Carlos could recall, and even when it was over, instead of repairing to his hammock on the deck to smoke a cigar, as was his ritual, Don Carlos remained at the table, brandy in hand, to chat with Catalina about her uncle Gilberto's adventures traveling the world as a merchant marine.

Carlos, meanwhile, sat quietly in his chair, watching their lighthearted conversation and squirming under the turmoil of his emotions. Here was the man whom he had come to know in so many ways: as his antagonist, the man he could never please; his hero, the man who commanded so much respect; his example, the epitome of a self-made man, and as his savior, for taking him into his home. Now, for the first time in his life he was seeing him also as his rival and he didn't know if he should feel jealous of him for his easy charm or hateful of him for his blind selfishness.

At that point, a servant arrived with a note that he assumed was for Don Carlos, but which turned out to be for his oldest son.

"It's for you." was all the father said, handing it to Carlos with annoyance.

It was from Doña Rosa, Alberto's mother, and of course one of Don Carlos' former mistresses. A neighbor had written it for her and it said that something terrible had happened and could he come right away?

Carlos was more than disappointed to be taken away during such an important moment in his life and as he excused himself from the table he grumbled that it had better be something really serious. He was still grumbling when he crossed the central plaza and Cliserio, a clerk at his uncle's store, redirected him to the government palace. There, in the lobby, he found Doña Rosa crying disconsolately and beyond any ability to make sense. Two neighbors who were with her explained that Fernando was upstairs being charged with the murder of his stepfather, Don Romulo Gallardo, the notorious prosecutor.

Carlos tried to go up to speak with Fernando but was not allowed because the official interrogation was still under way. So, while waiting downstairs he conducted a loose interrogation of his own among the neighbors and witnesses to the chilling event.

Apparently the whole thing had started weeks before, when another neighbor, whose house faced Don Romulo's back garden and who had gotten himself into some trouble with the law, decided to ingratiate himself to the powerful prosecutor. To that end, he visited the cantankerous old man at his office and told him that he had seen Fernando periodically sneaking back into his house.

Don Romulo flew into one of his famous rages. When he finally calmed down, he directed the informant to keep an eye out for Fernando and to notify him immediately if he should witness such a transgression once again. The man agreed and on that very morning did just that. The two men rushed back to the house, whereupon Don Romulo instructed his spy to give him a moment to hide in the bushes at the rear of the house and then pound on the front door with all his might. He did so and within seconds, the rear upstairs window opened and Fernando climbed out and down the vine. Yet, before he reached the ground, the old man set upon him, hitting him with the heavy, carved silver handle of his cane. The witnesses agreed that Fernando fell to the ground with blood already oozing from his head and the old man continued to beat him mercilessly with the cane until, finally, the youth managed to trip him with his legs onto the ground. The witnesses said that Fernando tried to take the cane from his stepfather but by then he only had the use on one hand and easily lost the struggle. Again the old man attacked him with the cane, ignoring Doña Rosa's screams from the window above. The commotion brought several more people to the scene. Fernando was cornered in the shrubbery and still under attack when he finally reached into his pocket and produced a small knife which, out of desperation, he used to threaten his stepfather. However, instead of retreating, the angry prosecutor lunged at him again. Then, suddenly, Don Romulo dropped his cane and grasped at his own throat. His starched white shirt was already turning red as he tumbled to the ground, mortally wounded by a cut that cleanly severed his jugular vein. Dazed, wounded and exhausted, Fernando sat down beside him on the ground and became the last image the old man ever saw.

The authorities arrived soon after and arrested Fernando in spite of many protests from the witnesses, whereupon Doña Rosa sent for Carlos.

At the municipal palace, several hours passed and still no one was allowed up to see or speak with Fernando. Besides that, the authorities apparently had no interest in speaking to the witnesses. Carlos realized then that they were only interested in forcing a confession from Fernando. He'd heard that they sometimes tortured people to obtain a quick and neat confession.

Carlos ran out of the government building and down the block to the offices of Don Sixto Carvajal, a powerful attorney whose uncle had been Governor of Chiapas years before. He found him as he was closing for the day.

Breathlessly, he related the story to the attorney, trying to include all relevant details, and then asked him if he would please represent Fernando. By contrast, Don Sixto was calm and deliberate, in part no doubt because he suffered from a stutter since birth.

"Don Romulo was a powerful man." he said. "A case like this will. . . will. . .will be very difficult."

"I was told you were the best lawyer in town." Carlos lied.

"That's not what I meant. I mean that th. . th. . this case is bound to be complicated and therefore will cost a lot . . . a lot of money."

"My father is Carlos Cansino," Carlos explained, "I believe you know him. He will pay you whatever it takes."

Don Sixto looked Carlos directly in the eye. "Did he say that?"

Carlos swallowed hard. "Look," he explained, "the mother of the boy under arrest was once my father's mistress. Do you think my father wants all that brought out in public?"

"Very well. In that case we'd better ge. . .get started."

They rushed to the government building where the same officers who earlier refused to let Carlos through now bowed to Don Sixto and moved from their path. Fernando was being held in a small, windowless room at the end of a hallway. The attorney burst in and surprised two police officers who had the tall, slender youth pinned against the wall. He was bleeding from the head and face and his right hand was dark purple and nearly twice its normal size.

"Gentlemen," Don Sixto announced in a clear, loud voice. "I represent this young man."

"You'll have to wait until we finish the official interrogation." answered one of the officers with disdain.

"In that case, I want bo. . both of your names and the name of your superior. I also want a written. . . and signed affidavit from each of you explaining exactly how long you have held my. . . my client here and a detailed copy of exactly what transpired during that time."

The officers looked at each other. "Hey, we're finished." one said, throwing up his hands, "He's all yours." Then they headed for the door.

"Just a minute!" Don Sixto called out. "I want a doctor. . . a doctor here to provide medical attention to my client, and I want it with. . . within thirty minutes. Otherwise, I promise you that San Cristobal will have two less policemen. . . and two more street sweepers!"

The two officers glared at him but left without a word, slamming the door behind them.

Carlos and the attorney helped Fernando to a chair.

"Can you talk?" Don Sixto asked him.

"Yeah." he moaned, forcing the sound through his broken, swallen jaw.

"Did you tell. . . tell them anything?"

"Only what really happened. Not what they wanted to hear."

"Good." The attorney took paper and pencil from his engraved leather briefcase, sat at a table near his client and began to make notes from Fernando's answers to his questions.

On another table, Carlos noticed an ebony walking stick with a bronze tip and a carved silver handle lying upon sheets of white paper. On closer examination he saw that the handle was carved into the head of a wolf with its mouth open and its fangs bared, and it was spattered with blood. Alongside the cane was a small pocket knife with bone handle and some writing on the blade. Carlos leaned over it to read: Made in USA, followed by the stamped likeness of a stag.

Suddenly, Carlos felt a jolt, like a tiny explosion inside the back part of his head causing a shiver to run down his spine, and he had to sit down to keep from falling over. Then, still dazed, he recalled his recurring dream of the wolf and the stag, and he realized it had nothing to do with his own struggle to become a man.

154

Chapter 12

On a sunny Saturday morning in the fall of 1931, Catalina Olea rushed across San Cristobal's central plaza, dodging and weaving through the many workers busy putting up the decorations for the annual Ladies' Day Festival. She was on her way to the Cansino's house to get together with her two best friends, Isabel and Adrianna, so that they could make preparations of their own. After all, this festival was in their honor, and although she was not quite fourteen, she was as mature as her older friends and understood the significance and implications of such homage as well as any young lady in town.

Filled with excitement, she crossed the street and continued past secluded little shops set beyond arched corridors and headed for Villa Real street. All the shops were decorated with white ribbons, white crepe and rice paper cutouts that hung from the ceilings and along the walls, while the counters, window displays and shelves were covered with tufts of cotton and white confetti that trailed strewn out into the street. Some of the shops were decorated so profusely that they reminded Catalina of the Swiss mountain cabins loaded down with snow that the Hess girls had shown her in postcards. Even the candy vendors arrayed along the portal stairs were already selling only the white varieties of candy, such as sugar-dust cookies, coconut shreds, marzipan balls, and *turrón*--egg whites whipped with honey to a froth and baked to a solid yet airy texture that melted in one's mouth with every bite.

Most adults smiled a knowing smile at Catalina as she passed, which made her blush with happiness. Passing the side entrance of the church of St. Nicholas, she muttered a prayer that the butterflies would arrive the following morning so that the festival could begin on a Sunday, and then looked hopefully up at the sky and found a small grouping of distant cirrus clouds as the only sign of white in a blue celestial sea.

Of the many festivals celebrated in and around San Cristobal every year, the *Señoritas'* Festival was one of the few without a definite starting date. Instead, its start was dictated by the yearly arrival of the white butterflies; millions of white butterflies. They would appear suddenly; clouds of them, so thick sometimes that they would obscure the sun. And they would invade the town, landing first on the rooftops like snow, then covering the eaves protruding over the sidewalks and the patios and the timbers of any rooms left open even for a moment. They usually arrived on the first of August, which happened to be Catalinas' birthday, but sometimes missed the mark by one or two days, and once, in the previous century, they had been late by one entire week. Some people attributed those delays to the weather while others speculated that it had to do with the phases of the moon, but no one knew for certain. No one was even sure of the butterfly's origins. Certain travelers said that they had spotted them flying north along the coast of Chile and speculated that they came from the Argentine Pampas or the frozen plains of Tierra del Fuego, but others swore they had encountered clouds of them in the middle of the Atlantic, coming apace from Africa.

They had been coming to San Cristobal for as long as anyone could remember and local folklore claimed that they first appeared on the day that *Friar Bartolomé de las Casas* took the pulpit to publicly chastise the King of Spain for allowing his minions to perpetrate such horrendous crimes upon the gentle indigenous people of the new world.

How it went from that to a celebration honoring young women, no one really seemed to know, but speculation was that the curious little animals reminded townspeople of their young girls dressed in white, celebrating their confirmation into the Catholic faith.

Catalina wasn't concerned with all that; just glad to be a part of it. When she reached the Cansino house, she didn't bother to knock, knowing that the door was never locked and that besides, she was expected. She walked through the dark foyer and rather than enter the parlor on her left, continued out to the patio, intending to go directly to Mariella's bedroom beyond the deck's protruding stairway. That was when she first heard the strange set of sounds; so strange that they made no sense to her, so she continued slowly down the corridor adjacent and open to the patio. Then she heard them again; louder now, closer. It sounded like a gasp, followed by a loud slap and then a long, diminishing moan, and it was coming from beyond the wild berry vines that reached up to the second story along the walls and to the deck. She instinctively walked around the bushes and past the old moss-covered fountain, and was suddenly petrified in place by what she saw.

There was Don Carlos Cansino, with his shirtsleeves rolled up to his elbows, holding a long whip in his right hand which he drew back and raised then brought down with a mighty swat onto his son's bare back. Carlos had his arms up, hands tied at the wrist to the lower branch of an old avocado tree, and he heaved a gasp before each strike, loading his lungs in preparation for the pain that he then exhaled with a moan through his clenched teeth. On the other side of the patio, beyond the cement sinks that the servants used to do the laundry, several of his sisters stood watching, transfixed, pale and expressionless.

Catalina let out a frightening shriek before Don Carlos could deliver the next stroke. He turned, surprised by her scream.

"Stop!" she yelled with anger.

"He's only getting what he deserves." explained Don Carlos, as he made to resume the punishment.

Immediately, Catalina interposed herself between father and son, and stood there glowering defiantly up at the man. "You stop, now!" she demanded, spitting the words at him.

Don Carlos was flabbergasted and momentarily at a loss to reply. It was clear that the young girl would not budge, so he threw the whip to the ground, picked up his coat and walked away.

"You're lucky this time, Carlos," he huffed, heading toward the house, "It seems you have a savior."

Quickly, Catalina struggled to untie Carlos' hands but could barely reach the ropes even on tiptoe. She looked over at his sisters and found them still standing there, motionless.

"Get over here and help!" she yelled at them, but they didn't move until they were sure that their father had gone inside. Then, two of them rushed up with a stool while another retrieved a knife from the kitchen and they cut him down.

They helped him to his room and Catalina asked for some warm water, Epson salt and clean cloths, which the sisters and the servants quickly retrieved. Meanwhile, she asked Carlos to lie face down on his bed. He protested that he was all right. "I said lie down!" she ordered, glaring at him now with impatience, and this time he obeyed.

His back was crisscrossed with red stripes and purple welts, some of which were bleeding at the edges. Then, with a tenderness Carlos had never known, she applied compresses to his wounds for over half an hour. He didn't dare turn around to look at her, afraid that seeing his reddened eyes she would guess that he had cried, but if he had he would have seen her own tears flowing quietly from her pretty eyes.

"Try to sleep," she whispered, "I'll be back this afternoon with an ointment that my nanny, Maria, makes from the roots of the Maguey." She walked out without making a sound other than the creaking of the wooden door.

For Carlos, the next several hours were filled with pain, joy and anticipation. He was even glad for the burning sensation in his back, for it was proof that this was not one of his strange dreams but the wonderful reality that he had finally become more than just another silhouette passing anonymously through Catalina's life.

Catalina returned in the late afternoon and was met at the front door by Mariella, who warned her that her father was upstairs in his hammock on the deck.

"So?"

"So, unless he's asleep, he'll see you when you cross the patio. But if you go around the block and come in through the stables, you can sneak into Carlos' room without being seen."

Catalina was astonished. "Mariella, I'm not the one who should be ashamed. Your father is. I hope he does see me." Then she immediately headed for the patio with a resolute stride. "It would do him good to think about what he has done."

Several of Carlos' sisters watched her from the parlor, but none was brave enough to accompany her. From the corner of her eye, Catalina noticed cigar smoke rising from the deck and defiantly put greater weight into her steps. She found Carlos' room dark, save for a small candle flickering on a shelf at the far wall and the dying streaks of sunshine that filtered through the worn and weathered boards of the old wooden door.

Carlos pretended to be asleep, but he was sure that the pounding of his heart had already given him away. He heard her place the candle holder on a nearby table and pull a small wooden chair up alongside his cot. Then he heard her unscrew the metal lid from a glass jar and somehow knew, without the slightest doubt, that it was a short, round jar of milk-white glass which had once held a fragrant skin cream from Paris, and that the lid was the color of lapis lazuli. He would have bet his life upon it.

Carefully, she removed the sheet covering his back and he pretended to awaken. "This might hurt a bit." she whispered, as she began ever so gently to cover his back with a cool ointment.

"It's okay," he said. "pain doesn't bother me too much."

Nothing else was said for a long time. He wanted to talk to her. His mind was racing, but he could not find the proper things to say. Eventually he relaxed enough to appreciate the incredible gentleness of her touch. It was almost a caress, and it brought him the sad realization that no one had ever touched him with such tenderness in all his life. A strange mixture of emotions started twisting in his stomach and welling up into his chest. Anger and self-pity pressed against the bottom of his throat and he fought to keep it from emerging. Then, from out of nowhere, the realization that the only thing that had sustained him all those years had been the similar touch of a strange woman in his dreams who had the exact same sweet voice as Catalina, overwhelmed his defenses and he began to cry. He pressed his face into his pillow in the vain hope that she wouldn't notice.

She kept silent and moments later replaced the sheet over his back. He panicked, thinking that she was about to leave him and he wanted desperately to explain away his weakness, but was still unable to find the words.

There was no sound, save for the rhythm of her breath and then a sigh.

"Why did he do this to you?" she asked, almost in a whisper.

"Because I helped one of his mistresses." he said.

Surprised by the answer, Catalina asked him to explain. So he told her the story of Fernando and Doña Rosa and the charge of murder and the trial. He even told her about the premonition of his dream. By the time he finished, another hour had passed, the evening sun had disappeared and much to his surprise, he was lying on his side, facing Catalina, just an arm's length away, and talking to her as if they were old friends.

"This morning he received Don Sixto's bill," he said, "It was a big surprise and a lot of money, but at least Fernando is free." He smiled in triumph and Catalina returned his smile, shaking her head, incredulous of the things men do. For a moment they were quiet once again, then startled by the door as it swung open and Lucinda entered with an oil lamp, followed by Mariella and a maid carrying their dinner in a tray.

"Time for dinner, you two." one of them said. "The rest of us have eaten."

"Oh, no. I can't." said Catalina, suddenly aware of the time. "I have to go."

"Relax," Mariella told her. "We've already sent word to your aunt, that you were having dinner with us and we would bring you home tonight."

Leaving the oil lamp they left the room as fast as they had entered, and then Lucinda peeked back in. "I don't think this is quite what they imagine." she said, with a chuckle.

That was the first time Carlos and Catalina shared a meal together, by themselves. They chatted as they ate, first about their likes and dislikes, and about what their respective schools were like. Carlos exaggerated the pain caused by the simple movement of his arm and Catalina fed him his soup, one spoonful at a time.

Suddenly, her brown eyes widened with surprise and she gasped.

"Oh, my God! Look!"

A tiny butterfly with white wings the size of a man's thumbnail had fluttered into the room. They followed its jerky trajectory around the room and twice around the oil lamp, until it landed upon Carlos' shoulder.

Catalina drew near, filled with admiration and wonder. "Oh, she's beautiful." was all that she could say.

"They say that if the first butterfly lands on you, you will have good luck." Carlos explained.

"Really? I've never heard that."

"It's true." he assured her, just as the little animal flew off once more. They followed it with their gaze once again, around the room until it landed, this time on the back of Catalina's hand.

"Oh, my God. What does it mean?" Her eyes filled with the moisture of her emotion.

"It means that your happiness is in your own hands." he said.

It flew off one last time, to join with several others that had entered through a crack on the upper corner of the door.

"They're here!" she said. "They're here!" She rushed to the door and found hundreds of the little butterflies fluttering about the patio in the moonlight.

"They're here!" she yelled with complete abandon and ran around the patio displaying her joy. The maids and servants emerged from the kitchen and smiled broadly at the sight. Just then, all of the Cansino girls ran out from their rooms to join Catalina, screeching with delight.

Spontaneously they skipped about and danced around the mango and avocado trees, under the stairway to the deck and around the old fountain holding hands. Some of them started banging on old pots and pans and their noise was soon echoed outside in the streets as the town awoke to their discovery. Moments later, church bells began to peal.

Carlos had made his way to the door to watch their celebration. He stood there, transfixed by the sight and holding in his hands a little milk-white jar with a lapis lazuli colored lid. Once, when Catalina danced past the door, she gushed: "The festival will start tomorrow, just as I prayed that it would."

He grabbed her by the arm and pulled her back to him, and she looked straight into his eyes as if daring him to speak his mind.

"Would you accept a white rose from me tomorrow?" he asked.

She smiled, and coyly answered, "Maybe." before disappearing among the others into the frolic of the night.

Chapter 13

An interview with Mexico's Minister of Foreign Affairs, directly from his offices in Mexico City, was playing on the radio. He was asked what consequences he thought the Japanese attack on The United States might have upon Mexico, and he said that, almost certainly, President Roosevelt would declare war upon the Japanese, and that at such point Mexico would have to review its existing treaties with all the parties involved in the growing conflict. The radio static made it difficult to make out the minister's exact words, so Carlos got up from his leather chair, adjusted the reception knob one way and the other in vain and then poured himself a small glass of brandy from an adjoining cupboard. From there he could hear the clackety rattle of his wife's sewing machine coming from an upstairs room.

Drink in hand, he walked over to one of the windows facing the patio and stood there for a long time, gazing out at the golden highlights of the garden drenched in a soft afternoon sunlight. A meandering path led to the fountain at the center, and another wound its way through the geraniums and the fuchsia to the well on the far corner. Near the fountain, on a cement bench, Quichel, the nanny, sat rocking the baby buggy and singing a Mayan lullaby to Maria del Carmen, his eighteen month old daughter. Just beyond them, Felix, his four year old son, was chasing a large blue and white butterfly which seemed to be teasing him, flying slowly from flower to flower, sometimes just inches beyond his reach.

What should have been a quiet moment of contentment, was for Carlos just another moment of frustration and despair. Another year was passing and the thought that had tormented him most for many years only grew stronger: The world was passing him by. Now this war had exploded and he wondered whether it would become the latest obstacle in his search for control of his own destiny.

Felix finally caught the butterfly. Holding it very carefully by its iridescent wings, he took it to Quichel and placed it on her wrist. When he released his grip, the lovely little animal didn't try to fly away. It stood still except for the slow opening and closing of its gorgeous wings, as if to show its confidence through the relaxed rhythm of its breath.

Carlos watched Quichel talking to his son, apparently pointing out some features of the tiny creature, and Felix listened with all the attention that his tender age allowed him. The scene could not help but take Carlos back to that day, more than ten years before, when a tiny butterfly brought him and Catalina together, amid the pain and sorrow of his youth, and turned the night into such magic and so much happiness that if he could have saved the overflow he would be happy still.

He still remembered that he hardly slept at all that night and was up in the morning with the dawn. Incredibly, the pain in his back and the soreness of his bruises had nearly vanished and he wondered now as he did then whether that was a consequence of his excitement or the effectiveness of the balm in the little white jar. In the end, he always preferred to accept that it was neither, but rather the healing power of love.

His sisters, three of whom would be taking direct participation in the festival that year, along with Catalina and about forty other girls between the ages of thirteen and seventeen, were also up early and creating a commotion in the main section of the house. This would be their day of confirmation as good, apostolic, Roman Catholics. Even more importantly to them, it would be their official conversion from girls into young women and with that came their acceptance into the town's social whirl, such as it was.

Carlos also recalled having had to iron his best clothes because all the maids were busy helping his sisters to prepare. Before breakfast, he laid his outfit neatly on his bed and rode a horse bareback to the marketplace, hoping to still find a bouquet of white roses. He was lucky to find one of mediocre quality and glad to pay four times its normal price for it with money he had borrowed from Petra, the old house maid.

Already the vendors were positioned in the square and all along the parade route, and the festive atmosphere was as thick as the clouds of white butterflies that continued their annual arrival. He kept the roses hidden, knowing that his sisters and his friends would tease him without mercy if they even suspected his intentions.

That was one of the last years when the festival was still held in strict accordance to tradition. Even then, the various factions had been arguing for months about it. Several of the wealthier families had been pushing to amend the rules, so that instead of using oxcarts as the parade vehicles--which was how it had been done from as far back as anyone could remember-- they could use their horsedrawn carriages and Sunday buggies. Some even wanted to use their automobiles, but that was too radical an idea even for the wealthy carriage proponents.

The organizers knew in their wisdom that if they allowed that change, the entire festival would soon become just another ostentatious showcase for the rich; a new chance to show off their expensive Arabian horses, extravagant silver-laden harnesses and gold trimmed carriages with pretentious family crests upon their doors. As if it wasn't enough that they were already sending their daughters into the parade wearing gowns designed in Paris and genuine ivory *peinetas* to hold up their lace Mantillas imported from Salamanca, Spain.

These wealthy aristocrats made up half of the organizing committee, while the rest were middle class Ladinos: small land owners and businessmen. The committee chair was traditionally held by a priest, representing the church. In this case it was father Felipe, from Santa Lucia, who had to call on all his powers of persuasion to keep an incipient class struggle from turning into an all out riot. In the end, he was able to appease the wealthy by once again postponing the general public's demand that the parade's honoree positions be open to all young ladies between the ages of 13 and 17 who resided within the town's limits, instead of only those attending the best schools. This proposal, brewing for years, was anathema to the upper class. As Don Pablo Velasco put it:

"Next thing you know, even the Indians will want their daughters to be admitted!"

So, the Ladies' Day Festival went on as usual that year. The whole town was up early that morning. They awoke to find their homes transformed by the millions of white butterflies swarming through their patios and gardens and into their rooms, there to land and take up every last spot of the uncovered ceiling beams. They would hang there, upside down, for two or three days except for momentary flights every few hours, perhaps to exercise their tiny wings.

There were many theories and explanations for the phenomenon of the butterflies and the reason for San Cristobal being their particular destination. Most of them, by the devout, had to do with some religious mystery or miracle, while the more scientific of mind put forward theories that they found to be more in keeping with their bent. Decades before, the German naturalist, Doctor Benjamin Becker, had done a detailed study that he himself financed and which lasted several years, and he came up with the finding that the trees in a large pine grove, which existed in the Valley of Hueyzacatlán for centuries, had developed some special chemical in their sap which not only attracted the butterflies but also stimulated their reproductive cycle. This chemical was unique to the pines in this grove, and those were the pines that were used to build the roof frames of the houses of San Cristobal, so that by the turn of the new century very few of them were left growing in the forest and their very soil had been mostly covered by new housing.

The more highly educated people in town accepted this explanation but the general public scoffed at the idea of treesproducing chemicals as if they could think and plan. To the younger generations, even those who had been Dr. Becker's pupils, the more mystical explanations were far more romantic and appealing.

The Cathedral bells rang out at exactly ten that morning, signaling the start of festivities. A dozen ox-carts ambled out of the staging area behind the Church of Our Lady of Guadalupe and proceeded down Villa Real street toward the central plaza. Each cart, except the first, carried four of the chosen girls, all dressed in white with some touch of blue, (allowed because the butterflies themselves exhibited blue on their feet and their antennae), and sitting on hay bales that had been covered with flower petals. Each cart had been distinctly painted and decorated by the many volunteers from schools and social clubs. One girl sat at each corner of the cart, facing forward during the slow, solemn journey to the church, but smiling broadly in most cases, unable to hide their excitement and their pride.

The leading cart, led by a marching band, carried a wooden structure in the shape of the framework of a church, built with the pine wood that attracted the butterflies so much. The frame was already covered with them, so that it looked as if it was painted white, and as it rolled down the street it attracted more of them in waves. People were lining both sides of the street, applauding each cart as it passed and drenching it with white confetti while the girls gazed about, searching for their relatives and friends, and young boys ran from one vantage point to another, noisily keeping up with the parade. Among the throngs of people and between the vendor's carts and stands, some photographers set up their tripods andcameras and waited for the perfect moment or a particular young girl.

Carlos took a position on a doorway near an intersection. He had his bouquet of roses wrapped in newspaper and he held it carefully at his back so that no one would see it. He was nervous from the time he put on his starched shirt and gray suit and his nervousness increased with every passing moment so that by the time the carts started by, his knees were trembling.

His sisters Adrianna and Mercedes passed by on the fourth cart and Isabel was on the next one, but Catalina had been put on the eighth one because, like most people, the organizers assumed she was years older than she was. When Carlos spotted her, half a block away, in her white satin dress, she might as well have been the only other person on that street. She was all he saw and all that mattered. She looked even more beautiful than he had imagined her and he knew then that he would not back down. The only question now was whether she would reject him.

He tried to catch her eye as she passed, hoping to get a hint, but she didn't see him. By the time the last cart reached the central square, the entire plaza was packed with people. The Cathedral was already full and overflowing when the young ladies in white walked up the central aisle, as if to reinforce the significance of that day in their lives, and took their place of honor at the front, near the altar.

By then, Catalina and the three Cansino girls had joined up once again and all of them were caught up in the joy and electricity of the moment. Catalina had expected all of that, and had been looking forward to it as much as anyone, because she understood the importance of being told, even if only by implication, that you are someone special and that your particular qualities are appreciated. What she had not expected was that she would walk up that aisle smiling, not to show her joy and happiness, but to hide her tremendous sadness and her shame.

Somewhere along the parade route, as she scanned the crowd in passing, looking for Florinda and Gilberto or other people she might know, her eyes met the dark eyes of a young Indian girl about her own age. She was sitting on the edge of the sidewalk, next to a woman who was probably her mother, selling peanuts from a woven sack. As their eyes locked together for an instant, a fleeting moment, the smile that was so natural to Catalina was answered with a weak, sad, distant smile that spoke in torrents directly to her heart. There had been no reproach in the young girl's eyes, soon averted to the ground, but somehow an exchange of feelings had transpired, the likes of which sometimes takes years for two people to accomplish.

The priest delivered to the standing-room-only crowd a florid sermon that included reference to revelations, but Catalina had just experienced an instant revelation of her own and now she wanted to stand up right there in the middle of that church, in front of all that crowd, and ask him, ask them all about it; even shout to them! Isn't that young girl just like me, like all of us? Doesn't she have longings and feelings and the ability to enjoy all this just as much as we do? Why are we denying her that? Why do we force her and all her sisters and her people something she has as much right to have as any of us?

Adrianna was surprised by Catalina's tears but assumed that they were tears of joy because the sermon was certainly not that moving. The entire ceremony, including the part where each of the honored girls was asked one or two questions regarding their faith by one of the attendant priests--which they all answered in the prescribed manner--lasted just over an hour. Then they were escorted in solemn procession back onto the ox-carts for the climactic parade around the central plaza.

This was the moment the girls had all been waiting for with tremendous anticipation. According to custom, this was when any young man who wanted to offer his complete and undying devotion to one of the young maidens, must do so publicly, in order to show the sincerity and purity of his intentions. This was done by stepping out into the street, in front of God and everybody, and offering the young lady in question a bouquet of white roses that signified his affection.

The young lady would, according to custom, accept the bouquet with an appreciative smile, but nothing more was demanded of her. She would simply go on and place the bouquet at her side the moment that a new one was offered. As the bouquets piled up around her, the whole world could see the extent of her popularity.

Naturally, the overwhelming fear each of them had was the possibility that they would be offered none, but that was always avoided by the parents and relatives who would send forth the brothers or cousins with what came to be known as the 'insurance bouquet', which was the next worst thing.

However, if a young lady, upon being presented a bouquet by a particular suitor, wanted not only to accept but also reciprocate his offer, she would take a single rose out of the bouquet and hand it back to him. In essence, this meant that they agreed to work toward the exclusive benefit of their relationship in hope that it would mature toward an eventual marriage. Of course, it was not a legal or binding contract, but merely a show of mutual affection strong enough to withstand public scrutiny.

Carlos, like the many other suitors in the crowd, stood trembling at the revolving door of ecstasy and misery, knowing full well that the majority of offers were turned down amid the laughter and all the jeering of the crowd as well as the more explicit cat-calls by one's peers.

Some were not bothered by all that, and much to the amusement of the crowd, would even go to te extreme of begging on one knee for the return of that precious single flower. But Carlos was not like them. He was too proud and far too easily embarrassed. At that moment he was cursing his own lack of foresight for having eaten a full breakfast, since it was getting very hard to keep it down where it belonged. He thought of running away and making up sone excuse later. Then he saw her coming and noticed that she had several bouquets at her side already, and shuddered at the thought that she might accept someone else's pledge of loyalty and love. He jumped out onto the street, right in front of the large brown oxen patiently towing her cart. The crowd responded with oohs and ahhs. Catalina watched him with a bemused smile as he approached. His sisters were screeching with delight and his heart was pounding like the time he almost drowned in the raging waters of the Usumacinta. He extended his hand with the bouquet and Catalina took the flowers with great care. She looked at the roses with appreciation and back at Carlos with the fullness of her smile but nothing else. The crowd roared. The old man leading the oxen made a clicking sound with his mouth and the cart jerked onward. Carlos suddenly felt himself in the center of a whirlpool, about to faint, his vision already blurring. But somewhere in the recess of his mind he heard his sister Isabel's voice yelling at him.

"Carlos, Carlos, look!" she was pointing insistently ahead.

In a daze he managed to turn, and refocusing his eyes he saw an image that would become the last image he would recall on the moment of his death, nearly fifty years later: Catalina with a white rose in her hand extended toward him.

Chapter 14

Spring slipped into Summer. In San Cristobal, 7,000 feet up in the mountains, the climate was far more temperate than in the surrounding regions of the state, so the seasonal changes were more subtle, but just as well defined. First of all, the colors changed, not only in the foliage of the trees and disappearing brightness of the flowers but even in the light itself. The sunshine, perhaps as a reflection of the hills, took on a yellow haze, lemon at first and turning orange and amber as it headed into autumn. The aromas also changed, driven as much by the customs of the people, who had become used to eating certain foods at particular times of the year, as by the evolution of nature's bounty and the fruits that it provided for the drowsy valley. By August from the patios and back yards of many houses rose the warm, sweet smell of boiling quince and baking apple, laced with brown sugar, tinged with cinnamon and strained hot into delicate wooden containers from Tenejapa, then left to cool and gel on window sills, mixing there with the feminine perfume of ripe guayaba from the orchard trees. Strains of mango syrup danced in the evenings among the earthy aroma of dried figs and aged plantain.

Those changes were ultimately reflected in the people. The vitality of spring slowed into a rhythm of contentment. Brisk morning walks turned into afternoon strolls and vigorous mountain climbs gave way to lazy summer picnics.

Even Carlos was able to set aside his quiet desperation, helped in great part by the fact that if his life still had no definite direction, it now certainly had a cause for which to fight.

He had no intention of returning to work at any of his father's properties, so he assumed that he would soon be asked to leave the house. Therefore, it was imperative for him to find a job. Meanwhile, Don Carlos knew that his son, having pledged himself to Catalina--a move he thoroughly approved though he kept that approval to himself--Carlos would now need his help to land a respectable, well-salaried position in their town. For the time being, father and son carefully avoided one another and played a waiting game.

In the afternoons, when the French Academy's closing bell rang and the girls streamed out into the narrow street, frantically whispering secrets to each other and squealing over the simplest things with exaggerated delight, a small group of young suitors would be waiting at the corner, and Carlos was the latest addition to that group. Escaping as fast as possible from the whistles and comments from his sisters and their friends, he and Catalina would stroll along the aqueduct, through Santo Domingo Park or anyplace where they could be relatively alone and unmolested. Nevertheless, they were careful to refrain from any overt acts of familiarity, such as holding hands, because they knew that it would get back to their families in exaggerated form almost before it happened. Gossip and rumors were a constant threat.

At first, as they slowly got to know each other, Carlos went through enormous pains to assure Catalina that he had great plans for the future and was prepared to achieve success somehow, no matter what the cost. He spoke in hazy concepts of diffuse dreams and passionate yearnings, and she listened patiently. But he would have been far less effusive and abstract if he had known her innermost reactions.

Catalina was dismayed by his ideas. She had heard them all before and knew their folly. It was like the old days, years before, listening to Gilberto at the dinner table. She just couldn't understand why the males of the species would always set their sights on distant pastures instead of cultivating the land under their feet. Still, she decided to be patient, already aware that time and fate, divine or otherwise, were far more powerful than the delusional aspirations of mere men. And time was on her side. She made it plain to him from the beginning that nothing more would happen between them for at least four years, until she was eighteen, if he was prepared to wait that long, and that during that time they would simply work to strengthen their relationship and confirm their love.

He went crazy. Apparently four years was an eternity. He would die of love before that. How could someone who professed to love him, want to torture him in such a way?

She laughed, as much at his romantic notions as his wild exaggerations, but in the end relented by taking off one year. Now he was happy. She had empowered him as no one else on earth could do. He had a goal, a definite direction, and to that end he could take on the world, and perhaps his father too.

At home Catalina related those matters to Florinda, as she did with all that happened in her blossoming life. There had never been, nor would there ever be any secrets between them. They spoke in the kitchen, over dinner, in lowered voices so as not to disturb Gilberto, who was seriously ill and resting in his bedroom. Their relationship, partly mother to daughter and mostly sister to sister now, was the ideal relationship between two women. Florinda had complete confidence in the child she had been rearing and observing with growing admiration, as she emerged into womanhood, surprising her continuously with a maturity and poise that her own mother, Magdalena, had only demonstrated during the last year of her life.

"Do you think I did right?" Catalina asked her sister.

"Yes." Florinda answered, choking up a bit at the thought that the first step had been taken toward her eventual flight. "I think he's a good boy." she added. "Just be patient with him."

Afterwards, while Maria Hernandez helped Florinda clean up in the kitchen, Catalina sat with Gilberto for a while. He was gaunt and frail; a mere shadow of the man he had been just a few years before. She often read to him until he fell asleep. His favorite stories were from a book he gave her: '1001

Arabian Nights'. This time she first told him about her decision.

"He's not good enough for you." Gilberto grumbled. Then he looked at her with half-opened eyes and a faint smile. "But then again, nobody on earth is good enough for you. So, I guess he'll have to do."

She leaned forward and ran her hand over his forehead, pushing back the front locks of his unruly mane.

"You tell him" he warned, straining because he was having difficulty breathing, "that if he ever hurts you, he'll answer to me."

She had to turn away to hide the feelings that the tears welling in her eyes would have betrayed. They both knew that he would not live to see her marry, and that injustice tore at her inside.

Maria Hernandez had Catalina's bath ready when she emerged from his room. It was one of the chores Maria most enjoyed. For her it was like being an integral part of something special and momentous. Up to that time, Catalina was the closest thing she'd ever had to a daughter of her own, though that was something she would never dare mention because people would think that she didn't know her place. Nevertheless, she loved the tremendous feeling of pride that invaded her being when she tended to the needs and wishes of that beautiful young maiden with the body of a porcelain statuette and--as she often told Doña Florinda--the smile of God. Once her charge was comfortably soaking in the steamy water, Maria looked around like a thief in the night, pulled a tiny pink bar of perfumed soap from her blouse and handed it to Catalina as if it were a state secret. The young girl took it gratefully, knowing that Maria had bought it with her own money and that she was taking a great risk by disobeying Florinda's orders against such displays of vanity.

In fact it wasn't a great risk. Florinda already had a high regard for Maria and her natural instincts, and would often defer to her, but the point was that Maria thought it was a risk and took it, out of her love and admiration for that child.

Meanwhile, Carlos' love for that same child impelled him to increase his efforts to obtain a job, even to the point of swallowing his pride and soliciting a post from people he didn't like or for whom he had little respect. After three weeks he received two offers. One, from the newly established State Education Department of Chiapas, was for a position as a rural teacher. It meant going off into the mountains for months at a time to teach the children of the Native Indians to read and write. The second was from the city government and it would make him a special assistant to the man in charge of a variety of architectural projects. It paid more than twice as much as the teaching job, included his own office in the municipal government building, a paid vacation and several other perks. He accepted it immediately and upon returning home he asked Adrianna to pass the good news on to Catalina. It was a Friday and he had to start work the following Monday, so he immediately began to read through all the books he could find in his father's library about the local government building codes. His father was at the dairy farm all weekend and Catalina sent congratulations but could not visit due to Gilberto's illness.

On Monday he reported to work bright and early and while putting up his coat in a closet adjacent to his office, two young attorneys ran into each other on the corridor outside. Carlos could not avoid overhearing their conversation, part of which was a discussion about him and his new job.

According to one of the men, the position had been made up and would consist of nothing more than using him as an errand boy.

"Wow. Old man Cansino must have paid a lot of money." the other man remarked.

"Well, I don't know. Maybe. But I'm not even sure he was at all involved."

"Then, why else would they do it?"

"As I heard it, the deal is this: Old man Cansino owns a large plot of land out near the lagoon, but can't afford to do anything with it. A lot of people want to buy it but he refuses to sell. By doing him this favor, he might change his mind."

Carlos was livid. He confronted the administrator as soon as he arrived and the man neither admitted nor denied the allegations.

"Well, I'm sorry to disappoint you," Carlos told him, "but this is one bone you'll have to throw to someone else." He left the building and headed straight to the offices of the State Education Department down the street.

That official was surprised to hear him accept the teaching position as it was clearly beneath his social stature.

"Are you sure you want this job?"

"Do I qualify for it?"

"Can you read and write?"

"Of course."

"Then you qualify."

"Then I want it."

"Then you've got it."

They shook hands and he agreed to set off on his first assignment at the end of the week.

When Catalina emerged from the academy she found Carlos waiting for her. They walked to the marketplace, just a few blocks away, and sat at one of the stands to share a glass of tamarind water. Carlos explained the entire drama, exaggerating things a bit and clearly feeling proud of himself and rather noble. Catalina listened quietly until he finished.

"I understand what you did and why you did it," she said, "but in the future, when you need to make some decision that will affect your future, I'll expect to be consulted, as long as that future includes me."

Duly chastised, Carlos apologized to her, and for the first time told her directly that he loved her.

"I know." she said, taking his hand. "Now walk me home to see my uncle."

Carlos asked to visit with Don Gilberto, and Florinda immediately gave permission. The room was dark with all the curtains drawn and the air heavy with the smell of medicines and camphor. Carlos pulled a chair up to the bedside as an oil lamp was placed nearby, and he was astonished at how emaciated Don Gilberto looked since the last time he had seen him. Catalina stood behind Carlos while Florinda and Maria receded into the darkness near the door.

"How are you feeling, Don Gilberto?" Carlos asked.

"Not bad, for a dying man." He answered in a low, hoarse voice.

"Oh, don't say that. I'm sure you'll get through this just fine."

Gilberto coughed several times and Catalina gave him a spoonful of syrup.

"I knew your father in school." Gilberto said.

"Really? I didn't know that. Were you friends?"

"We didn't like each other. Had a fight once. . . in the schoolyard.

I bloodied his nose." The old man turned his head to see Carlos' reaction.

"Thank you." Carlos said, "I've wanted to do that myself many times."

Gilberto smiled and paused for a moment to build up his breath.

"You know, Catalina is not my niece."

"Yes, I know, Sir."

"She's my daughter!" he growled. Carlos didn't know what to answer. "Just as much as if she had my blood." he explained.

"Yes, Sir. I know." Carlos answered just as he felt a tear fall on his shoulder.

"Blood is not that important." Gilberto continued. "People are important. You remember that."

"Yes, Sir. I will."

"Caty." the old man called out.

"Yes. I'm right here." she said, drying her tears and leaning towards him."

"Go away." he told her, "for a while."

Catalina tiptoed out of the room behind Maria and Florinda, and they closed the door behind.

There was a long silence. Finally, Gilberto leaned toward Carlos so he could look him in the eye.

"Carlos," he began, "I've been all over the world and I've known people of all types. And it took me all this time to learn one secret." He paused again to catch his breath and Carlos placed another pillow behind him for support. "Every person. . . EVERY person, without exception, gets one great opportunity in life. Yeah, sure, we get a lot of opportunities. But only one GREAT opportunity. And if we mess it up, that's it. We never get another. Do you understand?"

"Yes, Sir. I think so."

Gilberto smiled and leaned back. "Good luck to you, Carlos." he said. "And take good care of my daughter, or I'll come back and bloody your nose too."

"I will, Don Gilberto. I promise you that."

Gilberto closed his eyes and waved Carlos away with a weak movement of his hand. Carlos stood up, turned down the wick on the oil lamp and walked out of the room.

Nine weeks later, in a village deep in the southern Chiapas mountains, Carlos received a letter from Catalina, informing him of Don Gilberto's death. His immediate impulse was to jump on his horse to ride back for the funeral. Then, realizing the letter had been written weeks before, he sat down on a large rock overlooking a bluff and remained there for a long time, feeling helpless, as the long shadows of dusk wrapped him with an evening chill that he identified with loneliness. He wished that he could have been with Catalina to help her through her grief, and that he could have known Don Gilberto better. And he felt no joy in realizing that he was now in fact becoming a man.

Chapter 15

It was sunny on the morning when the ox-cart carrying Gilberto's coffin ambled up the clay road to the old cemetery. Catalina would have preferred rain, considering it more appropriate. She and Florinda, dressed in black including veils, walked behind the flower-laden cart, ahead of a solemn procession of townspeople.

A mass was celebrated for him in the church of Santo Domingo because it was his favorite church and, even though he was not a devout Catholic, he loved the mournful sound of its bells .

"That's real Italian bronze!" he used to say. "Their sound doesn't enter through your ears; it goes directly to your heart."

The church was nearly half full during the service, which surprised Florinda, because out of the legions of friends that he once had in San Cristobal, all but a few deserted him when he fell on hard times.

"You would think that poverty was contagious." he once remarked, not with bitterness but amusement.

When they came out of the church, Catalina was able to look at the faces in the crowd from behind her thick veil and it was clear to her that many of them were only there to gawk and find material for their gossip. As they loaded the coffin on the traditional cart, she heard one man's remark: "He could have used that Packard now."

Only about 35 people made the walk up to the cemetery with them. As they set off, the church bells tolled and Catalina felt their deep, bass song reverberate inside her chest even as each note hung for a long time in the air. It was the saddest sound she had ever heard. She looked at the coffin and smiled, already aware that this was a sound she would never forget.

It took them about half an hour to reach the cemetery. Several times, as the cart went through ruts and ditches, the coffin slid around, dropping flowers on the road. Once, a bouquet of white roses fell at Catalina's feet and she picket it up and placed it back upon the coffin. Moments later it slid off again, bounced on the edge of the cart and right into her arms. This time she kept it, and she began to cry.

Gilberto had been her father in almost every sense, and she couldn't think of any friend who had a better one. Although he wasn't given to expressions of affection or shows of emotion, other than to act stern, it was clear to everyone that he doted on her.

Catalina recalled that in her younger years, when Florinda scolded her and sent her to her room as punishment for something she had done, Gilberto would usually enter quietly, moments later, and sit beside her without saying a word. He would stroke her hair for a moment, with an awkward but very tender hand. Then, after a while of searching in vain for the right words, he would put a candy in her hand or some money under her pillow and walk out as quietly as he came.

Father Miguel Escutia, one of three priests at Santo Domingo, presided over a short graveside service. He was well known in town because he had established and taught catechism classes for young men. Also because he kept himself surrounded with young boys, whom he often took on field trips and excursions. The rumor was that he had been caught in compromising situations with some of his pupils on more than one occasion, yet as odious as such sins were considered by the general population, everyone turned a blind eye to his transgressions. Most people did it because he was a priest and therefore must be incapable of doing wrong. No matter what the indications or the facts might be, they must be lies. The civic leaders turned a deaf ear to the allegations because the Escutias were one of San Cristobal's most respected families. No one knew why the church leaders also ignored the matter, though some cynics speculated that it was because such perversions were widespread among the clergy from top to bottom. Catalina would have preferred some other priest to preside over the funeral but was mollified by the thought that Gilberto had a very low opinion of all priests. "The ideas behind all of all the world's major religions are good," he used to tell her, "It's the people who claim to represent those ideas that screw it all up."

Finally, when the coffin was ready to be lowered into the grave and it was time for a final goodbye to Gilberto, Florinda deferred to Catalina, who took the biggest rose from her bouquet and placed it on the lid. She kissed the coffin and stepped back. Florinda also kissed the coffin and then whispered some words into eternity. She recalled then the very moment when she first saw him, at the store in Chilón. Hello was the first word she said to him, never suspecting that two years later he would become the center of her life and remain so for so many years. Now it was goodbye, and now she wondered what would become of her.

Maria Hernandez had remained back at the house to finish preparing the meal for all the mourners. She enlisted the help of one of her friends from the marketplace and they borrowed tables and chairs from the neighbors. The meal, which was essentially a collection of Gilberto's favorite foods, required the efforts of all three women working through the previous night.

Some of the guests had known Gilberto from childhood and others had attended school with him. One man told Catalina that he had accompanied her uncle on many of his trips to Yucatán, Tabasco and Guatemala.

"We had some great adventures," he recalled, "but for him it was never enough. He always wanted to see what was on the other side of the next hill, and when he started talking about going to Africa and places on the other side of the world, well, I just didn't have the guts. But I'm glad he came back, 'cause there's nothing sadder than dying in a foreign land, all alone, among strangers."

Long after midnight, when all the guests had gone, Florinda, Catalina and Maria sat in the parlor to rest a while, for the first time in days.

"He was a good man, Doña Florinda." Maria said, "He worried a lot when you were sick. Walking up and down the corridor all night. That's how I will always remember him."

"I think I'll remember him the way he looked that day when he came home with the Packard." Catalina said. "He was so proud he could hardly fit into the room."

"Yes," Florinda agreed with a sigh, "little did he know."

Florinda had been critical of that purchase from the moment she first saw the huge machine and realized what Gilberto had done. But Catalina thought it was the most wonderful purchase, and that her sister was just angry because she had not been consulted. She remembered the many times that Gilberto took them for a ride around the town. Everyone would turn to look at them and smile and wave. Crowds would instantly gather around the car whenever they parked along the central square. Children would strain to peek inside or touch the shiny chrome or stand on the running boards and pretend the car was moving. The boys especially would oooh and ahhh and make motor noises as they ran around, turning imaginary steering wheels with their hands.

Sometimes the three of them would take a stroll around the plaza, stopping to buy ice cream along the way. Pedro and Danilo, wearing matching uniforms, would remain with the car, cleaning the fingerprints and shooing the kids away. When they returned, Danilo would open the door for them and countless smiles faded into longing stares, watching the majestic Packard drive away.

Catalina was too young and too innocent to notice the darker aspects of the feelings that the beautiful machine evoked. The envy and resentment that it stirred in many hearts was palpable to Florinda from the start, and increasingly evident with every passing day. This was a serious affront to most of the wealthy, aristocratic families. How could some upstart, some nobody, dare to parade under their very nose as if he were better than they were? And with his very own personal chauffeur and valet brought from Mexico City no less! Who does he think he is?

Gilberto was unconcerned with the stuffy old guard.

"Those fossils have been out of touch with reality for years." he would explain. They're still trying to impose on us a social code of behavior that even their snobby relatives in Spain were forced to discard long ago."

He was only interested in establishing a business and he didn't need their permission or anyone else's. That was what he thought. He met with the mayor, the chamber of deputies and various town leaders to lobby for improvements to the roads. He pointed out and listed the great benefits that such a simple change would make to the town's economy, its beauty and its quality of life. He enumerated places he had seen with his own eyes throughout the world which had done just that to wonderful results. And the beauty of the scheme was that the cost would be minimal because its main requirement was unskilled labor, of which they had a surplus. Besides, they could use all the men in jail for no cost other than to shorten their sentences accordingly.

His enthusiasm was infectious and his plan was well-received in the beginning. Government departments began to mobilize; the proposal could be voted upon soon. Meanwhile, Gilberto let it be known that the Packard was at anyone's disposal for a leisurely ride around town and the outlying areas where the roads permitted. All at a nominal price.

Several people immediately took him up on his offer, so that soon he had to make a schedule to keep track. But the well was quickly poisoned. Word spread that the powers that be, the voices that counted, the people of class and style, considered the act of renting such a vehicle, a vulgar and pretentious display. The customer pool started to dry up and Gilberto had to lower his price to the point where he was losing money just to keep his two employees occupied.

When the time arrived to consider his proposal, the vote was postponed for some unexpected reason and eventually postponed several more times. Meanwhile, dire warnings, originated anonymously, spread through town like wildfire. Roads would provide criminal elements from other regions easy access to the town and quick escape. Taxes would be levied on everyone to pay the mounting costs of upkeep and the resulting noise from automobiles would scare the animals to infertility. Cows would stop giving milk as they had done in the Mexico City area and poisonous animals would stow away in vehicles and infest the town.

It went on and on, and the more outlandish the claims, the more the people tended to believe them. But Gilberto would not even consider giving up. He fought back any way he could: speaking at town meetings, where at first he was heckled and booed, and later simply ignored; passing out flyers, which almost got him jailed for not having some obscure permit; and writing letters to *El Progreso,* San Cristobal's newspaper, which turned out to have no interest in progress after all.

When the original six months were up, Gilberto had to give Pedro and Danilo each a hefty raise just to keep them on the job a little longer. Things were bound to turn around for him, he thought.

"Even people who deserve bad luck don't get this much."

However, the company with which Gilberto contracted to supply him with oil and gasoline kept finding problems and reasons to escalate the price, so that he was soon paying three times as much as had originally been agreed upon. At the same time, the few families in San Cristobal who had automobiles, continued buying their fuel and supplies from a company in Comitán, even though it would have been cheaper and more convenient to buy from Gilberto.

The Packard, so reliable until then, suddenly began to have a rash of breakdowns, according to Danilo, when in truth, he and Pedro had been selling off the spare parts, piece by piece and claiming to have used them for repairs. Eventually, they even sent the extra differential and transmission back to Mexico City, selling them for a fraction of their price. The money was mostly used for the purchase of alcohol and women at a brothel in the neighboring town of Teopisca.

By the time Gilberto found out, even the spare tires and original tool kit had disappeared. He fired both of them and then traveled on horseback to Tuxtla to find their replacements. But only minutes after they restarted the Packard, its engine coughed and chattered and made ghastly noises never heard before, then suddenly stopped with a final gasp amid white clouds of steam and smelly blue smoke, and then just sat there, amid a deathly silence, save for the trickle of various fluids to the ground. Danilo's sabotage had been extensive.

It was all over. Gilberto was completely broke and he started drinking heavily for the first time in years. The Packard sat forlornly in a corner of the yard for a long time, collecting dust and cobwebs among the chickens and ducks that often lined up on its roof and running boards to take the sun.

In those days, Gilberto would often leave the house, telling Florinda that he was going to find some work and they wouldn't see him again for days. On several ocassions he was carried home so drunk that he was incoherent. Then, one day, Catalina was returning from an errand to the barrio of Mexicanos and she found him lying on the street. People passing by would just walk around him or step over him as if he were merely some dead animal. Two Tenejapa Indians, returning home from the marketplace, noticed Catalina's distress and offered to help. They carried Gilberto home on their shoulders, and when Florinda tried to pay them they politely refused. They smiled, and bowed to both women, and resumed their long journey home.

It was also in that time that Catalina twice saw Gilberto become abusive with Florinda. He had begun coughing up blood and when Florinda tried to take a bottle of *agua ardiente* from him, he whirled around and slapped her hard across the face, sending her spinning to the wall.

Later, when Maria Hernandez was treating her in the kitchen with hot compresses of Epson salt and olive leaves, Florinda took hold of Catalina's hand.

"It's not his fault." she reassured her little sister, "He's just sick, he can't help it."

The second time, Catalina was going into their room to show them her homework and she found them in the midst of a heated argument.

"Just stay away from me, you stupid whore!" he yelled.

It was the only time Catalina ever heard him speak to anyone like that and it froze Florinda where she stood. That time it took Florinda much longer to get over the pain.

His health deteriorated with every passing day and before long he was continuously bedridden. To pay the doctor bills and for the medicines that he refused to take most of the time, Florinda pawned her jewelry and any other valuables she could find around the house. She sold the piano to a neighbor for a fraction of its worth and in time she started to sell off pieces of furniture because her dressmaking and preserves were not enough to make ends meet.

She was unable to pay Maria Hernandez her salary for nearly a whole year, and Maria refused it on the few occasions when a small portion of it was offered.

"What do I need money for?" she would say, and quickly walk away.

All of those things provided grist for the San Cristobal rumor mill but the three women in that house had long since learned to ignore it.

One rainy day, Catalina was sitting in the kitchen, near the door, reading a book and watching the rain droplets splashing into the puddles of the yard, when a large man with a bald head and one earring walked into the house. He was carrying a sack of coffee beans which Florinda had him place against the patio wall, under an awning. More sacks, of sugar, flower and other comestibles, were brought in by the same man and his two helpers and stacked in the same place. That was followed by a scrawny table and four chairs, an old bookcase, a dresser and a vanity with a cracked mirror. And finally, a large bird cage with eighteen canaries and four parakeets. When Catalina set her book aside to go out and satisfy her growing curiosity,

Maria Hernandez, who was preparing the fire to cook dinner, stopped her without even turning around.

"Don't be a busybody." was all she said.

Catalina sat back down. Then she watched the large patio doors being opened to the street and the strange men go out and return carrying large coils of thick rope, which they attached to the Packard's hefty frame, after shooing away the chickens sleeping under it. The other ends of the ropes were attached to a massive carriage that was backed into the yard and which was towed by a team of five mules. A hand pump was used to put air back into the tires and after one of the men moved some of the levers inside the automobile, it started to roll, slowly and silently, but moving for the first time in well over a year.

Catalina watched it roll away just as the rain got stronger and lightning flashed in the mountains far away, and she felt as if something important was being taken from her life. During the next 55 years, she often caught herself glancing at a passing car, but she never saw another as beautiful as that.

Chapter 16

On the night after he disclosed to Catalina his decision to become a rural teacher, Carlos resolved that however difficult the circumstances and however hard the work, he would find a way to make his first paid job a resounding success. He would return to San Cristobal in such triumph that Catalina would want to forget their arrangement and marry him at once. His father, not that it mattered, would probably feel compelled to welcome him back with public expressions of fatherly pride. Expressions which Carlos would of course disdainfully reject. These thoughts ran through his mind all night so that by the time his body and mind were ready to rest, the bright light of morning brought them cruelly back to the current reality of his life.

Before earning a penny as a teacher, Carlos had to go out and put himself in debt. He borrowed money to buy a horse, a saddle, saddle bags and a Colt revolver with holster, a Winchester rifle and one hundred rounds of ammunition. He could have taken one of the horses that theoretically were his from his father's stables, but he wanted to show his father with unquestionable clarity that he didn't need or want a single thing from him.

He set out early on Monday morning. He had said his good-bye to Catalina the previous night but she sent him a roasted chicken and some rice along with tortillas in an enameled pot with a lid, tightly wrapped in a white cloth, together with some silverware in a napkin with a little note attached that simply read: Be careful. Write. I love you. Catalina.

Those seven words, memorized immediately and forever, danced in his head, producing the positive attitude, sunny disposition and renewed energy he needed to attack the road towards Ocosingo, before veering off east into the mountains along a narrow path. His destination was Tzuchijá, a tiny Indian village whose exact location no one seemed to know. He knew that it was in the general direction of Tenosique, just before the Tabasco border, close to the waters of the Usumacinta, and he assumed that the closer he got to it, the easier it would be to get directions.

The first day of travel was much easier than he expected. The land was mostly flat and the road easy to follow, although heavy with brambles. The Native Indians that he met along the way were all quite respectful, if not overly friendly, as they made their way to San Cristobal's marketplace to sell their wares.

At noon, he stopped to eat at the edge of a small creek and bought some oranges and limes from a passing merchant. In the evening, darkness descended suddenly, making the path difficult to see. He became wary and suspicious of the night sounds and eerie noises, and his imagination began to exact a toll on his composure. Branches looked like snakes and the rustling in the bushes might be a mountain lion preparing to pounce or a bandit lying in wait. Soon, he was riding with the reins in one hand and his gun in the other.

Eventually he spotted a distant light, and then another. He thought that he had reached the town of Altamirano, but it turned out to be the village of Chanal, only half way there. Nevertheless, he was glad to be somewhere. He asked for a place where he could get something to eat and was pointed to one of the huts along the road. It was one of the few that had an oil lamp inside; most others were lit only by the embers of an open fireplace.

He was served a bowl of beans with pieces of pork and several tortillas hot off the *comal*. A bowl of *horchata*, the common drink made from corn meal, was refilled as often as he wanted and the entire dinner cost him less than the tortillas alone would have cost in San Cristobal. Several other travelers, all Indigenous people from the surrounding mountain villages, were having dinner at that place. They sat quietly on logs or squatted on the ground along the smooth earthen patio and ate in silence, glancing periodically at the strange young man with yellow hair. They were surprised as much by his appearance as by the fact that he was traveling alone.

He tried to converse with them by asking their destinations or about the conditions of the roads but was met by blank stares. Assuming they didn't understand Spanish, he tried the bits he knew of local dialects. They answered him politely but as succinctly as they could and quickly returned their attention to their meal. Carlos was left to wonder wether they were suspicious or afraid of him; or perhaps just didn't like him.

When he finished and paid the lady for his meal, he gave her nearly twice what she had asked for and inquired about a place to spend the night. He was led to the back of the house, to a small room, more like an alcove, closed on three sides and only separated from the patio by a bamboo curtain that served as a door. The tiny room had a wooden platform covered with hay and a blanket to serve as a bed and a small wooden chair at the foot of it. There was little room for anything else.

Through the bamboo he could still see the stars and the part of the patio lit by the oil lamp. Some children were playing there now, and the men still eating were now talking and laughing without inhibition. His horse had been unsaddled and fed as per his request.

Carlos had been made uneasy by the fact that all the men carried a machete at all times. It was nothing new or unusual, and it had never bothered him until that night. Nevertheless, the night was pleasant, his stomach full and the bed quite comfortable after the long ride, so he relaxed, undressed and fell asleep without noticing it, but with his gun under his clothes, which he used as a pillow, and his rifle at his side.

When he awoke in the morning, the sun was already slanting through his bamboo curtain and the chickens were busy pecking throughout the patio grounds. His first thoughts were of Catalina, and he wished he could tell her immediately about his adventures to that point. He was truly on his own for the first time in his life, answerable to no one but himself and he wanted to boast about it to someone. He washed from the waist up at a cattle trough and was served breakfast the minute he sat down. While he ate, several children stared at him with great curiosity, and he remembered that his hair, no longer truly blond, still had streaks that glinted golden in the sunlight and that the grayish-blue color of his eyes was also something they had never seen.

The remainder of that second day was not as generous to him. Somewhere around noon, with the heat bearing down upon his back, he stopped at the edge of a ravine and saw a small valley stretching out before him. The path he was following turned south and circled around the valley in a wide arc. Carlos decided to cut across by hugging the wooded northern hillsides, not only because it would be much shorter but also because he would be shaded by the foliage.

At first, the angle of the hillsides was shallow but it slowly became steep as he continued. The trees and bushes gave way to saplings and vines that became increasingly dense and intertwined. Eventually he had to dismount and lead his horse through the thick, tangled brush, breaking branches in the thicket with his hands for he had never thought to bring his own machete. At the same time, the slanting ground beneath his feet was changing, turning spongy like moss-covered loam that sat, several inches thick, over wet, slimy clay the sun could never reach. With every step, the conditions grew worse, so that soon he and his horse were battling just to remain upright. He fell first, several times, coming back up smeared with mud and slime and an armful of red army ants on one occasion. It was worse when the horse fell, because it would flail wildly with its hooves, digging itself deeper in the muck and getting stuck among the labyrinth of tree roots. By the time Carlos decided to go back they were in such thick vegetation that the horse couldn't turn around and they had to continue until they found a clearing big enough to make the turn.

Finally, they returned to the place where they had left the trail that went down and arched to circumvent the valley. Both horse and rider were tired, dirty, frustrated and disgusted, and they had lost a total of five hours.

When he passed some Indian families in the valley they looked at him and greeted him with a passing vow, but he imagined them all bursting into laughter as soon as he was out of sight and he started to laugh at his own foolish inexperience. By the time he reached the river that ran along the valley floor, his plan to bathe away the mud and wash his clothes was made less urgent by the fact that the water was ice cold and the sunshine, already weak, would soon be disappearing altogether. It was a tough choice, eventually decided by the fact that his body was covered with welts from insect bites and itching to distraction.

He dove into the water, surfacing with an involuntary gasp, but by forcing himself to remain in the river he found that the numbness of his flesh soon made the cold irrelevant. He washed his horse, saddle and all, and in a clearing on the far bank made a campfire between some boulders underneath a stand of willows. The fire was weak but good enough to dry his clothes and the horse blanket over night. He ate the remainder of the chicken Catalina claimed to have cooked for him with her own hands and fell asleep thinking of her.

It took him three and a half more days, each one of them a similarly harrowing experience, before he found the village of Tzuchijá; a collection of thatched-roof huts sitting precariously on a hillside, overlooking a bend of the Usumacinta river.

When he first rode into their village, the people all retreated to their homes and warily peeked out at him from within. He walked up to several of the huts and called out for someone-- anyone--who spoke the Ladino's tongue. No one would even answer him until a voice surprised him from behind.

"What do you want?"

It was a tall Indian man with a scar across his face. Carlos introduced himself and explained that the government had sent him to teach the town's children to read and write. The man stared at him without answering. He looked like a man in his late twenties to Carlos, although with Indian people it was often difficult for him to tell. He was stout and muscular and his eyes were solid black.

"What is your name?" Carlos asked him, extending his hand.

"We don't need read and write." he answered, ignoring his hand.

"Well, the government has a different opinion. So, its not up to you or . . ."

"You go!" the man yelled, grabbing the handle of his machete at the same time. Carlos stepped back, wondering whether to reach for his gun, and listening for any noises at his back.

"Okay, I'll go." he told him. "But you know what will happen. If I don't do my job, twenty soldiers will come next week." Carlos started to walk away, then turned again and pointed at the man.

"And they will make YOU read and write." Again he turned, this time walking resolutely to his horse.

"Wait!" the man yelled. "Wait." The man turned and walked to a grouping of huts. Carlos watched as several other men emerged from the huts and gathered in a central clearing to talk among themselves. He recognized the dialect as Tojolobal, but he could understand few words. After some discussion, the man with the scar motioned for Carlos to join them.

"What we have to do?" he asked.

Carlos sat down on a rock and motioned them to do the same. Most of them did. He asked the man his name again.

"I am Antza-já."

"Well, Antza-já, please tell your people first that I am not here only because the government sent me, but also because I really believe that if your children learn to read and write they will help your people and have a better future."

Antza-já translated to his people and one of the older men answered him forcefully.

"We live here long, long time and never read and write."

196

"That's true." Carlos answered. "It's also true that the best Jaguar hunters are those who know how the Jaguar lives and what he does and why."

He waited for Antza-ja to translate and noticed that the people now seemed to be taking an interest even if only out of curiosity.

"The Ladinos, like me," he continued, "are coming more and more. Most of them are good but some are bad. The bad ones will try to cheat you, steal your cows, take your land. If you learn their ways, you can stop them."

Again they talked among themselves, this time with several of the women joining in. "We will read and write." was their decision.

"Fine." Carlos said. "We will begin tomorrow."

He was provided with some food that evening and with a hut at the very top of the hill which lay abandoned for some reason. He made himself a bed out of pine branches which he covered with his horse blanket and he used his saddle for a pillow. He was still awake around midnight when a howling wind that shook the roof and penetrated every crack on the mud and bamboo walls of the hut revealed the reason for the availability of his new home. However, by the time sleep approached he was more troubled by the mixture of feelings in his mind than the wind rattling his walls. He felt proud of himself for his accomplishments but hypocritical for telling the villagers that he was really there because he wanted to help them. That had never really entered his mind until he said it. And he felt stupid for putting himself through all this hardship for such little money, and lonely for being so far away from Catalina. Then he remembered that he was doing it all for her.

Chapter 17

Gilberto's death left Florinda and Catalina devastated and completely broke. They celebrated a novena, praying a rosary for the salvation of his soul each night in the company of friends. On the final night they were joined by Florinda's brother Arturo, his wife Adela and their three children. It was the first time Catalina met any of them except Arturo whom she barely remembered, but although they remained with them for only two days, Catalina felt a happiness she could have never expected. It was only then that she realized how much she had missed by growing up an only child.

During dinner on the final day Arturo proposed that Florinda and Catalina return to Chilón.

"There's nothing left for you here." he said. "In Chilón you have not only us but all the rest of your family. You will want for nothing."

Arturo was now the mayor of Chilón, following in his father's footsteps. Jacinto was also married and with four children of his own, whereas Nicandro had three, though he still lived in Salto de Agua, and by all accounts, Doña Juanita's house up on the hill had once again become the center of life in Chilón.

Florinda was tempted to accept the invitation on the spot, but instead immediately rejected it. She guessed that Catalina would not stand in the way of such a return, even while feeling devastated by the loss of her social surroundings, her education and her relationship with Carlos, and Florinda could never sacrifice her little sister in that way. In the end, she promised Arturo that they would visit Chilón for a few weeks during the summer. She told him not to worry, and lied that everything was fine, but he left her some money just the same.

The following day, Florinda put the house up for sale and it sold within a month. She bought a smaller place on Villa Real street, just two blocks away from the central plaza. It had a patio with a corridor that ran along only two sides of its perimeter, because in fact the house was half of the original home, which had been crudely divided by a wall running straight through the center. It had a small back yard that sloped up at the far end, just as its mirror image and now neighboring home. It was comfortable and with more than enough room for the three of them, but the reason Florinda bought that particular place was because it had a large parlor facing the street, with two balcony windows. It was a large room, accessible by a side door from the foyer and a double door from the corridor and patio.

"This room will now become our store." she announced.

She hired some carpenters and masons to build a partition that turned the rear of the room into a storage area and had one of the balconies turned into an entrance door with a brick staircase. A counter was installed, running across the room from side to side and the partition was covered with cabinets and shelves. Catalina and Maria were as exited by the project as Florinda, and all three of them spent every available moment for weeks, preparing for the grand opening. They cleaned and painted, scrubbed and polished. Catalina was in charge of all the signs and Maria Hernandez of setting up the barrels and crates in the back room to store bulk quantities of goods--it was amazing to see what strength she had--while Florinda arranged the front in such a way that sometimes she would think she was back in Chilón, working with Magdalena at her side.

During the day, while Catalina was in school, Florinda and Maria invaded the marketplace, to purchase goods, check prices and place orders with suppliers, and at the end of the day, after working several hours beyond dinnertime, they would drop on their respective beds like heavy stones into a river. Yet, on a couple of occasions, Catalina was awakened in the dark hours of the morning by the clatter of Florinda's Singer sewing machine. The frenetic pace of those days was a welcome distraction to all three of them; something to keep their minds off their great loss.

For Catalina, it was a change in her life that seemed to set off other changes. She had little time to spend with the Cansino girls now, which she missed for many reasons, not the least because they were her best connection to Carlos while he was away. But her friends were also changing and in ways she neither expected nor liked. Increasingly, life was becoming a war to them; a constant series of egocentric battles. Their feelings for and actions towards everyone, including their friends and even their own sisters, were dictated by the rumors and gossip that flowed through the town like a winter gale. The consequence was not only that two friends could suddenly become enemies, full of rancor toward each other, but that they expected everyone around them to take sides and help feed the flames of enmity. The rift would grow with insults, innuendo and disclosures that everyone would eventually regret, but reconciliation would only come about when a new rift developed and the sides had to be quickly realigned.

It was all senseless to Catalina, so she was glad that her busy new schedule gave her a reason to slowly pull away. At the same time, it was becoming clear that the new, frantic pace of life was taking a toll on Florinda's health.

The store, which they named *El Destino*, opened on a Sunday morning, catching the eyes of church goers with the colorful children's dresses that they hung on each side of the entrance.

Florinda and Catalina waited behind the counter and Maria Hernandez stood at the doorway between the storage area and the patio. All of them nervous and pretending to be calm and each of them secretly afraid that no customers would come.

"Of course," Florinda mentioned, "it's Sunday and people won't expect us to be open."

"That's right." agreed Catalina, "Besides, they don't even know what we have in here. So, those that do come in today will only want to look around."

The first prospective customers, an elderly couple, entered as the bells of Guadalupe were tolling for ten o'clock mass. They roamed around the store, looking at everything with great curiosity and whispering to each other. Three sets of eyes followed them discreetly but with every passing moment, three hearts sank.

Just then, two Zinacanteco Indians walked in but stopped abruptly near the doorway as if they had forgotten why they entered. They were both tall and muscular and impressive in their colorful garb. Their hiking staffs, with long metal tips, reached well above their heads. The old couple was transfixed and drew closer to each other.

"Kusha kan, Marchante?" Florinda asked them with a smile.

Relieved to hear their dialect they proceeded in and asked for several different things: salt licks for cattle, parafin bars, a dozen hand rolled cigarettes, some candles and a bag of *kishimposh*.

Catalina didn't understand the last request until Maria handed her a bag of raisins. Florinda took their money and made change from a box under he counter, than she thanked them in Tzeltal, their dialect, and wished them a safe trip. They thanked her, vowed and walked out with a satisfied smile.

The couple, still standing at one side, was impressed.

"Where did you learn their language?"

"Oh, I was brought up among their people, in the mountains." Florinda explained. "How about you two? Where are you from?"

"We're from Spain, just passing through your fascinating country on our way back from vacationing in Guatemala."

They ended up buying cheese, preserves, smoked ham and a pair of native hats. When they left, Florinda turned to Catalina with a smile of disbelief.

"Imagine." she said, "coming here all the way from Spain, just for a vacation. What's this world coming to?"

"Times are changing." Catalina admitted with a sigh, not sure wether she liked that change or not.

Meanwhile several other customers ventured in and business remained brisk until closing time. Earlier that afternoon, Father Jose Rivas, from the church of El Carmen stopped by and gently pulled Florinda aside.

"Are you planning to open every Sunday, my dear?" he inquired in a whisper.

"I don't know yet, father. It depends how well we do during the week."

"You know, the church does not look favorably on it." he warned her.

"Well, I'll be happy to close Sundays, just as soon as the church starts paying my bills."

The priest forced a smile. "That pie certainly looks delicious" he commented.

"It is." Florinda answered curtly, no longer pleased with his unforeseen visit. "I made it myself and expect to sell every bit of it."

He shuffled his feet for a moment. "Really? Well. . . I guess I'll be looking for you in church, Florinda." he said, and he walked out.

Their first day of business turned out better than all expectations. The excitement kept Catalina awake late into the night even though she was so tired, and it was just as well because she had promised Carlos to write to him at least twice a week and now she had so much to tell him. She knew by then that her letters took at least a week or two to reach him and it would be a month before she received his answer. That night she wrote to tell him all about the first day at El Destino, and Arturo's visit and the fact that she thought of him often.

Carlos received her letter ten days later, delivered by a mule driver who had gotten it from an itinerant merchant, passed on to him in Ocosingo by a government official to whom it was originally entrusted. Carlos paid a fee for it, based upon the time and distance even though theoretically it was done as a favor by people who were traveling to that location anyway. He read it in the classroom which he and the villagers had built in a more sheltered area of the hillside.

He had a total of 17 students, ranging in age from six to 22 years old. However, the attendance varied from day to day and absenteeism became a daily problem, especially with the older students who were often required in the fields or with the cattle on the range. It was understandable and Carlos became as flexible as necessary. In return, the villager's attitude toward him improved with every passing day.

"I just wish they could learn faster." Carlos complained to Catalina in a letter. "Their view of the world is so different from ours. They don't seem to attach as much importance to the future as we do. Or maybe it's just me. Maybe I just don't understand them. Maybe I'm just not cut out for this type of work."

Catalina's letters were always full of encouragement. She knew already that his moods were a virtual teeter-totter, up and down from day to day, but that her steady hand could keep him balanced. However, his impatience was another matter. Florinda assured her that he would grow out of it in time, but she was not so sure.

Carlos was in Tzuchijá for five months before he was allowed to return to San Cristobal for two weeks, one of which was taken up by travel. He was astonished to find Catalina looking older, more mature and even more beautiful than he remembered. They spent as much time together as possible during his week's stay. They went to the Sebadúa Theater where they saw a film starring Rudolf Valentino, who was the Idol of the day. They visited friends, and strolled through their old haunts.

Catalina told him that she had decided to leave school in order to help Florinda with the store, and even though he reminded her that they were supposed to make such life-altering decisions together, he was flattered by the fact that he was the first person she told.

People in town now recognized them as a couple and even their peers treated them with something akin to respect. Many of his friends addressed him, only half jokingly, as Professor, and during a birthday party for Isabel, Don Carlos surprised everyone by introducing Carlos to some guests with what sounded very close to pride: "This is my oldest son," he said, "He's a professor."

Carlos returned to Tzuchijá with renewed enthusiasm. All aspects of his life were getting better however slowly, and every passing day brought him closer to the day when he and Catalina would never separate again. If only he could make more money.

Even his work in the classroom was finally making noticeable progress. All his students knew the vowels and several could read and write their names in true Castillian Spanish. Best of all, he had penetrated a threshold, a wall of fear and suspicion that these people had for all things foreign and with good reason. And he began to understand that it was a wall built over decades, maybe centuries, to counteract the betrayals and the suffering the white man had inflicted upon them. He was astonished to learn that their whole village had been forcibly relocated twice within the last fifteen years. Once because the white men decided unilaterally to divert the river and later again because some foreigners thought there might be valuable minerals under their fields. He realized that this kind of treatment could be traced inescapably back to the time of Diego de Mazariegos and that these noble people, who exhibited neither greed nor ambition, but merely the wish to spend their short time on earth in harmony with their Gods and nature and each other, were more than justified to hate him and his kind. Yet, in a short time, they had opened their homes and their lives to him and already treated him as a good friend.

Time passed, the seasons changed and Carlos started making plans for his next trip back home. He had been in that village over a year. The corn he planted in the field behind the classroom had grown tall and been harvested by all his pupils on their own time. He had come to know them all and knew they could be as mischievous as children anywhere.

One of his students was a skinny, eleven year old, with the unfortunate characteristic of unusually large ears that pointed mostly outward from his head, rather than back. His name was

Nicolás, but his schoolmates teased him mercilessly and called him 'rabbit'. One day, Carlos decided to put a stop to it. "None of us is perfect." he told them. "I have a crooked nose, because I broke it once. And we can find something odd about each one of you. So, it isn't nice or smart to call Nicolás a rabbit just because his ears stick out a little bit."

When the laughter died down, Tzi Pec, a twelve year old girl stood up at the back and raised her hand.

"We don't call him rabbit because of his ears." she said. "We call him rabbit because he turns himself into a rabbit." Her classmates explained.

"Oh, you mean he acts like a rabbit or pretends that he's a rabbit."

"No." they all insisted. "He can turn himself into a rabbit."

Nicolás, squirming in his chair, denied it, and the matter was dropped. However, the topic kept returning during the next days as the children assured Carlos it was true and explained that Nicolás' father was a Shaman with knowledge of powerful magic. Yet Nicolás steadfastly denied that his father had taught him any of his tricks. So, one day, shortly before Carlos left for home, he dismissed the class except for Nicolás. The young boy sat at his place quietly but clerarly nervous. Carlos asked him to perform his trick and assured him that no one else would know about it.

"My father will get mad at me." Nicolas said. It was the first time he had admitted that much, so Carlos sprung his trap.

"Look, Nicolás, if you show me your magic trick, I promise that I won't tell anyone. But, if you don't show me, I will tell your father that you did."

Almost in tears, the child agreed. Carlos sat back, expecting his young pupil to use his hands to disfigure his face in some way, as children often do. Nicolás stood up and stepped back into the darker corner of the room. Carlos watched him carefully. Suddenly, the boy ran forward a few steps and dove to the ground, curling up as if to do a somersault, but as his feet came around and hit the earthen floor with a thud on the hard ground, he vanished from sight. Instead, a large, brown jack rabbit was sitting in his place, in that exact spot, with its ears standing straight up and its nose wiggling to sniff the air. Carlos felt the hair in the back of his neck stand straight up. He leapt from his chair and was out and running through the corn field in a flash. When he finally stopped and looked back, trembling, he saw Nicolas hurrying out of the classroom with his writing tablet under his arm.

Later, when Carlos finally got up the courage to return, he searched the classroom from top to bottom with his oil lamp but the only thing he found was a set of rabbit tracks on the spot where the animal had been. Carlos refilled the oil lamp and kept it lit near his bed all that night.

The following day Nicolás arrived promptly and took his seat without a word and only a glance at his teacher who in turn averted his own eyes. The matter was never mentioned again by either of them and many years would pass before Carlos confided the story to a soul.

Soon after that, Carlos spent three weeks in San Critobal and it rained nearly every day. He became a fixture at the little store of El Destino, even helping Catalina turn the balcony into a proper storefront window, adorned with samples of the merchandise that could be had inside. In the afternoons he and Catalina would sit at a little table in the patio corridor sharing hot chocolate and *pan dulce* that Maria Hernandez baked especially for them in the old earthen oven in the yard. They would talk about things of little consequence, hold hands and just watch the rain falling on the patio, just a few feet away, and steal a kiss when certain of their privacy. Those would become some of their favorite memories of their courtship.

Catalina had already left school, much against her sister's wishes, but Florinda was eventually reconciled to it, made easier by the fact that they enjoyed each other's company so much. Then, when Carlos was preparing to return to the mountains he was abruptly called to the Education office and given a new assignment by his supervisor. He asked who was going to take his place at Tzuchijá.

"No one right now. We have other priorities." he was told.

"Wait a minute." Carlos protested, "We made a promise to these people. Are we just going to break that promise?"

"Carlos, we don't make the rules. These orders come from Tuxtla and they're not negotiable.

Carlos considered quitting on the spot. And he considered it many times more during the following year. In that span of time he was transferred four more times without explanation or reason. He came to feel that it was not worth the trouble to do his job since it would all go to waste in the end, probably at the whim of some ignorant bureaucrat sitting in some distant office, whose sole qualification for the job was that he had powerful connections in the government. By the time he was sent to his fifth different village, Carlos was thoroughly disenchanted. He began to do exactly what the other rural teachers did: Put in the time and collect his salary. Periodically he would produce false reports claiming 'tremendous educational strides being made', and send them in as required. These were reports that the villagers happily signed with an X in order to forgo the constant disruption of their life's routine.

It was in that way that Carlos suddenly found himself with a lot of time on his hands, to do anything he wished except return to San Cristobal to be with Catalina. He began to roam the countryside, taking horseback rides to neighboring villages, venturing further afield each time. On several occasions, natives offered their services as guides to the "homes of the ancients." Years before, in San Cristobal, he had heard about the mysterious ruins of ancient Maya cities being found deep in the jungles of Chiapas, but such reports were always followed by admonitions of the dangers that surrounded such places: poisonous animals, head-hunter tribes, grave-robbers and treacherous terrain. Now it all added up to an adventure he was unable to pass up.

He took what precautions he could: filling his medical kit with quinine, iodine, epsom salt and a variety of herbs used to fend off malaria, treat dengue fever, cholera and other diseases prevalent throughout this tropical zone. A local curandero gave him a plant that, when chewed, could stop bleeding within minutes, and a dry root that could empty his stomach and his intestines in less time than that. He still carried a milk-white jar with a lapis lazuli top, filled now with an ointment to ward off insect bites which Maria Hernandez had prepared for him on his last visit home. In addition to his gun, rifle and ammunition he now carried a machete that the elders of Tzuchijá had presented him on his 20th birthday. It had a carved and decorated handle to match its leather scabbard.

He set off on a sunny morning with two Kiché Indians to guide him. They travelled on horseback along a narrow trail into woods so dense that day turned into night several times before the sun actually went down. The noise made by the countless birds and monkeys inhabiting the tree canopy far above them was deafening at times, yet Carlos preferred it to the moments of sudden silence that often stopped them in their tracks.

"What is it?" Carlos would ask.

"Shh! Jaguar!" The guides would answer, and they would remain motionless, barely breathing, until the birds resumed their chatter.

The horses were often spooked by seemingly no reason.

"Snakes." One guide would explain. "Horses don't like."

On several occasions, the forest gave way to muddy swamps but fortunately they emerged into a clearing just in time to build a campfire and sleep for a few hours. They awoke at dawn the following day and resumed their trek early in the morning after a breakfast of roasted iguana, fried plantains and black coffee. Long before noon the temperature was sweltering, their clothes were soaked and sticking to their skin and the air was filled with more insects than Carlos had ever imagined could exist upon the earth. He was already regretting his choice of adventure since he could have been lying on a hammock watching the clouds pass and the fog roll in from the edge of a quiet mountain village.

Fortunately, by the early afternoon they arrived at the town of Frontera Corozal, on the west bank of the Uzumacinta River: a hot and muddy shanty town made up of dilapidated wooden shacks, most of which seemed to be either cantinas, restaurants or a combination of the two. Corozal was also a noisy, bustling place, with music blaring from jukeboxes at every turn and crowds of people with their chickens, horses, pigs, and other livestock, pushing through in every direction. It was a town whose only reason for existence was to serve as a border crossing into Guatemala, across the swollen river. There he was told that the remainder of the trip would have to be by canoe since the jungles that surrounded the Maya ruins were impassable beyond that point. Carlos hired a large dug-out canoe that came with two additional guides. They agreed to leave in the morning.

He had dinner at a riverside establishment that was doing as much business in the back room brothel as it was in the front bar. Throughout his meal he observed men of all sizes and descriptions and in one degree or another of inebriation, stumble past his table eyeing him defiantly as if to size him up for a possible confrontation. He tried to ignore them but made sure that his holstered gun was in plain sight. By the time he finished eating he was longing for the safety of the jungle.

Before looking for a place to spend the night, he wrote Catalina a letter telling her exactly where he was, with whom, and what he expected his destination to be as well as the date of his return. He entrusted the letter to an affable old merchant taking a load of alligator hides to Ocosingo. Carlos had heard that other men making the same journey upon which he had embarked had disappeared, never to be seen again.

After a restless but uneventful night sleeping on the back room floor of a fruit stand, along with several fellow travelers, Carlos was glad to be moving on. He and his guides replenished their supplies at a dusty marketplace and packed them into the center of their canoe. That vessel, nearly five meters long, was carved out of a fallen ceiba tree which the Maya call Kapok and venerate as the sacred tree of life. This he learned from one of the guides when he asked why the wood had a pinkish color.

The swollen river was relatively smooth at first although it moved them along at a fast pace. It was the color of chocolate milk due to the silt that the rains had introduced through the erosion of the riverbanks. That created a danger since they were unable to see and thus avoid the branches and even trunks of trees felled by the storms into the river and which lay just beneath the surface.

Periodically the canoe would bump into such obstructions, usually with a mild thump but on occasion with a loud thud and a violent change of their direction which in one instance caused them to lose some of their supplies. The guides seemed to enjoy such surprises but Carlos grew more nervous by the minute, aware that his ability to swim was very poor.

Unfortunately the situation only worsened with the passing hours. The currents became stronger and less manageable while the alligators that had been an odd sighting at the start, with every bend in the river grew in numbers and in size. The river banks slowly gave way to sheer walls that grew ever higher into majestic canyons that only served to churn the waters into rapids and remind them of their impotence in the face of nature's awesome powers. At times they were totally out of control, along for the ride like a leaf in a windstorm. They plowed into waves that threw them from one side to the other, spinning into eddies, only to be thrown again into the maelstrom.

Somehow they all made it through the worst part although most of their supplies were lost, along with three of the four oars they originally carried. Relieved and grateful to be alive, they spent the next hour baling out water with their hands and flowing along in relative calm.

They stopped at a sandbank where, after scaring away several alligators lazing in the sun, they rested for a while eating mangos, jicama and dried beef. Carlos was feeling much better by then, already thinking of the letter he would write to Catalina detailing those adventures.

One of the guides from Corozal estimated that they would reach the ruins of Pa'chan within a few more hours. He was the only one of the guides to have been there before.

They returned to the river already with the confidence of veteran boatmen using the paddle up front and an old board that they found on the water as a rudder at the back. They made good time as the river became wider, at least a hundred meters in some places, and the currents smoother. Carlos even took the time to count the many species of birds nesting in the shore trees.

Suddenly and without fanfare the guide at front used his oar to turn the canoe hard to the left into a cove. They made their way through a thicket of mangroves that at one point became a virtual tunnel, forcing them to duck as far down into their boat as possible. Then the canoe slid up an old makeshift wooden ramp covered with mud and came to a stop.

"We are here." was all the guide said and they disembarked. They chopped their way through a wall of shrubbery and vines and climbed up a precariously slimy hill, pulling themselves up using the vines and protruding roots of trees above them. When finally they decided to stop to catch their breath they found themselves leaning against huge moss-covered stones covered with intricate carvings of a hieroglyphic nature. Beyond them stretched a large mesa, several acres in size and which had recently been cleared. It was surrounded on three sides by tremendous pyramids topped with imposing buildings reached by grand staircases and through ornate entrances. Carlos and his guides stood there quietly for a long time, gazing in awe at the sight and trying, each in his own way, to imagine the things that must have transpired there centuries before and to visualize the countless souls who must have worshipped there, in those mysterious temples.

Along the esplanade massively majestic stelae kept a silent guard upon the grounds. Standing ten to fifteen feet in height and up to two meters in diameter, they must have weighed several tons, yet somehow managed to appear light and delicate due to the exquisite carvings covering each of the four sides. Most were depictions of warriors or gods in full dress surrounded by mysterious inscriptions that probably described their amazing powers and astounding deeds.

It certainly astounded Carlos to think that these works of art were done hundreds or perhaps thousands of years before. The group climbed one pyramid, hundreds of steps, and entered what looked like a temple at the top, and in the dying evening light discovered luxuriant murals covering the walls in bright, almost iridescent colors; panoramas of warriors, priests and maidens engaged in rituals lost to the ages.

The guides spoke amongst themselves a bit, but for the most part remained silent, clearly in awe but also proud to know that this was the work of their ancestors.

The five men explored the various structures slowly, almost in reverence, trying to absorb all the wonders that lay before them, sometimes together but often veering off in separate directions as if in hope of finding something more astounding than the others. Carlos decided to to tackle the tallest pyramid of all, daunting though the climb promised to be. He paced himself, examining the carvings on each step and the huge animal heads protruding at intervals along the steep stairway. When he finally he reached the top, he rushed into the central chamber of that temple anticipating the murals that would surely be there. In stead, he received the fright of his life as something suddenly stirred in the shadows of a corner and came at him. With a gasp he jumped back instinctively and reached for his gun, stopping himself in the next instant as the menacing figure stepped into the light of an oil lamp. It was only a man, not very tall, wearing a tattered sombrero and extending a hand of welcome to him.

He said his name was J. Speer Taylor, that he came from a place called Rhode Island, in the United States and that he was an anthropologist doing field work for his studies of the Ancient Maya Civilization. He was slight, had blue eyes and a reddish beard. He wore wire-rimmed glasses, spoke broken Spanish and had a pronounced limp due to the fact that one of his legs was several inches shorter than the other. And he would change Carlos' life for ever.

Chapter 18

Jasper Speer Taylor, known to everyone as 'Jap', was thirty two years old, had a quick smile and boundless energy. When he and Carlos first startled each other, he wasted no time in introducing himself, extending a warm handshake, as if to an old friend, and inquiring, in his broken Spanish, about Carlos' reason for being there and about his profession. He was delighted to hear that Carlos was a teacher.

"Excellent! Excellent!" he said, and quickly took Carlos by the sleeve to show him what he had discovered. From a satchel lying on the floor in a corner of the temple he took out a package and unwrapped it with great care. Carlos expected to see some kind of treasure, perhaps gold, jade or other precious stones, such as he'd heard were often found in these places.

"Look! Look at this!" Jap urged, unable to hide his excitement. Carlos looked, even squinted, only to see part of an old bone with dirt still clinging to it. He was unimpressed.

"Come, come!" Jap motioned for Carlos to follow him out into the light. That was when Carlos first noticed that he walked with a pronounced, almost comical limp that made his entire upper body tilt down to one side and up again with every step. His left leg was in fact much shorter than the other. Carlos pretended not to notice.

"The lines." Jap said, "The lines." and he pointed to some lines that looked like nothing more than scratches on one part of the bone. Jap struggled to find the Spanish words he needed to explain his thoughts to Carlos and attempted several that made little sense, spurting out in English, Spanglish or Tzeltal. He became increasingly frustrated. Finally, he turned and began calling to someone named Chan'uk down below, who appeared moments later. To Carlos' surprise, Jap began speaking to Chan'uk in the Kiché dialect as fluently as if it was his native language.

Using Chan'uk as his translator, Jap was able to explain the reason for his excitement: He said, essentially, that the bone he and his aides had discovered in a nearby grave which they had been excavating for weeks, belonged to a Maya nobleman; that the lines cut on the bone were so fine and so precise that they could not have been caused by stone tools during an act of cannibalism as other scientists had theorized from previous and similar discoveries. From his experience at the University, he explained, he could recognize that bone tissue had grown around and even over some of those cuts, which meant that the person had lived for some time after they were made. Then he led Carlos and Chan'uk to a corner of the temple and with an oil lamp drew their attention to a lower section of the mural where a seated figure appeared to be holding a small knife to the mid-section of a prone body from which blood was flowing. Jap said that all the experts agreed this was the depiction of a ritual sacrifice, but he himself had never subscribed to such a theory. It was his belief that it depicted a Maya doctor operating on his patient, and that the bone would help him prove his theory with the help of X-rays and other techniques available back in the United States.

"That's not a knife." he assured them, That's a scalpel. These people," he continued, "were incredibly advanced in certain fields."

He waited for Chan'uk to translate for Carlos and then continued. "A thousand years ago they were using a calendar more precise than ours is now and their astronomical calculations went back thousands of years and forward thousands more, allowing them to precisely predict not only celestial events like eclipses, but also weather patterns and even cataclysmic episodes like floods, droughts and earthquakes."

Carlos was skeptical. "Really?"

"Come," he said, "Let's go have dinner and we'll continue talking then."

Jap started down the stairway in a sort of sideways fashion, like a crab, and Carlos was amazed to see how fast yet smoothly he descended the steep and narrow steps and realized that instead of letting his disability hinder his progress, as most others would have done, he was, in the most natural way, using it to his advantage. Chan'uk just smiled in recognition of Carlos' amazement.

They had dinner in a large tent that served as the team's quarters on the site. Through the meal Jap continued to expound with great enthusiasm upon his theories and his admiration for the people who had created the temples that surrounded them.

"Did you see the incredible colors in those murals? Those murals are a thousand years old. Even now, we have nothing to compare. Our colors fade in the sunshine within a few years. There is a treasure of knowledge here, Carlos, waiting to be discovered and deciphered." he explained, "But it must be done carefully. We must peel back the many layers that have accumulated over centuries in order to get to the truth. For example: this place is called Yaxchilan, which means the place of green stones in the local Lacandon dialect, but that's only because when the place was rediscovered, they found the stones already covered in moss. The real, original name of this place is yet to be revealed."

Jap's knowledge seemed to be eclipsed only by his thirst for more knowledge and his energy surpassed only by his infectious enthusiasm.

However, Carlos was impressed even more by something else. Jap seemed to possess a genuine belief in the equality of all men, and therefore the need to treat all men as equals. Carlos arrived at that conclusion, not from anything Jap said but rather by his actions. When Carlos, upon Jap's invitation, gathered up his four guides and brought them to the tent to eat, rather than showing them a cursory acknowledgment and then sending them off to eat with his own Indigenous helpers, as any Mestizo would have done, Jap greeted each of them with a warm handshake, asked their names, which he committed to memory, and insisted that they all sit together at the makeshift tables that he set up. Then, during dinner, which he personally served to everyone in equal proportions, he did his best to include them all in conversation, making it as convivial as could be expected. At first, it made the guides, and therefore also Carlos, very uncomfortable. But the actions of this man were so genuine and natural that by the end of the evening the entire group, in spite of the language barriers and tremendous cultural differences, felt more together than separate and certainly more at ease with one another.

In the morning, while the guides packed the provisions that Jap made available for their return trip to Corozal, and his own helpers returned to their anthropological work, Jap took Carlos on a tour of entire site.

They climbed what was then already being called 'The Grand Staircase to the Acropolis': a huge stairway, still partially covered by the dirt and overgrown by vegetation accumulated over centuries, but clearly more than thirty meters wide and well over a hundred meters in length, made up of some 150 steps; an assemblage of thousands of cut stones with intricate carvings facing out into a timeless world. Huge, carved stelae, rose from the center of the staircase at intervals and Jap theorized that during certain celebrations tens of thousands of people, wearing dazzling costumes, must have climbed that magnificent stairway, as if to heaven.

The staircase led directly to the main terrace, from which the two men were able to access all the major points of interest at the site. By then, the two men, so dissimilar, were quite at ease with each other, which made their communication much easier if still not very precise.

In the end, before pushing their canoe back into the Usumacinta, Jap warned them about the whirlpools that sometimes appeared without warning and had in fact taken the life of another anthropologist the previous year. He handed

Carlos a piece of paper with directions to his headquarters in Ocosingo and, through Chan'uk, told him he had an open invitation there. "Tell Carlos that I will be expecting him." he said. "and that my wife and I will teach him English and he can teach us Spanish in return."

During the trip back to his work, if it could still be called that, Carlos thought often about the strange man with the pronounced limp. He had turned out to be the most interesting person Carlos had ever met, and he resolved to take him up on his invitation as soon as he had an opportunity.

However, that opportunity did not arise for many months as several other things occurring in Carlos' life intervened as if to prevent it.

Chapter 19

Carlos and Catalina were officially engaged on her 17th birthday. Carlos wanted the marriage to take place within a month and Catalina wanted six months to make the preparations, partly in the hope that by then the latest wave of anti-Catholic government measures would have abated. They compromised to three months, and began their plans for a Spring wedding. By then Carlos would have concluded his latest teaching assignment and be back in San Cristobal. He applied for a month's leave of absence which they would use for their honeymoon in Guatemala and to move into their new home.

They scheduled the ceremony in the Cathedral and each of Carlos' sisters was given an assignment. Alicia was put in charge of the flowers, Lucinda and Mariella would take care of the bridesmaids' dresses, Isabel and Adrianna would help Florinda with the food for the party afterwards, which would also take place in the Cansino home. Carlos would arrange for the music and the paperwork for the civil ceremony which would take place one day before. To that end, he spent several hours one morning filling out forms at the civil registry offices. He also made the arrangements for the honeymoon in Guatemala and rented a house on an outlying section of San Cristobal for them to move into upon their return.

Rumors regarding some break in the tension between the government and the church intensified for weeks. Then, one morning, thirty armed soldiers stormed the Catholic monastery behind Santo Domingo church, ransacking the place and hurting several seminarians who tried to prevent their entry. The soldiers were searching for a French nun who had previously eluded them in Tuxtla along with a dozen children from her private orphanage in Chiapa de Corzo, the ancient capital of Chiapas. Mother Lissette had long been outspoken in her criticism of the Mexican government's policies toward its large orphan population and had become a thorn in the ruling party's side. Unable to silence her, they revoked her passport and ordered her expulsion along with the apprehension of her charges until a disposition could be arranged for each of them. The government had learned that they were all hiding in the monastery but the nun was warned in time and managed to elude the authorities once again. Speculation about their whereabouts became San Cristobal's topic of the day.

"It looks bad." Carlos said. "And its going to get worse."

Reports surfaced two days later about Sebastian Pijul, an Indian who had worked at Santo Domingo as the bell ringer and handy man for over forty years. They said that he was suspected of acting as a guide for the fleeing nun and her orphans, and that he had just been found somewhere in the surrounding hills with a bullet in the back of the head. The army disposed of his body in some undisclosed location to prevent the inflamed emotions that a proper burial might have induced.

Hundreds of outraged people gathered at the plaza and took turns at an improvised podium to denounce the military, the government and all their apologists. The military troops watched and listened from windows and rooftops but did not interfere. The following morning the citizens found six of the town's churches padlocked and chained shut. Pasted on the doors were official explanations claiming that each of these 'establishments' had been found to harbor anti-government activists and to have abetted their activity and that these places would therefore remain closed until further notice.

Meanwhile, the churches that remained open were limited to providing one mass per week on Sunday morning and absolutely nothing else.

Several people filled with indignation tried to organize a new protest and were immediately arrested. No one was allowed to see them and authorities refused to comment on their cases. Rumors immediately began that these prisoners would be transferred to Tuxtla during the night and no one had forgotten that during a similar situation four years before, six people were killed while "trying to escape."

A meeting was convened at the Cansino house to decide what to do about the wedding. The gathering in the parlor, included Catalina and Florinda. Father Rufino Galvez, who had been scheduled to perform the wedding ceremony was also present. After some discussion and a long exchange of opinions that was getting them nowhere, Don Carlos Cansino took the floor.

"What it comes down to is this: The wedding can be postponed until this crisis is all over, or it can go on as scheduled but done in secret, which means a far smaller scale, taking great precautions and great risks." He turned to Carlos. "The decision is yours."

Carlos thought for a moment. The large room, packed with people, was as quiet as if it had been empty.

"Unless Catalina has some objection, I would like to proceed with the wedding as scheduled, except of course that it will be at midnight instead of noon."

All eyes turned to Catalina. "I agree." she smiled and leaned against Carlos' shoulder.

"Well," Don Carlos concluded, "that's that. We have one week to finalize the preparations, except that now security has to be taken into account. As far as anyone needs to know, all the preparations you are making are for a birthday party. Everyone knows we have one here nearly every week." There was general but subdued laughter and as they walked out of the room the priest reminded them that the government had snoops everywhere, including many locals, and that it was best for one to assume that he was being watched at every moment.

"What a terrible way to live." someone commented.

During the next few days all previous arrangements were modified. The wedding would take place in the left wing of the Cathedral, away from the street, rather than the central aisle. Lights would be dimmed, there would be no organ music or singing of any kind. The crowd would be limited to about fifty people and they would all enter through the back door, having crossed through the yard of the neighboring convent of St. Nicholas. Several people would be posted at key locations including the bell tower, to warn them of any military raid.

Then, two days before the church wedding and one day prior to the civil ceremony, Carlos was summoned to the civil government offices. When he entered the offices his heart was pounding so hard he thought he might faint. He had no idea what this was all about. He was ushered into an inner office and told that someone would be with him in a moment. As he looked about the room, his mind was racing through the possibilities and he tried to calm himself in order to provide the proper answers. He was prepared to deny any intention to marry in church, and even to say that although a Catholic, he was not very devout, which was the truth. He wondered why Catalina was not summoned but he was thankful that she wasn't. Then he double checked his pocket to make sure he had brought the money for the bribe that would probably be required.

Finally a man entered from the side door and greeted him with a handshake and a smile, and Carlos assumed it was a ploy to get him to lower his guard. His name was Roberto Bilbao and the wooden plaque on his desk said he was a magistrate.

"I understand from these documents that you work as a teacher." he said as he sat down across the desk from Carlos.

"That's right." Carlos answered defiantly, "I work for the state department of education.".

"Excellent, excellent." The man opened a file and leafed through several pages. He resumed talking without looking up.

"And you are scheduled to be married tomorrow, right downstairs. Is that right?"

"Yes, that's right."

The man read through more of the file, scratching his trimmed beard as he did so.

"And your name is?" he looked up from his papers.

"Carlos Cansino."

"Your full, legal name please."

"Carlos Ernesto Cansino."

"Born in Monte Bello on November 10, 1914?"

"Yes. That's right."

The magistrate furrowed his brow. "Well, I'm afraid we have a problem, which may delay your marriage."

"What problem is that?"

"According to all the legal documents on file, birth certificate, etc. you are registered as Carlos Tamayo."

"That was my mother's maiden name."

"Yes, but there's no record of her marriage to Carlos Cansino."

"No, they were never married. But my father legally adopted me when I was four or five years old."

"Yes, that's what we call Legal Parentage Acknowledgment. We searched for that but there's no record of such papers ever filed on your behalf."

Carlos felt his heart sink. "Are you sure?"

"I'm afraid so. We double checked and cross-referenced with Don Carlos Cansino's files."

Carlos sat back on his seat and took a deep breath. He looked pale so the magistrate provided him a glass of water.

"So, this means I can't get married tomorrow?"

"No. It means you can't get married as Carlos Cansino, but you could still marry as Carlos Tamayo. You'd have to refile all these papers today. In fact, right now. But I would see that they clear this very afternoon."

"Yes. Let's do that. I will be happy to pay you for your trouble."

"Nonsense." he patted Carlos on the shoulder. "It's my job. And we need to get you back to your job. Education is the only thing that will take us beyond these types of problems."

225

Carlos spent the next two hours filling out papers and holding back the waves of anger that kept rising from his nervous body to his spinning mind. He purchased copies of his birth certificate and other documents in his file and walked out into a hazy day with rain clouds gathering in the east. As he walked the six blocks to his house, his anger was rising again and his steps became strident. He entered his house and ran into his sisters Gloria and Mercedes in the foyer. They were trying on their bridesmaid gowns and asked for his opinion, but he walked past them into the parlor, slamming the door behind him.

Don Carlos was sitting on the sofa across from Doña Helena in a rocking chair. They were entertaining friends; a couple and their little daughter, visiting them from Tapachula. Don Carlos' two oldest daughters, Alicia and Lucinda were seated opposite the couple and beside their daughter.

When Carlos entered, the only one he saw was his father. He walked right up to him and threw the handful of documents at him, shocking everyone to silence.

"You son of a bitch!" he yelled, swearing at him for the first time in his life. "You lied to me all my life as a child," he continued, "but you should have had the guts if not the decency to tell me the truth now."

Don Carlos was as shocked as anyone in the room.

"What are you talking about?"

"This!" Carlos yelled, "That!" He picked up some of the documents and shook them in front of his father's face. "That's my birth certificate, where it says that thanks to you I am a bastard and that you never acknowledged me to be anything else!"

"There must be some mistake." protested Don Carlos.

"No, there's no mistake. All you wanted was a servant, and you lied to obtain one that wouldn't require a salary. But it's clear now that you're a bigger bastard than I'll ever be."

Carlos turned and stormed out of the room only to immediately return to the doorway. "I don't want to see you at my wedding!" he pointed to his father, "I'll never set foot again in this house, and don't you ever set foot in mine."

Don Carlos threw his hands up. "Carlos, it's just some mistake. I'll have my lawyers take care of it."

"Rot in hell!"

Carlos left as angry as when he entered. He sent a servant for his belongings the next morning while he and Catalina were married in the civil court offices. He had already asked Florinda if they could hold a simple gathering at her house after the church ceremony and she agreed after asking him to think it over. Catalina was not as forgiving.

"Your way of solving a problem is by making it worse." she told him.

"That's easy for you to say. You're not a bastard."

"No. I'm an orphan!" She said, and walked away, leaving him with his mouth open.

The civil marriage was attended and witnessed only by Florinda, Isabel and Adrianna. When it was over, Carlos tried to kiss his wife, but Catalina, still angry, turned and walked away.

Carlos had already moved into the house that he rented although the upstairs rooms were still being painted. He was helped to dress in his formal suit by Fernando Suarez, who had come from his new home in Comitán to be his best man. All afternoon Carlos had been ranting and railing against his father. "He's ruined my life." he said. "He's ruined my marriage."

He paced the floor with his barrage of complaints. "Now, even Catalina is angry at me."

Fernando listened patiently for an hour, without saying a word. "I ought to do to him what you did to your step-father." Carlos concluded.

Fernando jumped up, grabbed him by the lapels, lifted him into the air and slammed him against the wall.

"Don't you ever say that, you idiot!" He flung him down on a sofa. "I'm tired of listening to your complaints." He then grabbed him by the tie and brought their faces to an inch of each other.

"You've got two choices," he scolded, "You can spend the rest of your life bitching, moaning and complaining like a bitter and helpless old lady, making yourself miserable, making

Catalina miserable, making everyone miserable around you; or
you can accept the fact that this is YOUR life, better than
some, worse than others, and take control of it, like a man,
making of it what YOU want."

He released his grip on the startled groom, who remained
speechless for a moment. Then he poured some wine which the
two of them were drinking moments later when some of
Carlos'old school friends arrived. The whole group then settled
back for the evening to drink and reminisce about school and
their adventures, pranks, small victories and inevitable regrets.
Then, fifteen minutes before midnight, they headed out in
pouring rain to the Cathedral.

Running across a side street under a shared raincoat,
Fernando observed that they wouldn't have to worry about a
police raid.

"Those guys are too lazy to come out in this weather."

Most of those attending were gathered in the church
sacristy, having trickled in by small groups as directed. All of
Carlos' sisters were present, except Alicia who was still
incensed by the disrespect Carlos had shown to her father.
Carlos laughed when he heard that.

"She's just scared that he won't pay for her wedding if she
ever finds someone to marry her."

That remark, quickly reported back to Alicia, would cause
her to seethe with hatred for Carlos and refuse to have anything
to do with him for the next three years. Meanwhile, Mariella
refused to sit near Adrianna because of some other remark that
her sister was rumored to have made. Adrianna, the maid of
honor and several other young ladies in attendance spent their
time and attention swooning over Fernando, even though he
was rumored to be in love with a young lady from one of the
wealthiest families in Comitán, where he now lived.

"If he really cared for her, he'd have brought her."
Reasoned Adrianna, and the others eagerly agreed with her
deduction.

Father Rufino's sermon, according to Antonio, was the best
he'd ever given, "because it was given in a whisper, heard only

by those who strained to hear it and not loud enough to disturb the rest of us."

A large automobile that Fernando rented, and which reminded Catalina and Florinda of Gilberto's Packard, took the bride and groom, maid of honor and best man along with Florinda to her house. The rest of them walked the three blocks in a boisterous group, no longer worried by the government's paranoia.

It was the biggest crowd ever to squeeze into Florinda's little house. Fortunately the rain stopped and some guests were able to overflow comfortably into the patio. There was plenty of food since it had been made for a larger crowd, and the music from the victrola was enough to set a happy mood without infuriating the few neighbors who had not been invited.

In the early hours of the morning, after all the guests had gone, Catalina and Florinda had to face the moment both had been avoiding. But instead of the goodby that would have underlined the fact that this was a moment of tremendous and painful change in both their lives, they kept telling themselves that they would be living only a few blocks away from each other, though it was really more like ten blocks, and that with Carlos' work taking him away so often, they would still be able to spend much time together. There was even the possibility that Catalina would continue working at the store.

That night, after the newlyweds headed off to their honeymoon, Florinda and Maria Hernandez sat at the kitchen table for a long time, reminiscing about their favorite memories of Catalina as a child, growing up beside them even as she grew into their hearts, and they sipped home-made wine and cried together like the dear old friends they had become.

Chapter 20

When Carlos returned from his honeymoon he was again reassigned to a different village. This time it was to Chenal'ho, a fast growing Indian community on the road to Ocosingo. He was told that there was a dire and immediate need for the education of the Indigenous people there because there had been a growing number of clashes between them and the Ladino merchants.

"Those Indians think they own everything there." His supervisor complained, "They don't understand the laws of property, land ownership and free access to trade." he explained. "That's where you come in. Don't worry too much about teaching their kids to read and write. Teach the adults to obey the laws."

Carlos didn't bother to argue. By then, he knew well where the real ignorance lay, and who was to blame for the ever growing friction between the Indians and Mestizos. During a previous assignment he had witnessed Ladino justice first hand: A group of men arrived on horseback to that village, which had existed in a small wooded valley since time immemorial. They were led by a man who claimed to be from the state government land development offices, and he was backed up by several men in military uniform and fully armed, as well as a group of men whom Carlos recognized as *mayordomos*, middle managers from one of the largest lumber companies in Chiapas.

The village leaders were assembled and the man spoke to them through his own interpreter: "Amigos, as you all know by now, we live in a nation ruled by laws, and those laws apply equally to all of us and we must obey them. That's what prevents problems and disputes." He spat out a wad of tobacco and continued. "All people who own land in Chiapas must have a legal document like this." he held up a sheet of paper, "This is called a deed. Now, any of you who have a deed to this land, go and get it right now so that we can verify it and be on our way."

No one moved, so the man started to laugh. "I didn't think so." he said, turning to the men who had arrived with him and were clearly enjoying his demonstration. Then he turned to the villagers again.

"You see, this deed right here tells me, without any question, that this land that you have all been using belongs to the Schiller Land Company, and has for many years."

Some of the villagers frowned and looked an one another.

"Now, fortunately," the man continued, "Mister Schiller has no intention of making you pay him for the use of his land all this time. However, he now has need to put this land to his own use and purposes. So he has agreed to give you a week to move your belongings and leave his land. Where you go is up to you. You're free to go wherever you want, but I would advise you to go back to those hills," he pointed to some distant mountain tops, "as far as you can go, and find some good land there. But when you do, you must go immediately to the land office in Tuxtla to make sure that no one owns that land. Then you can get your deed and won't have to worry any more. Okay? That's all I have to say, except that when Mr. Schiller's workers get here next week, if any of you are still here, you will be arrested."

Carlos was incensed. He introduced himself and told the man that these people had lived there for as long as anyone could remember. That he didn't think that paper was valid and that he himself would travel to Tuxtla if necessary to straighten out the matter.

The man listened to him patiently, then he put his arm around him and pulled him aside.

"Look, Mr. Teacher," he whispered, "I'm sure you've heard that two schoolteachers were killed last month near Tapachula, on their way back home. Another apparently hung himself from a tree right in front of his schoohouse in Chiapa de Corzo. It's been a bad year for schoolteachers, so I would just advice you to be very careful. You never know what you might find at the next turn of the road."

In the end, the villagers themselves asked Carlos not to endanger himself further. They moved away and he returned to San Cristobal. Now he was being sent, not so much to teach the Indians as to help the government keep them in their place. He went obediently, feeling angry and emasculated.

What he found in Chenal'ho was worse than anything he had seen before. Most of the Indians had already been dispossessed in one manner or another. Generally, they were first offered a pittance for their land, then, when they refused the offer, their access to water was revoked, or if the water happened to run through their land it was diverted or poisoned, so that not only would their livestock die, but many times their children also.

A great number of the Indigenous men were hired to work in the mines and rubber plantations on and around the Sierra. They were hired under contract, usually for at least six months, where they could earn far more than they could ever earn in town selling goods they could no longer produce. Their needs in those almost inaccessible places were met by the company stores. Food, clothing, tobacco, soap and anything else, could be purchased merely with their signature or X placed on a piece of paper that became their personal account.

When payday arrived, at the end of their contract, most of them would find that they owed money to the company and would have to continue working until they paid it off. Some of them had not seen their family in well over a year. Those who had managed to escape such economic slavery could be found in town, lying on the streets completely drunk on the strongest and cheapest firewater that the Ladino merchants could provide. Years earlier, it became clear to the Ladinos that alcohol had a far stronger and more immediate affect upon the Indians than upon the whites, and that they became addicted to it much sooner. Now, the Ladinos in power were using alcohol as another tool to 'keep them in their place'.

Domestic abuse among the Indians, virtually unknown before, was now rampant in their midst. Stories of drunken Indians hacking each other to death with their machetes were now commonplace. To keep such violence from crossing into white society, laws had been passed forbidding Indigenous people from owning or carrying firearms. In Chenal'ho, every white man and even young boys, carried a gun, just in case. Whenever an Indian was shot, it was assumed to have been in self defense.

Carlos' disillusion and his feelings of impotence soon gave way to renewed bouts of depression that often lasted for days. He would stay in his room, unable to eat or sleep, wondering what his and Catalina's future would now be, and angered by the fact that just when he should have been the happiest he felt more like a failure than ever before.

Finally, Carlos emerged from his room early one morning, took a long bath in the cold waters of a nearby river, ate a hearty breakfast and rode out of Chenal'ho for ever.

Two days later he arrived at the address in Ocosingo that Jap had given him and nervously knocked on the door. When he was about to knock a second time, the door opened and he was faced by a lady with blond hair, much lighter than his own hair had been, and very light blue eyes. She stared at him for a second and then burst into a smile.

"You must be Carlos Cansino," she said, to his surprise. "Come in, come in. We've been expecting you. Jap will be so glad."

She said her name was Annie, and she led him past an obstacle- filled hallway and through rooms crowded with boxes that were crammed with an assortment of odd things that included masks, plants, stones, papers and primitive musical instruments. From the second level they clambered up a makeshift stairway through an opening on the roof to a deck that had been added to take advantage of the sun.

Jap was sitting around a small table, engaged in conversation with three other foreigners, but he sprang to his feet and welcomed Carlos with a hug. He introduced the other men as colleagues from the United States. After an exchange of hand shakes they all stood in a circle, smiling awkwardly, since none of the guests knew Spanish.

Annie quickly took Carlos by the hand, explaining to the rest that she was going to show him around the house. It was a large house that felt more like a museum, with collections of rocks on one table and arrowheads on another. Shells of all types, from sea and river, filled an entire wall of one room, while tunics like those worn by the Lacandon tribe filled another. They crossed a central patio to a light, airy room filled with drawing tables and several easels.

"This is what I do." Carlos understood Annie to be saying.

She showed him a plant, just a very ordinary looking plant, like some type of herb. Then she held it up next to a drawing of that very plant, much larger and with amazing detail. Carlos was impressed.

"A work of art!" he said.

"No, no." she corrected him. "A work of science."

She explained that it was a very rare plant, not known to exist anywhere else. Not even in Veracruz. However, the ancient Mayas used it for medicine. She looked through another box of drawings until she found a reproduction of a figure painted on a wall in Tulum. The figure was holding just such a plant.

Annie had hundreds of such drawings, as well as reproductions of the stelae and the glyphs at various sites. They spent a long time going through them and Carlos was able to add some information about some of them, which Annie carefully wrote down.

When the three visitors left, Jap joined them in the art room. He said that his friends had brought some disturbing news from abroad. Apparently there were some ominous things taking place in Europe centered on some political movement in

Germany. Carlos was glad that he was not asked his opinion because he had not understood a thing.

They had dinner, prepared by and Indian maid from Guatemala, and afterwards relaxed with some sherry out in the patio. Jap brought out a set of postcards and photographs of various places in the United States and Carlos was enthralled by the rows of huge buildings, many stories high, and the wide avenues filled with cars. The people strolling on incredibly wide sidewalks were all attired in the latest fashions. There is no poverty there, he thought. Jap pointed to a horse pulling a carriage and pronounced 'horse' slowly for Carlos to repeat. He did so, several times, until he managed to pronounce it just right. Then he said to his hosts: "ca-ba-llo". They repeated it and Annie had no trouble with it but Jap kept swallowing the o, so that it sounded French. "No, no, Jap. Ca-ba-llo. Yo, Yo. Caballo."

That was their first English/Spanish exchange lesson of which there would be many more during the visits that Carlos made to the Taylors in the ensuing years.

In the meantime Carlos had become adept at manipulating the system that had for long manipulated him. He filed reports about native unrest in areas that interested him or villages where he thought he could still do some good. Often he would be posted there within a week or two, but on some occasions when he wasn't, he just went there anyway and later claimed that the office of education must have lost the copies of his orders. Like that, one year passed into another.

Felix, his first child was born in Florinda's house during the worst winter in memory and due to flooding, mud slides, raging rivers and washed out roads, Carlos was unable to be at Catalina's side as he had promised. So his first born was six weeks old when he first saw him. Fortunately, both child and mother were in good health.

As time went by he managed to make inroads with the bureaucracy in Tuxtla, actually becoming friends with some of the supervisors. That translated into better postings and more frequent visits to his growing family in San Cristobal. His salary, however, had grown very little since he started teaching and Catalina decided to move back in with Florinda and Maria Hernadez. The money that they were paying for a nanny and to rent the house could now be used to pay for the needs of their child, according to Catalina. It was an argument he couldn't refute, although it felt like a reproach to Carlos; as if to underscore the fact that he couldn't properly provide for them.

He always looked forward to his visits home with an almost childish anticipation. Along the way he would buy a new toy for Felix and stop in the valleys to pick flowers for Catalina. The days they spent together during those years would become the happiest times Carlos ever spent in his native San Cristobal. Sometimes they would stroll through the various sections of the old town, with Felix if the weather was just perfect, along the aqueduct, past the river and the bridge of sorrows, to the marketplace. Almost everyplace would evoke some memory of their courtship and anyone watching them walk by could see that they were still very much in love.

In those days, Carlos' father was out of town more often than not, taking care of his properties, although the looser tongues claimed he was actually taking care of his mistresses. In any case, it allowed Carlos and Catalina to visit his sisters and Doña Helena. Otherwise, Carlos still refused to set foot in that house. His oldest sister Alicia, married and living in Comitan, already had two daughters. Lucinda was giving all indications of ending up a spinster while Mariella had turned out to be the wildest of that first group. She changed boyfriends as often as she changed her hairstyle and drew great pleasure playing one suitor against another. Some people thought that she would end up running away to marry whoever she chose even though Don Carlos had already warned her that he would disown her on the spot.

No one yet knew what to make of Antonio, the youngest of the clan. He was extremely bright but completely uninterested in school academics; Very popular but not particularly interested in friends, and he still had not shown a great deal of interest in the opposite sex.

"Oh, give him time, Carlos." Catalina would say, "He's only twelve. Let him have his childhood."

"Yeah. Maybe he'll also have mine."

On rainy days Carlos was content to just spend hours sitting on the parlor floor of Florinda's house, playing with Felix and accompanied by the clatter of the Singer sewing machine nearby as Catalina practiced various dressmaking stitches that Florinda taught her. Later, Maria Hernandez would serve them chocolate and home made cookies right on the store counter of El Destino, so they could watch the world pass by.

Then, as the end of each visit home approached, Carlos would begin his slide into depression. Catalina assumed it was just the same sadness that came over her due to their coming separation, and she was partially right. But it was also caused by the fact that during those visits Carlos would inevitably run into some of his old friends or classmates and see how well they were doing with their lives. By then, some of them had their own business, others had received one degree or another. A few had gone to Mexico City in pursuit of real money and important positions. It was all a cruel reminder of his stagnant life and his bleak future, and it ate him up inside.

When his next visit home was still too far away, Carlos would do the next best thing. He would find an excuse or a motive for a trip to Ocosingo and include a visit to Annie and Jap.

On one of those trips he found himself shopping for groceries in the local marketplace with Jap. Carlos felt uncomfortable performing what he considered woman's work, but Jap went about it as if it was the most natural thing on earth. Sometimes he would even venture out wearing short pants, like a young schoolboy, but to Carlos' astonishment, the stares and snickering that such a sight elicited didn't seem to bother him at all.

With all the tact and delicacy he could muster, Carlos pointed out to his friend that such activity caused people to talk. Jap roared with laughter.

"What do I care if people talk? Am I breaking some law? Am I hurting someone? Of course not! I'm just living my life in the best, most comfortable way I can find. If some people have a problem with that, that is their problem, not mine."

Carlos thought long and hard about Jap's point. He could see the sense in what Jap said, but felt it just couldn't be as simple as that. Apparently Jap mulled things over too, because when they finished shopping and sat down to rest on a park bench he broached the subject again.

"Look, Carlos," he said, "to some people here I may seem like an eccentric or an oddball, but in my country no one would give my behavior a second thought. You see, the difference is that your territory was ruled by a European monarchy for ages and so your people were infected by that most hideous invention upon which a monarchy depends: class division."

Seeing that his friend's attention was thoroughly engaged, he continued, "By the time you threw off the monarchical yoke and gained your independence, the little idiosyncrasies that support the class system were thoroughly ingrained."

The two men bought some oranges from a passing vendor and the friendly lecture continued just as Carlos hoped it would.

"Living in a class system entails--for all but the lowest class-- looking with awe, respect and reverence, and perhaps a little envy, at the classes above you, while also looking with disdain and an air of superiority down at the classes below you. That maintains the class system equilibrium. So, when someone snickers at or derides someone else; makes fun of someone's faults as if they had none of their own, they are in fact--wether they realize it or not--trying to maintain their place in a class system that should have died long ago with the advent of independence. Real independence would include that."

The municipal tower clock struck one and the two men hurried back with the groceries that Annie and the cook were waiting for since noon. The three of them had lunch out in the patio and afterward relaxed under an improvised canopy next to two scrawny olive trees that Jap had planted years before and which now swayed gently in the afternoon breeze.

"We won't get too many more days like this." Annie predicted.

"No. The rains will be coming soon. We'll need to start closing things up at the site. The problem is, we can keep the rain out of the graves but not the grave robbers."

"Why not leave a guard there?" Carlos suggested.

"No. Looting is getting to be a big business." Jap explained. "The people behind it are ruthless. They would kill a guard without remorse."

"They have in the past." Annie added sadly.

To change the mood, Jap changed the subject.

"Now, what were we talking about before, Carlos?"

"Well, I've been thinking about what you said, and now I have a question."

Jap cleaned his glasses. "Go on."

"You said that things are different in your country, but wasn't your country also born of a monarchy?"

Jap sat up in his lounge chair. "On the contrary. Our country was the result of a rebellion against the monarchy. Our first settlers came to America to get away from such a system. They hated it so much that they decided to establish a system that would be the very opposite of a monarchy: not only independent but with freedom and equality."

"Well," Annie interjected, "at least, that was the theory."

"No, no. I believe they achieved it, although with two major and regrettable exceptions."

"That's what I meant." she added.

"And what exceptions were those?" Carlos inquired.

"Well, first, our dispossession, massacre and incarceration of the Indian tribes. And secondly, our enslavement of the African people,"

"Oh, yes. I do remember reading in school about your President Lincoln and the war."

"Yes, Abraham Lincoln passed the laws against the brutal and uncivilized practice of slavery, but the resulting misery has yet to be dealt with to a satisfactory conclusion. Prejudice is still a cancer in our land, and the closest thing we have to class divisions. And although Lincoln is hailed in history as the great emancipator, there was a man who did far more to stop the evil practice of slavery in America. I'm sure you know who I mean, Carlos."

Carlos thought for a moment. "Oh yes, of course. Simon Bolivar. The Great Liberator."

Jap started to laugh and Annie smiled. "I was afraid you would say that. But no; the man who did the most against slavery was much closer to you than that. His name was Bartolome` De Las Casas."

"Oh, Friar Bartolome`, the Defender of the Indians! He was the first bishop of Chiapas, and he lived in San Cristobal."

"That's right. But he did more than that. It's been estimated that thanks to his tireless efforts, which lasted most of his adult life, he saved some thirty four million Indians here in the Americas from the powerful claws of slavery."

"Really? Thirty four million? I didn't know that."

"Well, I guess he just didn't have as good a press agent as our President Lincoln, but it is true and I hope some day his memory and the record of his achievements will be resurrected by history."

Carlos was reminded of an afternoon, almost a decade before, when in the park of Friar Bartolome` and beneath his very statue he discovered the power of his strange dreams. He kept the memory to himself and in that way the three figures in the little patio of a corner house in Ocosingo, deep in the forests of Chiapas, remained quiet for a long time watching the long shadows climb the walls and then the hills to finally disappear with the breeze into the dusk. Those were the moments and the conversations that kept Carlos coming back to visit his old friend with the pronounced limp during those years.

Chapter 21

The teaching situation did not improve much during that time. Carlos thought about going to Mexico City and applying for a teaching position there, but he knew that 'proper schools' did not consider rural teachers to have any teaching experience at all. Besides that, he had already concluded that teaching was not what he wanted to do with the rest of his life. He didn't have the passion that teaching requires. And he no longer had the patience.

His son Felix had turned out to be a precocious but sickly child and the medical bills started to eat into the savings that he and Catalina had built up as a result of her move back to Florinda's house. Catalina then started dress-making in earnest. She made ordinary house dresses for her friends at first, but her friends then requested clothes for their children. She acceded with great reluctance, afraid that she would fail, but everyone was delighted with the results and most of all with Catalina's good taste. Soon they were turning up at El Destino with fashion magazines in hand, pointing at the latest styles from New York and Paris and begging for copies of them that they could wear at the next church social or society tea.

Florinda ordered the seldom-used dining room to be cleared out and she bought another, larger table where Catalina could draw and cut her patterns. Orders started coming in from strangers, even some from neighboring towns. Catalina had to work long hours to keep up, but she had never been so contented. It wasn't only the money she was making, though that was certainly welcome, but it was the pride and fulfillment it gave her to know that she was tangibly contributing to the future of her family.

Of course Carlos did not see it that way. To him this was only further and painful proof of his failure as a husband and a father. They argued about it in their letters to each other, and in the end Catalina just decided to ignore him and she plunged back into her enterprise with renewed energy.

What neither of them foresaw, however, was the coming of their second child. Catalina stubbornly worked right up until her eight month of pregnancy, but at that point had to close up her business. Their second child, Maria del Carmen, was born with the dawn of a day in early spring. This time Carlos was at Catalina's side until the last moments, and then allowed back into the bedroom with the first cry of his new daughter. To prevent the child from developing a propensity to illness, like that of her brother, the doctor ordered a strict adherence to the *quarentena* for both mother and daughter: forty days of quarantine.

Of course, in spite of Florinda's best intentions, there was little chance that such a rule would ever hold. Carlos' sisters were the first to break it, trampling into the room like a herd of buffalo on the very first day to view the latest addition to their family. After that it was difficult to refuse any of Carlos' or Catalina's friends from paying a visit.

"We might as well put in a revolving door!" Florinda scolded.

Meanwhile, and quite secretly, the happiest person in the house was Maria Hernandez, for she knew that she would soon get to hold in her strong brown arms and subsequently raise the daughter of the only daughter she would ever love as her own upon this earth.

Don Carlos Cansino sent word that he would like to visit his new granddaughter but Carlos adamantly refused permission. Weeks later, after Carlos returned to his work, Catalina took her child and personally presented her to the aging patriarch of the Cansino clan.

The months passed and things returned to normal. Catalina slowly took up her sewing again but to a much more limited degree since she now had two children demanding a portion of her time. Before anyone noticed, Christmas arrived, and for Florinda's household it turned out to be one of the most joyous anyone could remember.

El Destino sold Christmas decorations at a rate previously unseen in San Cristobal. This included wreaths that Maria Hernandez and Catalina made from fresh pine branches that Carlos and Antonio brought back from the valley woods. The distant mountaintops were appropriately white with snow that winter and in the afternoons when the cold wind swirled down the cobblestone streets, the clients of the often crowded little store were served complimentary cups of hot chocolate and fresh baked cookies.

At one point, Catalina noticed that some of the Indians passing by the store were reluctant to enter after seeing the many Ladino customers inside. So she filled a tray with cookies and cups of chocolate and went out to offer it to them. They refused at first, convinced it was a trick, until Maria Hernandez assured them it was free and offered from the heart. After a while, more than a dozen Zinacantecos, Chamulas and Tenejapas, men as well as women with children at their side or on their backs, were sitting on the sidewalk or leaning on the walls of El Destino, contentedly drinking their chocolate.

The sight made Catalina's eyes well up with joy just as Maria made an observation: "Now the Ladinos won't want to come in."

"I don't care." Catalina answered.

But they did come, and the store kept its doors open late each evening right up until Cristmas eve. Carlos and Antonio spent that day decorating the patio and clearing a space for the marimba band that Carlos hired. The women prepared the food that they had been cooking from the night before, all the while dreading that few people would show up and all that food would go to waste. They had steamed several dozen tamales wrapped in banana leaves. Several hams came out of the oven covered with browned slices of pineapple held in place with cloves. A large crystal bowl of hot punch made with pineapple juice and rum with cinnamon adorned the center of the table, surrounded by trays of *churros* and delicate *hojuelas* in the shape of flowers, covered with sugar and honey.

Hours later, looking at the crowd overflowing the patio and the corridor into the various rooms, Florinda and Catalina worried that they might run out of food. At one point the marimba band played a set of waltzes that took Florinda back to the celebrations in Chilon during her youth.

This celebration ended at eleven thirty only so that everyone could attend the midnight Christmas mass. The federal government had been slowly loosening its grip on the church for the past year and the church was quick to take back its territory and all its responsibilities. As a consequence, the Cathedral filled up to overflowing with believers, nonbelievers and all those in between. The parishioners had spruced up the old church and everyone agreed it had never looked better, and the crowd joyously sang hymns that they had only mumbled in the past.

Catalina, cradling Maria del Carmen in her arms and flanked by Carlos and little Felix, offered a prayer of thanks to God for granting her the wish that she had made in that very church during the Festival of the Señoritas, eight years before: To allow her a family of her own, healthy and surrounded by happiness. At that same moment, her husband was praying for a sign to guide him out of the misery of his failed life.

That sign did not come to him as a thunderbolt from the sky, but rather as a mist seeping imperceptibly into his consciousness over a long period of time and it had taken root in his mind long before he was aware of it.

In stead he returned to the drudgery of his work in yet another village that didn't want him any more than he wanted to be there. Now he also had to contend with an additional danger in the countryside. A new round of national and state elections was to take place the following winter and already the opposing parties were agitating to win the support they would need for the final campaign. By then the preferred and most efficient way to garner that support was no longer with longwinded speeches that most peasants couldn't even understand or promises that everyone knew would not be kept. It was gathered through the barrel of a gun.

Groups of armed men representing one faction or the other would ride into a village demanding support and loyalty to their cause; a loyalty which the people had to prove by donating what money they could gather and then painting the party's slogans and insignias on their walls.

Since few of the villagers could read, the slogans were painted or circled with the faction's colors: red, white and green for the ruling party or blue for the opposition challenging the government. Travelers were often set upon at some bend in the road and asked which party they supported. A wrong answer could sometimes mean a bullet to the head. Word of such attacks spread quickly and soon even the main roads were nearly deserted.

However, rotting away amid the boredom of some godforsaken village was nearly as bad, so Carlos decided to risk it and headed once again to Ocosingo. To be sure he stayed off the roads as much as possible and he kept his gun loaded and within easy reach.

This time he found his old friend Jap packing dozens of crates for shipment to the United States.

"Annie is already up there," he explained, "but once she gets everything catalogued, she'll be back here again to help me. We've got an awful lot to do."

Carlos helped him pack the remainder of the boxes and in the evening they sat down to dinner by themselves. Amalia, the cook, had gone to spend some time with her family in Guatemala. Jap was feeling melancholy and spent most of the evening reminiscing about his youth. The two men ate little but made up for it in wine and they talked late into the night. Jap said that he was an only child but had a happy childhood growing up in a seaside village of Rhode Island. His parents were both university professors so he had grown up surrounded by books. Perhaps because of that, he found school too easy.

"There was no challenge. I became bored and lost all interest."

"What did you do?"

"Well, I got interested in sports. Baseball! Baseball was big back in those days. Every kid dreamt of playing for the Yankees and I was no exception. Believe it or not, I was pretty good. Of course, it drove my parents crazy. My grades plummeted and I was nearly kicked out of school."

At that point Jap got lost in his private memories for a moment and Carlos refrained from interfering. Finally, he removed his wire-rimmed glasses and wiped the moisture from his eyes.

"Anyway, one day I was riding home from the ballpark in my bicycle and I was hit by a car. My hip was crushed and I was taken to the nearest hospital. There, a young doctor injected me with the wrong solution, causing further damage to my nerves and muscles. I'm sure he meant well, but you may have noticed the end result."

He got up, opened another bottle of wine and refilled both glasses.

"I was in bed for almost a full year. There was nothing to do but read and I went through most of my parents' library. I guess it's like they say, Carlos: Everything happens for a reason."

That night, Carlos slept on a sofa in a nondescript room that was now only half full of boxes. He woke up with a hangover and found Jap already at work, fresh and spry as ever.

"I've been waiting for you." he said. "Let's go have breakfast. I know a good little place just down the street."

It was a little restaurant hidden in an alleyway behind the plaza from which emanated such wonderful aromas that, both men agreed, could awaken the appetite of the dead. During their meal the two friends resumed their conversation, talking about one thing or another, from the weather to the wars already raging over Europe. There was little Jap didn't know something about, and although Carlos did not understand it all, he loved to listen and to learn.

At one point, and for no particular reason other than to recharge the conversation, Carlos asked Jap to name the worst thing about his country. Jap thought about it for a moment.

"Prejudice." he said. "There's still a lot of prejudice, especially against negroes and especially in certain areas."

"Why?"

"Well, my father used to say that prejudice was made of two parts ignorance and one part fear. And you know, he was right, God rest his soul. The most prejudiced people I've ever met were clearly ignorant, but most of all they were all cowards."

"And what's the best thing about your country?"

"Now that's an interesting question." He took a sip of his coffee, furrowed his brow and scratched the stubble on his cheek.

"You know, people have often called the United States 'the Land of Opportunity' and it's become a cliche`, but there's a lot of truth to it. Even cliche`s can be true. They also call the U.S. a nation of immigrants and that is certainly true. Everyone in my country, except for the Indians, is either an immigrant or a descendant of an immigrant. Unfortunately many of them tend to forget that after a generation or two. That's when fear and ignorance creep back in. Anyway, I've traveled to many parts of my country and have seen it with my own two eyes. Jews in New York, Irish in Boston, Italians in Philadelphia, Polish in Chicago, all immigrants who were willing to work hard--no one said it was easy--and they are all prospering. Annie and I went to San Francisco for our honeymoon. It's a beautiful city. They have an Italian neighborhood there that'll make you think you're in Italy. But best of all, there's a Chinese area there, called Chinatown, and I was told it is the biggest chinese community outside of China. And its thriving! That's the best thing about the United States. Anyone willing to work hard has a good chance of prospering. You know why? Because it doesn't matter where you come from or who your father was or what he did. No one cares about that. We fought a war to get away from those stupid class distinctions."

That was the exact moment when all the things that had been stirring in Carlos' troubled mind coalesced into one sublime idea. His and his family's future waited for them in the north, in the United States. He realized it that very moment.

Although he spent two more days keeping Jap company, when they parted they both somehow knew it was for the last time, and for the rest of his life, no matter how hard he tried, Carlos could not remember what they did or talked about during those two last days after that breakfast.

Chapter 22

Before returning home, Carlos went to Tuxtla, the state capital, to gather whatever information he could find regarding travel to the United States, the availability of work there and the required documentation. To his dismay, it all turned out to be much more difficult than he expected. First of all, very few people from Tuxtla had actually traveled to the U.S. and those that did had done so as government representatives with special and very limited visas.

"You can go there as visitor or tourist," he was told at the government office of travel and tourism, "provided you have money, but that's only for a specific time period and you won't be allowed to work."

To work there, he was told, he would need an American work permit, which he could only get if he had a valid contract from an American company requiring his services, but that company would first have to prove to its government that no American citizen was available to perform those duties.

"That's almost impossible to get, unless you are a scientist or academic in whom they have a special interest."

"What about all the laborers who go there to work on the farms?" Carlos asked.

"Well, they go there illegally. They sneak across the border. But that means that they can be arrested at any time, or worse, they can be exploited, robbed, attacked, whatever--and they have no legal recourse from either Government. Those are desperate people taking tremendous risks. Sometimes they are never heard from again."

Several other places told him basically the same thing, including an office connected to the the American Embassy in Veracruz. At the end of a frustrating week, when he was preparing to leave Tuxtla, Carlos was contacted at his hotel by a heavy-set man in a business suit.

"I understand you are interested in going to the United States to work."

"Yes, that's correct."

"Well, I can help you with that."

They sat down in the hotel lobby, across from each other, separated by a coffee table. The man introduced himself as Angel Serafino Santos, which elicited a laugh from Carlos.

"You should have been a priest."

"Yes. I believe my parents were hoping for that. Instead I became a lawyer. The pay is much better, at least in the short term."

He had offices in Mexico City, Tuxtla and Hermosillo, Sonora, he explained, because he mostly dealt with import/export matters.

"When do you want to go?" he asked.

"As soon as possible." Carlos told him.

"Okay. Well, there are several ways of doing it. All of them cost money."

"Of course."

"I'll tell you the way I recommend for you because I can see you fit the profile and it is the quickest, safest, and one that I can guarantee because it's legal."

"It sounds too good to be true."

"Indeed it does." he agreed, leaned closer and explained. "The Mexican government is continuously sending groups of people on official business to the U.S. It may be a commission to study the salinity of the rivers, or the latest technology to build dams, or any number of such things. It can also be some high government official going to some bilateral negotiations. In any case, these people need an assistant, a secretary and so on. These people travel with special visas such as this one."

He pulled some papers from his briefcase and placed them on the table.

"It looks pretty official." Carlos said.

"It is. That's the beauty of it. We make you a visa with your photo and other data, and you walk in as part of the group, or committee or whatever, wearing your best suit and tie. Then you all board a bus and head for whatever destination is scheduled. It might be 50 miles from the border or 500, to San Antonio, Dallas or wherever. Once there, you're on your own."

"And the cost?"

"Well, keep in mind that we have to pay one of the group to stay home, and the rest to keep quiet. So, fifteen hundred pesos. Half now and the rest upon crossing."

Carlos shook his head. "Way too much. What are the other ways?"

"Well, you could go by cargo ship from Veracruz. But that takes much longer, is more dangerous and there are no guarantees because the rate of success is 50/50 at best."

"I'll tell you what; if we go with the first option and you make it one thousand with two hundred down, we have a deal."

Serafino laughed. "Can't do it." he said and put the papers back into his briefcase.

"Well, thanks anyway." Carlos told him and he walked up the stairs to his room. Then he took two hundred pesos out of his wallet, put them in his shirt pocket, took out his straight razor and began to shave. There was a knock at the door. Carlos opened it with shaving foam still on half of his face. Serafino smiled at him.

"Okay." he said," You win."

When Carlos got home two days later, he was upstaged by Catalina, who greeted him with the news that their third child was on the way. They celebrated with champagne and Carlos spent the afternoon playing with his two children with a childish abandon, no longer burdened by an uncertain future.

At his urging, Florinda closed El Destino an hour earlier than usual and they all sat together at the table to enjoy Maria Hernandez's famous *cocido*: a beef broth with chunks of carrot, potato, cabbage, zucchini, chayote and green peaches. He tried to persuade Maria to join them at the table but she felt embarrassed at the very thought. It was one thing to sit with Doña Florinda and Catalina on occasion, but never in the presence of el Patron. In stead she claimed to have already eaten, thank you, and she took some of the squares of beef from the pot to roast them on the open fire so that Don Carlitos could roll them into a tortilla with a pinch of salt and pepper and a few drops of lemon, as he always liked to do.

Florinda opened a bottle of peach brandy and they all remained at the table long into the night, listening with amusement to Carlos' stories of adventures and misadventures in the pursuit of Indian literacy.

Maria Hernandez moved the baby, Maria del Carmen, into her room, crib and all, placing her near her cot and across from Felix's bed. This was ostensibly so that el Patron could better rest, but it was more so that he and Catalina could have the privacy they always craved after their separations.

It was only when they were getting into bed that Carlos took his wife into his arms and told her the secret he had been dying to reveal.

"WHAT? Are you crazy?" Her words rang out, bouncing off every rafter in the house. That was the beginning of an argument that lasted hours, during which he tried time and again to convince her that he was doing it for them, for the good of his family. He insisted it wouldn't be much different than his leaving for the Chiapas mountains, maybe even safer, and that he would be earning much more money.

"We don't need more money!" she yelled, "We have enough money! What the children need is a father!"

"What good is a father if he can't make enough money to support them?"

"You're doing okay. Besides, I'm making more dresses now. I've even got an order for a wedding dress."

"A wedding dress isn't going to buy us a house!"

Suddenly aware that they were yelling, Catalina lowered her voice. "Look Carlos, I have never asked you for any luxuries; not for jewels, not for fancy clothes, not for cars, and I have certainly never asked you for a house. All I've ever asked for is for a safe and loving place to raise our children. And we already have that."

"No we don't!" He yelled, then lowered his voice at her gesture to do so. "No we don't, Catalina. This is no place to raise children. We're surrounded by gossip and lies from people who think they're better than us just because their great-grandfather had some stupid title and ours didn't."

"Oh, Carlos, that's just silly stuff that can easily be ignored."

"Not when it keeps you from getting a job you deserve."

They continued like that, back and forth, but getting nowhere.

"Fine." She concluded. "I'm going to bed. We'll talk about it in the morning."

"Fine."

They fell asleep, each clinging to one edge of the mattress, as far from each other as possible. The following days were grim around the house. No one smiling or saying any more than what was absolutely necessary. On Friday, to underline his resolve, Carlos left the house with the announced intention of quitting his job as a teacher and picking up his final paycheck.

Meanwhile, Catalina sat down with Florinda to plead her case, which Florinda knew all too well. The older sister listened with great patience until Catalina's vehemence bordered on tears.

"Don't ask me to take sides, Caty," she told her. "That would be the worst thing I could do."

"Well, I'm not going to let him uproot his family just to satisfy some stupid and unrealistic dreams."

"Look, he says he's just going there to make money, so let him go."

"He's lying, Flo. I know that what he ultimately wants is to take us away from here."

"Listen to me. Let him go. There's a chance that he'll find out he was wrong. The grass is only greener until you jump the fence."

"Carlos is too stubborn and too proud to ever admit that he was wrong."

"If that turns out to be the case, you can deal with it then. All I'm saying is don't reveal your battle plans before you reach the battlefield."

Carlos returned in the afternoon with his final paycheck and a printed commendation for his 'exemplary contribution to the educational system of the great state of Chiapas', which he dropped into the fireplace as if to erase with fire the first decade of his working life.

The tension in the house dissipated steadily during the ensuing days, just as long as the subject of contention was avoided. During her errands to shop for dress-making materials, Catalina took every opportunity to casually inquire about any interesting job openings that might be suitable for "a friend of the family". Florinda did the same from her place behind the counter of El Destino.

Then, on a dreary Monday afternoon, came a knock on the front door from a messenger delivering a note for Carlos. Everyone held their breath, fearing the worst, except Carlos, who opened it eagerly. It was a notification of the death of his brother, Fernando Suarez, who had died at his home in Comitan from a gunshot wound.

Chapter 23

Carlos left for Comitan immediately. The dirt roads were in terrible shape due to the rains and he had to change horses twice along the way. He arrived the following day at the address on the note. Fernando's landlord, the owner of the home, expressed his condolences to Carlos and led him to a small apartment at the rear of the building. He unlocked the door and silently walked away.

Carlos entered as quietly as he could. He had never been there, though he had meant to visit many times. It was a small room, kept very orderly and neat. Between the entrance and the room's only window on the left stood a small roll-top desk and matching chair. Carlos threw open the window's curtains to let in more light and stared out at an empty lot and some grazing animals in the fields beyond and he sighed at the thought that this was the view that his older brother must have gazed out upon on countless afternoons.

Two steps behind him was the bed. It seemed a small bed for someone as tall as Fernando, and with its white linen sheets and navy blue bedspread, it was neat and tidy except for the tiny white feathers and wooden splinters scattered over it and on the otherwise spotless floor. The remainder of the pillow was still in place, blown open by a single shotgun blast and covered in blood that was already dry and turning brown. The old headboard was also spattered with blood, especially surrounding a three inch hole near the center; a hole that Carlos stared at for several minutes.

Beyond the foot of the bed, in the shadows of an alcove, was a bookcase filled with an eclectic assortment of books that included: The Theories and Inventions of Leonardo Da Vinci; The Physics of Flight; The Fifty Greatest Castillian Poems and Love in the Spring. Carlos leafed through some of them, always carefully putting them back in their place. On the middle shelf were some smooth and colorful river stones and assorted sea shells. Behind them stood an empty picture frame and in the corner sat a bowl full of ashes and some small but still recognizable remnants of letters. To the side was the door to a very compact bathroom. The bath tub, under an old glazed window, still showed signs of recent use as did a moist, wrinkled towel on the floor beside it. There was a small sink under a weathered mirror and in a small shelf recessed into the wall was a shaving kit with straight razor, sharpening stone and a tiny jar of mustache wax, all neatly in their place inside a silver case. On the inside of the lid was an inscription: To F.S. from A.M.L. followed by a tiny heart made of gold.

There was a large and heavy wooden trunk, only half filled with neatly folded clothes upon which someone had placed the shotgun and spent shell. Carlos went back to the roll top desk and opened it. There, in the center, was a three page letter, folded into quarters, with a single word written on top: Carlos.

Carlos sat at the desk by the light of the window and opened the letter with great apprehension in his heart and reverent tenderness in his hands.

My good brother:

Before I can ask for your understanding I must beg you to forgive my ultimate failure as a man. My lack of courage to face life at its darkest and most painful was the last thing I ever expected from myself. If there is a hereafter, I do not know what the cost of my cowardice will be, but my last hope on this earth is that you and all those I have held close to my heart will remember me and judge me for my actions prior to this awful day,

Fernando.

It went on from there but Carlos was unable to continue. His tears were obscuring the words and falling on the page, blurring the ink. The cries he was struggling to hold back suddenly burst from his knotted throat without control. His head dropped to his arms resting on the desk and he cried as he hadn't cried since childhood.

When he finally regained his composure, he carefully refolded the letter and put it in his inside coat pocket. Then he washed up at the sink and went outside, locking the door behind him. The landlord gave him directions to the morgue and Carlos headed there without delay.

Fernando's body was prepared for burial while Carlos found a pick-up truck whose driver was willing to attempt the drive to San Cristobal.

He paid for the best casket available and viewed his brother in it one last time, then ordered it sealed since the trauma to the head was so extensive. The casket was loaded onto the pick-up, along with Fernando's wooden trunk and another box with the rest of his belongings. It was nightfall by the time they left Comitan. The driver suggested that Carlos tie the horse to the pick-up and ride in the cab because the rain was coming, but Carlos declined and rode his horse behind the truck the entire way.

They arrived in San Cristobal on the afternoon of the next day. Catalina had already arranged for a mass to be held at the cathedral, in one of the side chapels, on the following morning, so the casket was placed in the sacristy over night, under lock and key.

Carlos was hungry, wet, muddy, exhausted and emotionally drained. He took a bath while his dinner was heated and served, but fell asleep as soon as he exited the tub and slept for eleven hours straight.

When Carlos, Catalina and Florinda arrived at the cathedral at eight in the morning to make the final preparations for the mass at nine o'clock, they were astonished to find the little chapel already full and starting to overflow. With the bishop's permission the casket was moved to the central nave of the cathedral, in front of the main altar where the mass was subsequently held, starting at exactly nine with the tolling of the bells.

Carlos was amazed not only by the size of the crowd but by its makeup, which included people of all types, Indian and Ladino, rich and poor, young and old, and although there had been bigger funerals in San Cristobal, no one could remember one at which so many school girls and young ladies openly and vehemently cried. No one cried more than Fernando's mother, Doña Rosa, who even fainted during the ceremony. She arrived with the twins, Amerigo and Amalia who had already grown into young adults.

Yet, the biggest surprise was to see their brother, Alberto Sanchez, arrive from his home up in the mountains, just in time for the mass. Afterwards, there was a gathering at Florinda's house attended by Doña Rosa and her children, Antonio Cansino and all the Cansino sisters plus many people who had known Fernando in one place or another. It was clear that the shy young man had made a good and lasting impression on everyone he met. To Carlos, the proof of that was in the fact that everyone now pretended to believe that Fernando had shot himself by accident while cleaning his shotgun, even though the truth had spread like wildfire and had reached San Cristobal ahead of his casket. The truth was being hushed up because anyone who commited suicide could not be buried in the Catholic cemetery. According to church doctrine he would also not be admitted into the kingdom of heaven.

Alberto Sanchez spent most of that afternoon sitting alone in a corner of Florinda's parlor or chatting quietly with Carlos.

The fame of the 'Grim Reaper' preceded him and most people only glanced at him out of curiosity and fear. Years before he had settled down in the village of Chincultik, between the Guatemalan border and the seven magic lakes of Montebello. He was living with an Indian woman and he casually mentioned to Carlos that they had a little daughter. It was the first Carlos had heard of it and he congratulated him, but he also warned him that he'd heard rumors about relatives of one of the men he had killed looking for him in order to get even.

"Ahhh," he dismissed it with a wave of his hand. "Those rumors have been around before. People know where I live. I'm not hiding. Besides, its been years since I had to kill anybody, and just as before, it was only in self defense."

It always amazed Carlos to hear his own brother talk about taking someone's life in such a cold and casual way. It aroused a strange mix of feelings inside him that included fear, revulsion, envy and pride.

"Why don't you come to the U.S. with me?" he told him, almost without thinking.

"What for?"

"You can make a lot of money."

"I don't need money. I've got an old shack where I can sleep and I'm surrounded by people who accept me and who are just as dirt poor as I am. What more do I need?"

"Well, with a year of work you could come back with enough money to buy a farm or a ranch, raise cattle or horses."

Alberto mulled it over for a moment. "Look, Carlos," he answered with a tired voice, "If you want me to go because you think I might be of some use to you, I'll go. I don't care either way."

Carlos smiled with satisfaction. "Great! I'll contact you as soon as I get the word."

Somehow, Antonio heard about the plan and decided he too would like to go along. He pestered Carlos for days.

"You're dreaming." Carlos told him. The old man would never let you go."

"Yes he will. I can always get my way with him. Besides, I'm eighteen now and I can do anything I want. I've already

261

told him I won't go work on that stupid farm or his old ranch. He's even threatened to throw me out of the house a couple of times."

Carlos said he'd think about it. There was a certain appeal to the idea of three brothers setting off on what could be the adventure of a lifetime. In the end, they agreed that they would do it in honor of Fernando.

Catalina hit the roof. She said that she had never heard of anything so stupid. It was bad enough that he was going, but to take along an irresponsible child and a murderer was just beyond belief.

Rather than argue with her, Carlos went out for a long walk. He visited with friends, stopped to eat at a new restaurant on the plaza and ended up in the park of Friar Bartolome`, sitting in his favorite bench, watching the sun go down through the clouds and the trees. It was only then that he took out Fernando's letter and read it calmly to the end.

The main part of the document was an explanation of the events that led to his destruction and he ended the letter with advice he had been saving up for his brother. Advice about life, acknowledging first that he might no longer have the right to impart it.

Fernando had left San Cristobal, not only to seek a better future but also to get away from his step-father's former colleagues, who were making his life miserable ever since he was acquitted of the old prosecutor's death. Through their considerable influence they made it impossible for him to get a job. Even a place to live became a major problem as they had him evicted from several places by spreading innuendoes, planting evidence and spreading lies.

They didn't do it out of any past friendship or allegiance to the infamous tyrant, but out of fear and self preservation. In a secret session after the trial, one them had spoken for them all: "If we allow some vindictive delinquent to get away with murdering an honorable member of the courts, then none of us will be safe. Any one of us may become the next target of the rabble. Our work is by its very nature thankless. We must not allow it to also become dangerous."

Fernando chose Comitan for no other reason than a conversation he overheard where someone mentioned that it was a nice place. He walked most of the way, slept by the side of the road and was given a ride on an oxcart into town. After a few weeks of hardship his perseverance paid off with a job as a stable groom at one of the better hotels. The pay wasn't much but he managed to save some of it by sleeping in the stables. In time, his hard work, sharp mind and unswerving honesty rewarded him with one better job after another, so that he eventually was earning enough to rent his own apartment. Soon he was able to buy new clothes for the first time in his life, and he took care of his wardrobe as if it was a treasure, which to him it was. It allowed a shy introverted youth to walk with a confidence and pride he had never before experienced. With new shoes, a felt hat and a well placed handkerchief the handsome dandy became a familiar figure in the nicer parts of town.

One fateful day, on the grounds of the central park, near the bandstand, he saw a beautiful young lady amid a group of her friends. Their eyes met for an instant and she instinctively turned away, but just as quickly turned back to him again and they exchanged smiles. He blushed with a warmth that rose from his belly to his cheeks and then instinctively averted his eyes. When he again looked up she and her friends were already walking off. He felt angry that his natural shyness had betrayed him, but he was wrong. She had been captivated by it and she daringly turned once again and smiled an unequivocal smile that would cause him long, wonderful, sleepless nights.

He looked for her in the park for several days, to no avail, and he had started to give up hope when they met once again in a French pastry shop. She was accompanied by her parents and a younger sister and all of them were elegantly dressed. Her parents looked very stern so he kept his distance, choosing a place several tables away to have his coffee and admire her. They managed to smile at each other several times without being detected. When the family finished their coffee, they walked past by him and she touched his hand with her fingers as if by accident and he thought he would die on the spot from the joy in his heart. The family strolled through the center of town, looking into shop windows and admiring the variety of sidewalk stands. Fernando followed them from a distance until they eventually reached a two story home in one of the nicest parts of town. A few moments later, he walked discreetly past the house, glancing at the windows and the door but unable to see inside. After a brief moment he walked by again and just by chance looked up to see the curtains part in a small window and the woman of his recent dreams appear just long enough to smile at him and wave.

Her name, he soon found out, was Amalia Mendez Luna, and she was the oldest daughter of a Spanish business man and a society lady from Mexico City. Fernando was first able to actually talk to her outside a private school where she taught ballet to the children of the town's society. That meeting removed any doubts in each of their minds about the nature of their feelings. Their infatuation was quickly turning to love.

For much of the first year of their relationship they met surreptitiously to avoid problems with her very strict parents. But as Amalia's behavior became more erratic; as her usual punctuality diminished and her whereabouts grew less predictable; her parents became increasingly suspicious and friction at her home began to take its toll. The two young lovers decided to face the problem head on. Amalia brought Fernando to her home and introduced him as a special friend.

Fernando was treated with cold courtesy at first, but as his visits continued, rather than familiarity overcoming their objections, as Amalia had expected, the parents made it clear to Fernando that their daughter was destined for much greater things, and that while they were sure he was a 'nice boy', there were those with far more to offer lining up for the privilege of their consideration.

Fernando took on a second job and opened up a bank account. He was determined to prove to them his worthiness. There was nothing on earth he would not do for the first and only woman he would ever love. However, her parents only made it increasingly more difficult for them to meet. Fernando did not realize that he was traveling upon the wellworn and destructive path that desperate lovers from Mexico to Buenos Aires had been forced to endure for centuries, since the days of the Conquistadors, just as others had long before that in the old world.

Soon, Amalia's parents were inviting wealthy young men of their choosing into their home to meet their daughter. Amalia wanted nothing to do with any of them. She rejected them tactfully in the beginning but as the parade of suitors became more insistent, she took to locking herself in her room.

Eventually, Fernando and Amalia decided that their only option was to elope. They made plans using Amalia's little sister as currier for their letters since their meetings in person had been made almost impossible. Then one day the police arrested Fernando at his place of work and charged him with intent to kidnap with further charges to be added later. Amalia's parents had discovered one of his letters.

In spite of his pleas of innocence and insistance that Amalia, who at 22 was of legal age, could clear the entire matter with her testimony, he was thrown into prison without further explanation. Then, when he demanded an attorney he was placed in solitary confinement.

Unknown to Fernando, high priced lawyers, hired by Amalia's parents, were working every angle, legal or otherwise to keep him incarcerated, and claiming to need more time to assemble the evidence, were able to delay proceedings for months. At the same time, the local paper carried a series of articles about this case that one would have thought Jack the Ripper had been apprehended.

Fernando languished in prison for a full six months trying everything he could think of to get word out to Amalia. The torture of each passing day was not knowing what was happening to her or if she even knew of his situation. To keep his spirits up he convinced himself that they would have to set him free sooner or later and that Amalia's love for him was so strong that she would wait for him no matter how long it took.

He was right about her love. As for his freedom; it came in the middle of his seventh month. His cell door flew open and he was escorted to the prison gates where an assistant to one of the lawyers against him explained that their diligent work had discovered insufficient proof and the charges had therefore been dropped. He started to make some kind of apology but Fernando pushed him aside and ran home to bathe, shave and then rush to see Amalia.

His landlord welcomed him back and gave him the packet of mail he had been holding for him. Once in his room, Fernando couldn't decide wether to bathe first or read his mail. Exitedly he ripped off his dirty clothes with one hand while he opened the letters with the other. There were several letters from Amalia. In the first she was desperately trying to find out where he was and why she hadn't heard from him. By the third letter it was clear that she had learned of his imprisonment and promised to do all she could to free him. Reading between the lines of the fifth letter it was obvious that the situation between her and her parents had become very ugly. That was the last letter from her.

There were some bills which he discarded without opening, and a manila envelope which he decided to open because it looked just like the one the lawyer's assistant had offered to him. Its contents included part of a newspaper and, to his great surprise, a note from Amalia:

My dearest darling:

Please forgive me. But I had no choice. I was presented with proof that a deal had been made which would keep you in prison for ten years. Please don't try to contact me. It is too late for me.
May God provide you the blessings you deserve,

All that is left of my love,

Amalia

The newspaper clipping was from the society section of a Mexico City daily. It was a month old and it contained a photograph of Amalia Mendez Luna in a wedding gown, holding hands with her groom while her parents and several other people stood triumphantly behind them. Beneath the photo, a caption mentioned that the groom was the son of a well known industrialist. Everyone in the group was smiling, except the bride.

Chapter 24

Carlos moped around the house for days, downhearted and depressed. Even his playful young son Felix was unable to lift his spirits. Then came the night when he had that nightmare of the planes bombing and strafing the steel ships, killing countless men in the exploding sea. It depressed him further.

For some time the radio had been reporting about the Germans waging war in Europe, so he figured that this graphic premonition meant that war was now coming to America. Whatever else it might mean, he could not guess.

He refused to tell Catalina what his nightmare had revealed, knowing it would only provide her with another reason to stand in his way, but even her suspicions were enough to cast a nervous gloom upon the entire house. He knew that he had to find a way out of his depression for everyone's sake.

On the far end of Florinda's patio stood a large shed that extended into the back yard and which was used for storage. Building materials, damaged furniture, yard and gardening equipment, ladders, a plow and other long forgotten things were kept there. Carlos suggested to Florinda that the shed be turned into an addition to the house. It could be divided into at least two good sized rooms, and it would add value to the property. He volunteered to do it since he had nothing better to do while he waited for word from Serafino. Florinda readily agreed, especially since the house was beginning to feel small and Catalina was again expecting.

Carlos hired a helper and set to work that very day. They cleared the shed completely, getting rid of most things and putting the rest in a corner of the back yard. The shed's roof was stripped and its frame strengthened and re-tiled. The brick walls were mended and plastered. The electric wiring was expanded to several areas before the wooden ceiling and room partitions were installed. Water was piped in from the backyard well into a sink where it could be pumped by hand. An oak wood floor was installed and the windows re-framed. Finally, the new front and rear doors were fitted with the help of a carpenter from the barrio of Guadalupe, and the walls were painted.

All of this took three months to complete and everyone was as delighted with the results as Carlos was proud of the achievement. Watching Carlos work during that time gave Catalina and Florinda hope that he might change his plans. They even had suggested that he start his own building company in town. He never told them that two weeks into the project he had received a message from Serafino Santos, advising him to be at the border in El Paso within fifteen days or he would forfeit his down payment. He didn't bother to answer, knowing he could not leave until he completed the work of remodeling. Besides, if Alberto was to come along, they would need to find more money.

The news of the attack on Pearl Harbor came just as Carlos was putting the final touches to the old shed that he had transformed into comfortable living quarters. Maria Hernandez was already transforming the long neglected yard into a lovely garden with paths leading to both the well and the fountain. The chicken coop was moved to the far wall, behind the well.

They turned the back room into Carlos and Catalina's new bedroom, with enough area left over for a sofa and Carlos' old leather chair facing the reconditioned chimney in one corner. The front section became the nursery and playroom for their growing brood.

It was around that time that reports began about the growing need in the U.S. for foreign workers. Rumors soon followed of a possible agreement between the two countries for

Mexico to provide some workers under contract. It was exactly what Carlos had been hoping for. It meant that he and Alberto could now go legally and at far less cost. He immediately sent word to Alberto, telling him to be ready at a moment's notice.

A week later, Carlos was sitting at a table in the parlor with Felix on his lap playing with some tiny metal cars. At his son's urging, he would take one of the little toys and move it around, finally crashing it into the others. Across the room Catalina sat in a rocking chair, feeding a bottle of milk to Maria del Carmen. She could see that Carlos' mind was far away and he was just absentmindedly moving the toys around. Maria Hernandez cleared the last dinner dishes from the table and then concentrated on her work in the kitchen.

"Maybe he's not coming." Catalina said, trying to make it sound like a comment instead of a hope.

"He'll be here." Carlos assured her. 'He said he would, and he never breaks a promise."

"Well," Catalina answered with a sarcasm that she knew was ill adviced but which she couldn't' hold back, "that must be the only thing he doesn't break."

Carlos looked up at her. "If that's how you feel about him, you should be happy to be rid of him."

Catalina shook her head in disgust but decided it was too late to argue the matter. She said no more. Some minutes later, there was a knock at the door and she felt her heart break rythm. Maria answered the door and Alberto appeared out of the shadows of the corridor. He looked much the same as the last time Catalina had seen him: thin and wiry, with a drawn and melancholy face, and that strange sadness in his deep, dark eyes. But at the same time he looked different. Although he was a year younger than Carlos, he appeared older by a decade and it confirmed Catalina's suspicions that he aged faster than anybody else.

She moved to stand up when he appeared but he stopped her.

"Don't get up." He bent down and kissed her cheek and then ran his bony hand over Maria del Carmen's hair. "My

271

niece is growing fast." he said, and Catalina shuddered from the thought that he in fact was her child's blood relative.

By contrast, Carlos' eyes lit up when he saw his brother. "Alberto! We've had dinner ready for you hours ago."

Alberto apologized and explained that the road from Zintalapa was overall a mess and nearly impassable in places. He had been living in a village near there for several years now, ever since he was involved in a brawl which left two people dead at a notorious cantina on the outskirts of San Cristobal. Some people claimed that Alberto had been accosted by bandits intent on robbing him of the money he had just won in a card game, but others had different accounts. In the end, no charges were brought against him or anyone else.

"It doesn't matter." Catalina told him, "Maria can warm your dinner up again in a few minutes."

"No, please, don't bother." he insisted. "I had something to eat on the way here."

He accepted coffee and pan dulce, eating it with slowly while Catalina took the children to off to bed.

"Any second thoughts?" Carlos asked him.

"No. I said I would go, and I'll go."

"But you're not convinced its the right thing to do?"

"I don't know. You obviously do and I'm sure you know best. I'm just wondering how you arrived at that conclusion when we've both seen that most of the people that have gone to work in the Norte have returned, usually right away and with their tail between their legs. I've talked to some of them--good, hard-working men--and they all had nothing but stories of disillusion to tell."

Carlos smiled. He had been doing his homework. "I know. But there are several differences now. First of all, those men went over there without papers or permission. They had to sneak across the border illegally. That meant they could be caught at any time and just thrown out. There was no security. Secondly, once they were in they still had to find work. Not easy if you don't even know the language. And even when they found work, they became the scapegoats for every Gringo too lazy to work who could point to them as the reason they weren't working."

Alberto took a sip of coffee and a long drag from his cigarette. "And now?"

"Now all that has changed. Not because the Gringos have changed and they suddenly love us, but because their situation has changed. They are in the middle of a war and have to send their men to fight in Europe and other parts of the world by the thousands; maybe hundreds of thousands. These are the men that were working the farms and the factories. So, now they need us. Just look at these papers."

He handed his brother the documents he received from Tuxtla and Alberto gazed at them without much interest.

"Basically, that amounts to a legal invitation. It's called the Bracero program. They need our help. They guarantee our jobs for a specific period of time."

"We have jobs here."

"Sure. Jobs that pay next to nothing. Look at me. I was riding all over hell, risking my life for a government that doesn't really care, trying to teach people who aren't interested, for a salary that barely paid the rent on an old house."

"Well, San Cristobal has always been a good place only for the rich. It just took you longer to realize it because you thought you were one of them."

Carlos was angered by that remark but held his tongue because it would have taken their conversation in a different direction.

"That's not true. In any event, money is important everywhere, not just here. And that's what this opportunity represents. We can save almost every cent we earn up there because the Gringos will provide our room and board. What we earn won't be much if we spend it there, but it will multiply ten times out here, because the cost of everything is lower and the exchange rate higher."

"Well, I'm just saying that the higher your illusions take you, the more painful the fall."

"Alberto, look, I'm not saying it's going to be easy. The work is going to be hard. No question about that. But hard work is nothing new to you and me."

"What about Antonio? Is he still going? 'Cause I don't think he's done a day's work in his life."

"Oh, he still wants to go, but I don't think father will let him."

"Well," Alberto concluded, "That's that then. I say we go." He drank down the last of his coffee when he saw Catalina approaching with the coffee pot.

"How about a slice of apricot and mango cake?" She asked. "Florinda made it."

"I'm too skinny to eat much, but I won't pass that up." Alberto told her.

When Catalina leaned over to serve him, he reached out and his coat opened up enough for her to see the handle of a gun. It startled her enough for them to notice.

"Catalina, what's the matter?" Carlos asked, rising to take her arm.

"It's nothing. It's just. . . the baby kicked." She put her hand on her belly and sat down.

"How much longer?" Alberto asked them.

"Two months." his brother said.

"Yeah. Not much longer." agreed Catalina. "You guys should wait until then."

"I wish we could," Carlos answered, "but we would miss the deadline for the program."

It was decided that they would leave for Tuxtla on Monday. Alberto would spend the weekend at Doña Rosas' until then. That night, when Carlos leaned over to kiss his wife goodnight, she turned to face him.

"Sometimes I think you're just running away from me." she sighed.

"Don't be silly. How can you think that?"

"Well, from the day of our wedding, we've spent more time apart than together."

"Yes. But not because I wanted it that way. Leaving you and the children is always very difficult for me. You know that.

But the only thing more difficult is to think that we could spend the rest of our lives stuck in this God forsaken town, where nothing ever happens."

She sat up. "How can you say that? Look how much Felix has grown. But he's growing up without a father. How can you allow that?"

"What I can't allow is for him to grow up without a future." he explained. He took her hand and kissed it. "Sweetheart, wether we like it or not the world is changing, but no one notices it here. In the United States people are allowed to grow."

"So, it's true." Catalina sighed. "Your plan is to take us away from here forever."

He didn't answer and they didn't say another word that night. Catalina's eyes glistened in the moonlight for a long time before she fell asleep.

Antonio and Alberto arrived together on Sunday. Antonio was in high spirits, excited by the prospect of the trip. Carlos took him aside.

"Does father know you are going? Did he say you could go?"

"Yeah. He doesn't care. He just said that what we're doing is stupid. He says we're going to shine the Gringo's shoes when we could stay here and have others shining ours."

"Sure, that's easy for him to say. But I don't think you should go. You're too young. You can go with us next time."

"Carlos, if you don't want me to go with you, that's okay. I'll go by myself. But I'm going wether you like it or not. I've made up my mind."

"Oh really? And what are you going to use for money?"

Antonio pulled a roll of bills out of his pocket. "I have about two thousand pesos here." he said. Carlos was speechless. "Here, you hold it for me so that I won'd lose it."

Carlos took it and that was the end of that. They joined Alberto at the dinner table. It was hard to tell what Alberto was feeling because his expression never changed. They had a few drinks before dinner and a few more during the meal.

"A toast!" announced Antonio. "May this adventure be the most unforgettable of our lives!" They touched glassed and drank.

"Now its your turn, Carlos."

Carlos looked at Catalina, who had been unusually quiet all day.

"I toast to family. To my wife and children and to yours, Alberto.

May we remember during the hardships ahead, that they are our reason for enduring them."

"Well said, brother. Now, how about you, Alberto?"

Alberto filled his glass and raised it. "Here's a toast to manhood."

He drank it down in one motion. Antonio cheered, then handed a glass to Catalina.

"Now let's hear from womanhood. Its' your turn, little sister."

Catalina put down the glass, then poured herself some *horchata*.

"I toast that you will all return safe and sound, and soon." The three brothers applauded.

Afterwards, the men retired to the parlor. Carlos tried to impress upon Antonio that this was not a game or a vacation, but a serious, difficult and even dangerous endeavor.

Catalina was in the kitchen helping Maria with the dishes when Alma, an old friend from their French academy days, walked in through the side door.

"Hey. How's the baby?" she whispered.

"Hello, Alma. It's getting more active every day."

"Aha! I told you it was a boy. Or maybe a very pushy girl."

Alma's attention was caught by the loud voices in the den.

"What's going on over there?"

"They're getting drunk. Celebrating the fact that I'll be left alone again. Want some coffee?"

"Sure. Isn't Carlos going to wait until the baby is born?"

"He can't. That work program has a time limit. Here you go. Made with beans from your lover's plantation."

"Oh, very funny. I only went out with him once."

276

While Maria finished washing the dishes the two young women stood by the kitchen entrance sipping their coffee.

"Look at them," Catalina told her friend, "Have you ever seen three brothers more different than those?"

"Well, you shouldn't be surprised. Half brothers." Alma noticed Catalina's cup trembling ever so lightly on the saucer. "Hey, are you still worried?"

"Wouldn't you be worried if your husband was going away for a year, accompanied by a man who had already killed several times. The fact that it's his brother only makes me think of Cain and Abel."

"No. He respects Carlos. He listens to him. They say that Carlos is the only one who can control him."

"Sure, now. But what'll happen when he goes into another of his rages? He's carrying a gun."

"Oh, lot's of men do nowdays." Alma reassured her. "And he'd be a fool not to, with all the people out to get him. That's why it's better that he go away from here."

"Do you know what people are calling him?"

"Yeah. The grim reaper. But you know what people are like."

The next morning dawned sunny and clear, so Catalina decided to have breakfast served outside. Carlos was already seated when Alberto appeared. Catalina greeted him and asked if Antonio was up yet?

"What? Oh. Ahh. . . he went home, to say good bye."

"Oh, that's nice. You should have gone with him, Carlos."

Carlos ignored her suggestion and began to serve himself.

"You guys knew that Don Carlos has been ill, didn't you?" she continued. Alberto shrugged and glanced at Carlos, who was still ignoring them.

"God only knows if he'll still be here when you return."

"I haven't seen him in years," Alberto said "and I'm sure that's the way he prefers it."

Catalina continued serving and casually probing. "Carlos, what about you? He's always asking for you."

"You know very well that he's dead to me." He answered, with obvious annoyment.

"But, Carlos, this is a good opportunity for the two of you to make up. After all, he is your father."

Carlos slammed his hands on the table with such force that Maria nearly dropped a plate of food.

"That's enough, Catalina! Just drop it."

They ate breakfast in a subdued atmosphere. Antonio arrived at the end and they all sat in the patio, enjoying the sun and drinking fresh orange juice with mango slices that Maria made for them. Felix ran up to Carlos and asked if it was true that he was leaving again. He said that he didn't want him to go, but Carlos told him he would return soon and would bring him back whatever toy he wanted.

"I want little soldiers, like my cousin Miguel has."

"All right, I'll bring you soldiers, and rifles and even cannons so that you can have a real war." Carlos told him.

The radio in the parlor was on, although no one was listening to it, and it was reporting that several thousand allied troops had died, battling in Burma.

When Carlos went to the bedroom to finish packing, Catalina gave him a small photograph of herself and the children which she had taken at Don Enrique Borjes' Studio weeks before.

"I don't want you to forget us." she said.

"Catalina, you and the children are my life. That's why I'm doing this." He promised to keep the photo next to his heart and to kiss it every night.

"What if you meet a Gringa?"

"If you knew how much I love you, Catalina, you wouldn't waste your time worrying about such silly things."

A car arrived to pick them up at noon to take them to Tuxtla. Catalina, Florinda and the kids stood out in the street until the car disappeared. In the privacy of the kitchen, Maria shed a tear.

Carlos and Alberto made themselves comfortable in the car's rear seat, leaning back and covering their faces with their hats in order to sleep. However, Don Zerafin, the driver, had to put up with Antonio's chatter for the six hours that they were on the badly deteriorated road to Tuxtla.

"Do you know where the United States is, Don Zerafin?"

"No, Sir, I don't. I only know its very far away."

"Yeah, very far. Almost on the other side of the world. And they have buildings so tall that they disappear in the clouds."

"Imagine that."

"Yes, and streets that are paved with pure gold."

"Ayy caramba! They must be very slippery."

Carlos smiled under his hat and fell asleep.

Chapter 25

In spite of the usual tropical heat and stifling humidity of the Chiapas lowlands, the Tuxtla Gutierrez Train Terminal was teeming with people when Carlos and his brothers arrived. They piled their baggage at the edge of the platform, just as others had done, and Carlos told his brothers to remain there while he squeezed through the crowd to the ticket window. The two sat down until Alberto noticed that Carlos had pulled a roll of bills out of his pocket and was confidently counting it as he worked his way toward the booth. Carlos approached the ticket window unaware that he was being followed by a tall man of olive complexion, wearing a Panama hat and holding a brown leather jacket over one arm. Once near the head of the line and directly behind Carlos, the stranger glanced around at the crowd pushing against them, then slowly slid his jacket back just enough for the point of a knife to emerge. He was about to press the knife into Carlos' back when he was startled by something pushed hard against his genitals. He grunted and looked down to find a revolver pressed against his crotch, and he heard the click of the gun being cocked. He found Alberto, staring straight into his eyes, and he recognized the immutable look of death reaching for his soul.

"No, no, no. . ." was all that he could manage in a stutter.

Alberto calmly held out his empty hand and the man carefully placed the knife upon it. It was a butcher knife, so sharp that it took the stranger a second to realize it when it slashed a ten inch gash straight down the inside of his thigh. He gasped but made no move. Alberto leaned forward and whispered in his ear: "If I see you again, I'll kill you."

The man turned around and pushed his away through the crowd, not yet limping but already feeling the warm blood running down his leg. Carlos, like the rest of the jostling crowd, never noticed a thing. When he returned to their luggage he asked Antonio where Alberto had gone.

"I don't know. Just to walk around, I guess."

"I wish he wouldn't do that. He'll just get himself in trouble." Carlos said.

"Well, I'm sure not going to tell him what to do."

Their train was scheduled to arrive at seven, but if it had it would have been the first time in a month that it arrived on time. So, they settled back to take in the colorful sights and the tempestuous atmosphere of the old railway station. It was full of people from every class and every walk of life, from businessmen in suits, to barefoot peasants wearing rags no longer recognizable as clothing. Families with several kids and couples with one child, some Ladinos and some native, mixed with the masses and the vendors, who hawked their goods from small stands they had set up in every available corner of the station platform while others carried their wares in boxes strapped around their shoulders or in baskets on their heads.

They sold tamales, tacos, fruits, bread and candies. There were also ice cones, popsicles, juices and bottled carbonated drinks, including one called Coca Cola. Other vendors sold toys, trinkets and curiosities, made by hand and ranging from tiny wooden guitars and violins, a few inches long and operational, to the more common hats, mats and animals made of woven straw.

There were beggars everywhere, blind, disfigured or deformed, holding out their hands for alms. But it was the children, hustling through the crowd, selling newspapers or gum and fighting like pack dogs over a potential customer, that attracted Carlos' attention. Some were barely older than his son, Felix, but they were already struggling to survive the misery of a poverty they had been born into and would probably never overcome.

Moments later the three brothers were approached by a young Indian woman selling popsicles out of a tin-lined wooden box. They noticed her immediately because she was stunningly beautiful. She had jet black hair, pulled back tight into a bun, deep dark eyes, rosy cheeks and a disarming smile that she flashed without mercy at her admirers, which included almost everyone in sight. For some reason Carlos caught her eye and she went straight to him, ignoring several other prospective customers.

"Hey handsome," she brazenly addressed him. "Won't you buy a popsicle to refresh those sweet, neglected lips?"

The men nearby, amused, started to whoop and whistle. Carlos blushed.

"How much?" he asked, trying to recover.

"Nothing for you." she said, running her finger down his cheek. " It would make me happy just to give you something."

At that point the hoots and whistles really became loud and more people gathered around to view the spectacle of the sexy young woman masterfully using her guile.

"In that case," Carlos told her, "give me one and sell me two for my brothers."

"What flavor would you like?" she asked arching one eyebrow and with a flirtatios tone.

"Do you have anything that tastes like you?" he said, attempting to hold his own.

"Sure." she said, batting her eyelashes, "But that would cost you more than money." The crowd laughed with appreciation.

Carlos bought three popsicles and happily gave her the tip that she had earned with so much pleasure. Just then the train pulled into the station with screeching brakes, clouds of hissing steam and a deafening whistle. Instantly the milling crowd jumped into action. People rushed for their belongings and ran for their train car, bumping and trampling into each other. The mobile vendors ran between and around them, into the train to make their final sales, knowing that once people were comfortably seated they were more inclined to buy. Others sold from outside through the windows, right up to the moment when the train started to move, at which point they ran alongside, concluding final sales.

Amid the whirl and excitement of those moments, the train dove into the darkness of the night and everyone eventually relaxed and settled in for the long ride.

"I guess this is it." Antonio said, as he laid his head on top of the luggage in the seat beside him.

Yeah, this is it, Carlos thought. The moment I've been waiting for all my life. Suddenly that idea scared him and the doubts crept in. What if he had been wrong all along? What if this was a mistake? After all, he didn't know exactly what it was that he was seeking. It was more a feeling than anything else. A feeling other than that of suffocation. He recalled all those nights at Doña Benilda's *posada*, near Palenque, when he and Jap stayed up for hours, long after their exchange of language lessons, talking about the things that interested them most. Jap wanted to know anything and everything about the Indian people: how they live, what they grow, what do they believe, who is in charge of what? In between, Carlos would ask him about his country. What was it really like to live there?

Neither one could fully understand the other's fascination, but it was a fair exchange. Reading between the lines of Jap's long explanations, Carlos was convinced he heard the promise of a life without the shackles imposed by a narrow-minded society clinging to notions of inherited privilege. He was thinking about that and absent-mindedly playing with his popsicle stick when Alberto looked at him from under his hat.

"Let her go, Carlos. Let her go."

Carlos realized he was referring to the woman who had given him the popsicle and he chuckled. He threw away the little stick and fell asleep.

The train pulled into Veracruz late the next morning. They had to transfer to another train that would arrive that night if on time, or the following day if as usual. So, they had some time to explore the old colonial city. They were amazed to find a marketplace bigger than the one in San Cristobal, and that fruits were also cheaper and even more diverse and abundant. Along the harbor they saw ships that were bigger than most buildings and they were transfixed by the vast amounts of things that were loaded and unloaded from each one. Antonio wanted to know why such a ship, made out of iron and steel did not sink from its own weight, but neither of his brothers could answer him with any confidence although Carlos had some notion of water displacement theories.

Eventually they ended up in the central plaza; a large public square surrounded by massive colonial stone buildings that each provided an open corridor within arches held up by Roman columns. The various shops and restaurants along the corridors overflowed out into them to display their products or provide their services so that a stroll along those passageways meant zigzagging past tables full of fresh fruit or stacked crates loaded with newly baked bread, and ducking or sidestepping waiters with trays of food for the waiting diners. The mingled aromas were enough to awaken the appetites of all within their reach.

The three brothers chose an available table in front of a seafood restaurant as much for its intense fragrances as for its location near a group of musicians playing tropical tunes to entertain the tourists for whatever money they could get.

Other musical groups and small bands strolled through those corridors so that the music was continuous every afternoon into the night. Fresh seafood was the town's specialty and that was what all three of them ordered. In the dying sunlight and a gentle sea breeze, tourists and locals could spend a relaxed and contented afternoon.

"I like this place." Antonio said, "Maybe we should stay here instead of going so far."

"I thought you wanted to make money."

"Well, we can make money here. I've been thinking about that and I have an idea. Want to hear it?"

"Do we have a choice?"

"Well, since the fish and fruits are so plentiful and cheap here, all we have to do is figure out a way to transport it to other areas, making sure that it gets there fresh."

"Put ice on it." Alberto suggested.

"They already do that." added Carlos.

"Yeah. But the ice melts." Antonio explained. "And when it does, everything spoils and you lose everything and go broke. That's the problem. But if we just figure out a way to make the ice last longer, we'll get rich."

Carlos laughed. "Don't you think that if it could be done, someone else would have already done it?"

"No, I don't."

"Oh, I see. All of a sudden you're Mr. inventor."

"Why not? Anybody can be an inventor. You don't need a license." Antonio protested, angry with his brothers for laughing at him.

"Look," Alberto explained, "The only place where ice doesn't melt is inside those big ice houses where they make it."

"Exactly!" Antonio agreed. "That has to be the key to the whole problem."

"Sure," Carlos added. "All you have to do is put the fish and the fruit inside the ice house and then put the entire ice house on the train."

Alberto and Carlos laughed uproariously at the idea and Antonio, frustrated, dropped the subject. His brothers let him pout for a while and then Carlos put his arm around him.

"Look, little brother, we're not making fun of you. It's just that you're still young. You've got a lot to learn. And one of the things you'll learn is that there are no short cuts to getting rich."

"Not legally, anyway." Alberto added.

"The only way to get what you want in life," Carlos pointed out, "is through your own hard work.".

"Oh," Antonio concluded, as he got up from his place at the table. "That must be why mules are so well off."

He walked away and his two brothers looked at each other with a smile and shook their heads.

For the first time that month the train north arrived, if not on time at least on the assigned day. Perhaps because it was much bigger or maybe because the evening was so placid, but the Veracruz train station seemed far less frenzied than Tuxtla had been. People walked calmly to the ticket booth and gave way to each other with a polite nod. On the other hand, the warm camaraderie and the democracy that allowed the classes to mix and socialize had been sacrificed for the cold, respectful divisions that were so much a part of the region's society.

They had a choice of first, second or third class. Antonio wanted first class but his older brothers pointed out that their aim was to make money, not throw it away. Third class would mean sitting on the floor, next to peasants cradling piglets and crates of chickens. They bought three tickets, second class. That meant wooden bench seats instead of the plush, padded ones and more people crammed into each car than first class.

Carlos noticed that most of the people in their car were lower middle class laborers. Some even barefooted, though many wore sandals rather than shoes. And although they talked and laughed among themselves, there was an unnatural reticence in their voices, as if something was holding them back. He suspected that it was because he and his brothers were there. Their Ladino skin was certainly whiter than the tropical tans. At one rear corner of the car, three men sat, each carrying a guitar of a different size. There were some couples and a few children but most were men, weathered, more by hard work in the sun than by time.

They traveled in that unnatural quiet for some time, passing countless farms where the earth was deep black and fertile and lush green vegetation covered the land. Palm trees were scattered, not only along the beaches but even in the inland hills.

Those who could afford them wore the fancy, short-sleeved *guayabera* shirts popular in the region to take advantage of the warm, sea breezes of the night. Young, barefoot boys riding donkeys, carrying sacks of fruits or vegetables, were a common sight along the roads and trails. The placid atmosphere started Carlos wondering whether the United States could really be better than that.

Most passengers were already asleep but woke up when the train entered Jalapa. They would be there only a half hour, so few people bothered to get off, except to stretch their legs. A host of vendors poured in with steaming hot food while others presented their offerings from outside at the windows. This would be their last stop of the night, so Carlos and his brothers bought tamales for dinner, made with pork in tomato sauce and cooked wrapped in banana leaves, just like back home. It would be the last time in a year that he would eat such a delicacy.

Noticing that the three men at the back hadn't bought anything to eat and were just sitting forlornly in the corner, Carlos called the tamale vendor.

"Give those three men in back anything they want." he directed.

"We'll pay for it."

The men's eyes lit up. Several people turned to look.

"Music makes us happy," Carlos explained, "so we should do the same for our musicians." People nodded in agreement. The three men were very thankful and moments after the train left Jalapa, they took up their instruments and entertained their fellow travelers with soft, romantic, tropical ballads that spoke of love for women as well as for this lush corner of their land.

During the following days, they repeated those serenades for the appreciative audience that had coalesced into much more than just fellow travelers. They had become friends. Even Carlos and his brothers, in spite of their lighter skin and Spanish features, were accepted without reservation. And Carlos began to understand why Alberto had always preferred the country's native people over the mestizos who, ashamed of their mixed heritage, pretended to be something they were not.

During a short, night stop at Mexico City, where they were able to see little except the vastness of the place, the train was separated and the first class cars taken away. That didn't affect Carlos' car, except that since now second class became first, they were charged more for the privilege.

It turned out that the three musicians, named Jose, Camilo and Lautaro, were also on their way to work as braceros in the United States. They had all been born and raised in the same village outside the city of Veracruz. Through many years of toil, their fathers had had bought small farms in the valley which in time and in each case they passed on to their male heirs.

"And now you're going to work the Gringo's farms?" Antonio asked them.

"It appears to be our fate. Patroncito"

"But who will take care of your farms?"

"Oh, those are distant memories for us." Camilo explained with a melancholy laugh.

"We lost them years ago." Jose added.

"Lost them, how?" asked Carlos.

"About 15 years ago the rich people of the interior discovered our lands. They saw how fertile it was and, with the help of the local *caciques*, started to buy it up."

"Yeah. Before long, they had control of all the best parcels in the valley." Lamented Camilo.

"By the time we sold," Lautaro added, "they gave us a pittance."

"Why did you sell?"

"Those who didn't sell had their water cut off." said Jose.

"Our wells were poisoned." Camilo chimed in.

"Without water, land is worthless." Lautaro added with a sigh.

"Unfortunately," Carlos concluded, "that's the sad story of our country. The rich are sucking the very life blood out of it, and even these crazy revolutions have been unable to stop it."

Everyone remained quiet for a moment. Then, feeling guilty for starting it all, Antonio changed the subject.

"But you still have your music."

"Yes," Camilo laughed. "We Veracruzanos are born listening to
music. Lately, many of us have died the same way too."

"What do you mean?" Carlos asked.

"Well, music is good for the heart, but it doesn't fill stomachs." Camilo pointed out.

"We should write a song like that!" exclaimed Jose with laughter.

Carlos was surprised and asked if they also wrote songs.

"Yes, sometimes," Jose explained, "but we just write them in our head, because we don't know how to write with a pencil."

"Well, don't feel bad. None of us know how to play a musical instrument." admitted Antonio.

Ironically, Camilo and his friends, as well as most of the other people on that train car, had been wondering about the reason Carlos and his brothers were going to the United States to work as braceros: common laborers. They were light skinned Mexicans, more Spanish than Indian, in a country that rewarded those things far more than any other. They were wondering about that, but in the end, were too respectful to mention it.

The train spent the next few days crossing the state of Hidalgo, and climbing the mountains of Queretaro, zig-zagging down through canyons, over decrepit river trestles before starting to climb again.

The lush green vegetation of the south gave way to brownish forests and increasing patches of yellow hills and dark blue distant mountains. Soon they were speeding across the drying plains of San Luis Potosí and by the time they reached Zacatecas the train's engine expired in a cloud of steam and dust. They had to wait for two days in the middle of nowhere for a spare engine to arrive from Mexico City and Carlos began to fear that they might not reach the border in time.

The engine arrived just in time to take them into one of the worst heat waves Durango had experienced since the beginning of the century. It felt like a sauna inside their car. But when they opted to open all the windows, they quickly changed their mind. The wind felt like flames reaching in to lick one's skin. At Torreón they turned east, straight into the desert, but although hot, it was an improvement on the days before.

One morning, Antonio shook Carlos awake as the train approached a station in the middle of nowhere but were clearly coming to a stop.

"Carlos, look! There's something going on out there. Some kind of celebration."

Disgruntled by the disturbance of his sleep, Carlos rubbed his eyes and squinted out the window. There were some horses and several automobiles behind the little run-down shack of a station. On the weathered boards of its platform was a small crowd of people and the sad approximation of a marching band, all gathered around a white-haired man wearing a three piece, blue-gray suit and a top hat. He was flanked by six men, armed with rifles and he was the only one talking, gesticulating with some exaggeration as if giving a speech. When he stopped the people around him applauded. Some of the crowd was made up of peasants, hat in hand in spite of the heat, and the rest were overly dressed people, including a dour looking group of women wearing floor-length gowns and holding tiny parasols.

"He must be important. Who do you think he is?"

"I don't know, Antonio. Probably some local *cacique*."

The old man waved his cane at the train as if to specify a particular section and several of his guards came aboard the car Carlos and his brothers occupied. They looked around suspiciously at everyone.

"We need a dozen seats!" one of them bellowed.

The passengers looked around nervously, not knowing what to do. The man decided to be more direct. He pointed to a group of men sitting across the aisle from Alberto.

"You four. Out!"

The men stood up without hesitation, grabbed their belongings and walked out onto the platform. Then the man pointed at a family sitting nearby; a couple with three children. They stood up, got their things and walked down the aisle. But the oldest child, a boy of about sixteen, decided to protest.

"We have our tickets." he said, turning around. "Look!" He took his ticket from his pocket and approached the man who was giving the orders. In one swift move the man bashed the butt of his rifle against the boy's mouth, sending him to the ground, bleeding profusely.

"No!" his father yelled as he ran back to his son.

"You'd better teach him to obey." the guard told him, as the man helped his son to his feet, sopped his blood with his handkerchief and walked him out.

"Three more." one guard reminded the leader who then scanned the remaining passengers with a scowl. He looked at Alberto, sitting low in his seat, with one hand on his belt and the other underneath his vest, close to his heart. Alberto stared directly back into his eyes. The soldier turned away and noticed the three musicians.

"You three. Go play your guitars out there for a while."

The three looked at each other with dismay and started out."

"No!" the white-haired man ordered as he clambered in. "The musicians can stay!"

Three others, near the exit door, were chosen and escorted out. The old man walked ceremoniously down the aisle. "I like music." he said, to everyone in general, and he sat down on one bench chair, laying his leather gloves on the seat beside him, while two young men in suits and carrying briefcases sat directly in front of him. The six bodyguards took up their stations at each end of the car and the train started to move again.

The passengers fell silent and pointedly avoided looking at the old man, while he scanned them carefully and made his assessment.

"I am Maximo Urquiedo," the man said in a loud voice, addressing everyone, confident that they were all interested and hanging on his every word. "These are my lands. Everything, as far as you can see is mine. So you are all my guests, and even though I didn't invite you, I gladly extend my hospitality." He looked around with a benevolent smile and several people felt compelled under his gaze to thank him. Alberto ignored him but Antonio was transfixed. Carlos, meanwhile, had to bite his lip to keep from blurting out what was already boiling inside him.

"I'm going to Monterrey." the old man continued, "For a very important business meeting. And you? Where are you all going?"

No one wanted to speak. Finally a man sitting near him, in his direct line of sight, cleared his throat and answered him.

"We're going north. To the United States. We're farm workers."

"Ohhh," the old man said, "You're going to leave the fruits of your labor in another land, instead of investing it in your own country. What a shame."

Carlos could no longer control himself. "At least there they offer us a decent wage for our labor." he told him.

The entire train car seemed to hold its breath. The surprised old man turned slowly around in his chair in order to face the person capable of such temerity. He sized up Carlos with an ominous smile but Carlos stood his ground, staring back at him. Alberto was impassive, Antonio mesmerized. The passengers kept rapt attention.

"Oh, are you also going to be a bracero?" he asked.

"That's correct." Carlos answered defiantly.

"But you don't look like a laborer. What is your profession?"

"I'm a rural teacher."

"Ahh, no wonder. A teacher, frustrated by his own inability. And now, instead of continuing the struggle, he runs away like a dog with his tail between his legs."

Don Maximo's guards laughed.

"Better dog than vulture," Carlos answered, "living off his fellow creature's blood."

The leader of the guards jumped forward toward Carlos but the old man waved him off.

"It's all right." he said. "This gentleman has had some education, and I want to hear his complaints. . . before we throw him out."

The old man turned fully to face Carlos.

"So, what are you claiming? Are you a communist? Are you a socialist? Tell me what thorn has pricked you."

Its too late to hold back now, Carlos thought.

"I'm just a man who is tired of watching the destruction of my country by thieves and parasites who become rich at the expense of honest workers like these." He gestured at the passengers in general and a low murmur of approval rolled through the car.

Don Maximo started to nervously rub the handle of his cane and he forced himself to smile a disingenuous smile.

"I was wrong." he said. "I thought you were an intelligent man but it turns out you are just a common fool!" He stood up and raised his voice to lecture his captive audience. "This nation has progressed thanks to men of vision and courage like myself, not charlatans like this one. In Coahuila and Nuevo Leon, I employ more men than the federal government itself! In fact. . ."

"It's one thing to employ, another to exploit!" Carlos interrupted.

"Enough!" The old man glared at Carlos. "Throw this animal out!" he ordered.

Two of his guards immediately rushed toward Carlos, but before they reached him, Alberto jumped up and grabbed the old man from behind. He had him in a choke hold with one arm and the muzzle of his gun pressing against his temple with the other.

"Nobody move!" he yelled. "First mother fucker that moves, this son of a bitch dies."

The old man waved his men away. The guards froze in place.

"Antonio! Disarm them!" growled Alberto.

Antonio carefully took away the rifles and guns from two men while Carlos did the same to two of the others. Meanwhile, at the far end of the car another guard slowly reached for his gun but froze when he felt something hard pressed into his back. It was the end of Camilo's guitar.

"None of that, my friend." Camilo told him, removing the gun from his hand.

All the guards were disarmed, and half an hour later, when the train pulled into another desert station and stopped to fill its water tanks, the passengers in the other train cars watched with amusement when six men off boarded and stood in line on the platform and saluted while wearing nothing but their underwear.

294

"Where are the photographers when you need them?"
Someone was heard to lament.

About ten kilometers later, as the train crossed the hot
barren desert, Don Maximo's two young attorneys were
unceremoniously tossed out, naked, into the sands, followed
soon after, by the patriarch himself, wearing only his tie.

Their clothes, guns and other belongings were divided up
among all the people in the car. Half of the six thousand pesos
that Don Maximo was carrying was entrusted to the uncle of
the young boy hit with the rifle butt, after he proved his
relationship with a photo and promised to give the money to
him upon his return from El Paso the following week. The rest
was split up among everyone else and used for food and drink
during the remainder of the trip. It became the happiest train
trip any of them could recall.

Chapter 26

Catalina was standing at the parlor's doorway to the patio gazing sadly at a tiny iridescent green hummingbird feeding on the mango tree. She was so engrossed in the moment that she never heard Alma approaching.

"I know what you're thinking. Oh, I'm sorry. Didn't mean to startle you."

"It's okay. I was just thinking how much I envy the humming birds. Their lives pass by so quickly, while mine drags unbearably on."

"It's natural that you miss him. After all it's only been a week."

"It wasn't supposed to be like this, Alma. I thought a marriage was for two lives to enjoy life together. It was bad enough when he was in the mountains; at least there was an end in sight, but now, I can't even imagine how far away he is or where our life is headed."

"Come on. It'll be worth it in the end, Cati. You'll see."

"I don't know if I can last that long. It's not just the loneliness. It's the uncertainty. Where is he? Is he okay? Is he sick? Has something happened to him? Is he alive?"

"Don't torture yourself, Catalina. You have to be strong, for your children and for all the rest of us who love you. We'll always be here for you."

Catalina's eyes filled with angry tears.

"He's the one who's supposed to be here for me."

Weeks later, on a sunny afternoon in the large central patio of a Spanish Hacienda-styled home, a large crowd of people gathered to celebrate a child's seventh birthday. The orange, plum and fig trees were all decorated with bright streamers and banners hung from wires that crisscrossed above tables of food, the central water fountain and the marimba band. Three colorful piñatas hung patiently in one area while several children chased each other, throwing confetti and streamers, and running among the couples dancing near the band. Felix ran up to his mother, seated with friends at one table.

"Mama`, mama`! The present."

"Yes, its right here." Catalina assured him. "Is it time? Here. No, wait! Remember: you hand it to him and then wish him a happy birthday."

"But I don't like him."

"Shh! Don't say that. He's your friend. You behave, Felix."

With a frown, Felix ran off. Catalina looked at her friends and rolled her eyes.

"Oh, Caty," Alma said, "Your son is darling. You're so lucky."

"And look at the husband she got." Leticia grumbled. "I don't know how you did it, Cat."

Catalina just smiled.

"On the other hand, my husband may not be so great, but at least

I get to enjoy him." Leticia dropped the line casually as she walked away.

"Don't pay any attention to her." Marta said. "You know what a bitch Leticia is. Besides, every whore in San Cristobal has enjoyed her husband."

"Yeah, she's just envious." clarified Anna Luisa. "She hasn't gotten over the fact that your Carlos never gave her a second look."

The band struck up a well known romantic melody and several young men dashed up to ask the women to dance. One by one they were all escorted to the dance floor until only Catalina remained. She sipped champagne as she gazed at the couples. All her friends, schoolmates, and contemporaries seemed content with their partners, husbands, lovers or admirers. She envied them all, and was so deep in contemplation that she didn't notice when a distinguished, white haired man appeared beside her.

"Would my daughter care to dance?"

"Oh, Don Carlos, you startled me. I didn't know you were here.

Did you just arrive?"

"Yes. I decided it might be better to die dancing than sleeping."

"Oh, don't say that, even as a joke. Besides, you look quite well."

"You don't have to lie to me, Catalina."

"No, really! In fact Carlos wanted to visit you before he left, but we were told you were ill."

"Another lie. We both know that Carlos won't even visit me in my grave." He took out a cigar. "When does he return?"

"Within a year, God willing." She answered, softly.

Don Carlos lit his cigar. "What a fool." he said, exhaling a cloud of smoke, but Catalina had no answer.

Days later, Catalina was remembering that moment, sitting on a chair with extra cushions to alleviate her back ache. She was knitting in silence as golden rays of sunshine slanted into the room, filtered by gossamer curtains that billowed with the delicate air currents from the patio. Felix was playing on the floor with his toy cars. Alma was sitting near a window, at her easel painting the mango tree and the fountain beyond it.

"Do you think they've crossed over yet?" Alma asked.

"I don't know. When the letters arrive they'll be a month old. Little consolation."

"You shouldn't be so negative. It's because of your condition. You'll see. As soon as you give birth the world will be rosy again."

"On the contrary. Afterwards you feel even worse. You'll see, when you have your children."

"Hmmpf! First I have to have a man."

"What happened with the coffee man?"

"Oh, that man's only love in life is his coffee plantation. Besides, I wasn't born to be a servant."

At that instant, Maria Hernandez placed a tray with coffee and cookies at her elbow.

"I was, Miss Alma," she told her with a smile, "It's not so bad."

Alma turned bright red. "Oh, Maria, I didn't mean that." she said with a sheepish smile. Maria returned to the kitchen and Alma covered her face with her hands. "I am so stupid." she said.

Catalina chuckled. "Who was it that said that life's great lessons come in little moments?"

"Oh, shut up!"

Minutes later, Maria entered the room once again.

"Doña Catalina! The man for the repairs is here. In the patio."

"Thank you Maria , I'll be right there."

Catalina struggled to get out of her chair.

"No. Don't get up." Alma told her, "I'll see to it."

Alma walked out to the patio expecting to see some old peasant worker. She was surprised to find a tall and very handsome man tying up his horse and two loaded mules under the mango tree. He turned and greeted her and she stared at him, at a loss for words, her mouth absentmindedly open. He had curly, black hair, green eyes and eyelashes that most women only dream about.

"I just wanted to tell the lady that I have all the material now," he said, with a deep and resonant voice, "and also that if it is not inconvenient, I can leave it here, next to the wall, covered up, and begin the work right after the rains."

Alma was thinking that he must be a mulato, but if so, he was the most perfect mixture of the two races that she could have imagined. Suddenly, she realized that he had stopped talking and was waiting for an answer and she tried in vain to remember what he had just said.

"What? Oh, ahh, yes. Whatever you like. I mean. . . you know best."

From the parlor, Catalina leaned over to see them through the window. Felix came running to her.

"Mami, mami, can I turn on the radio?"

"Yes, but not very loud. Your little sister is asleep."

Just then Alma virtually floated back into the room.

"My God!" She said. "That man is simply gorgeous."

Catalina started laughing. "No wonder you're still single. One minute you spurn a man of means because he works too hard and the next you're swooning over some poor laborer."

"Poor laborer? Didn't you see him? He must be the Greek God of laborers. Besides, you didn't marry for wealth, although you sure could have."

"Yeah, and look at what that brilliant decision has cost me. Oh, leave it there, Felix! I love that melody. I think it's another Agustin Lara composition."

"It's called 'Upon the Waves'," Alma said, "which is how I feel right now."

Both young women sat quietly for a moment listening to the tune.

"So, what are you having done to the house?"

"Well, the roof is leaking in a couple of places and the window frames are beginning to rot."

"Isn't that going to be expensive?"

"Oh, I'm not going to pay for it. The landlord will, although he doesn't know it yet."

"What do you mean?"

"Well, Carlos paid the rent for this whole year in advance. So, when we moved back in with my sister in order to save money, we assumed Mr. Senteno, who owns this house, would reimburse us for the remaining five months. But he refused."

"Why?"

"Because, he says that that wasn't stipulated in the contract."

"So, what are you going to do?"

"We found out that what he wanted to do was rent the house out to someone else, therefore conveniently doubling his money."

"What a rat! Why don't you take him to court?"

"Because that would take forever, and he knows that. In stead, we decided to move back in so that he can't rent it out, and now I'm having all the necessary work done on the house and he'll have to pay for it because that IS stipulated in the contract. I'm sure that when he sees how much it is all costing him, he'll change his mind and return our money and I can go back to my sister's house."

"Wow. Pretty sly."

"I'm just fighting fire with fire."

The music on the radio stopped and a man's voice crackled with a bulletin delivered with some urgency.

"In the day's news, the North American General, Douglas McArthur, insisted Wednesday in a press conference that plans for his campaign have not changed. However, the latest Japanese victories would seem to indicate otherwise."

Just like that, the contentment in the room turned to sadness and worry.

Catalina greatly appreciated Alma's company during those days. Whenever she was alone she was susceptible to bouts of depression even if she could not identify the exact cause. The whole world was in shambles, with the war causing such death and destruction that each new report seemed to be as bad as it could get, until the next one, which somehow managed to get worse. There were rumors that Mexico would soon have to choose sides and be dragged into the mess. She still had no word from Carlos and it was difficult to keep her imagination from running wild. Her only solace when alone came when she could direct her mind to memories of her honeymoon in Guatemala.

They had spent two weeks in the picturesque village of Quetzáltenango, on a lush hillside in the Guatemalan mountains. They stayed at Doña Rosalias', a quaint guest house, even for that area and those times. It was built up above the cobblestone street that wound up a hill into the forest. The walls, like the roof, were made of thick thatched grasses, tightly woven through bamboo poles, and they were open at the top as well as the bottom, giving the entire house a charm and almost total lack of privacy that made for instant familiarity. It was run by Doña Rosalia herself, and her two daughters. Three women of ample girth who could find the lighter side of every situation, no matter how dire, and made friends with every one without distinction. They had several pets which had the run of the house, including a mischievous monkey that loved to dance to the music of the jukebox, a toucan that begged for food by knocking its bill against the shins of unsuspecting diners, and two iguanas that had a habit of jumping down from the rafters intopeople's beds at the most inopportune times.

Catalina loved walking arm in arm with Carlos, through the streets of the little town, where everyone seemed to know them after just a couple of days and would wave and smile at them as they passed by. There were dozens of colorful little shops and a tiny marketplace where they often lingered just to visit with the native people who seemed to sense their happiness and tried to share in it.

It was like living in a storybook where everything was as it should be. Those had been days when Catalina thought life would never change and she would stroll arm in arm with her mate forever.

Because of those memories, Catalina talked Alma and Maria Hernandez into letting her accompany them to the marketplace. They strolled into the heart of it and Catalina felt revitalized by the sights and aromas.

"Just look around." she observed, "We have everything here that anyone could possibly want."

"Yes, that's true." Alma agreed.

"Then what the hell are men searching for in distant lands?"

She didn't realize how loud she was speaking until she noticed several people laughing at her words and nodding in agreement.

"I think they're just trying to get away from crazy women like us." Alma conjectured, laughing along with the others.

They stopped to buy carrots from an old Indian woman who had two little girls sitting quietly beside her. Alma asked for the price.

"Twenty cents a bunch for you, Ma'am."

"Are you kidding?" Alma broke in. "Look at these. They're drying up already."

"No, Ma'am. They're just right for stew. Very tasty, Ma'am."

"I'll give you fifteen cents. No more." insisted Alma.

The vendor woman hesitated. She looked sad.

"Twenty cents is fine." Catalina told her. "We'll take three bunches."

Alma was shocked, Maria surprised. Catalina paid for them and the lady carefully placed them in a basket that Maria was carrying. They walked on.

"Are you dumb? We could have gotten them for half the price. Isn't that so, Maria?"

"I think so, Doña Alma."

"Alma, these poor people have a very hard life. After they grow their crops they have to carry them down here from the mountains, and then they have to accept whatever we give them because of course they can't carry them back. How can we begrudge them a small profit?"

"Yeah, but their suffering is not our fault."

"Oh, no? Then, whose fault is it? Who do you think has taken away their lands? How many of them lived in what is now your uncle Alejandro's ranch?"

"That's not fair, Catalina. That wasn't their land. They had no title to it."

"Of course not. Titles are our invention. All they had was a thousand years of living on it."

"Okay, fine. You know everything."

"By the way, Alma, did you notice how that woman called you Ma'am and then called me Miss?"

"Oh, yeah. Some Miss you are, with that big belly."

The three women walked into the indoor part of the marketplace laughing. Inside the main pavilion, Catalina and Alma sat down at a table and ordered chocolate with churros while Maria went to the butcher's stand. A blind Indian woman, led by a little girl, approached them.

304

"Alms for the disadvantaged." the woman begged, holding out her hand. Catalina reached into her purse and gave her some coins.

"May God bless you and your baby boy, who will come into this world in fifteen days." the woman stated as she and the little girl walked away.

Catalina was chilled by her prediction. Alma was not.

"She's just guessing." Alma told her.

"But she's blind."

"Yeah but the little girl with her isn't."

Moments later, Catalina gave money to another passing beggar.

"I see that you plan to single-handedly expiate the sins of our people" Alma remarked.

"Some months ago, I was visiting my friend, Doña Esmeralda, whom I love dearly." Catalina explained. We were having tea when there came a knock at the door. Her maid was out shopping, so she went to answer it. I heard some commotion, the door slamming shut, and then she returned. She told me that it was some beggar asking for food and that she had sent him away because it was a Wednesday."

"Yeah," Alma answered, "they passed that law last year, that they can only beg door to door on Tuesday and Thursdays. Before that, not a day passed without them coming around."

Catalina stared at her friend for a long time.

"What?"

"Do you realize what you are saying? Are you able to tell your stomach not to ache with hunger because it's Wednesday? And how would you explain that law to your children?"

Tears welled in Catalina's eyes and Alma looked down into her empty cup.

"What are we doing to these people?" Catalina asked softly. "What is happening to us? Maybe Carlos is right. Maybe this is what he's running from."

Two weeks later, on a rainy afternoon, inside Catalina's upstairs bedroom, Doña Leonora, the midwife washed herself on a basin. Maria Hernandez collected her equipment. Alma cradled the crying baby in her arms, admiring it. She sat on the bed at Catalina's side and took her hand.

"Well, you've done it again, Señora. You have another beautiful baby boy. Your garden is growing."

"Just another flower for Carlos to uproot." Catalina lamented. Doña Leonora said that Catalina needed to rest, so they all walked out to let her do so. Then, as soon as the midwife was gone, Alma returned to Catalina's side.

"We were in the marketplace fifteen days ago." Catalina said. Alma rolled her eyes.

"Yes, I know. The blind woman was right."

Chapter 27

The train entered Ciudad Juarez on a sweltering afternoon, clattering across dusty rail yards and blowing its whistle in triumph, as if it never really expected to get that far. Most of the original passengers had gotten off along the way and their places had been taken by more laborers accepting Uncle Sam's invitation, so that in the end most of the cars were packed with aggravated and disgruntled people standing in the aisles. They streamed out like ants, carrying their luggage in boxes, bags and bundles, and were confronted by a depressing sight. In the searing heat, gusts of wind sent dust and papers swirling through smoke filled alleys while battered cars and trucks jostled with dilapidated, horse-drawn wagons for space along the dreary streets. The buildings, in advanced states of disrepair, doors and windows agape, offered little shelter to crowds of people with sunken eyes and blank stares, who shuffled aimlessly along the broken sidewalks.

Carlos and his brothers, along with the three musicians, walked out of the station and turned in the direction that they thought would be the town center.

"What an ugly town." Antonio remarked.

"All border towns are like this." Carlos told him.

"Why?"

"Because nothing is permanent here. This is just a place where people stop on their way to somewhere else."

After a few blocks, they turned a corner and stopped dead in their tracks.

"Look at that." was all one of them could say.

Across the street, a cyclone fence that must have been twenty feet high, separated them from another world. They crossed the street and stood silently at the fence, grasping it with their fingers and staring in awe at the panorama beyond, as if it were a mirage or an apparition. Neat rows of houses, white picket fences, trimmed lawns and decorated gardens lay in front of their eyes and just beyond their reach. A child rode his red tricycle along the pruned hedges and irrigated lawns.

"That, gentlemen, is the United States." Carlos announced. They all smiled.

"I guess it was all true." Antonio said. "A place like that is worth gold."

At the dingy cafe where they had dinner, they were told that the immigration offices opened at eight o'clock each morning, so Carlos decided they would be there by six in order to be first in line, Antonio's moaning not withstanding.

They arrived promptly at six only to find several hundred men already milling around the building's entrance. Many of them had slept there, some were still lying on the ground.

At exactly eight o'clock the door swung open. In stilted Spanish, a short, portly man with small blue eyes used a bullhorn to direct them into groups. Another man behind him collected their documents, had them leave their baggage in the center of a courtyard and pointed some along a yellow line in one direction and others in the opposite way along a green one. They were sent into various rooms where men and women in white smocks gave them rudimentary examinations, checking their mouths for sores and peering into their eyes with a small light. They were stripped and sprayed with DDT and sent out into a yard where they all eventually ended up. Hours later, another man with a bullhorn stood in the center of the yard to address them with a rudimentary command of their language. He began by welcoming them to America.

"Isn't Mexico in America anymore?" Alberto quipped with a straight face.

For the next hour, the man reviewed for his bored and captive audience, the list of rules that would govern their stay. In the evening they were finally given their first American meal. Hot mush and black coffee was handed out to them right there in the yard. Hours later, trucks started arriving to take them to their destination.

The men raced to get in line. They were allowed to take only one bundle and it could be no more than medium size. The rest had to be left behind in a pile that quickly grew in size against the fence. When it was the musicians' turn to board they were told they could not take their instruments. They couldn't understand what they were being told so Carlos jumped out of the truck to try out his tenuous command of English for the first time. The officials understood him well enough and insisted that the guitars must stay.

"You tell 'em that they're here to work. Otherwise they can just go back home." the official said. Jose finally decided to give in. He walked to the pile of refused baggage and placed his guitar on top of it.

Alberto, inside the truck started to chant: "No! No! No!"

He was immediately joined by others and soon hundreds of voices echoed their refusal through the deserted streets around the yard. The officials became nervous but refused to change their stand. Then Alberto jumped off the truck, still chanting, and walked to the pile, took Jose's guitar and walked back into the courtyard. A few followed him, soon joined by others until another official came running out of the building waving his arms.

"Okay, okay!" he said. "Geetars okay! Come on. Geetars okay."

The men cheered their victory and returned to their trucks, holding the three guitars aloft, like trophies. Relieved, the official turned to his counterpart.

"God Dammit! You never know when to quit; Do you, Mercer?"

Dawn was breaking by the time all the trucks were loaded and heading as a caravan into the promised land.

Several hours later, in a pouring rain that had appeared from nowhere and after the long caravan had been broken up at various intersections and forks in the road, sending truckloads of braceros in every direction along the Texas, New Mexico and Arizona desert corridors, the truck in which Carlos and his brothers were riding stopped for gas. Some of the men lifted the canvas cover to look out, just as another truck pulled in on the other side of the gas pumps. It was a military truck and it was going in the opposite direction. It also had a canvas covering the back from where two soldiers jumped out to stretch their legs. The attendant, a wiry old man, disgruntled at having to brave the rain, emerged from the office and walked between the trucks. He looked at the braceros peeking out and turned in disgust. He went to fill the tank of the military truck and one of the soldiers approached him.

"That other truck was here first." the soldier told him.

"Let them wait." the old man said. "Just another load of fuckin' Mexicans."

Moments later the braceros noticed that someone inside the military truck was slowly lifting up a section of the cover to peek out. There were a lot of people crammed into that truck as well, but they were oriental and many of them were women and children. The two groups of people stared at each other silently, dark eyes inside dark trucks, prisoners both, just a few feet apart and separated by culture and destiny, but brought together by fate, in that desert for that one moment in time.

The rain was just a memory by the afternoon when the truck stopped on the crest of a hill. Ordered out, the braceros emerged slowly, muscles aching from the long hours spent crouching in discomfort. They were met by a small group of men who said nothing to them until the truck roared away. A spry man of about sixty stepped forward from the group to address the workers. He had bright red hair, dark green eyes and a deeply wrinkled face. He said his name was Eli and he spoke loud and fast. He asked if anyone spoke English and Carlos again volunteered.

"A little bit? Okay, fine. Yeah, that's good. Come over here. What's your name, son? Carlos? Okay, Carlos, I'm Eli, this here's my sons Alan and Billy Jo. That there's my son-in-law Vern and my foreman Decker. Now, anything any of them say, you boys do. Understand? Lessen I say different. Got it?" He started to walk down the hill and Carlos turned to explain the bits he understood.

"Hey, hey. Hold it there! What are you doing? You don't talk when I'm talking. Understand? I'll explain things to you and when I'm finished, THEN you explain it to them. Got it? Now come here."

He led them all down the hill to a large, weathered old barn that had been turned into a bunk house. Eli might have been describing a cozy hotel as he pointed out the wood-burning stove that doubled as a heater in one side of the cavernous room, and the bunks, some metal and some wooden, but all worn and rickety, which he declared to be comfortable and cozy. There was a well outside and some buckets hanging from a tree which apparently served as a shower. He didn't mention the holes in the roof, big enough to squeeze a man through, or the missing panels in parts of the wall, not to mention the broken window panes, covered with yellowed paper and cob webs.

He said that no one could leave the farm without permission and that with the harvest coming they would be working every day, dawn to dusk. They would be given two days off at the end of the month and be provided transport to the nearest town to "raise some hell." All their needs would be met and their wants provided for. All they had to do was sign for it and it would be deducted from their pay each month.

In his halting English, Carlos pointed out that, first of all, their contract said they would get one day off per week. Eli stopped him.

"Son, let me set you straight. I don't know about any contract other than my contract. You all do things my way or I call the law and they send you to your next job, somewhere down in Mexico. Understand? Good. Cause my crops ain't gonna rot just for some damned piece of paper. Now, get some rest. We start at four in the morning."

311

It was a splash of cold water to the men. A dose of reality and a portent of things to come.

"It looks like we aren't going to be fed today." one man ruefully observed.

"Of course not. We haven't worked yet."

Wind was beginning to whistle through the holes in the wall androof, and suddenly there was a rush for the best placed bunks, but the one closest to the stove was left for Carlos, or 'the professor', as many were already calling him. Later most of the men gathered around a group playing poker by candlelight that night. Carlos wrote his first letter to Catalina by the flickering fire of the stove and found it very difficult to tell her that everything was going well, when in fact he already felt pangs of disillusion, Antonio was feeling even worse.

"I guess we made a mistake, Carlos."

"No we didn't. This is the best thing for you. By the end of this year you will be tough, able to conquer any dream, and you'll have money in your pocket." he reassured him. Antonio didn't believe a word of it.

In the morning, after receiving a ladle of sticky oatmeal and coffee to wash it down, they were assembled at the edge of a sugar beet field that disappeared into the morning fog. Eli and his men gave them a demonstration of the task they would be performing during the first week. It involved straddling one furrow, bending over at the waist to reach the ground with either hand and using a sharp, short-handled hoe to trim unwanted growth from the base of the plants. It had to be done fast and accurately. They were not to straighten up until the end of the furrow, which was at least as long as a football field, because that would slow them down. At the end of the demonstration they were cautioned about accidents and Eli asked his son-in-law to remove his glove and show them all his two missing fingers.

Every one of the men had a back ache by the end of the first hour and it became severe by lunch time.

"Don't worry." Eli said, "You'll get used to it. The first day is the hardest."

Lunch consisted of baked beans in molasses, which none of the braceros had ever tasted and few of them liked, washed down with water or cold black coffee. Several were already grumbling about quitting but all of them returned to the fields for another seven hours. Darkness was falling when they returned to the bunk house and they fell on their cots like blocks of lead.

They could barely move the following morning and their back muscles hurt so bad that it was almost a relief to start working in that awkward posture once again. After a few days some of them started to get the hang of it and to fall into a rhythm. Much of it had to do to with reaching a point where pain was so acute it could no longer register in their minds. They became zombies, moving automatically, without awareness of anything like heat or pain or time. To reach that point each day, many of them raced one another, even making bets, and the rest fought to keep up. No one wanted to be last but Antonio usually was. The foreman or one of Eli's sons rode on horseback behind them, urging them on, never quite satisfied.

On the third day Antonio was falling behind more and more and Billy Jo started to yell at him from atop his horse.

"I told you not to stand up, you idiot! Get back down and hurry up!" His hand gestures made his meaning clear.

After the third or fourth repetition of such yelling bouts, Alberto stood up from his work and turned around.

"I'm not talking to you. What the hell you lookin' at?" Billy Jo yelled at him. "Git back to work!"

Without a word, Alberto walked back toward Billy Jo, staring straight at him and still holding his sharpened hoe. He told Antonio to take over his furrow and then stood in front of the horse, staring up at Billy Joe defiantly. In his mind he was now looking at General Aramenta again, back in San Cristobal, waiting for the agressor's next move. Billy Jo became nervous. His orders were repeatedly ignored and some of the other workers were stopping and turning to observe. His options were narrowed to two, and he chose to back away. He rode off, swearing away his anger, swallowing his pride. Then Alberto took over Antonio's row, slowing his pace in order to remain at the back of the group all day.

At the end of the week Eli rewarded them with a large bucket of cold lemonade with chunks of ice brought down to the bunkhouse by two of his house servants. He told the workers that they were doing a great job and then invited them all up to the "store".

It was a large windowless room adjacent to the main house which had probably been used as a garage in the beginning. It was fully stocked with clothes, hats, soap, cigarettes, boots and just about everything but food. The men peeked inside timidly but Eli was on them like a salesman, personally showing them the goods and turning them over to his wife or his daughter at the counter register as soon as they showed the least little bit of interest or approval. A yellow card was made out for each worker and all they had to do was sign their name after the description of the purchase. Those who couldn't write were told to just put an x on the card. Many of them bought blankets and Carlos wondered if that was why the holes in the bunkhouse had never been patched up. Others bought hair grease and combs, soap, shaving razors and new clothes in anticipation of their days off. In the end almost everyone bought something and they began to feel that things were not so bad after all. Harvest began that week under a blinding heat wave. The men had to work twice as fast to keep up with the tractor bins and ahead of the machines that mulched the leftover plants into the ground.

The completion of each day was a small victory for the men who were finally working as a team, often helping one another. That was also the week that Carlos observed a bus pull up to the main house. Alan, Eli's youngest son, emerged dressed in a soldier's uniform, and boarded the bus while the rest of the family watched him off, waving good bye. His mother remained in the porch, crying into her handkerchief.

The trio 'Los Locos,' as the three *Veracruzanos* were being called, serenaded their comrades every evening, and the nightly poker games became Alberto's domain.

"Hey, Carlos, why is Alberto so good at poker?" Antonio asked one evening.

"Because he can hide his feelings."

"Are you sure he has any?"

Carlos closed the subject with an admonishing glance.

At the end of the month most of the men rushed to the bunkhouse after work to be among the first to shower. Clean shaven and with hair pomaded and slicked back, they marched as a unit to the main house. A bus was already there to take them into town. A table had been set up in front of the store and Eli's daughter, Mary Lou, sat behind it with a ledger, pen and stack of yellow cards in hand.

Eli greeted them: "Okay, Seeñors, it's time for money-- *dinero*." He was waving some bills in the air and the men were amused and filled with anticipation. He called Carlos to his side to read the names of the men so they could step up and be paid. Cornelio Aldama was the first and the others hooted him as he stepped forward, hat in hand. Eli and his daughter looked through the ledger and produced his card.

"I see he bought himself a shirt and a sombrero. Hey, that's a nice shirt. You're gonna knock 'em dead in town. Here you go."

He handed him a couple of dollars and some change. Cornelio waited for the rest. Eli turned to Carlos.

"What's the matter? What's he waiting for?"

"Money. What happened to pay?" Carlos asked him.

"Well it's right here in black and white." He showed Carlos the ledger. "See here, this is the days he worked, so that's the money he made. He did real good. Now, over here its all government deductions. Everybody in the country has to pay that. It's got nothing to do with me. Even I have to pay 'em. That leaves this amount here, see? Then this is for his room and board, and this. . .

"No, no. Room and board?"

"Yeah, that's where he lives and eats. 'Cause otherwise he'd have to find a place to rent--I don't know where--and pay for his own transportation every day. That would cost a lot of money. I provide it for next to nothing. Then, he bought a shirt and hat. Here's what that cost. He knew that. Maybe a little cheaper in town but they don't give credit like I do. Now, some of these fellas bought some nice boots, so they actually still owe me money. But that's okay 'cause there's lots of work left. They'll pay them off in no time. And in the meantime I'm even willing to advance them a couple of dollars so they can enjoy themselves in town."

Carlos was dumbfounded, and the men, already sensing the situation, somberly awaited his translation. In the end no one was in the mood to go to town and they walked demoralized back to the bunk house.

"That son of a whore!" observed Lautaro, "The only thing he didn't charge us for is the air we breathe."

Someone said that they had never heard of such a thing, but Carlos told them that he had. He said that in the jungles of Chiapas, in the *monterias*, the Germans used to do the same thing to the Indians. They would contract them for six months and then their mounting debt would keep them working there at least six years.

"It's legalized slavery." he said.

"Well, I'm not staying here six years." Antonio said. "Let's just leave." Others agreed.

"Where will we go? We don't even know where we are. Who would hire us? The police could arrest us any time."

"Well, we have to do something."

A while later, Eli and his family heard some noises. He looked out of the window and saw the workers throwing all their purchases on his front porch. Hats, boots, shirts and even used bars of soap were dumped at his front door. Eli opened the door and started yelling.

"Hey, that stuff is used. I'm not taking it back!"

The men didn't say a word. They just kept coming and dumping all their things at his feet before walking back to the bunkhouse.

"That's the thanks I get for trying to treat you all like decent people!" Eli sputtered as he slammed the door.

"Ungrateful people!" Eli's wife concurred. "We should've never hired foreigners."

"We got no choice, Má. All our damn workers gone off to war."

"Well, what if these people leave?" asked Mary Lou. "What then?"

"Oh, we'll just get more." her father answered. "There's plenty of 'em."

"They'll be just the same." his wife warned.

"Well, what the hell do you want me to do?" Eli's screamed.

When Alberto returned to the bunk house, Ramon, who had lost some money to him the previous night, accosted him, demanding it back. Alberto calmly explained that he had won it fair and square but Ramon was adamant and angrier by the minute. Alberto tried to walk away but Ramon pulled out a knife and threatened him.

Several men stood watching, some of them rooting for Ramon because they too had lost money to Alberto. Alberto said okay, then took a final puff from his cigarette and flicked it at his adversary's eyes, then instantly threw him to the ground, disarming him on his way down. Carlos and others came running and found Alberto pressing the knife to Ramon's throat.

"Alberto, no! Let him go!" Carlos yelled. He knelt down, next to Alberto, whose body was tight as a coil. "I said, let him go." Alberto stood up and handed Carlos the knife. Ramon stood up on shaky legs.

"The next time," Alberto told Ramon calmly, "by the time my brother comes to help you, you'll be dead."

Carlos took the deck of playing cards and threw it into the stove that night.

After two days of rest, spent mainly sitting around listening to their private troubadours and sharing stories, they went back to the field, but they did it in a more leisurely pace and took breaks for water or the bathroom whenever they had the need. Eli and his men just watched in simmering anger.

One day, a couple of weeks later, Antonio took Alberto aside and told him of his plan to make more money for less work. He had been watching the tractor operator and was sure that they could teach themselves to drive it with just a bit of practice. He knew that the tractor was left unattended with the key in the ignition during lunch time. He badgered his brother so much that Alberto eventually, although reluctantly, agreed to join him.

They hopped aboard the old tractor and started it without any problem, but the large number of levers got Antonio mixed up and he began to pull and push them indiscriminately. Suddenly the tractor lunged forward and started down the hill. Alberto nearly fell off and Antonio tried to stop the machine but only made it turn and spin and lunge ahead even faster. They headed straight for the bunk house until the last minute when Antonio managed to make it veer off to one side. Nevertheless, it caught a corner of the building and ripped a large portion of it to pieces with a tremendous crash. The workers dropped their food and ran to see what happened. They found the tractor upside down in a ditch covered with pieces of the bunk house. Antonio had crawled out from under the mess and was calling back down for Alberto. Carlos and several others jumped into the ditch and dug through the rubble with bare hands. They found Alberto, dazed and bleeding from a cut above his ear but otherwise unharmed.

Carlos was furious at Antonio but Alberto accepted at least some of the blame.

"I should have stopped him, he said." Then he glared at Antonio, leaving him trembling even more than the accident had done.

The three brothers climbed into the bunk house through the gaping hole and appeared at the door a moment later, carrying their hastily packed belongings. They said a quick farewell to their comrades who wished them good luck in return.

At the road, they looked down one side and the other and headed across into the hills, still aiming north.

Chapter 28

The sun had set, turning long shadows into darkness, when a black Ford coupe bounced slowly over the cobblestones of a deserted street on the outskirts of San Cristobal. Alma was at the wheel of her father's car with Catalina at her side.

"Are you sure you won't come in with me?" Catalina asked.

"I'm not crazy. If I wanted to see ghosts I'd visit the cemetery. But how will you get back?"

"Don't worry. I'll be fine. It's not that far."

Alma drove off into the night while Catalina pounded the heavy brass knocker against the massive wooden portals. She waited. Nervous moments passed. She looked down each side of the street. The shadows seemed to move when a sudden gust of wind kicked up some papers and a crow cawed as it flew by. She knocked again, harder, almost in desperation. Finally, some chains rattled inside and the door creaked open a few inches. A small, hooded figure whose features could barely be discerned answered with a quavering voice.

"Who is it?"

"It's me, Catalina Cansino. I came to see Doña Hermelinda."

The door closed again. More rattling of chains ensued, followed by the hollow thumping of a wooden beam upon the ground. The door opened with a sustained creak and Catalina entered into a large patio lit up only on one side by the slanting rays of a bluish moonlight. She followed the small hooded figure along a long, dark corridor but kept bumping into branches and things in the dark. Something ran past her feet and Catalina shrieked. On the other side of the eerie courtyard she could see a row of small, dark doors within the brightness of the white-washed walls. Two of the doors were ajar and the flickering candlelight within them revealed a hooded figure peeking out from each. When Catalina stopped to focus on them, the doors closed slowly with a final creak. By then, the silent figure guiding her had disappeared, and Catalina had to feel her way along the corridor, knocking on every door she came to.

"Doña Hermelinda! Are you here? It's me. Catalina." she kept calling.

Finally, one of the doors pushed open, revealing a dark, cluttered room glowing orange in the center from the light of a large, stone fireplace. An old woman's tremulous voice echoed from a rocking chair near the fire.

"Come in, my dearest. I've been expecting you."

Catalina swallowed nervously as a flush of hot air and the smell of dead geraniums wrapped around her. She entered and the door slammed shut behind her with a sudden gust of wind. The old woman, rocking slowly in her chair, had silky white hair and deep blue eyes. She looked very frail, very old and wrinkled, with bony hands covered loosely by white satiny skin that revealed the greenish branches of her veins. Catalina kissed her forehead.

"Good evening, Doña Hermelinda. It's so good to see you and to find you looking so well."

"God is very great. Sit down my dear. Over here, close to me, so we can talk in peace. Amaranta! Prepare the chocolate!" she ordered. "And now, my little girl, tell me about the currents of your life."

They talked for a while about trivial and inconsequential things and slowly found comfort with each other as the minutes rolled by. The hot chocolate was brought in, served in a tea set of the finest silver. Catalina took a sip of her chocolate and looked at the old woman with a mischievous grin.

"I ran into Don Carlos, the other day." she probed with feigned indifference.

"Yes. At the Vildosola's party." the old woman said, turning to glance at her guest. "And he wanted to dance with you."

Catalina gasped with astonishment.

"My God! How did you know that?"

"Oh, my dear. This town is so full of old secrets that there's no room left for new ones."

"Well, anyway, Don Carlos still looks very handsome, although they say he's very ill." Catalina continued, and she studied the old woman's face for any signs of a reaction.

"Carlos always was very handsome. He always will be. When he dies he will no doubt be the handsomest corpse that San Cristobal has interred. Nevertheless, you must be very careful with him even then, my dear."

Puzzled by the remark, Catalina sipped her chocolate and waited for an explanation, but as none came she decided to probe further.

"Why do you say that, Doña Hermelinda? You couldn't possibly still be holding a grudge."

"Of course not. All of that . . . was in another lifetime. I'm just warning you that the snake's poison continues to be poisonous after the snake has died."

Not knowing if someone might be listening in the shadows of the room, Catalina moved closer to her confidant and lowered her voice to a near whisper.

"What really happened between you and Don Carlos?"

The old woman looked deep into her empty cup for a long time. Her eyes became clouded by the old memories newly disturbed in her mind.

"The rumors that we were lovers are a lie." she finally said. "Carlos and I were friends since youth. For me, he was like a younger brother."

Catalina was enthralled to the edge of her chair.

"Our two families," the old woman continued, "belonged to the cream of society, at a time when that was an honor worth more than pure gold. We remained close friends long after both of us had married, and when my husband died, Carlos was there to comfort me." she paused. "Or so I thought."

Catalina noticed the old woman's eyes glistening.

"How old was your daughter when he took her?

"Barely sixteen." She struggled with those words as if they came from very deep inside and weighed an awful lot.

"Did your daughter believe he would marry her?"

"At that age, young girls believe what they want to believe. I'm the one that should have seen it. We all knew that Carlos was a womanizer. He already had several women and many children scattered about. But those were women of a lower class! Some even had been servants at his houses or his ranch. In those days, men measured their power with their pecker."

From out of the shadows, a scrawny hand appeared to refill their cups and Catalina nearly dropped her's from the fright. They waited in silence until the servant disappeared, staring at the dying embers for a while.

"They say that they lived together for a time." Catalina remarked.

"I don't know. I only know that he installed her in a house in Montebello, on the shores of those famous lakes, damned may they be, and that soon after the child was born he abandoned her."

The pain in the old woman's heart was beginning to show in the crackle of her voice. Catalina reached for her silky hand, placing it between her own.

"Is it true that when she tried to come home, you rejected her?"

Stung by the question, the old woman pulled her hand away with a surprising vigor, but her answer was equally swift and direct.

"Yes. And that's something I'll take to my grave." She paused for an instant. "The following Sunday she was seen at the church with her baby, and that afternoon they found her floating in the blue lake. Or maybe it was the emerald one. I don't remember now."

Tears were now trickling from the old woman's eyes, and from Catalina's as well.

"It could have been an accident." Catalina proposed.

"She was found wearing her wedding dress!" was the rejoinder. The two women stared at the last flickering flames for a while.

"And you never confronted Don Carlos?"

"What for? The damage was done. When he took my daughter's honor, he destroyed our entire family. We've lived inside this mausoleum since then."

Finally acustomed to the darkness, Catalina looked around at the old furniture in the shadows, carved with grotesque figures that now seemed to move in the dancing light. In the distance, a clock struck the hour, its gong reverberating through the house, and she tried to imagine her husband as a baby, living within those cavernous halls.

Several days later, Catalina was sitting in her room, breast feeding her baby while Felix played near her feet with his toys and Maria Hernandez walked around the sunny garden with Maria del Carmen in her arms. Alma was on the sofa, attempting to knit baby booties.

"What a tragedy!" Alma lamented. "I remember that my grandmother used to tell us that the Tamayos were one of the wealthiest and most respected families in San Cristobal. But one day they just closed their doors to the world forever, and no one really knew why."

"Yes. The rumors were that a horrible illness had attacked the entire family, leaving them disfigured or insane, and that the children born in that house were monsters; a punishment from God for something evil they had done."

"Who knows, Catalina? No one ever comes out of that house except the servants to the marketplace. It's not even known how many of the family are still alive. Talk about skeletons in the closet." Alma shivered at the thought and laughed.

"But, Alma, do you really think it's possible that all of this is some sort of self-punishment for what a sixteen-year-old girl did?"

"Oh, you innocent child. In this town, anything is possible. But what I want to know is this: How is it that Carlos ended up at his father's home?"

"Well, according to Doña Hermelinda, when her daughter drowned she took charge of the baby. So Carlos grew up in that home for several years. Then, one day, Don Carlos and his wife just showed up at her door, asking for the child."

"Mother of God! What did she tell them?"

"To go to hell, at first, but he was very persistent, so eventually she told him that she would only turn him over on the condition that he, Don Carlos, would publicly acknowledge him as his son and raise him accordingly."

"Which he pretended to do but didn't."

"Oh, you mean that thing about the papers? Well, personally I believe Don Carlos when he swears that it was all some bureaucratic bungle. After all, he did acnowkledge his paternity to the whole town at that time."

"Where does it all stand now?"

"Don Carlos had all the official papers corrected while we were on our honeymoon, but Carlos still refuses to even talk to him. The irony is that all of Carlos' sisters are angry now, because they think Carlos is just trying to get some of their inheritance, which Carlos really couldn't care less about. Not that there is much left."

"But why do you think Don Carlos did it? Guilt? Love?"

"The original acknowledgement? Only Don Carlos knows. But it didn't stop his son from hating him. It's a hatred that's eating Carlos alive."

"My God! So much hatred, so much tragedy. It's almost like a family curse."

"Oh, please don't say that, Alma. This whole thing has got to stop right here."

The baby was fast asleep.

Catalina received Carlos' first letter two weeks after it was postmarked in Prairieville, Texas, which in turn had been three weeks after it was written. It basically just said that they had made it into the United States without problems and had been working from the start. He didn't know exactly where they were but would send the address soon. For a school teacher, he wasn't much of a writer, Catalina thought. Two more months would pass before she received a second letter.

She kept busy making dresses in order to pay the bills and her clientele grew as word of her ability spread. Some people preferred her work to that of Florinda's because, although the workmanship was excellent in both cases, Florinda's taste was more traditional and staid. Catalina tended to use more modern lines, not to say daring, and brighter, more colorful prints.

As time passed and the baby became less dependent of her, Alma and the Cansino sisters kept trying to entice her out to social gatherings, parties, festivals and family outings. They were afraid that she was losing her zest for life; declining into early matronhood, as Alma put it. But in fact, Catalina just wasn't attracted anymore by such endeavors. She felt silly and out of place at parties or social gatherings, and wished she could be home with her children instead, preferably sewing while they slept, but near them nonetheless. Solitude had become soothing rather than lonely and the moments of relative peace at home now provided a blessed contentment.

What she enjoyed most of all were the tranquil Sundays shared with Florinda and Maria Hernandez, and the children. With a few well placed questions she could get Florinda reminiscing about Chilón and the days with Catalina's mother, Magdalena, or even prior to that, growing up in that village with her brothers and her friends.

I'm becoming an old maid, Catalina laughed to herself one day, with a husband and three children. On another occasion she was fending off Alma's invitation to a dance when Alma happened to look out at the patio and saw to her surprise that the repairman who had caused her many sleepless nights was out there, building new window frames. He was shirtless and his glistening perspiration combined with the soft afternoon sun to highlight the muscles rippling in his tall, lean frame.

"Oh, you devil! No wonder you don't want to leave the house. You have a much better distraction right here."

"Don't be silly. I'm a married woman. Here, take your coat, you'll be late for your dance."

An hour later, as the afternoon sun disappeared over the patio wall, Catalina stood in the exact same spot where Alma had been, and through the slit between the curtains stared at Felipe, the handyman, for a long time. In one of the compartments of the roll-top desk behind her, were the few letters from her husband.

During the days and weeks that followed, she paid less and less attention to him, even though Felipe was usually perched on one of the house's windows or another, working as quietly as he could and watching with interest the flow of her life as seamstress and mother.

Then, one day Catalina was alone in the sewing room, cutting a pattern for a wedding dress. There was a knock at the door and she assumed it was her client.

"Come on in." she said, without turning right away. When she did, holding up a sample of material, she was startled to find Felipe standing at the entrance to the room. He apologized for startling her and approached her with a nervousness clearly betrayed in his voice.

"It's just that I've noticed what nice work you do, making dresses and things, and I have a little daughter who will soon be five. So, I was wondering if you could make her a little dress. If you have time. There's no hurry, and of course, I would pay you for it."

"I will be happy to do it. What size is she?"

"I don't know. But she's a little smaller than your boy, except she's skinny."

"Okay. And what style do you want?"

"Oh, I know nothing of those things. But I'm sure whatever you choose will be just right."

"And when is her birthday?"

"The last of this month. But that doesn't matter. I can give it to her later."

"You certainly will not. It will be ready in time."

He smiled and thanked her and tip-toed out of the room. Catalina was amused to see how such a man could turn so meek, and surprised to know he had a daughter. For some reason she had never thought of him as a married man.

She made a frilly little dress in white and pale green and would not accept payment from Felipe except for the cost of the material. All that had completely slipped her mind the following week, especially since it had been raining and Felipe hadn't been around. She was in the patio corridor, admiring the flowers when she heard a tiny but very clear voice behind her.

"Thank you for my dress, Doña Catalina."

Catalina turned to find the nicest surprise she'd had in months. Wearing her new dress was a tiny wisp of a girl with big round eyes, olive skin and a tiny pink mouth. She was dwarfed by her father, standing behind her.

"Oh my God! What a precious thing. What's your name, sweetheart?"

"Lupita."

"Oh that's a nice name. It suits her. She's just darling."

"Yes, thanks to your dress." Felipe said.

"Yes, the dress suits her, but this little angel would look good in anything. Come here, honey. Let me look at you." Catalina was so taken with her that she couldn't resist taking her in her arms.

"She's light as a feather."

"She doesn't eat much, but she's healthy." her father explained.

"Oh, she's just a little doll. Her mother must be so proud of her."

"Her mother died giving her life."

"Oh, how sad. So, who takes care of her now?"

"My sister, mostly."

"Here in San Cristobal?"

"No, in Comitan. I try to get back there every weekend, so she can have some rest."

"Well I'm so glad you brought her, and you'll have to promise me to bring her back again, as often as you can."

He promised that he would and they left right away in order to catch the last bus to Comitan. Catalina was already looking forward to seeing her again.

Felipe brought her by some weeks later and again two weeks after that. Catalina said that Lupita was a wonderful playmate for her children. In time, Felipe and Lupita's Saturday afternoon visitsbecame almost a part of their routine and they continued long after Felipe had completed his work on Catalina's house.

Alma was the first to warn her that people would begin to talk, and Catalina became angry, insisting that her only concern and interest was the welfare of that fragile little doll. Then Felipe showed up a couple of times without Lupita, just to report that she had a cold or some other minor ailment. And of course, being a good hostess Catalina offered him some chocolate or some tea, and since it would have been impolite to turn her down, he stayed, for a little while.

Catalina would only admit that she had come to admire Felipe, for being such a good father and she also appreciated him for being such a true friend.

"If people want to talk, that's their problem." she told Florinda.

"But God is my witness that Felipe has never made so much as the slightest advance toward me."

"And what will happen when he does?" Florinda asked her.

Chapter 29

The three brothers hiked north for six days over endless prairies and along dried out riverbeds. They ate whatever they could find and slept anywhere that gave them shelter. They trudged into countless communities to look for work but usually found people kind enough to provide something to eat yet suspicious or mistrustful enough to close their doors to them afterward, until they disappeared from sight. Soon they found out that the best places to find work were the small farms, because they had all been left shorthanded by the war, but the work never lasted very long and the pay was barely enough to keep them going until they found another job. They discovered hitch hiking and rode in the back of trucks carrying anything from chickens and pigs to sand and gravel.

Each of them was beginning to consider the entire adventure a fiasco, but they kept it to themselves, realizing that the last thing they needed in those days was to fall out with each other.

One morning they were walking along a country road when a black 1936 Ford coupe pulled over to the side of the road, right in front of them. Carlos and his brothers stopped in their tracks. Their first thoughts were that it was the police and almost in unison they looked around to see where the others would be coming from as well as which direction might be open for them to turn and run.

The driver of the car got out and walked toward them. He was a man of about 45, with a three day stubble and reddish brown hair, partly covered by a brown felt hat that had seen better days. He was slim, of average height and wore a white shirt with the sleeves rolled up and which wrinkled and folded up against his perspiring torso to reveal that it had either belonged to a larger man or he had lost a lot of weight since buying it. His gabardine slacks were baggy on him too, and one could have said that was the style, but they were worn and shiny at the seat and knees, pointing to their use for harder work then that for which they were intended. And he surprised all three brothers when he spoke to them in perfect Castillian Spanish.

"Where are you gentlemen going? Are you looking for work?"

They reluctantly admitted that they were, expecting him to pull a badge out of his pocket, but he said that he was doing the same and suggested that they ride together. His little car had leather seats and they were the softest thing any of them had rested on in weeks.

The man told them that he had been working in a factory somewhere, making parts for radios, but that the military had taken it over to convert it for war material production. He wanted no part of that, he said, because he was a pacifist, so he quit. For the two previous weeks he had worked odd jobs but was looking for something more permanent for the next six months or so, and then he would just take off to travel.

"Travel to where?" Carlos asked him.

"Anywhere the road takes me." he laughed.

At the next town he pulled into a cafe and bought them the first full meal they had eaten in a month and they were so grateful that they didn't mind his constant chatter. He loved to talk and did most of the talking long into the night, as they continued north.

His name was Elwood Bryars Pennington III, and he showed them his driver's license to prove it, but when all three brothers failed to pronounce it, he just laughed and said that everyone called him 'Cappy' because he had been the captain of a fishing boat for a few years, sometime back.

"Working off the coast of Alaska," he said "mainly going out for salmon."

He spoke five languages fluently and had been to every continent, except Antarctica. He had worked in farms, factories, canneries, sugar mills and countless other places, aboard ships, trains and airplanes. He was skilled in several trades, including carpentry, glass works, lock smithing and forestry. "I just don't like any of them for more than a short time."

They eventually ended up outside Pratt, Kansas, working on a ranch so large that they had to climb the highest nearby peak to see its boundaries. Their job was mostly the repair of old barbed wire fences and the installation of new ones. It paid okay but it was hard work over rugged terrain and it left their hands and arms crisscrossed with cuts that, to prevent infection, they seared with some iodine solution.

After that hey picked fruit in windy orchards along Junction City, Kansas, and dug irrigation ditches for some farms outside of Ottoville, Iowa. And every time that Carlos saw Cappy working just as hard as they did, he wondered why, when he could easily have some well-paid office job. It never occurred to him that people often wondered the same thing about him.

One day, on a bulletin board outside a restaurant, Cappy noticed a flyer offering work on the railroads for experienced as well as inexperienced men.

"It's hard work," he told Carlos and his brothers, "I've done it. But the pay is as good as we're likely to find these days, and the benefits are even better."

Two days later all four of them were sitting in the Dixon, Illinois offices of the Illinois Central Railroad Company, filling out long applications. They had to sign a contract for at least one year, and if they left before then, they would lose a third of their pay, which would be held back until the year was up. They signed without any hesitation even though they had already been away from home nearly a year.

Two days later they were handed uniforms and work boots, and put aboard a train to work the lines outside Chicago. They were given 2 weeks of training at a camp in a forest, along with forty other men. The wind blew down on them from the snow capped peaks as they learned to unload, transport and install sections of rail and switching gears by hand. Five men were badly hurt in accidents during the training period, but Cappy, Carlos and his brothers all made it through without a problem. They were given their first paychecks and a weekend off and seeing that they were already earning more than twice as much as they had in any of their previous jobs, they decided to go into Chicago and spend some money on themselves for once.

Cappy drove straight into the center of town. Long before that, his three passengers had been mesmerized by the constellation of lights, the frantic traffic and the general hustle and bustle of the area. Looking at the skyline, Carlos recalled his old teacher, Mr. Cupertino Meneses, when he would rhapsodize about the skyscrapers, the trains and the automobiles, and he knew now that he had indeed been talking specifically to him. They parked the car inside a large building that was made exclusively for that purpose. There were dozens of autos inside along several stories and Antonio remarked that they looked like metallic cattle in a corral.

They walked down an avenue that had one fancy restaurant or hotel after another with a few department stores sprinkled in between which had huge decorated windows, displaying the most stylish clothes and fanciest accessories any of the three brothers had ever seen in person. It was a wonderland for them, spoiled only when one of the hotel doormen, thinking they were bums, chased them away.

Cappy took them to a public sauna and afterwards to get haircuts and be shaved. They bought new suits, ties, shirts, shoes and even cuff links, and were ushered in to dinner by the doorman who only hours before chased them away. They finished the evening at a Jazz night club where every brass fixture was shiny and every waitress young and pretty. They spent that night at a fancy hotel, sleeping like babies, except for Antonio who remained awake, desperately trying to think of a scheme to make fast money so that they could always live that way. He kept himself company with a radio that seemed to play only Glen Miller's music, interspersed with reports of heavy American casualties incurred in battles with the Japanese in New Guinea, while in the European theater, rumors grew of a German occupation force extending in all directions. Meanwhile, at home, it reported, the rationing of basic foods was being intensified. Antonio did not understand a word, but loved the music.

Carlos had a dream that night, in which he and his brothers were still looking for work, trudging through the mountains. Eventually, tired but thirsty, they spotted a beautiful and placid lake and headed down to it to drink, even though they sensed some danger. When they reached the water an began to drink, huge monsters, like gigantic crocodiles came rushing after them from behind the rocks.

In the morning that was all he could remember of the dream and he ignored it, convinced it was just nonsense brought on by the liquor of the previous evening.

Nursing hangovers, they did some sightseeing on Sunday and returned Monday morning to report for work. Cappy was offered a job in Chicago which paid more and was mostly indoor work, but he turned it down so that he could remain with Carlos and his brothers. They had become good friends by then.

The only thing Cappy didn't like to talk about was the more intimate details of his private life, but from bits and pieces that he let slip by, Carlos managed to put some of it together. Apparently he had married and settled down many years back. He and his wife bought a home on the banks of a river he referred to as 'the Hudson' and they had a child. Five years later, however, his wife suddenly died. The tragedy affected him so much that Cappy returned to his old ways and aimless life on the road, as if searching for something without knowing what. He seemed to have a need just to keep moving, as if something was chasing him. He started drinking heavily at that same time, just as he had before his marriage, so that by the time Carlos and his brothers met him, he was going through a small bottle of whiskey every single day.

When they returned to the barracks of the railroad company they found thick, hooded overcoats on top of their bunks, and then the foreman walked by with a big grin and pointed out the window to the snow-covered mountain peaks in the distance.

In fact they worked in the valleys for the the first two months, but when winter came, storming down the hillsides, all four were sent up into the mountains, to repair tracks and clear snow drifts off the rails with shovels and sometimes picks where the snow had turned to ice. They often worked in blizzards when the wind would howl and the temperatures dipped to forty degrees below zero, snapping rails like pieces of glass. They slept in small wooden cabins with boarded up broken windows and walls made of thin wooden panels lined with tin, rather than the thick logs the training station had. The cabins were set every ten or fifteen miles along the rail road lines in the mountains, put there for the workers as they traveled by. Their only heat came from old stoves in which the snow would constantly douse the fire by blowing down through the flue, so that they usually slept fully clothed, wearing sweaters and coats, wrapped like Egyptian mummies, motionless upon their freezing bunks.

One morning the foreman, passing by on a utility train car, handed them buckets and lanterns and sent them into a succession of dark mountain tunnels to find and retrieve the pieces of two men that a train had run over while they took shelter from the howling winds.

"It happens all the time." they were told. "You'll get used to it."

They went in, praying that the reports were wrong and that it had been some animal. They found nothing for a long time, then Antonio let out a cry and ran back past them. One wall was completely splattered with blood and guts. It had all started running down and then froze into bright shiny patterns. They soon found scraps of clothing and then pieces of arms and a hand. One section of torso was too big for the buckets and they had to carry it between them with bits and pieces dangling and falling off.

That night they sat together in a half circle around the stove. They were freezing, and demoralized. All of them had lost weight and looked like ghosts, pale and haggard. Antonio was adamant that they should leave, but Carlos pointed out that if they did they would lose nearly two months worth of pay. Cappy had been offered the job in Chicago once again. His health had deteriorated more than the others and Carlos demanded that he take the job. They argued about it but all three brothers voted that he go that very day. He finally agreed but he insisted that they keep the car.

"You've all been dreaming of California and this will get you there." he said. However, Carlos convinced him that if they didn't crash it somewhere and kill themselves, the police would confiscate it and jail them on suspicion of its theft. Back at the rail yard they heated up some water from roof icicles gathered right outside the door and used it to melt the oil and the radiator water before starting the car. The three brothers stood together and watched Cappy and his Ford disappear into the mountains, knowing with dead certainty that they would never see him again. Then they jumped into a boxcar on the next train that came along. With the wind biting their faces, they stared at the snow-covered pines flashing by. It looked like those Christmas postcards they had seen in town, but now they knew those tranquil scenes had another side to them. Even after losing a third of their pay, they still collected much more money than they had ever made working in farms. On the wall outside the next railroad station they saw a map of the United States with all the railroad lines criss-crossing it.

"Where to?" Alberto asked.

"California." his brothers answered.

Chapter 30

It took Carlos and his brothers eighteen days to reach California. They changed trains a dozen times, catching the wrong one on several occasions, and then having to double back. Along the way they encountered dozens of other men hopping trains, going in one direction or another. At some of the small stations there were far more people hiding in the bushes, preparing to sneak aboard the freight cars than there were people on the platform waiting to board the passenger cars. Some of the 'train jumpers' were hoboes, mostly white, doing it as a way of life--a hard and lonely life--but that was the price they were willing to pay for total independence. The majority, however, were men just like Carlos and his brothers, usually a bit darker on the skin perhaps, with higher cheekbones. They were Mexican or Filipino, mostly, but also Afro-American, American Indian and Chinese; filled with the same passion inside; paying the heavy price for a chance at a better future for their families.

One of them, over a campfire, somewhere in Arizona, casually told Carlos: "I know I'm going to die here, maybe run over by a train, just like my brother, or shot by one of these train policemen bastards, but it really doesn't matter now, because I've already sent some money to my family, and even if it isn't much, its made a difference."

The Bracero Program contract included a clause that the U.S. Government would keep ten percent of the workers' earnings in safekeeping for them and release it to them at the end of their stay. For many of them it was all that they would have to take back home, so they were looking forward to that. But the more experienced workers--those that had been working in the country even before the program--were not counting on it.

"We'll never see any of that." they said. "No one is even keeping track of it."

Some of the more experienced train jumpers gave Carlos and his brothers plenty of advice, sometimes contradictory, but it was their directions that finally got them to their destination.

At one of the thousands of places where the tracks crossed a road, the long dusty train slowed down enough for the three of them to jump off, each carrying his belongings inside a canvas bag. Rolled up inside were their clothes, including the new suits they had worn only once, some postcards and a few other trinkets they had bought as souvenirs.

They were welcomed by nothing more than an overhead banner stretched across the dusty and deserted street proclaiming: Welcome to Suisun--Heart of America's Farmland. Pop. 717.

There wasn't a cloud in the sky, nor a bird for that matter. The ten o'clock sun was scorching the clay streets, cracking them open, and small clouds of dust rose up with every step they took, and hung in the air with no wind to disperse them. The buildings were all made of wood and mostly painted gray, or a drab green, like the army vehicles that seemed to appear on every road. In spite of the stifling heat, the buildings were silent and tightly closed, window shades drawn. The only people visible at first were three old winos, sharing a bottle under a tree, oblivious to the heat or to the world around them. The scene wasn't exactly the California any of the three brothers had imagined.

They walked a couple of blocks and found two laborers conversing in Spanish.

"Excuse me, friend." Carlos interrupted, "How is the situation here, as far as work?"

"Very good, comrade. There's always work here." one man said.

"It's because we're in the very center of the valley," a second man added, "surrounded by big farms and ranches."

"Is the pay good?" Antonio asked.

"It is if you're a good worker, brother, cause it's all piece work."

"I see." Antonio said, without really understanding.

"Yeah. In other words," the second man explained, "they pay you to pick the fruit, not to stand there gawking at it." They all laughed and one of the men took a bottle from his pocket and offered them a drink. Carlos thanked him but declined, as did his brothers.

"What are they picking now?" Alberto asked.

"Well, nearby it's pears. But there's lots of other stuff."

"Up north its grapes," his partner said, "up around Lodi." he pointed in the general direction. "Down south you have your peaches, apricots, tomatoes; and in the Salinas Valley they got great weather with the sea breeze, but picking lettuce is no fun."

"We're much obliged." Carlos told them, "Oh, one more thing: can you recommend a place to stay?"

"If you go up this street, you'll find several places."

"Yeah," warned the other man, "but some of them won't take Mexicans."

They walked along, past several places with 'rooms for rent' signs hanging in the windows, but none of them appealed to them because they were all dark and sealed off from the heat and the world. Alberto sensed that they were being watched from inside as they walked by, just as he used to feel in the rich parts of San Cristobal. Then, suddenly, at the end of one block they were confronted with a sight that looked completely out of place. It was a large, wooden, two story building, standing alone, taking up one small block and looking more like a fort than a residence. It had one huge entrance which was more like a tunnel, leading into a central patio. But it was alive and inviting, its windows flung open with abandon, clothes hanging out of some of them. The joyous sound of children playing emanated from its core, sounding much like a schoolyard.

At the center of the patio stood a majestic palm tree, so tall that its top fronds could be seen from a distance above the building's cantilevered roof. That explained the sign above the entrance: *Casa de la Palma*. Below it was a small, hand painted sign proclaiming: Vacancy.

The brothers walked in without hesitation. The rooms on the ground floor opened to the patio and most of them were indeed open. The children ran in and out of them with impunity. Chickens and geese wandered freely pecking at the patches of grass. The rooms on the second story opened to a large, common, covered deck, like an internal veranda, that circled the entire patio from above.

"You guys looking for a place to stay?" a woman yelled at them as she hung sheets on a clothesline.

"Yes." Carlos said.

She studied them for a moment.

"Take number six, upstairs." She told them. "We'll talk later." One of the older girls led them through an alcove to the stairway which took them to the inner deck by which all the apartments on that floor were accessed. Carlos and his brothers were delighted to find that number six was actually two rooms, with twin beds in each and, wonder of wonders, their very own indoor bathroom. All three stood side by side in the middle of one room, staring with awe at the claw-foot bathtub. The sight brought a trace of moisture to their eyes. They looked at each other, and then scrambled for the bathroom door. None of them made it. Each was too busy keeping the others back. They wrestled all over the room, tearing each other's clothing in the process, while several of the children watched with amusement from the door.

Finally, tired, perspiring and wrapped together like a pretzel, they stopped to rest and Carlos made the other two a proposition.

"All right, all right," he said. "We'll do this fairly. We'll draw straws, just like Cappy taught us."

"We don't have any straws." Antonio said.

"There's a broom right over there. Hand it to me."

Antonio went to get the broom, Carlos stood up and extended a hand to help Alberto, then pulled it suddenly away, leapt over a bed into the bathroom, slamming the door shut and locking it behind him. His two brothers hung their heads in shame while the children laughed and walked away.

"The devil knows more because he's old than because he's the devil." Alberto remarked.

After all three had taken long, refreshing baths in cool water, they sat around, still wet, looking at the flat green and orange patches of farmland, stretching out as far as they could see.

"Man," Antonio said. "Why didn't we come here first?"

"Shut up!" Carlos ordered him, and Alberto smacked him on the head with a pillow.

They spent the evening sitting around the veranda, which was as wide as were the rooms themselves. It was somewhat dark, due to the roof sloping down over it, but there were small lamps on the various tables scattered on the deck between old sofas and easy chairs. Red and yellow Chinese lanterns hung from the rafters, giving the entire deck a cozy feeling that increased in inverse proportion to the evening's loss of light.

The evening weather was so pleasant that first night that many of the tenants had their dinner out on the veranda, including some from the apartments downstairs. It made for a warm, communal and intimate atmosphere that none of the brothers could have dreamt of just a week or two before. The freezing nights they had spent in the mountains just weeks before were now quickly receding in their memory.

All three brothers were as curious about their new neighbors as they all must have been about them. A Hindu family lived in apartment number two, across the way. The man wore a turban, which they had only seen in the movies before that so they decided to refer to him as Ali Babá.

In number nine lived another elderly couple, who must have been more than eighty years old. In time they would learn that the man was a clock and watch maker, who had a little shop, two blocks away, where he had worked for over fifty years. More interesting to them was the fact that the woman was not his wife. She was his sister-in-law who had come west for the first time from Wisconsin for her sister's funeral, twenty eight years earlier, and had been with him ever since.

"I guess she wanted to keep it in the family." Alberto was to observe, without even cracking a faint smile.

Yet, their most interesting neighbor, or more accurately, the neighbor that interested them the most, turned out to be the tenant at number ten: a blonde woman, no more than twenty five, very attractive and apparently living alone with her two children.

The three brothers ate dinner at a little Chinese restaurant that first night and afterward Carlos returned to their apartment, eager to write Catalina a letter telling her of their good fortune. His brothers, meanwhile, decided to explore the little town.

By the time Carlos sat down with pen and paper on the veranda, all the tenants had gone inside. Most of the lights were out, though a few children could be heard still playing in the the patio. Somewhere down the street, a piano played long, romantic melodies.

My dearest darling, he began. You won't believe the wonderful luck that we have finally encountered. Then he stopped, because he remembered that he had started other letters to her with those same words, except that in those cases he was lying. Should he now tell her he was lying? Why would she believe that this time it was true?

He didn't know what to do. Then he suddenly realized that the young woman from number ten was standing outside her door, her hands above her head, clasping the protruding beam, her legs crossed at the ankles, face slanted up, eyes closed, as if bathing in the warm night air.

She wore a silky dress that revealed the youthful firmness and defined curvature of her body. Perhaps sensing his stare, she turned and looked directly at him. He was caught. Averting his gaze quickly would have compounded his guilt so he owned up to his act by staring openly at her for a moment longer. She did not back down either and for an instant their eyes were locked upon each other. Then he turned away, returning to his letter. He wrote a couple of lines but could not control the urge to look at her again. He turned, but she was gone.

Sometime in the night, Carlos awakened, covered in sweat and so frightened that his heart was pounding. He called for Antonio, who answered from the other room.

"What are you doing?"

"Reading a magazine."

"What time is it?"

"Two thirty."

"Is Alberto asleep?"

"No. He's playing poker in that cantina down the street."

"Go down and get him. We have to get up early tomorrow to look for work."

"He'll be here. They were starting to close when I left."

In the morning they hitched a ride to the biggest farm in the vicinity. Its main product was pears, which people said were ready for harvesting. There were six men waiting to apply for work when they arrived and another five came in after them. All were told to wait outside a bungalow so they sat down on empty crates along a fence. One by one they were called in for a quick interview with the owner's son. He had his foreman there to translate because few of the workers knew much English. Each man was asked a few questions about his past as well as his plans for the future, which seemed rather odd to most of them. Only Carlos recognized that the questions were intended to reveal the applicant's attitude toward hard work and he figured there must only be a few positions available if they could afford to be so picky. He also guessed that the owner's son must have just graduated from some academy of higher education and was eager to try new methods of dealing with their workers and new ways to run the company. He wasn't sure how he felt about that.

When the interview finished, each man was told to go back and wait outside. No one knew how many positions were available and Carlos began to worry that they might not hire all three of them.

After a while, the foreman came out and handed each of them, except Antonio, a set of tools that included a ring shaped knife which he explained was designed to measure the pears before cutting them. If they fit through the ring they were still too small to pick.

Carlos was not surprised that they hadn't picked Antonio. He could just imagine the flights of fancy that he must have woven into his answers. Still, he thought of demanding that they hire him or else he and Alberto would walk away. And he wondered if such a ruse would work.

"Antonio Cansino!" someone called, and Antonio jumped to his feet. A tractor was brought up and the driver turned it off and walked away.

"Okay, *muchacho*," the foreman said to Antonio, "let's see what you can do."

He hopped on, started the engine and moved the vehicle forward with pronounced, jerky motions. Here we go again, Carlos thought, and he covered his face. Antonio drove around in circles, as directed, and each lap was smoother than the one before, but it was also clear that he didn't know one lever from another.

Finally, the owner's son told him to stop and turn it off. Several of the other workers were laughing openly by then.

"You've got a lot of nerve telling me you could drive a tractor." the young man scolded. Antonio hung down his head and started to climb off, but the man stopped him. "I like a man with nerve." he said, "We'll get someone to train you. You're hired."

In the end, all the men were hired but Antonio was making 35 cents more an hour. After a couple of days of training he was weaving through the orchards with abandon, towing flatbed trailers full of pear crates or tanks of irrigation water. And every time he passed near his brothers, up in ladders on the trees, with huge bags of pears hanging from their aching shoulders, he would whistle some happy tune and exaggerate his joy.

He became difficult to live with, crowing and gloating all the time, until some of the workers, with Carlos' permission, threw him into a muddy irrigation ditch.

They earned about half of what the railroad company had paid them, but it was the best job they had held by far. They could even work only five days a week if they wanted. The sixth was optional. They decided to work six and to put that extra money toward the purchase of a car like Cappy's. Then they could cut back to five days and spend the weekends traveling around California. Their ultimate dream was a trip to San Francisco. Even in Chicago's stores they had seen post card packets that opened out like accordions with a dozen pictures of the Golden Gate Bridge, the cable cars and other incredibly beautiful sights in San Francisco.

Carlos had sent one of those photo packets to Catalina, which she concluded was just another trick to change her mind.

Meanwhile, Sundays in Suisun were a day to rest. They stayed around the Casa de la Palma watching the children play and sometimes even joining in. On Saturday evenings, Alberto and Antonio would head for the bar named Murphy's. Antonio went for a few beers and to shoot pool although he wasn't very experienced at either. Conversely, Alberto went for the whiskey and the poker; both of which were old friends to him. Carlos would stay home to enjoy the changing light of dusk from the veranda and to write his letters home.

Eventually the lady from apartment ten would appear, to look over the railing at her children or just to enjoy an evening cigarette. They would act coy and unconvincingly disinterested, casting furtive glances at each other, Carlos soon started paying closer attention to his appearance. He would take a bath as soon as he got home from work each day and then arranged for Sherry, the landlady downstairs, to wash and iron his clothes for a small fee.

One day he appeared at home with two bags of groceries which included an aromatic and more expensive soap than the one they had been using, shampoo, brilliantine and after shave lotion. He even bought himself a new, ivory handled razor with a gold plated spine. His brothers took to calling him Rudolph Brilliantino.

One especially warm evening, while they were having dinner, the lady from number ten came out and stood by her door, fanning herself with a magazine. Carlos raised a bottle of cold beer at her and she smiled. He took it to her.

"I knew it." Antonio remarked.

By then Alberto was spending most evenings at Murphy's poker table and when Carlos suggested that he find some other diversion he became annoyed.

"What do you want me to do?" he snapped, "Stay around here making eyes at the neighbors?"

Days turned into weeks. Summer turned to fall. One job would end and others would beckon. All three brothers sent home more money than anyone in San Cristobal had expected. Alberto's went to Doña Rosa, for safekeeping, and Antonio to his mother, Doña Helena, for the same reason.

The placid afternoons strolling through the town or along the main irrigation canal made them forget the previous hardships and a sense of almost belonging was already creeping into their their subconscious. Many people in the little town recognized them on the street and smiled, no longer afraid or suspicious of them as in the beginning.

Carlos became obsessed with the idea of that visit to the fabled city of San Francisco and promised to take it as soon as he had an opportunity, perhaps during the Christmas holidays. Whenever alone in his room he would stare at the postcard of the Golden Gate Bridge with the San Francisco lights gleaming in the background and reflecting on the sea and he would tell himself that this would soon be the place for his family; a home for the rest of his life. He knew it with a certainty and it filled his heart with joy. For the first time in his life he felt the oppressive tyranny of his birth lifting from his shoulders. It was the most wonderful, liberating feeling. He had found the place of his dreams, where the faults of his ancestors had no reach because such things didn't matter here. This was a place where, at last, he could be valued by his own actions and nothing more. His ultimate happiness, if not yet at hand, was certainly within sight.

Susan was the name of the blonde in number ten. One friday night, after his brothers had left for their usual hangout to again try their luck at billiards and poker, Carlos got up the nerve to ask her out to dinner.

She accepted but said they would have to wait until her girls were asleep. They sat on the veranda, watching the children play below, each nursing a beer and making awkward small talk. Both of them were uneasy for the same reasons. Both were married and wondering wether they were about to embark upon something they would later regret. Nevertheless, both of them had been suffering from loneliness for a long time and their meeting had brought it to the surface.

Two hours later Carlos was sitting on a sofa in Susan's small apartment. She was in the bedroom, covering her two sleeping daughters with a sheet to protect them from mosquitoes in the still, hot night. Then she joined Carlos on the sofa .

"Mari leen and Yoos teen?" he attempted.

"That's right. Marilyn and Justine. And I'm Susan and you're Carlos." she laughed.

Carlos pointed to a photograph on the mantle, of Susan and a young man in a soldier's uniform."

"And he?" he asked. "He is papa?"

"Yeah, that's their papa. Darren."

"Darren. Where is Darren?"

"Who knows?" she said with some disdain, "Somewhere in Europe, fighting someone else's stupid war for reasons I could never understand and no longer give a damn about."

Her face became angry and her look distant, so Carlos ran his hand gently down her cheek and she softened and smiled. A slow, romantic melody floated out into the night air from the piano down the street. Carlos stood up and took Susan by the hand out to the deck and they started to dance, all alone in the shadows and the moonlight.

Tears of bitter loneliness and relief started to roll down her cheeks and he kissed them away. Their lips met nervously for the first time and then she laid her head down on his shoulder. A short time later, Susan locked the door to number ten and left the key with her neighbor in nine, who promised to keep an eye on her little girls. Then they walked downtown to a new chinese restaurant for a late dinner.

When they passed by Murphy's Carlos mentioned that his brothers were in there. The bar was crowded and noisy because a lot of the monthly workers had returned to town, with money in their pockets and a hunger for liquor and for company.

One of them was Tom Silva, a tall, balding man with a loud voice and an arrogant manner. He fancied himself a ladies man and a great poker player but he had lost to Alberto once before and was now intent upon getting even. By ten o'clock Alberto had most of his money and the other players, along with some of the spectators, started giving Silva a hard time.

"You might as well give up, Tom. This kid's too good for you."

"Yeah, he's been lucky, but I got talent." Tom answered. "Luck changes, talent don't."

"Didn't he clean you out last time too?" another player asked. Tom ignored him.

"Tom's got talent all right." someone else yelled out. "He's even developing a talent for losing."

Everyone laughed except Tom, who just clenched his teeth, or Alberto, whose expression never changed, making people wonder how much he really understood. On the following hand, when everyone dropped out except Tom and Alberto, Tom suddenly wanted to raise the limit. Alberto refused.

"What's the matter, amigo. Ain't you got no *huevos?*"

"Hey, come on, Tom. Lay off of him." one player told him.

"I'm just trying to make the game interesting. Let's bet some real money, not just this piddly shit."

Alberto still refused.

"Okay, but I'm raising your ass and I dare you to raise me back."

"Hell, Tom, he can't even understand half of what you're saying."

"Well, it's not my fault he's a dumb wetback."

Alberto betrayed no emotion. "I call." he said calmly, and spread his cards on the table.

"Wow-wee!" someone yelled. "A straight flush, ten high. Tom, he just did you a favor, man!"

Tom threw down his cards and got up, all disgusted. "I'll be here tomorrow." he warned. "You guys better explain to this greaser that if he shows up, he better be ready to play for some real stakes."

He stormed out.

"Don't pay him no mind, Alberto." one onlooker said. "He's just had too much *cerveza*."

"It's a good thing," someone else commented, "'cause he's even a bigger *pendejo* when he's sober."

Another player quickly took Silva's place and the poker game continued.

Down the street, Carlos and Susan ate dinner in privacy since they were the last customers of the night. Afterwards they strolled back home, stopping to look at the posters in the town's only theatre. A cowboy movie was playing all week. Murphy's was still crowded and noisy. When they got to Susan's apartment, she retrieved her keys and went in to check on her daughters, returning to say that they were still fast asleep. Both of them were still apprehensive, wondering what the next move should be. Susan's bed was in the same room as her daughter's and her couch in the front room was very small. Carlos thought of inviting her into his room, knowing that his brothers would not be back for at least another hour.

In the end they kissed good night and agreed to see that movie the next day. Susan said they could have dinner before the movies because she could leave her daughters with her neighbor over night.

Chapter 31

Carlos was up early the next morning. He went for a walk around the town, ending up at the old section where weathered farmhouse barns still made a stand against the encroaching home developments. Crossing an empty lot where weeds had grown over the rusted hulk of a primitive plow, he came upon the church of the Holy Trinity, a catholic church built back around 1850 in response to the new tide of immigrants attracted by the gold found in the California foothills. It was an odd building, made of wood that at various places showed advanced states of decomposition.

Unlike the churches of San Cristobal, which were made of stone, built to last for centuries, this was clearly something temporary, though it had obviously been patched up many times over the years. He went in, mostly out of curiosity. There were just a few people inside, praying, lighting votive candles or dropping coins in the poor box, all done as quietly as possible but every sound and footstep echoed as if to underscore its significance. Carlos stood at the back, remembering the night of his wedding, so distant now in every way. And he wondered about the fate of all those people who had come through this place: Currents of people from all parts of the world, sacrificing everything, risking all. For what?

That afternoon he took a long bath after his brothers left and then dressed slowly, unable to concentrate. He took the photograph of Catalina and his children, kissed it and placed it face down inside a drawer. The evening sky was crimson when he left home and headed to number ten.

Murphy's was not quite as crowded that night. The pool table was covered and a few of the bar stools were empty, but there was a crowd of spectators around the poker table. Tom was winning and letting everyone know it when Alberto arrived.

"Well, well, look who's here." he crowed. "The Mexican bandit. Hey, Medina, tell this guy that he might as well keep walking cause there's none of this nickel and dime shit tonight. If he wants to play, he'll have to make it worth my while. I'll even let him choose the game."

Medina translated the gist of that for Alberto and all eyes were on him as he pulled up a chair and sat down. "Okay." he said to Silva, "We play. You, me, nobody else."

"That's fine with me. How much you wanna play for, seeñor?"

People crowded around, sensing something of interest was about to happen. Alberto asked Medina to translate his intentions.

"Tom, he says you'll each cut the cards one time and high card wins."

"Fine with me. What are the stakes?"

Alberto reached into his coat and, to everyone's surprise, he took out a knife which he stabbed into the center of the table.

"He says that the stakes are one ear." Medina explained.

"An ear? What the hell does that mean?" Tom asked.

"He says that if he wins, he cuts off your ear, and if you win you can cut off his ear."

"What the hell do I want with his ear?"

Alberto stood up and leaned forward, staring Tom Silva in the eye. "Wassumatta? You got no *huevos*? You *maricon*?" he sneered at him.

The crowd laughed with glee. They could hardly believe the nerve of this small, wiry young man.

"Hey, fine with me! If that's what you want to lose, okay."

Alberto calmly shuffled the deck several times and then pushed it toward Silva. Tom hesitated, reached for the cards slowly. The crowd became quiet and very attentive of the slightest move from either of the players. As usual, Alberto betrayed no emotion. Tom, on the other hand, was begining to perspire. He pushed the deck back towards Alberto.

"You first." he demanded.

Without hesitation, Alberto cut the deck and took the top card. He peeked down at a corner of it. Six of clubs. He looked back at Tom with the stillness of ice. Tom reached for the deck again. The sweat was beading up on his forehead. He looked around. A deathly silence had fallen on the place. Even the jukebox had been turned off. No one moved. Every eye was on big Tom Silva, waiting for his draw. Suddenly he pushed away from the table.

"Go to hell, you little bastard! I ain't never heard of anything so stupid in my life!"

Tom stalked out amid shouts, boos, cat calls, whistles and much laughter. There were even some chicken clucking imitations. Alberto removed his knife from the table, put it away and the regular game of poker resumed.

Carlos and Susan had dinner at a busy diner out near the canal. Then they walked to the Rialto to watch that cowboy film to which neither of them paid much attention.

At that very moment, thousands of miles away, Catalina was sewing a dress when Pancho, an old handyman that Florinda often employed knocked on the door and entered.

"Will you need anything else, Doña Catalina?"

"No, Pancho, thank you. That was the last errand. But tomorrow you'll have to help me with the shopping because Maria won't be back until Monday."

"Yes ma'am. I'll be here early. Good night."

Maria Hernandez was in Bachajo`n, visiting an old friend who was very ill. A moment later, Catalina was searching through her cabinets for some material when she heard a knock at the door. Oh, Pancho, what did you forget now? she thought.

She opened the door and was surprised to find Felipe instead.

"Felipe. What a surprise. Come in."

"I'm sorry to come by so late, Doña Catalina" he explained, "but I wanted to give this to Felix." He handed her a toy car made out of wood, with doors that opened and wheels that turned.

"Oh, how pretty. Did you make it? It's great. I know he'll love it, but he's not here today."

"Oh, no?"

"No. He's spending the day with his cousins. But he comes back tomorrow. Why don't you come by then and give it to him? It will mean that much more to him."

Felipe looked troubled. "No. I can't." he said. "I mean. . . I'm going away."

"You're going away? Where to? For how long?" Asking those questions so automatically made Catalina realize that her feelings were coming to the fore.

"For good." he said.

"Why? Has something happened?"

Felipe was fidgeting nervously.

"Well, I hope you won't think ill of me." he began, "but ever since I started working here," he hesitated for a moment. "I developed certain feelings for you; certain emotions to which I have no right, but over which I have no control. And now, the only solution I can think of, is to leave this place forever."

Catalina's heart was racing. She was hearing things that she didn't want to hear but which deep inside she had often longed for. And she was afraid, as much of her own emotions as of his. She didn't want to test her will power against such unpredictable urges.

"Felipe, why don't you come in and sit down?"

He walked in and stood by a window facing out to the patio, with his back to her.

"Listen to me." she said. "These things happen. They happen to all of us. But running away is not the solution. You can't run from something that's inside you."

He leaned his head down and she realized he was crying.

"Then what am I supposed to do? You don't know what I go through. It's torture. I hear your voice everywhere. I see your face in my mind day and night and I spend all my time trying to figure out new excuses to see you. I feel foolish, like an adolescent, awkward and lost."

"Felipe, I don't know why life does these things to us. Maybe it's to test us. Or maybe it's just that people always want the things that they can't have."

"It's not fair, Catalina. I didn't want to fall in love with you."

"I know." she said. "I know.

*   *   *

It was nearly one in the morning and Murphy's saloon had livened up. Antonio was playing pool with several other young men and it was standing room only at the bar. No one paid any attention when Tom Silva returned. He made his way straight for the poker table at the back but no one noticed him in the darkness beyond the tables' light until the chips, drinks and other items on the table went flying from the table. The few people at the table who did not jump back at first, were quickly on their feet and moving back when they saw Tom lean across the table with a gun in his hand. Alberto was the only one left, still sitting there, with five cards in his hand and staring calmly down the barrel of the gun.

"Now, you son of a bitch! Let's see you cut off my ear now!"

With his free hand, Tom Silva grabbed Alberto's shirt. Alberto didn't flinch nor struggle. Antonio was watching just like everybody else, and trying to think of what to do.

Then, bracing himself against the table, Alberto leaned back into his chair, pulling Tom with him. When Tom realized he was about to fall forward on the table, he released Alberto's shirt, dropping his hand to the table for balance. In that same instant, Alberto flung the table up from his side, sending the table over and Tom Silva with it to the ground. One bullet fired off with a loud explosion as Silva's arm hit the ground.

The loud report echoed and reverberated through the bar. People ran for cover in all directions. Tom Silva rolled over and came up with the gun still in his hand and fury in his eyes. He searched through the shadows for Alberto, pointing the gun in all directions. Women were screaming as tables and chairs tumbled over sending glasses and bottles crashing to the ground.

"Where are you, you son of a bitch!" Tom yelled at the top of his lungs. But even before he completed the phrase, the knife that had threatened his ear found its way into his chest. He collapsed to the floor with a moan. A second bullet went off into the ceiling as he fell.

There ensued a stunned silence in the bar which slowly gave way to a rumble of murmurs.

Carlos was in bed, making love to Susan, when a distant siren first pierced the stillness of the night. His youngest brother was running through the town's deserted streets. When he ran across an intersection he was just barely missed by a police car that sped by with siren blaring. Half a block before reaching their apartment he was already calling for his brother at the top of his burning lungs. "Carlos! Carlos!"

He ran into the patio and yelled his name again from the ground, then bounded up the stairs, repeating his cries. As he was about to run into their apartment Carlos came out of number ten, still putting on his shoes and buttoning his shirt.

"What the hell are you yelling about?"

Antonio was gasping for air and pale as a ghost. "It's Alberto. . cantina. . .a fight."

"God damn him! When will he learn to control his fucking temper?"

They ran down the street together, Carlos still stuffing his shirt into his trousers. More sirens filled the night air. When they got to the final block, they saw a large and growing crowd around the cantina. Once there, some people pointed Carlos and Antonio out to the police sergeant in charge, who ordered them brought to him while the rest of the people were pushed back.

"Is that guy, Alberto, your brother?" the sergeant asked Carlos.

"Yes. My brother. What happened?"

"Well, I'll tell you what happened. Your brother just killed a man. Apparently in a dispute over some gambling debt. Then, when two of my officers came to investigate, he shot at them, wounding one of them and taking both of them hostage. Now he won't come out."

"Okay, I talk to him." Carlos said.

"Yeah. But here's what you need to tell him. I don't want anyone else getting hurt. He needs to turn himself in, now! Do you understand?"

Carlos nodded and walked slowly to the bar's front door.

"Alberto!" he yelled. "Alberto, its me. I'm coming in."

"Only you. Nobody else!"

"It's just me." He entered to find the place in near total darkness. Only a neon sign against the bar mirror cast an eerie multicolored light upon the chaos of the room. He felt his way along through fallen furniture and broken glass. "Where are you?"

"Back here. But don't come any further. It's best if you go back, Carlos. Don't get mixed up in this mess."

"Don't be a fool, Alberto. You're my brother. Your problems are my problems. Listen to me! Everything will turn out all right. I promise you. But first you must release those two men."

"Forget it, Carlos! Get out of here. I'll deal with it."

"Don't be stupid, man. This place is surrounded by cops. It's not like Chiapas here. There's no escape."

Outside, in the street, the crowd waited, intently watching every movement, listening for every sound, making judgements, telling each other their impressions.

"What's taking him so long?" a policeman asked the sergeant.

"Just relax, Benson. Time is on our side. I don't mind wasting time. It's lives I can't afford to waste. That's my nephew he's got in there."

Carlos emerged slowly and alone. The officers with their gun sights upon him tensed up.

"Hold your fire men! Don't anybody shoot! Come on over here, son."

The sergeant took Carlos aside. They quickly ran into some problems communicating so a Spanish speaking officer was brought to them to translate.

"Ask him what the deal is? What's his brother want."

The crowd closed in, trying to hear every word.

"You people get back! This ain't a circus. Well, what's he say?"

"His brother claims that Tom assaulted him and he killed him in self defense. He says everyone in the bar saw it and they'll back him up on it."

"Explain to. . . what's your name? Carlos? Explain to Carlos that I've already talked to several people who saw the whole thing and they do say it was self defense. But that's not for us to decide. The courts will have to do that. Now, I think with all these witnesses he'll have a good case. The trouble is, he then went and shot one of my men, who could now be in there bleeding to death. Your brother is not helping his cause any. Listen to me Carlos. He has got to release my officers immediately."

The officer tried to translate the message verbatim but Carlos indicated that he understood. Then he replied to the translator point by point: "Tell him this: My brother was the one who asked that the police be called. When they arrived, he explained everything and all the witnesses agreed with him. The two policemen said that it was fine, and then suddenly they jumped him. One of them was shot with his own gun during the struggle."

This was all translated carefully to the sergeant, who insisted that all that would come out in court.

"No." Carlos was adamant. "I know my brother perfectly. He was betrayed by the police today and he won't trust you a second time. He says this has to be resolved right now, one way or another. And I know he means it."

The sergeant mulled it over. "Well, what does Carlos suggest?

"Tell the sergeant that if he lets me take my brother from here now, I promise that no one else will be hurt and that he'll never see us again."

"Is he asking me to break the law?"

"He says he's asking you to prevent an injustice and any further bloodshed."

The sergeant met with several of his officers for a few minutes, sending several of them away in their patrol cars. About fifteen minutes later, the remaining policemen watched from a distance as Antonio pulled up to the front door in a shiny 1940 Dodge Sedan. Carlos walked out of the bar helping one officer who was wounded on the leg. He handed him over to the police who already had an ambulance standing by. The sergeant was disappointed that the officer was not his nephew. Carlos then returned to the bar and reappeared minutes later with the other officer, blindfolded, in front of him, and Alberto, barely visible on the other side, holding a gun to the officer's head. They got into the back of the car and Antonio sped off into the darkness. The policemen quickly gathered around their sergeant to receive their orders.

"Oliver, you know these roads better than anyone. You'll be point man. No headlights if possible for the first ten minutes, just our running lights. I expect they'll continue south and stay off the highway at first. Julie, you call Sacramento and get those road blocks set up. And tell them not to shoot. My nephew is in there. Let's go."

They rushed into their cars and headed off in the same direction that the fugitives had taken.

By then, Antonio had driven into the main highway leading from Sacramento to San Francisco. He was traveling at over 90 miles per hour, heading south. Suddenly he pulled over to the shoulder in a cloud of dust. Carlos jumped out with the keys, opened the trunk, took out a crow bar and smashed both tail lights. He jumped back into the car and it disappeared again into the darkness of the nearly deserted highway.

"Are they behind us?" Antonio asked nervously. His foot was trembling on the gas pedal.

"I don't see them." Carlos said. Alberto remained quiet, calmly holding the gun in his hand.

"I think they're going to try to cut us off, up ahead." Carlos said, "So we'll be leaving this road soon." He kept looking out into the darkness, at the passing farm houses and the side roads.

"Okay, Antonio. Slow down. See that dirt road up ahead?"

"Yeah. Turn in there?"

"No, no, wait! Go past it. Stay on the pavement. Okay, stop. Now turn off your lights and back up into the road. I'll guide you if you can't see."

"I can see the bushes in the moon light."

"Make sure you stay on the right side of the road as you back in."

They backed into that dirt road for about a hundred yards and then made a u turn. They continued on that road among some groves and farms and over shallow hills. Eventually they stopped on the edge of a ravine. They locked the policeman in the trunk after telling him that the car was on the edge of a cliff and if he moved around too much it might fall off. They cut some branches from a tree and swept their tracks until they reached a rocky hill.

"Now what?" Antonio asked.

"We'll head back northeast toward Sacramento. Then we should be able to hop a train."

They walked for hours, through farm fields and irrigation ditches, no longer sure of their direction. Eventually they entered a foggy, wooded area and confronted a series of steep hills. By dawn they were descending one of them when they spotted the sandy shores of a lake. They realized then how thirsty the long walk had made them and practically ran down to the shore. After drinking their fill, they built a campfire and rested among some boulders near the edge, where they could still hear the soothing sounds of the water lapping the rocks.

Carlos sat atop one of the boulders and stared out over the placid waters and the slowly receding fog.

"Do you think they're still following us?" Antonio wondered.

"I don't know. We'll see." Carlos told him.

"I have a feeling they're not." Antonio hoped.

"Then why are you so nervous?" Alberto asked him.

"I'm not nervous. I'm just cold." he said.

Antonio had always envied Alberto for having so much courage. Nothing ever frightened him. He had always wanted to have that kind of courage but he never seemed to manage it. Now he stared at his brother, crouched next to him, calmly scratching the wet sand with a twig.

"So, why the hell aren't you ever scared?" He asked him directly.

Alberto looked at him from the corner of his eye. "It's very simple." he replied. "Many years ago I accepted something you two guys could never accept."

"What's that?"

Alberto turned and looked directly into Antonio's eyes.

"Destiny." he said.

The three brothers sat there in silence for a long time, absorbed in their own thoughts. Carlos kept thinking that all their work that year and all their suffering had been for nothing. They would go back home as fugitives. How would he be able to return? And he thought about the many times he dreamt of being surrounded by his family, all dressed up and walking hand in hand down some fancy street in San Francisco, perhaps somewhere overlooking the famous Golden Gate. Catalina would be wearing a yellow dress and a white gardenia in her hair. Their children would all have new shoes and little gray overcoats. And they would have a car just like Cappy's. Now, all of that seemed to be receding with the fog.

Eventually the fatigue and the excitement of the night caught up with them and they fell asleep one by one. Alberto was the first to fall asleep. He just curled up between two boulders and closed his eyes with a yawn, as if it was the most natural thing to do. Carlos soon followed, but although his sleep was deep, he tossed and turned continuously, periodically waking himself in the struggle.

Antonio fought it as long as he could, and even when he finally succumbed it was only to reawaken with every sound, be it the cracking of a twig or the water lapping on the shore. Each time, he scolded himself for being such a coward and tried to reassure himself that everything would be all right.

Meanwhile, in the still dark, fog-shrouded hills behind them, over a dozen men crouched behind rocks and fallen tree trunks, taking up positions. Some of them wore police uniforms and others were dressed like civilians, several of them in suits. From the center of the group, the sergeant peered down with a pair of binoculars. A soldier next to him, squinted through the scope of a rifle.

"Keep the noise down, you men!" the sergeant growled, "Sound carries far around here. See them?"

"Yup!" the soldier answered.

"See, here's the thing." explained the sergeant, "We could rush 'em, but I know they'll shoot it out, 'cause they're brothers, and they might take some of us with them. In stead, we'll wait for more daylight, then we'll take our shot if you think you can do it."

"Understood. I can do 'em from here. Ain't no problem." the soldier told him.

"The only one I'm interested in is the skinny one, with the brown jacket. You sure you can do it?"

"Yup. Just let me get my best gun for this distance." He walked back up to the crest of the hill.

About two hours later, Carlos woke up to find the first signs of daylight. He walked to the water's edge, washed his face and sipped water from his cupped hands. He gargled with it and spat it out. When he turned he found his brothers sitting up.

"You were tossing and turning. Were you having some of your weird dreams?" Antonio asked him.

"Yeah, I was."

"What about?"

"I don't remember." he lied.

362

Alberto rubbed his eyes. "I guess I've pretty much ruined all your good dreams, eh, Carlos?"

"Naw." Carlos reassured him. "Some dreams are only meant to be dreamt. Besides, we're not finished yet."

They remained quiet for a moment, then a shot rang out in the distance and echoed in the hills. Antonio jumped up.

"Is that them?" he asked, looking around.

"I don't think so," answered Carlos. "Probably just hunters."

Then, at the same time they both noticed Alberto with a grimace on his face, as if he couldn't breathe. He slumped slowly to the ground, still crouched as he had been sitting, and they saw the blood on his shirt and a bullet hole on his jacket, in the back.

"Alberto! Alberto!" Antonio was yelling as they rushed to his side. Carlos knelt on the ground and cradled Alberto in his arms. Antonio was turning one way and the other, desperately trying to think of what to do. When he heard a noise coming from the woods he reached for Alberto's gun, but Alberto grabbed it first and wouldn't let go of it.

Looking up at his older brother, Alberto tried to speak but could only make some gurgling noises and blood came spewing out of his mouth.

Antonio knelt beside him and started to cry and moan. "Please don't die Alberto. Please. Noooo."

Carlos kissed Alberto's forehead just before the light in his eyes went out and his tensed body went limp.

Up on the hill, the sergeant peered down with his binoculars.

"You're one hell of a shot, mister." he said.

"I can do the other two." the soldier said."

"Heck, they won't fight back now." said an old policeman who was standing behind them. "We can just go down and arrest them."

"No." said the sergeant, "That would only complicate matters: bad publicity, investigations, long drawn out trials. We don't need none of that. Justice has been done. Best of all, my nephew won't be so cocky now."

Carlos emptied Alberto's pockets. He found the photograph of a young girl that neither he nor Antonio had ever seen. It was wrinkled and faded and the writing on the back was too smudged to make out.

Antonio kept looking up at the hill with the gun in his hand.

"Why aren't they coming down?"

"They got what they came for." Carlos told him.

With their bare hands, they dug a grave for their brother on the sand at the edge of the lake. Antonio cried all during that time. When they finished covering the grave Antonio wanted to make a cross for him but Carlos stopped him.

"It's better if no one knows where he is." he said. "Let him rest in peace. . . for the first time in his life."

When they walked away they kept looking back. Carlos flung the gun as far into the lake as he could.

"I wonder what's the name of this lake." Antonio sighed.

"Lake Alberto." Carlos said, as they walked away into the fog.

Chapter 32

Catalina was in the children's bedroom, sitting by the window sill. Florinda was standing by the baby's crib. Outside in the sunshine, the baby slept in the buggy, covered by a shawl, while Alma walked around the patio with Maria del Carmen in her arms, showing her the flowers. At the fountain Felix was leaning over the edge, pointing out to his two friends the little fish hiding under the water lilies. Mariella and Isabel Cansino, having just made up from a long feud, were sitting on the bench, drinking cold ginger beer and exchanging new gossip.

"What did you tell him?" Florinda asked.

"That I cared for him too. And that it was precisely because we cared for each other that we should not do anything to destroy our friendship."

"What did he say?"

"Oh, you know, that he couldn't help his feelings and that it was all very difficult for him."

"Did he want to spend the night here?"

Catalina thought for a moment.

"What bothers me and scares me," Catalina admitted, "Is that I wanted him to spend the night here." Then, Catalina started to cry, openly and angrily.

"Why does that scare you?"

"What do you mean, why? Because it makes me feel like there is something wrong with me. That I can't be trusted. What's going to happen the next time?"

Florinda began to laugh.

"How can you laugh about this?"

"Because I'm glad to see that I have nothing to worry about with you. You are a young woman in the prime of your life and your husband is away. Your feelings are quite natural; nothing to be ashamed of. You were put to the test and you passed it with ease, and next time it will be even easier for you to defend yourself and your family, because fire is what tempers steel."

Florinda held her little sister in her arms for a while. She wiped Catalina's tears and kissed her.

"Well," she finally said, "I've got to go. I left Maria alone to mind the store."

Catalina walked her sister to the door and kissed her on the cheek.

"I'm just glad it wasn't your mother." Florinda chuckled. "She would have really made a mess of things."

Catalina cleaned up and joined her friends in the garden. They were discussing poets and poetry. Mariella thought Lord Byron was fine but she still preferred the new Chilean poet Neruda, particularly his 20 poems of love and one desperate song.

"Oh, what a surprise! Coming from someone who is desperate for love." remarked Alma.

"How dare you! You. . . you failed coffee planter." Mariella countered.

Isabel burst into laughter.

"What are you laughing at, Isabel? We still haven't forgotten the bible salesman."

"Catalina, did you hear what this shameless woman said to me?"

"No, no. I'm not taking sides. Besides, you know how I feel about gossip."

"What gossip? We're just discussing poets. Who is your favorite?"

"Yeah, in terms of the most romantic." Isabel clarified.

"Well, I guess it would be Shakespeare."

"Oh, no." They chimed. "Shakespeare is too difficult."

"Well, they say that all worthwhile things are difficult." Catalina told them.

"Oh, God. She's going to get philosophical now. Run for it, girls."

"You know, Catalina, you've been walking around all morning looking very strange. What's going on?" Mariella asked.

"Yeah, I'd like to know what happened to her carpenter." Alma wondered.

"Oh, that's right! I haven't seen her admirer in a while." Isabel realized.

"Wait a minute. Let's not start rumors just because he worked here and we became friends. He's very nice. Now he's finished his work in San Cristobal and has gone to live in Tapachula." She turned to Alma. "If you are still interested, I'll see if I can get you his new address."

"No. I'm not interested. He's not really my type."

"Honey." Mariella said, "he's a man. That makes him your type."

They went on like that for a while and then moved out of the sun into the shade of the corridor, to finish their ginger beer.

"All kidding aside, Cat, are you reconciled to moving to the United States?" Alma asked.

Catalina mulled over the question for a moment. "I was raised here, and my children will be raised here." she assured them.

"Have you told Carlos that?"

"Oh, its going to be his idea." She said.

The two Cansino sisters exchanged glances.

"Hmmn, It looks like our innocent sister is finally growing up." Mariella concluded.

Over a thousand miles away the two Cansino brothers were walking along a winding country road in California's central valley at that very moment.

"Carlos. How many miles do you think we've walked during this year in these United States?"

"I don't know. But I'm sure its more than most Gringos walk during their lifetime."

Around the next bend, they came upon a little church, nestled among the farms.

"Hey, why don't we go and say a prayer for Alberto's soul?"

"We don't even know if it's a Catholic church." Carlos pointed out.

"So what? It's Christian. It's got a cross."

They crossed the road and headed for the church. Three youths were sitting on the front steps of the church and when it became clear that Carlos and Antonio were heading their way, they were joined by two other young men, who had been playing ball out in front. The five of them blocked the entrance, standing shoulder to shoulder. The two brothers walked right up to them.

"Where do you guys think you're going?" one of them asked while he pounded his fist into a baseball glove.

"In church." Carlos told him.

"This is a white man's church." another youth told him with a grin. They stared at each other for a moment, and then the church doors opened and a priest emerged. He was a middle aged man with brown hair and a reddish, pock-marked face. He looked at the standoff without saying a word.

"We want to pray." Carlos said.

"Well," the priest answered, "I'm afraid the church is closed. Closed for repairs." He turned and closed the doors.

"What did he say?" Antonio asked his brother.

"He said this is a church that God never visits."

They turned and walked away. One of the youths yelled after them. "Go back where you came from, greasers!"

"Now, now. There's no need for that." the priest admonished him with a smile.

A few hours later the two brothers were standing at a roadside fruit stand, trying to hitch a ride. They lowered their outstretched arms when a convoy of military trucks passed, then raised them up again. Countless vehicles passed them by, so they bought two coca colas and drank them down, standing underneath a tree. A radio in the fruit stand was playing a Tommy Dorsey tune. When they finished, they replaced the bottles to the wooden crate and took their position at the side of the busy road once again. Even before they put out their thumbs, a big, green, dilapidated truck pulled up beside them. An old man behind the wheel smiled a toothless smile.

"Howdy. Where you boys goin'?"

"Mexico."

"Mexico?" he laughed and pounded on the steering wheel, "You boys are sure making a big mistake. Yes sir, a big mistake, 'cause this here's the land of opportunity. Well, come on, get in. Ain't got all day! I can take you as far as Oxnard."

They joined him in the cab and the old truck rumbled down the road amid a cloud of dust and blue smoke just as the radio in the fruit stand reported that some experts thought the war would end soon.

Carlos reached into his pocket and pulled out the photograph that Alberto had been carrying. He put it together with the photo of Catalina and his children, placed them carefully in his shirt pocket, over his heart, and buttoned the pocket. He was also carrying a postcard of San Francisco, and he stared at that for a long time.

"Too bad we never made it that far." Antonio said. "But it's too late now. Now it'll be good to go back home and leave this God forsaken place behind forever."

Carlos smiled but refrained from comment. From his lakeside dreams the previous night he already knew that he would in fact return, and not only to visit San Francisco, but to settle there with his whole family. And he also knew that he would die there.

However, it had not been revealed to him that his whole life would be only a small part of a great cycle of migration that began long before his birth, would not end for another century and would include new generations of his blood line. His descendants would complete the circle with their return to the old continent, to Europe, where their odyssey began more than a hundred years before.

A cycle, preordained like the currents of the sea that five hundred years before had carried, for good and ill, men like Bartolome' de las Casas and Diego de Mazariegos to the new continent of the Americas; to places like San Cristobal.

The End

2nd Edition, Volume 1

www.ingramcontent.com/pod-product-compliance
Lightning Source LLC
Chambersburg PA
CBHW031055260626
47172CB00001B/87